QUEER FEAR II

ARSENAL
PULP PRESS
Vancouver

QUEER FEAR II

edited and with an introduction by

MICHAEL ROWE

GAY
HORROR
FICTION

QUEER FEAR II
Copyright © 2002 by the Contributors

ARSENAL PULP PRESS
103-1014 Homer Street
Vancouver, B.C.
Canada v6b 2w9
arsenalpulp.com

The publisher gratefully acknowledges the support of the Canada Council for the Arts and the British Columbia Arts Council for its publishing program, and the Government of Canada through the Book Publishing Industry Development Program for its publishing activities.

Book and cover design by Solo
Cover painting by James Huctwith
Printed and bound in Canada

This is a work of fiction. Any resemblance of characters to persons living or dead is purely coincidental.

NATIONAL LIBRARY OF CANADA CATALOGUING IN PUBLICATION DATA:
Main entry under title:
  Queer fear II : gay horror fiction / Michael Rowe-McDermid, editor.

ISBN 1-55152-122-9

  1. Gays' writings, Canadian (English)★ 2. Gays' writings, American. 3. Horror tales, Canadian (English)★ 4. Horror tales, American. I. Rowe, Michael, 1962-
      PS8323.H67Q432 2002   C813'.08738920664   C2002-911149-8
      PR9197.35.H67Q442 2002

For Geoffrey Person, with love
and
For Janine Fuller, a personal heroine
with admiration and respect

CONTENTS

ACKNOWLEDGMENTS

I would once again like to acknowledge the friendship and support of my publishers, Brian Lam, Robert Ballantyne, Blaine Kyllo, and Kiran Gill Judge. Their enthusiasm for my work, and their willingness to push the cultural and artistic envelope makes me proud to be part of the process, and part of the family.

James Huctwith has again made his artistic gifts available to us with the cover painting, enriching this enterprise with his searing vision of the duality of light and darkness. I am grateful in the extreme for the privilege of having his work on the cover of a second volume of *Queer Fear*.

I am again grateful to be able to have worked with some of the finest non-fiction editors in the field of horror: Tony Timpone and Michael Gingold of *Fangoria*, Rod Gudino and Mary-Beth Hollyer of *Rue Morgue*, and Barbara and Christopher Roden of *All Hallows*. Their thoughts on the literature of our genre have informed me in the wisest fashion, and the best of what you find here will have been in some way influenced by their aesthetic sense, acquired by osmosis.

Many, many friends have been supportive of both *Queer Fear II* and its predecessor, and they may not know the degree to which their affirmation and love has been appreciated. This is where they hear it definitively.

In particular, I'm grateful to Jack Morrissey, whose kindness and hospitality brought Los Angeles alive to me in an entirely new way. Jack has always made me feel as though we might be doing something important with the *Queer Fear* series, and that it is worth doing well. Also in Los Angeles, Jon Larson, for keeping a special place in his life and his heart open to me, and to our friendship over many years. And in New York, Stew Noack, for all the reasons mentioned above, and others.

To the writers who have again entrusted me with their nightmares, and willingly shared them with you, thank you for again spilling your brilliant darkness onto the page.

And lastly, to my husband Brian (who doesn't even *like* horror), thanks for never letting me go down into the basement of that old, dark house by myself – in movies, in print, or in life.

... the communication
Of the dead is tongued with fire
beyond the language of the living.

— *T.S. Eliot, "Little Gidding"*

Unfathomable to mere mortals is the lore of fiends.

— *Nathaniel Hawthorne, "Young Goodman Brown"*

Just as courage imperils life,
fear protects it.

— *Leonardo da Vinci*

IN FURTHER PRAISE
OF QUEER FEAR

MICHAEL ROWE

I love cities, especially in autumn, especially at night in the dead hours before dawn.

Has a haunted house ever existed that could rival the macabre grandeur of those granite-and-steel canyons on a late October night, their long shadows tinted blood-red in the high-riding harvest moonlight? In the countryside it might be blacker and quieter, but here in the city, in the shimmer of reflected neon, you can see more clearly what walks beside you, and the distant rush of humanity – muffled car horns, the suspiration of traffic, the sound of people's voices – can mask any number of sounds, from breathing to screams.

Small towns and suburbs may be the place from which many gay men draw our personal histories, and, in some cases, the place to which we return, satiated by the freedom that an urban life offers us, yet hungry for something more elemental. But for most of us, the city is New Jerusalem, the shining metropolis on the hill.

The best – and the worst – of us flow to its gates.

In many cases, the city allows us to become what we are meant to be, free of the strictures and prohibitions of small-town life, where our every action has a reaction from others, and a harsh judgment. Assuming for a moment that a horror sensibility begins with an awareness of what constitutes dread, an argument could be made that for many gay men and lesbians, those first lessons in terror are taught to us as children who are – correctly – viewed as *different*. We come to the cities in droves, initially delighted to find a place where, for once, our difference at worst renders us blissfully invisible, and at best is celebrated in a variety of fields where the suburban virtues of mediocrity and assimilation are seen as undesirable.

But the city teaches its special lessons in terror. Like any tribe, gay men have our own urban legends, most of which link violence to desire.

Think of the infamous "salt and pepper" killers who were rumored to have haunted the streets of New York in the late 1960s. According to legend, two men disguised as policemen would "arrest" gay men coming home from the bars, and ask them a series of questions relating to their lifestyles. If the men gave the *wrong* answer, they would be dismembered.

I myself remember hearing a variation of that urban legend when I was in my early twenties. According to one, there was a gang of men who roamed the streets of the city driving a van with blackened windows. They were always dressed in full leather, and the van was set up as a fully-equipped s&m dungeon. They would lure unsuspecting gay men into the van, or kidnap them, and torture them to death. No one ever knew anyone to whom this ever happened, but it always sounded familiar. Certain elements were consistent: the killers were handsome men, they were always *tops*, and before they got down to their gruesome work, the victims were taken to undreamed-of sexual heights. Like the "salt and pepper" killers, they were presented as figures of authority in the classic sadomasochistic mold.

In some ways, these stories share elements with other urban legends, most notably the notion that desire and "immorality" are punishable by death, be it the babysitter who has sex with her boyfriend while a murderous psychopath slaughters the innocent children sleeping upstairs, or the gay man who indulges desires that society deems inappropriate or abnormal.

Of course, we all laughed when we heard these stories, but beneath the surface two diametrically opposed *frissons* were occurring: one was a desire for the pornographic violence imbedded in the tales, the other was something approaching genuine terror. It's an easy step, on a dark and rainy night, to link those stories to the many *Have You Seen This Man?* flyers tacked up on bulletin boards in the basements of those same bars, especially when walking home alone, remembering that those men also walked home alone, and were never seen again. When a Jeffrey Dahmer or a John Wayne Gacy slips a human mask over the monster's face, the world of legend and reality collides in a denouement that is as tragic as it is terrifying. A writer of dark fantasy is never satisfied with the bare facts, however, or the intrusion of reality into the realm of legend. For a horror writer, facts are merely a runway from which to launch the reader into a black, starless night. If we agree that horror fiction begins with the awareness of legends that permeate a given culture – be it trolls, ogres, dragons, demons, monsters, or the Devil himself – gay men aren't without our own cultural grounding in the language of fear, and our horror writers are not ill-equipped to articulate our own terrors in a way that speaks to our own people.

Sometimes, though, writers need to look back in order to look forward.

My partner Brian and I moved from the city to the small town of Milton, Ontario, for six years in the early part of our marriage. We wanted to be closer to Brian's parents who lived nearby. We bought a red-brick Victorian house on Martin Street, on the edge of downtown Milton. I'd never lived in a real small town before. Far from the city, we could always smell each season individually. Spring and summer's green bouquet crumpled into autumn's smoke and spice, which in turn gave way to winter's chill, the blue scent of new snow and frozen bark.

I walked everywhere, and would often walk our two golden retrievers through the woods bordering the millpond, and along the windswept country roads to a desolate cemetery on the edge of town at dusk. Those walks were a time for reverie, a time for my mind to wander and imagine, especially at night. There was mist in the woods, there were the cries of nightbirds high in the trees that screamed like children, there was the nocturnal ballet of bats that wheeled in the moonlight.

Although initially conspicuous in the town, Brian and I made close friends there, and for a time were able to observe the turn of life itself at ground level, through the eyes of people who let us into their world. Births, deaths, graduations, marriages, we participated in them all, and the experience was a fruitful one in many ways, not the least of which were, for me, literary. Not only was I a magazine journalist who also wrote for the local newspaper, *The Canadian Champion*, I had also begun to write about my world, and my observations of my place in it. Some of the essays I wrote about my life in Milton were collected in a book, and there is a multiplicity of other pieces that will likely remain unpublished, all dealing with the minutiae of small-town life in a way that served primarily as a prism through which I explored my place as an urban gay man in an alien world, like many a queer social historian before me.

In time, though, we felt the pull of the city, and after six years we said a lot of tearful goodbyes, packed up our memories, and returned to a life which, though occasionally anonymous, allowed us a measure of freedom from observation that had been lacking in Milton.

As a horror writer, however, small-town life had been universally fertile ground. Expatriate writers have always found that distance sharpened their sense of "home," and although I had moved a relatively short distance back to a city I knew well, Milton sharpened into focus.

I wrote a series of dark fantasy short stories that appeared in the *Northern Frights* anthology series and elsewhere, set squarely in the town of Milton, with no attempt to hide either the locale or, particularly, the people. Don Hutchison, the editor of the *Northern Frights* series, has said of those stories that they turned Milton into "the most fiend-haunted, werewolf-ridden, vampire-infested real estate outside of Jules de Grandin's Harrisonville, New Jersey and Charles Grant's Oxrun Station." Generous praise indeed from an editor of Hutchison's stature, and flattering to be sure. The fact that only other horror afficionados, either writers or readers, would *get* the literary references made it all the more honeyed. Horror fans – and I count myself as a passionate constituent of that elite literary number – can be a clannish and insular group with their own touchstones, passions, shared language, and pop-culture references, much like those shared by gay people.

In this second volume of the *Queer Fear* series, many of the writers have used the city as the place from which the horror grows, and those who have used small towns and suburbs have done so with anti-nostalgia, or by reminding the reader that no matter how rough life can be in the city, it is the place that nurtures and protects us, and when we venture too far from its sooty embrace, any defenses we may have built up in the course of our years there is suddenly rendered powerless in the face of the yawning suburban abyss where we are always alone, always vulnerable, always, somehow, metaphorically fifteen years old, and an outcast.

In the year or so following the publication of *Queer Fear*, I've had the opportunity to read volumes of mail, and speak with hundreds of gay men, about what, aside from the obvious horror *motifs*, resonated for them when reading the book. Variations on certain themes repeated themselves. "The past" was one theme; thwarted adolescent lust and desire. Another theme was the notion of leaving a bleak, desolate youth behind and reinventing oneself in the city. Nostalgia was a big theme: the horror films of the '70s and '80s, teenager slasher films in which we were not represented, and where we often identified with the heroine, the not-quite-pretty but infinitely sensible babysitter who saved the day while the bodies of all the pretty, popular prom queens and star quarterbacks littered the floors of suburban living rooms and remote summer camp cabins like so much shark bait. It was wonderful to discover that the notion of queer fear – gay horror fiction – was something that readers had not only been looking for, but which served to link an entire post-1960 generation through shared cultural memory, language, and flashpoints.

In the weeks following the devastation of the attack on the World Trade Center, I was sent to Los Angeles on a magazine assignment. The closest I have ever come to real dread – the deep, soul-cutting kind – was saying goodbye to Brian the morning I left the house for the airport, something both of us have done hundreds of times over the last eighteen years. All I could think of was the people who had said goodbye to their spouses the morning of September 11, 2001 and who, in a few hours, would be dead.

The feeling dissipated over the course of the drive to the airport, as I knew it would. Rationally, I wasn't afraid of terrorists, especially not that day, with security in every major airport in the world at a hysterical pitch.

No, it was the dread of that final goodbye.

Some critics of horror fiction elect to harp on the notion that horror writers and adherents access a negative, destructive force in the hard-wiring of human nature, and revel in it. In fact, the reverse is usually the case. Horror readers and writers are able to face and identify the real darkness in the world because they don't mistake it for their literature. Any of us can attest to the difference between "fear of" vampires, werewolves, or ghouls, and the very real dread of losing your most precious loved one in a blaze of fire in mid-air against a hard blue September morning sky.

I arrived in California in fine form, visited some friends, and attended the meeting of a waspish gay seniors book-club in Palm Springs. They had, to my surprise, picked *Queer Fear* as their book of the month. The discussion of the book afterwards, filtered through the perspectives of their advanced age and eclectic life experience, was lively, illuminating, and unforgettable.

I left Palm Springs the following morning and returned to L.A., where I met with my editor, and did the interview for which I had been sent to California in the first place.

I've come to love Los Angeles. It has always struck me as the quintessential haunted city, one of those eldritch locales where the past and the present meet in a Mobius strip that bridges time itself through the medium of celluloid. Nowhere else in America do the icons of the past loom larger. I've never been surprised at the reverence many gay men have for Hollywood. If youth, beauty, and fame – eternal life, really – are gods, nowhere else in America have they been worshiped as reverently, and for as long, in such an unbroken line. If we run for a moment with the notion that ghosts are the manifestation of accumulated dreams, hopes, terrors, heartbreaks, and triumphs of people who live and die at a fever pitch, where better than Hollywood to observe the restless dead? Think of the millions of young people, many of them gay, who have poured into L.A. for a century, dreams of fame and fortune clutched tightly. Think of the ones who have lived and died in the city of angels having never achieved the celestial heights they pined for. Think of the ones who *did* achieve it, who still haunt us in the flickering electric firelight of movie theaters around the world.

If ghosts are a manifestation of energy, it's a miracle we don't see more of them hovering in that shimmering golden haze of smog and surreal sunlight.

Later that afternoon, I was taken on a drive through the streets of Los Angeles and its surrounding neighbourhoods by my buddy Jack Morrissey, an Angeleno by adoption whom I met shortly after *Queer Fear* was published. We quickly became friends, and it was a pleasure to discover that many of the elements of what I had previously thought of as my own personal "gay horror sensibility" were, in fact, shared. Jack took me to the house of the late filmmaker James Whale, another gay man who left his grim, gray, working-class English world to remake himself in Hollywood, who gave the world *Frankenstein* and *Bride of Frankenstein,* and whose life was dramatized in an Academy Award-winning film starring Ian McKellen and Brendan Fraser, written and directed by Jack's partner, Bill Condon.

We made a pilgrimage to the residence which served as the exterior location of the *Nightmare on Elm Street* house. We also drove to the street, minutes from Sunset Boulevard, which was one of the main exteriors in *Halloween,* one of the seminal horror movies of any of us with a 1970s or '80s childhood. When I realized how disappointed I was that "Haddonfield, Illinois" was a couple of dusty streets in Hollywood, I became aware of three things in rapid succession. First, I was an adult. Completely. Second, I was going to die a horror-nerd. Third, I was oddly comforted to come to this conclusion in the company of a good friend who was another gay man for whom these movies (and their black magic) had been an integral part of youth. The fact that it was *Queer Fear* that brought us together made it all the more poignant, and in a way it didn't matter that Haddonfield, or the Elm Street house, were exterior film sets. They exist like a memory from my past, and Jack's past, and the past of so many other queer people whose world view has been shot through with the brilliant black and orange threads of perpetual October.

In the same way gay people exist outside the social mainstream, horror people – writers, editors, readers, fans – exist outside the bookish mainstream. Whenever one of our own breaks out of the tributary of dark fantasy fiction into the wider waters of mainstream acceptance, the news is greeted with a mixture of pride and triumph for the writer in question (whose generous gifts will now be shared with a much-deserved wider readership) and a bittersweet sense of something like betrayal along the *Don't forget your roots!* lines. We have seen this phenomenon time and time again, every time Stephen King, or Peter Straub, or Clive Barker, or Robert R. McCammon (who as of this writing has just published a stunning non-horror historical novel, *Speaks The Nightbird*) steps outside the fiery perimeter of tradional horror fiction.

One tradition we began with the first volume of *Queer Fear* was to introduce readers, both gay and straight, to a variety of fresh names in addition to genre stars like Douglas Clegg, Michael Marano, and Brian Hodge. These names were drawn from a variety of sources, ranging from literary writers, to comic book writers, to journalists, to neophytes making their debuts.

In *Queer Fear II*, in addition to a raft of exciting new writers, we are delighted to welcome a variety of writers from other fields including acclaimed Carribean-Canadian fantasy writer Nalo Hopkinson, Australian science-fiction writer Stephen Dedman, and the award-winning British ghost story writer Steve Duffy.

Poppy Z. Brite, another icon of the field, has effectively "retired" from writing horror fiction, and is now exclusively writing haunting, gay-themed, southern-inflected mainstream fiction. In an odd sort of way, horror's loss is our gain as gay readers, and it is our honor as the purveyors of queer thrills to be able to bring her two literary directions together here in a glorious dovetail that will chill and delight you.

Each one of the writers has left the safety of his or her particular "hometown" and made pilgrimage to the pages of this book. Many of the stories are set in cities, suggesting that there may be some truth to the notion that we bring our terrors with us when we leave the place we come from. Some of the stories are set in small towns and suburbs, suggesting that many of us have found some measure of peace in the metropolis, and only in looking backwards do we truly face our nightmares.

Individually, however, each writer brings their own private darkness to bear. Each one brings a brick, and what is constructed is a city of words, of stories. Every story is a building, and together they make a metropolis of terror.

The sun is down, and the autumn moon is riding high.

Take my hand. Shall we go for a walk in the dark?

Toronto, Vancouver, Los Angeles, Palm Springs, Toronto
September 2001 – July 2002

QUEER FEAR II

BUGCRUSH

SCOTT TRELEAVEN

Grant belonged to that peculiar species of troubled teen that arrives unannounced mid-way through the year, the product of a divorce or a parent being laid-off, and completely fails to fit in. It was just the kind of rank, suburban pathos that Ben adored, and he fell for the new boy immediately. Unfortunately, in the four months since Grant arrived in the school, Ben had only managed to draw a few semi-meaningful conversations out of him. It was more than the scowly, solitary youth afforded anyone else, and the privilege wasn't lost on Ben, but he wanted more. He was secretly convinced that there was something flirtatious in the predatory way that Grant would fix his wide, dark eyes on him while they fumbled with small talk. This wishful thinking was further corroborated by the fact that Grant was never seen in the company of women. Ben's friends were quick to remind him that Grant was never seen in the company of *anybody*, much less a potential girlfriend. Ben was undeterred. He had fallen for this boy's alluring blend of thuggishness and intelligence, even if his friends had mistaken it for latent brutality and self-absorption.

Unlike Ben, who had been refining a half-starved look since the eighth grade, Grant was a thicker, burlier sort of beast. To Ben he looked like a young Henry Rollins. A nonchalant stretch or a reach up to scratch his dark, cropped hair revealed a deliciously chiseled and lightly furred midriff, but that was all the skin to be seen. Even now that spring was on its way Grant seldom wore revealing clothes, and even when he did the only thing of interest that Ben could see was a length of gauze bandage which covered Grant's entire upper left arm. He told Ben that it was a tattoo in progress. Being already despised by the teachers, this unusual accessory made him an even more popular target.

When he wasn't in detention, which was rare, Grant could usually be found lingering around the smoking pit by himself. The school had a small cache of goths and freaks that Grant could easily have fit in with, but there was something about their fluffy and inoffensively coifed rebellion that either didn't suit or didn't appease him. Noticing this, Ben tended to feel embarrassed by his friends whenever Grant was around. They had tattoos, they had lip, nipple, and nose piercings, a few of them even sported mohawks, yet somehow they never managed to achieve that same outsider status that made Grant so appealing. Believing that he'd caught a glimpse of the true spirit of teenage rebellion, Ben decided that friends were little more than a retinue of posers and fakes, and in a very short time he had managed to drive a social wedge between himself and his peers, leaving him almost as solitary as his crush.

Now in the eleventh grade, Ben was used to loving other guys from a distance. Saying anything obviously flirtatious, or even being straightforward, was totally out of the question. His school was still largely untouched by the giant social strides made in bigger cities, and it was just too treacherous to risk being outed. The few friends he had managed to confess his crush to reacted with shocked and confused stares. While they could make concessions for Ben being queer, they all unanimously felt that he had made, as one friend had succinctly put it, "a bad object choice." Still, Ben was less concerned with his friends' opinions, and even less his personal safety, than he was with the possibility that one wrong move might drive Grant away entirely. Being deserted by the few friends he had left, or getting beaten up by a gang of jocks, didn't seem as traumatic as the idea of losing Grant. Eventually, Ben grumpily resigned himself to the fact that he would probably never get to reveal his crush to Grant, much less have it reciprocated. The most excitement that he had to look forward to was the unveiling of Grant's tattoo.

After class one day Ben noticed two boys that he had never seen before, hovering nervously on the edge of the school parking lot. They were both roughly his age, maybe a year or two older, and fit the bill of nondescript suburban teenagers: a grunge kid and a crusty-looking punk. The grunge kid was an ungainly, spotty teen in denim and plaid, with scruffy, long hair and a missing tooth which he took great delight in flicking his tongue through. The other boy was even more unwashed and weed-like. Replete with dreadlocks that had come from plain lack of hygiene instead of a salon, his wasted arms were disfigured by crude pin and Indian ink tattoos of skulls and spiders, and he would have looked perfectly at home clutching a squeegee. Ben was just about to disregard them when he noticed Grant, slipping discreetly between the parked cars, going out to meet them. When he saw the tattooed boy embrace him, Ben almost convulsed at the thought that he might be the artist behind Grant's tattoo. As Ben watched the three of them walk away from the school he knew that, whoever they were, they were totally unworthy of Grant's attentions. Somehow though, these two boys had managed to do the very thing that Ben had failed to: they were getting close to him.

For weeks the scene replayed like clockwork. The boys would arrive to meet Grant, then they would all abruptly vanish. Asking around, Ben could only uncover that the two boys were named Keith, who was the grunge kid, and Shannon, and that they were from a neighboring high school. No one knew anything else about them. What was even more peculiar was that at least once a week, Shannon and Keith would bring a third boy along with them. Always someone different, this rotating third youth tended to be cleaner and younger than the rest of the entourage. They always looked like grade nine kids, though once again, never anyone that Ben or his peers had seen before. It was baffling. Against all social odds Grant had gone from a skulking, social pariah on the fringes of the smoker's pit, to regularly hanging out with two, sometimes three, cute guys after class. There was something in the way that Shannon had embraced Grant on the first day that made Ben loathe him instantly. It was a cozy familiarity that Ben had felt entitled to, and was now being robbed of. He seethed with jealousy, watching them come and go, over and over again for days.

There was, Ben conceded, the slim possibility that Grant actually *was* a fag, and had hooked up with Shannon. The even smaller chance that Keith was in there too, somehow, was even more horrible. At the same time, it was so poisonously thrilling that Ben spent several nights lying awake, jerking off while imagining Grant, grinning and rapacious, fucking the shit out of the two. Masochistically, Ben sometimes let the scene in his head drift until the wasted figures of Keith and Shannon were there, sharing the object of his crush between them. As for the other mysterious boys that arrived, always too far away and too fleeting for Ben to remember in detail, they became extra arms, hands, legs, and mouths for his fantasy; fleshy insect hybrids, pinning Grant in place. Immediately after he came the mere thought of it made Ben as sick as it had made him hard. The vigorous masturbation sessions ruined his sleep and left him in a wake of exasperating hallucinations. He envisaged Grant lurking somewhere in the shadows of his small bedroom, leering and veiled with thin, viscous webs of sperm.

An unusually frigid rainstorm had moved in during the early hours of the morning and had left the smoking pit deserted, except for the diehards. Naturally, Grant was out there. After lingering inside with the rest of the lightweights for a moment, Ben zipped up his flimsy hoody, stuck a cigarette in his mouth, and headed out to where his crush was sitting. Having managed to sneak a couple of shots of vodka before leaving his home, Ben felt somewhat fortified. He had no idea what he was going to say or do, but he was resolved to be mercenary about it. His goal was simple: he wanted to be the third boy that Shannon, Keith, and Grant left the school grounds with.

Using the cold as an excuse, he huddled up close on the bench beside Grant. They started off with the usual, semi-painful small talk, but it was cold, and Ben knew that once Grant finished his cigarette he would go back inside. Time was of the essence, so he cut to the chase:

"So how do you know Shannon and Keith?" Ben asked, as if he knew them too.

Grant swiveled his head in Ben's direction, giving him the slimmest trace of smile. Ben tried to maintain an air of disinterest.

"From around," Grant said.

Ben nodded.

"They seem pretty cool."

"You think?"

"Sure. I mean, I don't really know them. . . ."

Grant knocked the edge of his cigarette against the back of the bench, putting it out mid-way through. Seeing this gesture, Ben's stomach tied a knot in itself. He sensed the conversation was grinding to a halt and frantically tried to find a new avenue for the conversation, then all of a sudden Grant said:

"Ben, check this out."

From inside the neck of his shirt he produced a small length of leather cord with a miniature copper pendant on it. Glinting feebly in the overcast light, it looked like a tiny metal insect of some kind. It was long, with a curled abdomen and squiggly scraps of metal protruding from the sides, suggesting the requisite six legs. The eyes were tiny, and it's formidable, curved mandibles had been dipped into red paint.

"What is it?"

"It's a bug. Shannon made it for me."

Ben never liked insects to begin with, and now he disliked them even more.

"It's fucked up."

Grant laughed. Ben became angrier.

"No, really. Why would you wear that?"

Ben reached over to touch the pendant. The metal was like a piece of ice in his fingers, but Grant's throat was so wonderfully warm he couldn't take his hand away. Grant obliged by stretching out his neck even more, putting his face up close to Ben's.

"Come on, Ben. You like it."

Ben felt his cheeks go scarlet. "No I don't. What is it? A scorpion?"

"It's just a bug."

"Like your tattoo?"

"My – ?" Grant looked confused for a second, then patted his left arm, adding, "Oh yeah. Just like it."

"Why did Shannon make this for you?"

"He's my friend," he offered.

"Oh." Ben's brain rolled the word around in his head. It could mean anything. Acquaintance, drinking pal, fuck buddy.

"You know what's weird. . . ? We were talking about you last night."

Ben's stomach tied its second knot. He dropped the pendant.

"Who was?"

"Me, Shannon, and Keith."

"Oh yeah?" Ben said, trying hard to sound indifferent.

"They were wondering how I know you. Weird, huh?"

"Why did they want to know?"

A small gnaw started in the base of Ben's brain. A tickle of information, a message. He wasn't sure what is was.

"They've seen you around a few times. Just wanted to know who you were."

"What did you tell them?"

Without warning Grant started to grin. Ben wanted to run his tongue across those lustrous teeth, and felt the blood start to drain out of his face and fill his cock. It was odd, though. Grant's eyes seemed to be completely disengaged from the smile itself. He had to run a hand over his mouth to make it go away.

"I said I only sort of know you. But I said you were cool."

"Really?" Ben caught himself. "Yeah, well, it's not like we really hang out."

"Shannon thought that we should sometime. All four of us."

Ben was stunned. It was exactly what he'd wanted to hear. He would rather not have had the suggestion come from Shannon. Still, a victory was a victory. For some reason, the nagging sensation at the base of his skull had stepped itself up a notch. His instinct was vying for attention with his swelling dick.

"So, uh, what kind of stuff do you like to do?" Grant asked.

"What kind of stuff?"

"Yeah. To get fucked up."

Ben nodded slowly as the question sunk in. It occurred to him then that maybe Grant, Shannon, and Keith were selling drugs to the mysterious one-off boys that kept showing up with them. If that was the case, and Grant was selling, then Ben was most certainly buying. Ben ran down a meager list for him – acid, pot, hash, ecstasy. Drugs didn't really interest him, but it was an inroad.

"Pot's cool . . . but we get up to some pretty weird shit, too."

"Like what? Like crystal and shit?"

Either seemed fine; Ben was on the brink of agreeing to anything.

"Nuh-uh. Nothing like that. It's some, uh, organic . . . substances. Hallucinogenic stuff I brought with me when I moved here."

"What, like 'shrooms?"

"No, none of that shit. More of, uh . . . kind of, uh. . . ." Grant was seized with the toothy grin again. His face wrestled with it for a few moments. "Hey, Ben, why don't you, uh . . . why don't you just come over tonight? We'll go right after school."

The voice inside, finally articulate, simply said "don't." So succinct and abrupt, it sounded like Ben's own voice and caught him off guard. Aside from possible heartbreak, he refused to believe that he was in any real danger from Grant. Ben curbed an almost visible shudder, and sounded perfectly calm when he agreed.

"Uh, sure. I don't think I'm doing anything."

"You can see my place," Grant said, rising from the bench. "Just keep it quiet, okay? It'll be fun."

Ben's cigarette had burnt itself down to filter. He flicked it away.

To Ben's amazement the other two boys weren't assholes at all. On the contrary, Keith and Shannon seemed to be genuinely happy that Ben was coming home with them. As they started to drift away from the school together, Ben could feel his rib cage reverberate with the heavy pulse of his heart. In his mind, for some reason, this felt like a date. Grant did most of the talking, filling Ben in on the details of his life previous to moving here with his Mom. Having no doubt heard it all before, Shannon and Keith lingered silently, a few paces behind. When they stopped briefly at a liquor store, Grant brandished some fake ID and ducked in, leaving Shannon to take over the conversation. He asked Ben about his family, his friends at school. There wasn't much to tell on either front, but Ben appreciated the gesture. Keith barely opened his mouth the whole time, except to poke his tongue out through the vacant spot in his smile. However much Ben tried to ignore it, the flickering pink morsel seemed to be telegraphing all sorts of lascivious things to him. When Grant finally re-emerged with a bottle of vodka, he made a show of stretching his arm around Ben before they resumed walking. Ben kept waiting for a hint of jealousy to creep into Shannon's expressions, but none came.

The modest townhouse that Grant lived in seemed to be more functional than comfortable. Grant's mother had flown back out west to finish off the arduous legal process of her divorce, and to divide up the spoils for their new home. She had been gone for the better part of two months, and much of the unpacking had been left to Grant. The kitchen was still in boxes, and he insisted they rummage through them to find his special set of shot glasses. With nothing in his stomach since lunch, the alcohol went straight to Ben's head. Sitting in a mismatched chair, he let his forehead touch the tabletop for a moment.

"I thought you liked vodka," Grant snickered.

"I do."

"Yeah, I know. I could smell it on your breath this morning."

Shannon and Keith exchanged a brief glance with each other and then burst out laughing. Shannon leaned over and poured a copious amount of vodka into a glass of orange juice and pushed it in front of Ben.

"That's pretty hardcore, buddy. I like that. Here. Knock yerself out."

Ben waved his hand to refuse the drink, then gave up. He started to laugh as well.

"I was, uh . . . expecting a rough day."

"Well, hang in there," Grant reached over and squeezed Ben's arm. "We're just starting."

Out of the corner of his eye Ben could see Shannon staring at him expectantly. He wasn't sure if Shannon wanted him to notice or not, and he found it unsettling.

"Hey, Shannon, I like the, um, bug you made for Grant," Ben lied.

"Oh yeah? Thanks, man. I made one for Keith, too," he said, and turned around in his seat to fish Keith's pendant out of his shirt. It was on a particularly long piece of hemp string, and Shannon felt compelled to shove his hands into Keith's shirt to grab it. Keith squirmed with delight.

"Shut up, Keith. Here. Lookit this."

It was identical to the one that Ben had seen around Grant's neck.

"I got one, too."

"Nice. So, what does it mean?"

Shannon cocked his head in Grant's direction.

"Mean? . . . Grant? Do you wanna field that question?"

Grant was sitting right beside Ben, almost pressed up against him, with an arm across the back of his chair. He leaned in and ran a hand up Ben's back. A trail of soft electric sparks followed Grant's hand up his spine.

"Ben's pretty smart. He can probably handle this. Here."

To Ben's astonishment Grant stood up and slid his shirt off of over his head. He tossed it to Ben. Catching a strong whiff of the boy's scent, he fought the urge to clutch it to his face. Grant's torso was broad and lean with faint tufts of black, wiry hairs running around his nipples and down the centre of his chest. The ubiquitous tattoo bandage was on his left arm as usual. Grant untucked a corner of the gauze, and to Ben's further amazement, started to unravel it.

"Grant, man," Keith muttered with uneasiness, "what're you doing?"

"Trying something new."

Shannon was also apprehensive. "I dunno about that, Grant."

Ben's eyes lingered everywhere on the boy's torso except his arm. More than anything he wanted to run a hand down Grant's stomach to that dense tuft of hair poking out over his waistband. The trail looked so smooth, it seemed to invite exploration. Fully distracted by Grant's pubic hair, Ben wasn't prepared to see what Grant had been busily unveiling on his arm, and when he did he leapt out of his chair with a cry.

"Holy fuck. What the fuck did you do?"

The upper half of Grant's arm wasn't tattooed at all, instead it was covered in weeping, white-headed sores. Each sore consisted of an abscess of some kind nestled in a vivid red welt. There were so many, and so tightly clustered, that it looked as if someone had smacked his arm with a wire brush. Ben put his hand over his mouth. He imagined for a second that he could smell the sores, but he was mistaken.

"What is that? Are you sick?"

He wondered if Shannon had botched the tattoo, and this was some kind of hideous infection.

"No, I'm not sick."

"Grant. Wrap it back up until you need it," Shannon flatly advised.

Grant slowly redressed his arm.

"They're only bug bites. We've all got them. Shannon, show him yours."

Reluctantly, Shannon stood up and turned around. As he lifted his shirt he revealed a similar patch of sores on his back between his shoulder blades. They were nowhere near as heavily concentrated or as nauseating to look at as Grant's. Keith rolled up a pant leg and showed off his own collection of lesions. Ben felt panic grip him. He wondered if by sitting on the furniture he was going to break out in a patch of his own.

"How did you get them?"

"They're bug bites," Grant repeated. "It's okay, I've had them before. They'll go away, it's not like a tattoo."

"Do they hurt?"

"Not at all."

Grant picked his shirt up from where Ben had dropped it and pulled it back on. Seeing that Ben was thoroughly freaked out, he motioned to Shannon who poured Ben another generous amount of vodka.

"They just look painful. They don't feel like anything."

"Kind of tingly. Nothing bad," Shannon helped.

"Did you fall into a nest of spiders or something? How do you get so many?"

"I didn't fall, I did it on purpose. So did Shannon. So did Keith."

"I don't understand. That's really fucked up. Why would you do that?"

"Well, you know . . ." Grant paused to pour himself a drink and then sat down again. This time, as he sat, he slipped one of his knees in between Ben's legs till it was almost pressing against his crotch. When Ben looked sufficiently distracted, Grant started over:

". . . I like you a lot, Ben. I liked you from the moment you first talked to me, so I'm gonna tell you a secret about the bites. When I was living out on the coast I would go for walks in the forest trails near my house. And sometimes, when I was hiking through somewhere that was totally secluded, I would lie down in the dirt and beat off."

Ben thought he heard Keith mutter, "hot," under his breath.

"So, this one time I was out there, lying in the trails, stroking my big old cock and enjoying myself, when all of sudden I feel a tiny little bite. Tiny, just like this."

Grant reached over to Ben and pinched him lightly with his nails. Ben yanked his arm back as if he'd been stabbed.

"Fuck off."

"That didn't hurt, did it?"

"No, but –"

"I'm just showing you it doesn't hurt. Relax. Anyway, I felt this tiny little bite – probably hurt less than what I just gave you – on the back of my leg. So I stop jerking, sit up and look at my leg, and there's this insect biting me. It looked like a little worm or something. That big," he held up his fingers to indicate something miniscule. "Before I know it, my leg is going numb and I start to freak. I think holy fuck, this little bastard is poisonous. Then I start to really panic. I'm like – no one will ever find me, and I'm gonna die out here. Worse still, what if my Mom finds me lying here dead with my dick out?"

Shannon snorted and murmured, "Lucky we didn't find you."

"There was nothing I could do because whatever that little thing pumped into me, had started working its way into my head, and before I could figure out what was going on I was suddenly having the best trip of my entire life. I went from completely freaking out to having this total, warm body buzz. It was so weird. I started to think, fuck, if I die that's fine, cause this is the fucking *best*."

"You can't be serious."

"Ben, I'm being totally serious. It was this amazing, numbing body high. And it's a short high, too, it's what, like, twenty minutes?"

Shannon and Keith nodded knowledgeably.

"Yeah, well, the most fucked up thing of all was when I finally came down, I was still hard. Honest. Isn't that insane?"

"So what'd you do?"

Ben could tell that Grant was delighted that he'd asked.

"I finished beating off!" he blurted. "And it was the best fucking load I have ever shot in my life."

For dramatic emphasis, he grabbed a handful of hair at the back of Ben's head and pulled him close, "The best load, man. I swear."

"All of this from that bug."

"Yep."

"Really?"

"Uh huh. I went back to that spot, like, a hundred times until we moved. I mean, it doesn't hurt at all, and it was so easy to get bit. And you know what the best thing is?"

Ben knew.

"You brought them here."

Grant nodded. "I fucking *brought* them here. Shannon and Keith tried it over the March break. I didn't think anyone else would ever be crazy enough to try it. Shannon was the first person I ever told about it." He turned to Shannon, "Tell Ben what you thought of it."

"It's really fucking good, Ben," Shannon said.

"There's nothing like it," Keith added. "I hate bugs, but it was so worth it."

Ben felt cornered. He didn't like the way things were unfolding. The wooziness brought on by the vodka and Grant's sexual advances made him decide to stay put for now. He wondered if the masturbation was a mandatory part of every encounter with the bugs. If so, that might change everything.

"I, uh, I don't think I could do that. . . . What about those other guys? Did they try it?"

Shannon, Grant, and Keith exchanged glances for a moment.

"What other guys?" Grant asked.

"The other guys you meet up with after school. They look like grade nine kids or something. Did they come over to try it?"

". . . Oh. Yeah. Yeah, they all tried it."

"Did they like it?"

Shannon leaned across the table. "Dude, everyone loves it."

Grant reassured Ben that there was no secret agenda at work to get him stoned or hooked, but Ben still felt like he was being coaxed. It became even more obvious when Keith and Shannon made a point of disappearing to another part of the house so Grant could have Ben's undivided attention. Apparently, not long after his discovery of the nest, Grant realized that he was going to be moving. The high he'd discovered was far too good to part with, so he started to experiment, bringing the bugs home in small containers. With a sufficiently cool, dark place, and enough blood to feed on, the bugs were quite content to live wherever Grant decided to put them. He explained that the adult bugs just grow into ugly gray beetles, which are more interested in eating damp wood than sucking human blood. It's their larvae that secrete the substance that gets you high. Storing a plastic container of the larvae in the bottom of a moving box for a couple of days was easy and they survived the relocation without any trouble. Grant had also found a perfect breeding place for them. A small, dingy shed in the backyard of his house. Ben asked if he was worried about his mother stumbling in there one day. Grant said that he simply told her it was full of bugs, and that had guaranteed that she would never set foot in there. He didn't have to specify what kind.

"Ben, why don't you come and look at them?"

Ben shook his head vehemently. "I don't want them biting me, man."

"Nothing's gonna bite you. Just come out and have a look. You can stay at the door if you want. I just want you to see them."

"What about Keith and Shannon?"

"Don't worry about them. . . . It's just you and me for a while."

⚬⚬⚬

In the murkiness of the backyard Ben could barely make out the shape of the shed. Made from a few sheets of plywood, it looked like it was on the brink of collapse. As they made their way towards it Grant kept his arm around Ben, as if he were protecting him from the cold. Ben sensed that, if nothing else, he wasn't going to leave that shed without Grant's mouth being on his. Grant started to recount how he'd met Shannon while cutting through a park, in the middle of the night. Shannon was sitting on a bench smoking a joint and invited Grant to join him. They seemed to hit it off, and after getting stoned together a few more times, Grant decided to introduce Shannon to the wonders of an entomological high. It sounded to Ben like the narrative had been seriously abridged. After all the stray touches he had been getting from Grant that night, he was ready to ask the more obvious questions: did he and Shannon have sex with each other, or what? Ben decided to wait for a better moment. It was too dark to make out Grant's expressions in detail, though he could tell that the grin was there, almost luminous.

"Stay here for a sec."

Ben was in no hurry to go into the shed, and was happy to wait. After turning a key in a heavy padlock, Grant disappeared into the doorway. Ben could hear him rustling around inside, swishing the ground with his foot, like he was clearing debris. Ben thought for a second that he might be stepping on the bugs, and imagined that Grant might suddenly bolt screaming from the shed, covered in writhing grubs. A dim orange light clicked on in the shed and Grant called for him to come inside. His limbs leaden with fear, Ben could only poke his head around the doorway. It smelled like the inside of a hamster cage.

"Ben, come inside."

"No way."

Grant was on the floor, sitting cross-legged on a towel. A battery powered utility lamp glowed beside him. Even though Ben could see his breath in the pale light, Grant had taken his shirt off again. Wreathed in soft, waxy shadows, he was more inviting than ever. Ben was still cautious.

"Where are the bugs?"

"I put them away. They don't like light. . . . It's okay. I won't get them out if you don't want me to."

Ben remained at the door for a second longer.

"Ben. C'mere and sit down."

Ben stalked in, and gingerly lowered himself down beside Grant. The ground was icy. The shed had probably been used for heavy work at one point; it was rife with bolts, metal loops, and chains, all fastened into the poured concrete floor. There was a sizable heap of paint rags in one corner. He couldn't see the walls, but the floor was certainly free of bugs. Ben sat down in the pool of lamplight, close to Grant.

"Aren't you cold?" Ben asked.

Ben saw it all unfold in slow motion, before it actually happened. Grant rolled his body forward and draped himself, heavy and warm, onto Ben.

"Now I'm not."

Grant started to kiss him. It came lightly at first, then all at once Ben's mouth was invaded by Grant's tongue. The sound of his own heart drowned out most of his thinking, though for a second Ben began to doubt if there were any bugs at all. Maybe it was all some dumb, creepy trick Grant had thought up to cajole him into the privacy of the shed. Shannon and Keith must have been in on it, pouring him drink after drink, and then disappearing. And yet the bites were real. Mid-thought, Ben felt Grant's fingers thrust beneath his T-shirt and start to pull it off. He flung the shirt into some dark corner, and pushing Ben down, slid on top of him. The cold air made Grant's bare stomach burn against his. This was bliss, bugs or not. One of Grant's hands was working itself down into the mossy hair under Ben's belt. The other one disappeared out of the lamplight for a moment. Then Ben felt it come back, sliding warm and careful under the back of his neck. And then something bit him.

"Fuck!"

Ben sat up, almost hurling Grant across the room. He reached back to locate the source of the pain and panic immediately overtook him. There was a small, spongy lump twitching away at the top of his spine. Slapping wildly at his neck, he shrieked for Grant to take it off, but the other boy stayed motionless. He had stood up and Ben couldn't see him fully, his face in blackness.

"Ben, it's okay," he was saying.

"Fuck, Grant. *Grant!* Take it off me. Take it off me, please. I don't want it on me."

Ben started to whimper. The body of the larva was small and oily, and Ben couldn't get a grip on it to pull it out. It felt like it was chewing, burrowing. He tried to stand up, only to discover that his legs had already been anesthetized with the poison. The numbing sensation spread quickly, like a reservoir of hot water being pumped in through the back of his neck and into his veins. His fingers started to lose their feeling next. When Grant noticed that Ben's movements were becoming sluggish, he knelt back down beside him.

"Ben, calm down."

He ran a hand through Ben's hair.

"Just chill. Let it take over."

Ben started to fall backwards, but Grant caught him, delivering him gently to the ground.

"See, you're okay." Grant moved his hand down to Ben's crotch and grabbed it. "You're still hard, too. That's good."

For the first time Ben found himself looking at the ceiling of the shed. In the circle of lamplight he noticed that a large, rectangular piece of chipboard had been balanced across the uncovered beams. The edges of the mouldy wood were overflowing with dozens of viscous, white cocoons, egg sacks which had spilled over from the piles of nests that were on the top. They dangled gently, stirred by the wind coming in from the open door. Ben thought he could see tiny gray forms peering over the edge of the plank, and then retreating. He was starting to feel calm. The warmth had flooded him completely now. It wasn't unpleasant at all. It was like floating at the bottom of a deep, hot bath, broken every now and then by a lazy chill coming up from the concrete beneath him. He could sense the high levelling itself off. He was still slightly lucid.

"Oh man," Ben slurred. "This feels so . . . nice. . . ."

"Isn't it? And you were so scared."

Grant started to slide his hands up and down Ben's body, lightly massaging the poison into his extremities, undoing his belt.

"I didn't even have to convince Shannon. He just did it, crazy fuck . . . Keith took a bit of work. But those kids, though. Man. You think you were a hard sell. At least you *know* what you want. . . ." Grant ran his lips across Ben's nipple. He seemed intensely pleased with himself. "This is some trick, huh? Bringing kids out here. Shannon's so smart."

Just then Ben remembered all the other boys. Grant must have brought them here, too. The chains that littered the floor around him were ominous for a second, but it was impossible to fix on a sensation that wasn't pleasurable. Whenever Ben veered towards a terrible thought a rush of warmth welled up to neutralize it. It frustrated him at first, then he gave in to it.

"Here, watch this." Grant stood up over him and started unwrapping his arm. "I'm gonna join you."

Reaching up he plucked one of the egg sacks off of the underside of the board. A few insects came to the edge to see their offspring being stolen, then retreated back, shrinking from the light. Grant held the egg sack in his fingers, and squeezed it gently at the sides. He knelt back down beside Ben and showed him the cocoon. Squirming around inside were three mucous-covered larvae. Ben couldn't feel disgust, just awe. Grant held out his arm and squeezed the edges of the sack some more, causing one of the maggots to slide out onto his arm. Ben noticed that it had six crab-like legs that had been tightly folded along its sides. As Grant held it up so Ben could get a better look, it's legs began to flail around spastically, grasping blindly in the air. He put the little worm back onto his arm.

"Check this out."

Ben watched with numb fascination as the maggot hoisted itself on stick legs towards a vein on Grant's arm. Under the influence of the poison Ben's perception kept shifting; he could feel its viscid belly sliding across Grant's skin, as if the belly were his own. Once it reached a suitable vein the maggot started to chew with a pair of strong mandibles, clutching tightly to the surrounding skin like a tiny, eager hand.

"Oh yeah. Here it comes."

Grant rolled his head back to welcome the venom.

"Best thing is," he said, letting his eyes drop down to Ben, "I've done it so many times I have a bit of a tolerance. . . ." He reached over and started to undo the buttons on Ben's pants. "I can get high, and while you lie there —" he freed Ben's cock, still hard, from his boxers, "— I can do whatever I want."

On top of the warm, floating miasma Ben was swimming in, he could now feel Grant taking him into his mouth. With the maggot and his crush both sucking away contentedly, Ben scarcely noticed Shannon and Keith lurking in the shed doorway.

"Hey Grant," Shannon drawled, "how is it?"

"He's sweet, man. You gotta try this."

Grant went back to work, but this intrusion had shaken Ben from his high. His limbs still felt like they were filled with heavy, wet plaster, but he knew he didn't want Shannon and Keith watching. He picked up a leaden hand to try and gesture for them to get out. It slid in a useless arc across the floor.

"Hey . . . guys," Ben managed at last, ". . . go away."

Grant stopped sucking and sat up.

"I think that someone needs another bug."

Shannon stooped down and picked up the cocoon that Grant had used. Ben could see another worm wriggling out under the pressure of his fingers.

"Where's the other one?"

"It's on the back of his neck."

"Are you gonna have one?" Grant asked Shannon.

"In a minute," Shannon said. "Let's take care of him first. . . ."

Shannon lifted Ben's head gently and held the gauzy egg sack up to his nape.

"Please . . . I don't want it."

Another rolling wave of warmth pushed Ben even further under.

"That . . ." was the last thing that Ben could get out. In his head he was trying to say "that's too much," but his tongue could only roll around, useless. The new rush dislodged him from his body entirely. Now he heard and saw everything as if he had been dragged to the bottom of a swimming pool. The boys looked like shadow puppets, their dark shapes shuffling around in the orange lamplight. Ben could see Keith standing with his legs splayed, making furtive, rhythmic gestures. Shannon and Grant had crouched over Ben's head, and were filling his mouth with their tongues. When he looked again, Shannon and Grant were lying awkwardly across his face, trying to get his paralyzed mouth to blow them. Ben thought it was impossible that he could still be breathing.

"Let's roll him over," Shannon said.

Keith sprang to help while Grant took off his pants.

"I get him next," someone said.

The sensation of being rolled onto his stomach was so abrupt that it brought Ben back into his body. The sudden repositioning had left his head partly thrust into a dark corner, and Ben could make out what he thought was the heap of paint rags in front of him. As his eyes adjusted, though, he could see that it was actually a large pile of clothes. His shirt was resting on top of it, but the other things did not belong to him. Jeans, shirts, underwear. Coats. Shoes. Keith and Shannon were tying his arms down. It took a full, sluggish minute for Ben to realize that those clothes had belonged to the boys who came before him. It also occurred to him that his face was lying out of the protective ring of light.

Straining his eyes, Ben could faintly see the swarm of beetles, refugees from the nests overhead, crawling towards him, carrying their hungry offspring. There was nothing he could do but try to shut his eyes and concentrate on the warmth of the body that was now lying on top of him.

He hoped it was Grant.

POLYPHEMUS' CAVE

DAVID NICKLE

The horror in the sawmill wasn't far from his mind the night he saw the giant. He'd thought about it briefly in Los Angeles, after he saw the telegram announcing his father's death. He considered the slow swing of barnboard doors across its great black belly each of the three times he'd had to stop to change flat tires on his brand new Ford Coupe. He thought about it again stopped in the afternoon sun at the top of a steep slope just west of the Idaho line, to deal with his boiled-over radiator. The water steaming from under the hood made him think about how the rainwater dripped from the tackle and chains in the sawmill's rafters as he lay face-down in damp sawdust. He retched yellow bile into the roadside dirt and started, maybe, to cry. The horror of that night was clearer in his mind then than it had been for years.

But a hundred miles ahead when the sun had at last set, the spruce trees at the side of the road spread apart like drawing curtains and the nude giant stepped into his path. The sight of it drove the North Brothers Lumber Company and its terrible sawmill from James Thorne's thoughts like a spurned beau.

The giant clutched a splintered rail tie in front of him like it was a baseball bat. He glared into the Ford's headlamps with a single eye – a great green orb flecked with yellow around a pupil as wide and deep as the Idaho sky. It hovered in the middle of his skull, beneath a great curling mass of black hair. James slammed his foot on the brake pedal and the Ford's tires bit into the road, sending stones rat-a-tatting into the depths of the wheel well.

My god, thought James. *He's big as trees.*

He leaned forward in the seat to get a better look. The giant crouched down and leaned towards the car. A leathery lid crossed his eye as he peered through the light at James. They studied each other in that instant. James felt as though that eye was looking through him: drawing the rest of his terror from him like sweet liquor at the bottom of a dark glass.

Then the giant made a noise like a dog's barking, his lips pulled back from teeth that seemed filed to points. With a swing of the rail tie, he splintered the tops of two trees on the far side of the road and disappeared again into the wood. Crickets chirped and treelimbs cracked, and James Thorne's heart thundered in his chest.

"He's big as the trees." He said it aloud, with a bit of a laugh. He wanted to say it to his pal Stephen Fletcher, a lean, young, black-haired colt of a boy who dressed sets back on *The Devil Pirates*. For the past month he'd spent many of his after-hours undressing James. Stephen was smooth and young and eager to please — and James wished Stephen were here now. But he couldn't take his lover home. Not anymore than he could admit to having him in Los Angeles.

James set his mouth and engaged the clutch. The Ford Coupe crunched across the gravel with a noise like breaking glass. He rounded a bend and came out in the great bowl of a valley in the Coeur d' Alene mountains. The road was still high enough that he could see the dim etchings of the familiar peaks against the night sky that surrounded Chamblay. In the valley's middle, miles distant, James could make out a glow among the trees.

This was new for him. When he'd left home, the Grand Coulee Dam wasn't even half built, and the only light in Chamblay came from candle, kerosene, and the sun. James smiled bitterly.

After dark on a moonless night, Chamblay could hide in itself.

The road carried James down a sharp slope and drew alongside the Northern Pacific line that served the town. The tracks gleamed silvery in his headlamps for an instant before he turned back parallel to the line.

This was the line that, according to his mother's cryptic telegram, had something significant to do with his father's sudden and untimely death.

"Mmm." He smiled a little, and thought about the giant in the road again — not just the eye, but his immense, sculpted thighs, the dark beard that tumbled halfway down the broad chest. . . .

"What a thing," he said. "What a marvelous thing. Put that in a picture, no one would believe it."

The giant, of course, would be the perfect thing for the pictures. Particularly pictures like *The Devil Pirates*. In the person of the brave and over-energetic Captain Kip Blackwell, James had battled a giant octopus, not one but two carnivorous gorillas, a host of man-eating midgets from Blood Island, and of course, several of the fearsome Devil Pirates themselves. For all that battling, Republic still wanted another batch of a dozen episodes before the serial ran its course. The giant man in the road, with the peculiar eye in the middle of his forehead, naked as the day he was born — he'd fill out four of those episodes, maybe more, all by himself.

James thought about that — about unsheathing his rapier against a giant more than twice as tall as he — leaping across the otherwise unconvincing deck of the *Crimson Monkey*, dodging the blows of the giant's papier-mâché club, slashing out theatrically with his sword to bring a dozen yards of sailcloth onto the monster's roaring head. Perhaps, to be true to the plot-line, they'd be battling over the honor of the lovely Princess Rebecca, who had disguised herself as a cabin boy back in episode three to join Kip and his crew on their frenetically eventful voyage.

"Wouldn't do to lose that fight," said James, thinking for a moment of what would become of his co-star, tiny Alice Shaw, in the amorous clutches of the giant. He slowed down as he drew through the closed-down business section of Chamblay, past the Episcopalian church his parents frequented, the schoolhouse where he'd learned to read – and finally outside the old clapboard house where he'd spent the first seventeen years of his life. James smiled and shook his head: the preposterous picture of a twenty-foot tall man mounting a five-foot two-inch woman provided a comic, if grotesque, distraction to the matter at hand.

He was still thinking about it – or about the giant, the magnificent giant that he might have seen or might, the more he thought of it, simply have dreamed – as he pulled his suitcase from the Ford's trunk, let out a long sigh, and made his way up the path to his mother's front door. The telegram that had brought him here sat folded in his jacket pocket and he made himself think of it. It was a reminder of what he ought to be feeling.

DEAREST JIMMY STOP I HAVE TERRIBLE NEWS TO DELIVER STOP YOUR FATHER HAS BEEN KILLED IN ACCIDENT ON TRACKS STOP PLEASE COME HOME STOP ALL IS FORGIVEN I LOVE YOU STOP YOU ARE THE MAN OF THE HOUSE NOW STOP PLEASE COME STOP LOVE ALWAYS YOUR MOTHER STOP

"Oh."

That was what James had said when the script girl had handed him the slip of onionskin paper from Pacific Telephone and Telegraph. He'd set his glass of water down. Read the words from the telegram once, and then again. Endured the girl's hand on his arm, the sympathetic cooing noise she made. He gave her a smile that was meant to look strained – the smile of a grieving son, bravely facing the death of his beloved old dad.

"Well," he said. He unbuckled the leather belt and scabbard. He draped it over the canvas back of his chair. He walked back behind the false-adobe wall of the Castillo de Diablo set to a spot where no one could see him. Crossed his arms. Put his hand on his forehead, and waved away a carpenter who'd stuck his head back there to see what was wrong. Then laughed, silently but deeply, until tears streamed convincingly in little brown rivers down the layers of orange pancake encrusted on his cheeks.

His dad was dead. Some terrible accident on the tracks. Well, wasn't that rich. The town would probably be having a parade for Nick Thorne, his strapping, iron-jawed Paul Bunyan of a father. . . . And now –

– now, he was the man of the house.

There was only one word for it.

Rich.

Three days after the telegram, in the middle of the night, James trod up the front steps to the family house. He didn't know much more now than he did then: he'd just sent off one telegram before packing up his car and heading off.

He found that he didn't want to know more than his mother chose to reveal in that fifty-word telegram. So he just composed one of his own:

DEAREST MOM STOP I WILL BE HOME IN THREE DAYS STOP DO NOT WORRY ABOUT THE COST OF BURIAL I WILL PAY STOP YOUR SON JAMES STOP

There was a light inside the house. He was not surprised to see that it was not electric. His father hadn't worked a decent job since the last time the North Brothers had run their mill, and that was years ago.

But the kerosene flame gave James an odd sort of comfort. The yellow, flickering light was proper and right for a town like Chamblay. Electricity was for New York and Los Angeles. This little place wasn't ready for it.

He paused to look inside. There was his mother, sitting in one of the hard, high-backed chairs. She held the black covers of the family Bible in front of her face like a fan. She heard him coming – he knew her well enough to tell that – but she pretended not to. As he watched through the window, she licked a forefinger and turned a page.

James leaned over and rapped twice on the window pane. His mother looked up. Widened her eyes in unconvincing delight, as though he were the last person she'd expect to see at the window on an August night some four days after the death of her husband. "Jimmy!" Her voice had a far-away sound to it through the window pane. She shut the Bible on its marker, set it down and hurried to the front door, which she flung open with a clatter.

"Oh, Jimmy!"

James patted his mother's back. "Hello, Mother," he said, as she buried her face in the crook of his shoulder and moistened his shirt with tears.

⚜

"Now tell me what happened," he said, as they sat across from one another in the dining room. "What happened to Dad?"

His mother smoothed out her print dress and looked down. "I'm sorry, hon – I guess I didn't put too much in that telegram. Thought you might have read the newspapers. About the derailment and such."

James shook his head. "I don't have much time for that, what with my schedule."

His mother smiled and patted his hand. "Well, you've got time to come home when I need you most. That's a blessing."

"They gave me ten days," said James. His mother's smile faltered, so he added: "I'm sure I can arrange a little more."

"Oh." The smile returned. "Well, good."

"Now. Was it the derailment? That –"

"That killed your father?" James' mother folded her hands in front of her and fixed her eye on the Bible. "Not directly. I can't believe you didn't hear of it. There was a newspaper man who came all the way from Seattle to interview me and take pictures. He said it'd play in all the Hearst papers, what with the circus angle. Biggest one since 1918, he said. I'd have written more if I'd known."

James frowned. "The *circus* angle?"

"It was a circus train," she said, sighing. "Twillicker and Baines Circus. Come down from Canada. Old steam engine, six rickety old freight cars and a couple of Pullmans. Wasn't even supposed to stop here. . . ."

"Ah." James nodded. He *did* remember the story now – the Twillicker and Baines wreck had come up a couple of times while he was in makeup. The circus train had derailed somewhere "up north." There'd been a kerosene fire. Some animals had gotten loose. A lot of people had been killed. There was a number, but he couldn't remember what it was. He shut his eyes – as much in shame as in grief. Maybe someone had said the word Chamblay in connection with the wreck. If they had, James just hadn't made the connection between the wreck and his home. Even when his mother told him of his father's death.

What did that say about him?

"There there, dear." His mother patted his hand. "It's been a long day's drive for you. I see that pretty car of yours outside. You don't want to hear about your father right now. Why don't you get some sleep? Lots of time to talk in the morning."

"I'll sleep later." James opened his eyes and took his mother's hand in his and looked her in the eye. It had been years since he'd fled Chamblay, and every one of those years showed in her face. Now grief was added to the mix. She looked very old. "Tell me about Dad now."

His mother nodded. "The train wreck happened in the middle of the night. They're still trying to figure exactly how, because there wasn't any other train involved. It made a terrible noise, though. Sounded like the ground was being torn. Your Dad – well, he went out to see what was what. You know how he could get."

James didn't answer. He *did* know how his Dad could get. Old Nick Thorne had a reputation to uphold in the town: he was the strongest and most capable man there was, after all. A terrible explosion sounds off in the middle of the night? He'd be out there in a flash.

"He joined the fire crew. The wreck was just a mile south of the station house, so he hopped on the back of the truck as it passed. Last time I saw him alive."

"Was he caught in the fire?"

James' mother shook his head. Tears were thick in the corners of her eyes. They gleamed in the kerosene light as her mouth turned down and her brow crinkled angrily.

"Trampled," she spat. "Crushed underfoot. By that damned *elephant*."

⚜

James' bed was as he remembered it: an iron-framed monstrosity, barely wide enough for one with a mattress that sagged deep in the middle. If two people got on that bed, its rusted springs would scream to wake the dead. Otherwise, there were few possessions left in the room. He stopped his mother from apologizing.

"I've been away a long time," he said. "It's fine. Now go to bed."

The room had a small window in it that overlooked the town. Light poured in from below, painting squares on the ceiling and walls. It reflected back from a small tin mirror nailed onto the opposite wall. His mother absently straightened it. James took her gently by the shoulder and led her to the door.

"Bed," he said firmly.

When she was gone, he undressed himself, hanging his trousers and shirt on a hook by the closet. He sat on the bed for a moment – listened to it squeak as he bounced a little. The briefest flash of nostalgia overcame him, then – of another night, when he felt the bristles of his friend Elmer Wolfe's neck against his shoulder . . . when the springs screamed, loud enough . . .

. . . loud enough. . . .

"Cyclops!" James snapped his fingers. That's what you called a giant with an eye in the middle of his forehead. He'd seen drawings years ago, in the old *Bullfinch's Mythology* they had at the schoolhouse. A huge, one-eyed man who lived in a cave and was ultimately blinded by a gang of Greek sailors.

James went to the mirror. The light from the window was enough to see himself by. But the mirror made him into a funhouse image – his chin was cartoonishly long; the thin mustache he'd cultivated for his Captain Kip role looked as though it'd been drawn by a drunkard. He leaned closer and it was better: the nearer you get to a bad mirror, the less the distortion.

Finally, he found he was literally looking himself in the eye. Just inches from the mirror, his own eye seemed huge. The light was wrong to make out the color – but it took little imagination to paint his iris yellow and green. To imagine the iris – big and black as an Idaho sky. He could lose himself in that eye. No, scratch that: he *wanted* to lose himself in that eye.

"Mmm," said James. His hand crept down to his crotch – took hold. He smiled. Shut his eyes. How would it be, he wondered, to lick that thing – that massive thing, while hands as wide as his back squeezed his shoulders; a thumb as wide as a post gently, maybe even painfully, spread his cheeks.

Eyes still closed, he backed across the room to the freshly-sheeted bed and fell into it – lost already in a fevered and vivid dream.

⚜

James and his mother spent the next morning at the Simmons Brothers Funeral Parlor in town. His mother had made nearly all the arrangements before he'd arrived. It was going to be a good burial, in the Chamblay Hill Cemetery, with a nice oak casket, and a polished headstone made of granite. It was far more than his mother could afford on her own. James made out three large checks while Mr Simmons prattled on about the tragedy of the train wreck and the evil of circus folk and the better place that Nick Thorne had gone to. When they were finished, James took Mr Simmons aside.

"Tell me," he said quietly, "what really happened to my father. It was no elephant — was it?"

Mr Simmons crossed his arms and lowered his head.

"An elephant," he said carefully, "was involved. But no."

"Not an elephant," said James. "But it was a big thing." He took a leap. "A cyclops, I heard."

Mr Simmons fixed him with a glare. "Circus folk," he said sharply. "Circus folk have all manner of queerness to them. Giants and midgets and clowns and trapeze artists. Big enough man can call himself a cyclops if he wants. I should stay well clear of them, if I were you, son."

"Where are they?"

"By the creek — camped like wicked hobos in the North Brothers common. But they won't be there for long."

James suppressed a smile. *Wicked hobos.* "I see."

Mr Simmons' glare faded. "I'm sorry," he said. "I've buried nine good men who lost their lives trying to put out the fire on that train wreck. Your father far from the least of them. Contrary to what some might say — a busy day's no pleasure for an undertaker."

"I'm sure it's not," said James.

"But son —" Mr Simmons put a pale hand on James' arm. "— Circus folk aren't nothing but gypsies, you know. They'll cut your throat and steal your wallet, give them half a chance. They'll overrun a town, steal its children. Don't go out there looking for vengeance."

"Vengeance?" James was honestly puzzled, and that was betrayed in his expression. "Why would I —"

"For the death of your father," he said, then added quickly: "Although I can see such thoughts are far from your mind. That is good, young sir. I apologize for thinking you a hothead. Other sons and daughters have been angrier about the goings-on with the circus folk. If I may say — your mother has raised a fine and temperate man. I am told that you do quite well for the family. In the moving picture business. I've a nephew in Spokane who's a great fan of the pictures. I shall tell him we've met."

"Give him my regards," said James. "And now — one more thing — if I could. . . ."

Mr Simmons smiled sadly. "See your father? I'd advise waiting till tomorrow. There's some work to be done. To make him as he lived. Do you no good to see 'im now, son."

James hadn't been about to ask to see his father's corpse. God, that was the last thing he wanted to see. He'd wanted to know more about the circus folk. About the cyclops. But Mr Simmons wouldn't talk more about that. He'd just think that James was fixing for vengeance, and try and stop him. So James just returned the sad smile and nodded. "Tomorrow, then," he said.

⊹

"You're far away," said his mother outside the house.

"Yes." James ran his hands over the knobby wood of the steering wheel. Stared into space at the far western ridges that were partly obscured in low cloud right then. "Sorry."

"That's all right, dear." She sat in the car, looking at him.

He smiled at his mother. "Listen. If it's all right with you, I'd like to take a little drive by myself."

His mother took a breath, patted his arm. "Of course, dear. You haven't been back here for almost ten years. And now you're back, it's to bury your –" She stopped, lifted her handkerchief to daub her eyes.

"Yes."

James let his mother go inside, then put the car into gear. He wheeled back through Chamblay's downtown. It was looking livelier during the day. Livelier, in fact, than it had in some time. He counted maybe a dozen trucks, covered with black tarpaulins. Big, dangerous-looking men in dark suit jackets leaned against their fenders, leering at passing townswomen. From behind the wheel of the Coupe, James leered at them. *Turnabout's fair play*, he thought, imagining himself in their midst – a giant in their midst – plucking first one, then the other, screaming into the air. . . . Ramming them face-down into the sawdust – into the dirt. . . .

God, James, he thought as the little fantasy took form in his mind, *you are a depraved one.*

Back in Los Angeles, Stephen had taken to chiding him about that very thing. "They'll let you go, you know, if the press gets wind of your shenanigans," Stephen said to him, curled against his stomach in the heat of a Sunday afternoon not long ago. "They'll cut you loose."

"No fooling." James had reached around front of Stephen, took hold of him lightly and ran a fingertip in the warm space between his thigh and his scrotum. He gave Stephen's nuts a sharp little squeeze. Stephen sucked in a breath – James could feel the cheeks of Stephen's arse tightening around him. "I guess we should stop, then. Maybe I should find religion. Or –" he pulled his hand away "– take little Alice up on one of her many offers. Knock her up. That'd settle it once and for all."

"Oh, go to hell," said Stephen. "You wouldn't know what to do."

"Wouldn't matter," James had replied. "She'd know what to do. And she *wants* to fuck me."

"Everybody wants to fuck you," said Stephen. "You're Captain Kip Blackwell, for Christ's sake. But I have to tell you, *Kip* – that unenthusiastic flirtation you play at with her in the canteen isn't fooling *anybody.*"

"It fools Alice," James had said.

"You think?"

James set his jaw. Put his foot on the gas pedal. He took the road to the mill – then, following the wood smoke and tireruts, made his way to the creek-bank where, according to Mr Simmons, the circus was encamped.

⚓

There was no Big Top; no shooting galleries or cotton candy stands or halls of mirrors. The remains of the Twillicker and Baines Circus were mostly people, and those people had spread out in a makeshift shanty-town along the grassy east bank of the Chamblay Creek. Little tents pitched here and there, charred swaths of orange and green and blue fabric. Some of the folk had dug out firepits in the needle-covered dirt. They were surrounded by trees, spruce and pine so high that from the camp's far side, they obscured much of the snowy mountain peaks to the west.

James stopped his car and got out. The place smelled of wood smoke and burnt fat. He tromped down the slope to the first of the tents – where a young woman sat beside an older man, broad-chested with a long, drooping mustache. He wore a battered felt bowler hat, and his arm was in a sling. She wore a pale blue cotton sun dress, mismatched with the torn fish-net stockings of a dancing girl.

"Hello," said James.

"Good sir," said the man, tipping his hat. "Clayton O'Connor, at your service." The woman smiled wanly. "And this is Clarissa."

James stood there awkwardly for a moment. They didn't appear to recognize him – which, as he thought of it, wasn't unusual: circus folk had a show of their own to perform Saturday afternoons. There'd be precious little time for the pictures, what with all the fire-eating and clowning and lion-taming to fill up the day.

"Good afternoon," James said. "James Thorne. I'm looking – that is –"

"The eye," said Clarissa, nodding. She wore a funny look.

"Do not mind her and her riddles, friend," said Clayton O'Connor. "She's new at the Sight."

James smiled. "*The Sight.* She's a fortune teller?"

Clayton nodded, and removed his bowler cap to reveal a balding crown covered in intricate tattoos. "An oracle," he said.

"Ah. Of course. Oracles speak in riddles, don't they?"

Clayton shrugged, held his hat in front of him. "It is a mixed blessing, good sir." He extended the hat a little further, like a bowl. "Prophecy is good, but it's nothing," he said, "without sound interpretation."

"I see." James laughed. "Prophecies are free, but interpretation costs a penny."

"Five pennies."

James' first impulse was to walk away – leave the tattooed man and his abstruse young oracle to prey on the next townie that happened by. But he dug into his pocket and came up with a nickel he thought he might spare. The oracle was a good schtick, and these people had just survived a train wreck; he couldn't begrudge them their little grift. He tossed the coin into the hat. "Interpret away," he said, and knelt down beside them. "Tell me . . ." He paused, looked across the creek to the dark evergreen wood. Some of the circus folk between himself and the river were taking note of him – of his new automobile. A dwarf limped up to it and gave the rear tires a malicious little kick. ". . .tell me about the cyclops."

Clayton looked into his cap – with his damaged fingers, he pulled the nickel out, turned it over and examined both sides.

Clayton paused a moment, then looked James in the eye. "You've seen it, have you sir?"

"The cyclops? I have." James took a breath. "Yes."

He shook his head. "And you're here anyway."

"I have to find him. It."

"Father," said the oracle, throwing her head back theatrically and gasping at the sky. "Here for his father."

"Hmm." James wasn't sure how good Clarissa was at oracling. But as an actress – well, she made wooden little Alice Shaw look positively Shakespearean.

"That has nothing to do with this. My father's dead."

James looked at Clayton, then at Clarissa. Her eyes fluttered shyly to her hands, a sly smile playing across her lips. Clayton raised his eyebrows in a questioning way.

Clayton nodded. "A lot of men are dead by that monstrosity's hand," he said. "That's why we're here."

"That's why *you're* here," said Clarissa, looking across the creek but pointing straight at James.

James ignored her. "All right, Clayton," he said. "Tell me about this thing."

Clayton looked at him. "That's more than interpretation," he said, rubbing two coinless fingers together as he spoke. "That's a tale."

Sighing, James dug into his pocket for a couple more pennies. When he'd added them to the nickel, Clarissa feigned a swoon across the log where she sat, and Clayton started talking.

✣

"The cyclops," said Clayton, "was with us for less than a season. Sam Twillicker found the beast deep in a cellar at a ranch in eastern Texas, where he'd been guesting over the Christmas break. Baines and Twillicker had had a bad run of luck with the Hall of Nature's Abominations the past season. The mermaid had come unstitched and spewed straw and cotton all over her case in the middle of our St Louis show in May. In the early morning hours of July 8, our prized geek Skinny Larouche ran off into a Kansas cornfield with a pair of chickens and the previous day's nut. Later that month, Alfie Fowler took ill with something in his intestine. In August, the bug moved to the gut of brother Mitch, and by Labor Day we'd lost our genuine Siamese twins. Perhaps, said Charlie Baine, the days of sideshows were winding down and they ought just fold up the rest of Nature's Abominations and concentrate on the Rings. But Twillicker didn't buy that; to him, a freak tent was as much a part of the show as clowns and lion-tamers and the high wire. So when his host in Texas mentioned the thing he was keeping in the cellar, and intimated that he had intended the thing's stay should be temporary – 'I'll have to kill it or be rid of it, and I'm not sure I can kill it,' he said – Sam Twillicker was intrigued.

"But Twillicker's no fool. He took care not to let his interest show.

"'We have an excellent strong man,' he said cagily. 'You've got a fat Greek with an eye out? I might put a patch on my Wotun the Magnificent, change his name to Polyphemus and call him the one-eyed giant – and not have spent a penny more.'

"'It would not be the same,' said the host. 'For mine – he has seen the Trojan women and sung duets with Sirens and walked the sea-bottom at the heel of Poseidon. How can you compare?'

"'You ought to have been a barker, my friend,' said Twillicker. 'For you could make the rubes see all those things and more in even my poor Wotun, with pretty words like that.'

"'Not the same as seeing it for real, though.'

"Late in the evening, Twillicker walked outside the ranchhouse, to do just that: see it with his own eyes. They climbed down a tunnel past a padlocked door in the Texas scrub, and stepped out onto a ledge in a room like the bottom of a giant well. The thing – the cyclops – was below them, lolling against the wall amid a carpet of whitened bones. Flies buzzed and flitted in the lantern beam that Twillicker's host shone down, and the creature looked up into it with its single great eye, so wide that Twillicker could see the pair of them reflected in it.

"'How big is he?' said Twillicker.

"'Twenty and five,' said his host. 'From toe to skull top, twenty and five feet.'

48

"'And that eye,' said Twillicker. 'Sitting unnaturally in the middle of the forehead like that. It's real?'

"'It better be,' said the host, 'for the beast has none but that to see by.'

"'My god,' said Twillicker.

"The bones rattled and crunched below as the cyclops stirred. Both men stopped their conversation as the thing drew himself to his feet. Standing, the cyclops was nearly eye-level. His breath came like a hot Mediterranean wind. His eye blinked. A hand, big as a door, came up over the lip of the ledge – Twillicker barely had the wit to step back into the tunnel before it could grasp him. The cyclops opened his great mouth and rumbled something that sounded like Greek. Hot, unbreathable air followed them up the tunnel as they backed away from the grabbing hand.

"'That,' sputtered Twillicker, as they climbed the stairs to the Texas night, 'that thing was going to eat me!'

"'Not likely,' said his host. 'The cyclops likes lamb better than man. But still – better he didn't get hold of either of us. Because that eye – that eye of his is a hungry eye.'

"'What do you mean by that?'

"'What I say. It's a big eye – a god's eye – and it hungers for the sight of a man's soul. It'll drink that sight right out of you, if you let it.'

"Twillicker spent another three days at the ranch – thinking mostly about what that meant. He didn't know about getting his soul drunk up – but he surely wanted to see that cyclops again. He wanted to see it something fierce; it took all his will not to steal down that hole again, and look at the beast once more. How many times, he wondered, could he haul a rube back and back again to see this beast, if it had such a draw on a seasoned ringmaster as Twillicker?

"He came back a month later with the right cash and equipment for moving the creature. By March, he had a rail car rigged up and fresh signs made. By the middle of April, the circus was on the move again, and Nature's Abominations was back in business.

"There were practical problems. For one thing, the cyclops was not a professional. It was more like keeping an animal than an employee – as they discovered when our roustabouts tried to use the cyclops' strength to haul up the big top outside Denver and three of them wound up in bandages and splints, raving for days from their trials at the cyclops' hands. The creature's unruliness kept him out of the Big Top as well. He couldn't be trusted around townies without thick bars between he and them, because unlike our old geek Larouche, depravity was no act for the cyclops. He leered – at everyone, in a measure, but he paid particular attention to the aerialists. One time –" Here Clayton paused, and patted Clarissa on the shoulder, "– one time he got hold of this girl here. Didn't he darling?"

Clarissa's eyes rolled into her head and she trembled for an instant. Then she blinked and nodded.

"Took five of us to get her back," he said. "Clarissa tore a ligament, and that was it for her on the trapeze. Looked at her for a little long – maybe drunk a bit much of her poor wee soul, hey girl? And she hasn't been the same since.

"But for that, no one could deny that with the addition of the cyclops to our roster, the Twillicker and Baine Circus had turned a corner. Every town we stopped in opened its purse to us and our monster. Rubes loved Hall of Nature's Abominations now that the cyclops sat in its middle. They forgave the two-headed ewe that floated nearly invisible in a milky brine. They didn't mind that the geek cage was still empty, or that the two Italians who played the Siamese twins didn't even look like relations. They hurried past Gerta the Doll Woman and Lois the Chicken Lady. Didn't heed the resentful glare that our own Wotun the Magnificent gave them, as they sat through his Nine Feats of Strength that raised sweat-beads big as dimes on shoulders and a brow that had one time seemed immense. They each paid their nickels and gathered in five-dollar crowds in the Hall's middle for the headline of our show – and listened, as Twillicker himself rolled the spiel outside the curtained-off cage of Polyphemus, Son of Poseidon.

"'He has seen the Trojan women and sung duets with Sirens and walked the sea-bottom at the heel of Poseidon,' Twillicker would bellow. 'He has fought Ulysses, battled Odysseus, and shook a fist at great Jove himself! Ladies and gentlemen – I give you – '

"And their breath would suck in, as the bright red curtains drew from the front of a tall, steel-barred cage.

"' – I give you Polyphemus! Son of the sea god Poseidon.'

"And the curtain would open, and the men would gasp, and the children scream – and the women, some of them, would faint dead away at the sight of the naked giant Polyphemus. His lips would pull back from a shark's-row of teeth, and his great arms would rise to rattle the bars of his bolted-together cage – and he'd take a taste of them with that eye of his.

"And then, as fast as it'd risen, the red curtain would fall back in place, and the next crowd would come through. By the time the circus was ready to pull up, all the crowds were filled with familiar faces. They all felt that same draw Twillicker had felt that first night. By the time the circus left a town, the coffers were filled to overflowing with fresh torrents of silver.

"The cyclops became a part of the circus like he'd always been there. The cat wranglers and elephant handlers and the roustabouts had all worked out a drill for moving him, from his cage to the railcar and back again – figured out how to feed him without getting too close to those giant hands, those lethal jaws – and devised a way to wrap the ropes and chains around his wrists and ankles and middle, so he couldn't squirm much. Charlie Baine looked at his books, and understood that for all the food he was buying for his Cyclops, profits were still higher than they'd ever been. As for the freaks, now relegated to second-class oddities in the shadow of Poyphemus? They rattled the change in their pockets and shrugged. Even Wotun couldn't complain much about being upstaged by the Greek giant. It was as good as pitching the tent next to the Grand Canyon. Folks'd pay to watch your show, just because it was on their way to the view.

"And the view," said Clayton, "doesn't ask for a cut of the nut."

"But the cyclops wasn't just a view," said James. "The cyclops felt differently."

Clayton winked at him. "No fooling you, sir. 'Tis true. The cyclops felt *differently.* And why wouldn't he? For we kept him like an animal, although he was a thinking beast. He stood in his cage, listening to Twillicker holler his spiel, enduring the stares of the glassy-eyed rubes. Submitted to the will of his wranglers. And always he watched. With that great eye he has. He watched and he paid attention. Listened to what Twillicker said, and made out the words. Listened to the rubes muttering amongst themselves. Heard the wranglers and the freaks and the clowns chatter on. Two weeks and a day before the tragedy here –" He gestured behind him to the camp. "– he spoke."

Clarissa the Oracle stood, her eyelids trembling in a sideshow trance. "*I am Polyphemus,*" she said in a deepened voice, "*son of the sea god Poseidon.*"

"Dear Clarissa started talking then, too. She'd given up the trapeze, and been fooling with tea leaves and Tarot cards instead. We thought she might open a fortune telling booth. When the words started to come – the poetry – it dawned on us all that little Clarissa should start calling herself the Oracle."

"From the Greek stories," said Clarissa.

"It was a theme," said Clayton. "The cyclops didn't speak much. But the words he did speak commanded respect. He seemed to speak the things in a man's soul. The things that did not wish speaking. Perhaps – perhaps he did what Twillicker's Texan host said he did: drank in the souls of men and women through his great eye, and spat up truth. For is it not true, that the cyclops were the sons of gods?"

"The sea god Poseidon," said James dryly.

"You mock," said Clayton. "But you shouldn't, because you've seen him." James couldn't argue with that.

"The talk continued off and on," said Clayton. "Sometimes it would be just a few words a day. Words we could understand. Words in strange tongues. All mixed up. It was a kind of parroting. After a time, the talk became incessant. He talked as the wranglers tore down his cage, roped his wrists, and led him to his rail car. It went on even after he was chained in, we all boarded, and the train was underway. Talked and talked and talked through the night, louder even than the engine whistle some times – softer than a whisper in your ear at others. Far into the next night, and into the mountains – the giant's voice lived in our skulls. That can be the only thing that drove Twillicker to do what he finally did."

James shivered as the wind shifted over the circus shanty-town. In the distance, he heard a rumbling sound of car engines. "And what," he said, goose flesh rising on his arms, "did Mister Twillicker finally do?"

"Unbound him," said Clayton. "They found Twillicker's body near the cyclops' car after the wreck. The giant killed him, we can only think – after Twillicker clicked the locks with the key we found on 'im. Perhaps the cyclops told him something he could not ignore. Or perhaps –"

"– perhaps the temptation to take a look was too strong to resist," said James quietly.

"Split up the middle was he, into Twillickers two," said Clarissa helpfully. "One good, one wicked – and –"

She stopped. Rubbed her arms. Looked back to the road.

"What's wrong, deary?" said Clayton.

"Wicked," she said, very quietly, as the first black-draped truck crested the hill and stopped to let its load of bat-bearing men out to the circus' hobo town.

"We should run."

⌖

"*You are all trespassing. By the authority of the Chamblay Sheriff's Office and the owners of the North Brothers Lumber Company – on whose property you are squatting – I'm placing all of you under arrest.*"

The speaker was a thick-set man with short bristly white hair and thick brown sideburns who stood on the hood of the second truck in. He wore a suit jacket and black wool pants tucked into rubber boots that came up to his knee. He held a long, double-barreled shotgun propped against his hip. Maybe two dozen men carrying baseball bats and wearing dark suit jackets surrounded him.

"*Don't make trouble for yourselves.*" The man lowered the megaphone and motioned down the slope with the barrel of his shotgun. His men started to move.

James was already ankle-deep in the river. Clayton and Clarissa and a crowd of others with the circus, were with him.

"Who the hell is that?"

"Pinkertons," said Clayton, huffing as he sloshed. "That one was here day before yesterday. There was trouble with a couple of the roustabouts."

Pinkertons. James shuddered. This wasn't the first time he'd heard of the detective agency; when he was a boy, a gang of Pinkertons ran herd on the men who worked the lumber mill. His father's most prominent scar, a puckered pink thing that extended along his forehead up past his hairline, dated back to the first time Pinkertons came to Chamblay.

Dating to a night . . .

When the bedsprings screamed, and . . .

. . . Jimmy tasted the sawdust in his mouth . . . .

There was no doubt about it. James' feelings about Pinkertons were . . . complicated.

The Pinkertons men moved through the camp like armed locusts. They knocked down tents and sent pots of hot water flying and splashing into cookfires. Three of them descended on a dark-chinned roustabout and pummeled him to the ground. Two were studying James' coupe, parked a dozen yards upslope. Another two chased down a pair of dwarfs straggling behind the exodus to the creek, while five more waded into the waters after the fleeing mass of circus folk. At the top of the slope, their captain stuck a cigarette in his mouth as he watched it all unfold.

"Get away from my car!" shouted James.

"Christ," said Clayton, a dozen steps ahead by now. "Hurry, boy. He'll crack your skull! Run!"

James was about to turn and do just that when the shadow passed briefly over their head.

The Pinkertons captain looked up. He dropped his cigarette, still unlit. The boulder crashed down in the middle of his truck, sending glass and metal flying through the air. The Pinkertons men who were following them turned and gaped at the sight.

Clarissa screamed then. "Oh, lord!" shouted Clayton, pointing at the opposite bank. James looked, and froze, creek-water lapping icily on his ankles.

The cyclops stood there, a bronzed giant in the sunlight. He raised an arm to shield himself against the flames, then waded into the creek and bent down and reached into the water.

James stood transfixed as the cyclops' muscles strained to yank a huge, river-rounded rock from the creek-bed. A lid the size of a window cover crinkled over his single eye and his sharp teeth bared in the sunlight as he hefted the rock to shoulder height. James swallowed and gasped as the beast straightened and the muscles rippled down his abdomen.

"What're you staring at? Come on, boy!" Clayton yanked James' arm and hauled him stumbling downstream. Behind them, there was a gout of water high as geyser as the rock crashed in the path of the five detectives who'd followed them. James ran as best he could through the fast-moving shallows of the Chamblay Creek. He didn't look back when the terrifying roar sounded out across the valley; kept moving when he heard the two gunshots, and the screaming. He finally stopped with the rest of them, when they reached a small rapids in the creek.

Clayton helped Clarissa onto a low, spray-soaked shelf of rock that split the creek. James hauled himself up, and for the first time looked back.

The circus camp was blocked now by a low rise of trees. A black plume of smoke rose above them and into the sky. There was another scream — distant and strangled — and then Clarissa pointed and cried out: "Look!"

A man was flying — his legs and arms wheeling as if for purchase on the air. He must have been a hundred feet up, before he started falling again. There came another roar. Clarissa covered her ears. Clayton shut his eyes against the tears. The others who were lucky enough to make it to the creek cowered in terror.

And as for James —

James Thorne found his hand creeping to the belt of his trousers. He pulled it away, and ran it through his hair.

"My god," he said unconvincingly. "The horror."

The camp was ruined when they returned, and the cyclops was gone. But he'd left his mark. People were down everywhere: strong men and acrobats and clowns and roustabouts and the hard men from Pinkertons. Some must have been dead, because it smelled like barbecue. The beast had marked his exit with a gateway of smashed and broken trees. Clayton bent down onto his knees and clenched his good fist. Clarissa knelt beside him. The two of them wept softly.

James stepped back from them: surveyed the place. It was a terrifying mess. Was this what the undertaker Simmons had meant when he said the circus folk wouldn't be here for long? Had he heard tell that the North Brothers had gone and hired Pinkertons to clear out the town? James felt a little sick: if he'd been more on the ball, he might have been able to muster a warning, rather than waste these people's time telling him tales of the cyclops.

The lame dwarf who'd kicked his car tire hobbled past, and pausing, glared up at him.

"Ain't you the movie pirate?" he said.

"Captain Kip Blackwell," said James. "That's right."

"Well, why don't you get your fat piratey arse moving and take care of that beast? Make 'im walk the fuckin' plank! 'Bout time someone did."

"I'm not a real pirate." James held up his hands. "Look," he said. "Not even a sword."

The dwarf bent down over one of the fallen detectives. "Well, fuck my arse, if this ain't your lucky day." He stood up, holding a baseball bat nearly as long as he was tall. He handed it to James. "Now you've got a choice — you can use this one —" The dwarf pointed to the bat. "— or this one!" James yelled as the dwarf swatted his groin.

"Ha! Unless you want to save it for the oracle bitch, who — hey!" The dwarf yelled as Clayton grabbed him with his good arm and lifted him off his feet.

"That's enough," said Clayton.

"Wotun! C'mon! Fuck you! Put me down!" The dwarf's feet pinwheeled in the air. James raised his eyebrows.

"Wotun?"

In one motion, Clayton set the dwarf on the ground and shrugged at James. "Not much of a strongman now, I'm afraid. We're all put in our place. By that thing."

James hefted the baseball bat. He looked to the crack in the woods the cyclops had left behind him and back at Clayton O'Connor, the former Wotun the Magnificent.

Clayton took off his bowler.

"You want company?" he said.

James shook his head. "No," he said.

"I can tell what you mean to do," he said. "Are you certain you dare to?"

James felt himself smile a little. "You have no idea what I mean to do," he said, and set off toward the edge of the trees, where the cyclops had marked his path.

⚜

As he tromped through the woods, James thought about his last day on the set. The last scene he'd shot before they let him go. Two of the Devil Pirates had tossed him into the Sarcophagus of Serpents – where Captain Kip would spend the next episode, while Princess Rebecca and the rest of the *Monkey*'s crew contrived his rescue and James Thorne contrived to bury his old Dad.

"Jimmy!" Alice Shaw hurried to catch up to him, as he stalked away from the plywood Sarcophagus left over from last year's *King of the Mummies* serial. He sighed and stopped.

"Alice," he said.

She stopped in front of him, set her fists on the velvet britches that were Princess Rebecca's single nod to disguise. "I just wanted – to offer my *condolences*."

"Thank you."

"Because we can all see how *torn up* you are. About your father's death."

James frowned. "Well, it's been a long time –"

Alice stepped closer to him, took his hands in hers as though they were sharing an intimacy. In a way, they were. "You know, Jimmy," she said, "you should really learn how to act."

"Alice?"

"You'd fool more people." Alice stepped back. "Why are you even bothering to go?"

James crossed his arms. "To bury him," he said.

"Something you wish you'd done long ago?"

He sighed. "If you like, Alice."

She wagged a finger at him. "I know what you are, Jimmy Thorne," she said. "The only question is: what did your horrible old father do to you, to make you this way?"

James wondered if he'd ever feel the proper things about his father's death. He felt as though he were circling those things as he walked – getting closer to the feelings of grief and loss and everything else that went with facing a father's death.

But the fact was, he wasn't thinking about that. He was thinking about the cyclops. And he wasn't thinking about how he'd kill him, either.

The path led him to the bank of the creek where it twisted around a cropping of rock and tree. With a trembling, he knew where he was:

The North Brothers Lumber Company's sawmill.

The last time he'd seen it, the mill was up and running. The whine of the sawblade would cut across the valley as teams of horses hauled giant logs up the round-stoned creek-bank to the mill's black and hungry mouth. Inside, men would unhitch the logs and haul them further along with complicated block and tackle. Nick Thorne would be first among them, the muscles in his thick forearms dark as mahogany, straining at the weight of the spruce and pine logs cut down from the mountain slopes all around them.

Now the place was still as a tomb, its wooden walls and roof gray as stone.

James swallowed. His hand was shaking as he set the baseball bat down in the pine needles beside him, and set out across the creek shallows. The mill's great black doors were open. Inside was dark as a cave.

⚓

The last time James had been inside the mill, the scent of pine sap was overpowering. Pine sap and machine oil and a bit of fear sweat.

Now, it smelled like a slaughterhouse.

At first, James was afraid the cyclops had brought humans here – some of those folk Mr Simmons had said had gone missing. But as his eyes adjusted to the dark, he saw that wasn't so. The smell was from something else. Animal carcasses hung from chains wrapped around the rafters. He first passed a couple of shapes like big cats, their skins torn off as they hung maw down to the sawdust-covered ground; something that might have been a boy, but James gathered to be a monkey carcass, hanging by a single, hand-shaped foot; and what was left of the elephant. The bloody trunk brushed James' shoulder as he passed underneath and a cathedral of ribs hung over his head. A cloud of flies that had been feeding there followed James for just a few steps then abandoned him as he left the cyclops' larder, and moved into the next chamber of the mill.

James stepped around a thick post. Looked down, where the floor of the sawmill sloped from wood down to dirt. Light leaked in through the warping barnboard of the mill's wall – reflected off a pool of oily water that had collected at its base. The cyclops crouched by that pool – poking with an extended finger at a dark shape in the water.

The cyclops rumbled something indecipherable, in a deep and lazy voice. Mottled sunlight from the pond flickered across the giant's flesh.

He stood high enough to brush rafters, while at his feet the shape rolled and sank beneath the water.

His nostrils flared and he made a bellows-like huffing sound as he sniffed. He turned to face James.

In two great steps, the cyclops had closed the distance between them. He leaned down, so that his eye – big as James' head – was just a few feet off.

James gasped. This close, the cyclops' eye was fantastical. Colors shifted across the broad surface of its iris like oil across a sunlit pool. As for the dark in its middle, that grew and shrank as the creature focussed on James –

– the darkness was hungry.

The Cyclops reached around with both hands, and tucked them under James' arms. He lifted him like he was a small child. The cyclops muttered ancient words as he turned James from side to side – studying him like he was a doll.

James kicked his feet back and forth in the air beneath him. He looked down: his toes were at least a dozen feet from the floor. He could barely breathe, the creature was holding him so tightly. He stared into the great eye, and the Cyclops stared back.

Memory drew from him like pus from a swollen wound.

He felt a sob wrack across his body. The cyclops ran a great thumb down his chest. When it settled, James gasped. The cyclops grinned.

James squirmed in terrified ecstasy. The giant's thumb was thick as a man's thigh, but far more nimble. The feeling was primordial – it was as though it yanked him back to the night when his old friend Elmer Wolfe slept over – and had found his way into James' bed – pressed close to him – and then the springs . . .

. . . the bedsprings. . . .

They screamed.

⚓

The mill was dark when Nick Thorne and Jimmy arrived there. It was in the hours before dawn – long before the morning shift would arrive. Nick pushed the boy around the side of the building, and through the great, blackened doors. It was dark inside.

"You want to lie with men, boy?" Nick cuffed his son hard enough to send him to the ground. "You like that, do you?"

Jimmy heard himself whimper – and hated himself for making so weak a noise. He was covered in sawdust. Face-down on the ground. His father smelled of liquor and sweat. "I'll show you what it's like. . . ."

Jimmy tried to press himself into the ground – as though he could escape that way, by enveloping himself in wood shavings. But there was no escape. His father's hand, thick and calloused from working a lifetime in the sawmill, pushed hard between his legs, pushed his nuts up hard into his abdomen. He gave a cry that sounded to him like a squeak.

"That's what it's like, queerboy." His father grunted, took back his hand, and undid his trousers.

"*That's what it's like, queerboy.*" The cyclops brought James close to his face. He opened his great mouth, and a tongue came out, thick as a marlin and rough like a towel – touched James' middle, taking a taste of him. The cyclops huffed, and smiled, and lowered James to his own middle. Now James was staring straight into another, smaller eye. James felt his feet touch the ground, and the giant's hand pushed him, guided him forward.

James rubbed his face against the shaft of the giant's penis. It was wide as a drum, and the leathery flesh trembled as he caressed it. The cyclops moaned. The hand stroked James' back. It wasn't squeezing him anymore. But James knew it held him there as surely as if it were a fist clenched around him. Shaking with fear and lust, and tears streaming down his cheek, he raised his own arms and embraced the immense shaft.

The memory kept coming. The vivid, awful memory of his father, the heroic Nick Thorne, buggering him for what seemed to be an hour on the floor of this place. To teach him a lesson, he'd said. The old man had rolled him over before he was done. Demanded . . .

. . . demanded. . . .

There had been a sharp cracking sound before he could do anything else, and his father had fallen down, clutching his skull. A man with a baseball bat was standing behind him. First ordering him off the property – telling him he was trespassing. Saying something about being an "agent of the mill." Showing a little eye-shaped Pinkertons badge on his chest. Then, seeing Jimmy half-naked in the sawdust, shutting his mouth. The baseball bat came up again, and down again. That was when Jimmy had said it:

"Stop killing him! He's my Dad!"

"Sweet Jesus," said the man from Pinkertons.

"*Sweet Jesus,*" said the cyclops.

James looked up. The cyclops moved his hand from his shoulder, let him step back.

"Shit and hell." Not a dozen feet off, the gray-haired man from Pinkertons stood, blood in his beard and his shotgun raised, along with a fresh troop of detectives. "It's a monster, boys. Kill it."

The cyclops let James go, and turned his great eye to face his attackers. James sat down in the wet sawdust and finally felt the tears – hot and salty and honest – streaming down his cheeks. They weren't the tears of mourning. Those, James realized, would never, ever come. The roar and light of gunfire and screams filled the cavernous mill. James was nearly deaf from it, weeping in the dark, when the cyclops turned his gaze back to him.

Now why, wondered James as he gazed up into the cyclops' encompassing eye, would anyone stick a spear into that?

James dropped two polished nickels on his father's waxy eyelids. Gunshots echoed through the valley as another wave of detectives assaulted the sawmill, and James thought about old Nick Thorne's death: fighting his way through the flames – looking everywhere but up – before he was plucked into the sky and flung down again, amid the screams of his fellows.

James stepped back and put his arms over his mother's shoulders. He tried to ignore the stares of the other mourners. He was a mess. He'd come directly here to the Chamblay Cemetery from the sawmill. His shirt and trousers were stained and torn from the night spent in the crook of the cyclops' arms, amid the heaps of dead men left over from the first Pinkertons assault. His chin was dark with morning beard. It was quite scandalous – showing up such a disheveled mess at his father's burial. He supposed he would have to get used to that, when he went back to Hollywood. There would be quite a lot of scandal then. Republic would more than likely, as Stephen had put it, cut him loose once it all came out.

It may as well come out. Because he couldn't go back to the cage of lies he'd made for himself in Hollywood – to being Captain Kip Blackwell of the Seven Seas – any more than Clarissa the oracle could go back to the trapeze now that the horror of her own tiny soul was drunk dry, or than Clayton O'Connor could trick the rubes into thinking he were a true strong man, or than Sam Twillicker could live another day once the cyclops had sucked his soul right from him.

But he would have to take this one step at a time. His mother looked at him with wet, uncomprehending eyes. "*What happened to you?*" she whispered.

"Quite a lot," said James as Mr Simmons' shaking hands closed the lid of his father's casket, and his sons prepared to lower the old man into the space they'd carved for him in the earth. James felt himself shaking too, around the great, empty space in him where the sawmill had crouched all these years.

"I'll tell you all of it this afternoon," he said.

DEAD IN THE WATER

C. MARK UMLAND

Martin was quite certain he had gone to bed last night the way he usually did. He saw himself creeping upstairs under cover of darkness, avoiding loose floorboards like they were landmines, and then with held breath sliding in next to the hateful Maria. Then he was sure he had fallen asleep under a cool oscillating-fan breeze, wearing his jockeys because he no longer slept naked next to her, while she slept on her side, equally un-naked, turned away from him, her raven-black hair fanned on her pillow.

He was positive it had happened that way.

But when he woke up, just as the first light of dawn was streaking the sky, Martin found himself walking on the centerline of the road that traversed Lake Laughton, a good five miles down the hill from his house. He walked alone, handling the centerline the way a driver might during a sobriety test for a cop, and he thought to himself that an abundance of whiskey before bedtime was wreaking havoc on good REM sleep.

Martin looked about. He saw the waterfront and moored boats behind an amorphous blur of white that he assumed was the morning light coming in through the bedroom window. He closed his eyes and imagined himself pulling the thin top sheet up to his chin He burrowed his head further into the pillow. He heard the ticking clock, the pleasant drone of the fan. He heard Maria's soft breathing.

He opened his eyes again.

The park and beach was to his right, a popular local holiday spot during the day for families, and a terrific area at night for teens to skulk about, drink beer, smoke shit, and get laid if lucky enough. Because of the recent heatwave townsfolk had been pitching tents near the water, contrary to municipal legislation, and at night brazenly skinny-dipping in the open – again in contradiction to the law of the land. Townies tended to gravitate toward the water, and on a normal day, even an early morning like this, the lakeshore was a hub of activity. Except for now. Now the area was completely barren. Water lapped politely against the sand and the hot air moved at a languid pace. An innocuous cloud hung over the middle of the lake, bothering no one. Two lifeguard towers stood on the sand, the remnants of a sandcastle were near the waterline.

And again he shut his eyes, still walking, still quite sure that the clock radio was about to switch on to that obnoxious local morning show and then Maria would sit up, give him a hard, baleful look, and lay back down. Then he'd climb out of bed to face the day, face ten hours shut up in an anonymous government office building, ten hours he would endure because Thomas waited at the end of it.

Martin became aware of small shockwaves as his feet struck hard blacktop. The low morning sun fell damply on his shoulders. A chorus of wheeling seagulls patrolled for dead fish. He stopped, looked around, blinked stupidly. Confusion competed for space alongside that kind of internal fog that infiltrates the recently-awakened. But the fog lifted quickly, dissipated by low panic and an emphatic query that resounded in his mind:

What the fuck?

The morning shimmered around him like a bucolic mirage. The pale light was faded and washed out and the air attained a kind of undersea murkiness. *Sleepwalking,* he thought. *Good god, I've been sleepwalking,* and then in complete alarm looked down to see if he was wearing more than just his jockeys. He was. The clothes he had been wearing the night before covered his body, *clung* to it actually as liquid moved along the surface of his skin. He wore a light cotton shirt – white – and khaki Dockers with the cuffs rolled up to reveal no socks and sandals. It seemed he had gotten himself decent for his somnambulistic stroll, had dressed in his sleep, put on what he had removed in the dark and left in a pile on the floor (and what Thomas had removed in the dark much earlier) as he crept into the bedroom, being careful not to awaken Maria, and praying quietly and insistently for the whirl of scents, of whiskey and cigarettes and Thomas' sweat, to not rouse her.

His mind saw more, but he wasn't quite ready for it. Not yet. Instead, his temporal lobe teased him with snippets of information – little disjointed shards of memory. A flash of bloody roast beef laying on a Corning dinner service. A decanter of red wine being lifted and tilted. Splashes of Merlot blossoming onto a pale yellow tablecloth. A glowing end of a cigarette. A tear sliding down a cheek.

⁍

Maria smoked cigarette after cigarette and chewed on her thumbnail. Her own meal sat before her, nearly untouched, but Martin had devoured his. He was anxious to get going.

When the meal was over, Martin offered a perfunctory "thanks for dinner" and went upstairs to change out of his work clothes. In the bedroom he dressed for Thomas; Thomas liked him looking smart and cool, top buttons undone to reveal tanned flesh, trousers just a bit tight, emphasizing his ass and making their removal a sensuous game.

Back downstairs, Maria looked up at him and said, "I'm getting tired of this, you son of a bitch."

"What's wrong?" he said, looking for, then finding his wallet on the mantle over the fireplace.

She laughed. "That question itself is a tragedy."

"For chrissakes," he said and turned away. This was an evening ritual, a horrible routine; a quiet, sullen meal before he excused himself to dress and go down to the tavern, usually followed by a throw-away lie that he was meeting someone – anyone – from work. Tonight it was Eric. Eric didn't exist, but over dinner he told her that Eric had been let go and was having a bad time of it and he was going to meet with him, talk things over, perhaps lubricate him with a little Canadian Club.

Who's Eric? she had asked.

Oh, you've met him . . . tall fellow, dark hair . . . I think he hit on you at the last company Christmas party.

"You're not doing yourself any favors," she said. "Night after night at the tavern, handing a small fortune over to the owner and getting pissed. So you can hide from me. Martin, you're going to become fat and stupid."

"Do you care?" he asked.

"Enough to bring it up."

As he made his way to the door he turned and watched her, sitting at the dining room table, staring off – a thousand-yard stare, the vets called it. For a microsecond he actually thought of scrapping the evening. Staying home, making some kind of effort, kind of like what she was doing with her serving a roast on a Tuesday night. Roast beef on *any* night fairly screamed effort.

Things had changed, of this there was no argument. There had been a quiet if determined deterioration over the past five years and he and Maria had not so gently drifted away from each other. What little time spent in each other's company was now done in fleeting intervals of great silence, and not a comfortable silence or a cushion of quiet with all of those wonderful unsaid things a couple shares shimmering between the lines like delicious secrets, but a great silence, unhealthy and forbidding. Paradoxically, theirs was also a silence that spoke volumes. It spoke of pain and unhappiness and discontentment and apathy, and it spoke resoundingly of how everything in their lives – no, that wasn't quite right – how everything in their *marriage* amounted to, especially these days but really since the beginning, a big steaming pile of shit.

He left her, sitting and staring.

Martin blinked in the sunlight and drew in a large, uneven breath. He didn't know what to do, except head home. He felt in his pockets for bus fare, for any coins at all. He was tapped out. Lint and a spare fucking button for the Dockers. Which meant a long walk home. Of course he had made it one way, but it had been downhill all the way. Plus, presumably, it had been cooler in the dark.

Now there was a thought – a big goddamn terrifying one. Sleepwalking five miles *in the dark*, for god's sake! Martin was frightened. The stillness of the beach area was unnerving. There wasn't anyone to be seen, anyone he could bum a buck fifty from, a bus driver he could convince to let him ride gratis. The bus station itself was another five miles west.

He turned toward the water, licking his lips thoughtfully, wishing for a tall icy drink in a sweating glass. The lake water wasn't filthy like it was down in Toronto, but he wasn't about to gulp it down. However, it was probably cooler by the shoreline and he contemplated a quick dip. Another naked townie breaking city ordinances.

He walked across the sand, slipped off his sandals and let his toes submerge in the quiet water. The lake was cool but it wasn't offering up anything in the way of a breeze. The jack pines and red spruce fortifying the shoreline creaked slowly; *they* had found some kind of air current, but here, by the castle and the thousands of bare footprints in the sand and someone's bikini bottoms discarded near one of the towers and a few empty tins of beer and packs of Players Light, everything was dead.

Martin stared into the shimmering water. He leaned forward, saw the top of his head reflecting back at him, and the previous evening continued in his mind.

⚜

The Bull Tavern was halfway down the hill and off on a narrow, leafy side street full of moving shadows. A silver thread of moon peered through the green canopy over the street as Martin turned into the place, and he hurried across the small unlit parking lot. But rather than entering the building, he stepped off the front walk and into the side alley. Stacked boxes of bottles for recycling and industrial-sized garbage cans neatly blocked his way; he turned sideways and slid past, catching a whiff of rotting food, and disturbing some sort of furry beast that had found its way inside one of the containers. The creature, a raccoon, hissed, leaped out, and beat a slow, waddling path toward a nearby park.

In the back was a small, paved-over square of backyard. A dilapidated stairway-cum-fire-escape crawled up the back wall of the tavern. Someone had piled junk on the bottom steps – boxes of broken metal tools, a cracked toilet, bald spare tires, and a small stack of yellowing newspapers, which were the easiest to move. He gave the bundled papers a good shove, wondering if Thomas had complained to anyone about people using his stairs as a junkyard, and climbed up, first two at a time, then – as anticipation got the better of him – three. He was sweating lightly as he reached out to knock on the door. He held back his fist, waiting a full thirty seconds until he was composed and breathing normally. He smiled in the dark. His breath would be labored soon enough.

He banged on the door.

"Enter!" came a far-off voice from within.

Martin pushed open the door. It resisted at first – the wood always swelled in the heat – but relented with a shudder.

"In here," said the voice.

He followed it, though he knew exactly where he was going. Past cobwebs that brushed his face like whispers and dust motes that drifted lazily in the air at the behest of a breeze coming through an opened window. A candle flickered in the corner, and he smelled a strong man-scent: sharp, musky, heavy with salt. Dried come on an ancient mattress. The mattress itself was on the floor, shoved against the wall. Empty whiskey bottles stood militarily on the windowsill. Beyond the glass, the humid night moved secretly in the wind that had come off the gently lapping lake.

"Hello," said the voice, and Martin swallowed hungrily, allowing hands to pull at his clothing, undo his shirt, release the top button of the Dockers and tug them down. The jockeys were next, and even before they were over his hips, Thomas had taken him into his mouth.

Martin tried to breathe in the small, close room that was suddenly without oxygen. The candle flickered and was snuffed out.

They had met four months ago. Four months; could time really pass that quickly?

It had been toward the dirty end of winter and at the bitter conclusion of a fight that was sure to go into the books, were such fights actually recorded. The fuel behind the confrontation was the same old thing. It had just happened, spawned from general unhappiness and springing upon both of them like some rough beast. Before either of them knew it, the sleeves were rolled, the spittle was flying, and in the climactic third act a quarter-full bottle of wine – a somewhat cheeky, if very young, Pinot Noir – was smashed against the dining room wall. Maria had been the culprit, the Nolan Ryan of wine bottles, and Martin had bowed out at this point – go ahead, sweetie, the title is yours – and fled the scene, fled the house, and ran along the street until his ribs ached. He stayed out for hours, stalking the neighborhood, crunching through blackened snow and wondering what had happened to his life, wondering when his misery had become so pervasive, so all-fucking-encompassing.

After a while he happened upon The Bull, a place he knew fairly well, and stepped inside. On the best of nights, this establishment was the place to be if you were young, horny, and gay – a twenty-first century den of iniquity where finding a partner was as easy as hailing a cab. He ordered a pint of lager, sat at the bar on an old, padded, round stool, and gulped it. The second one he accessorized with a double shot of Mr Daniels, the third and fourth came and went quickly, and by his fifth pint and third double of Jack he was quietly and miserably weeping into his glass. As he did this, all hunched over, wishing he could just disappear, a hand came down to rest heavily on his right shoulder and he heard a voice, remarkably familiar, speak close to his ear. He wiped his eyes as the voice, full of such incredible sincerity that he wanted to weep all over again, told him, *okay now, okay, s'okay partner* . . . and he had looked up, feeling the fool, feeling about two-and-a-half until he saw the eyes and face of the consoler.

The tavern had been unusually empty, even for early in the week. A tough, determined little burg, there was usually no down time, drinking-wise, in Laughton. But on this night only a few young men with custom darts playing rounds of cricket, a quasi-stupored guy in a flannel shirt at one of the tables, two distinguished older gentlemen playing chess in the corner, and the leather-clad barkeep himself, who looked like he could have been the bouncer as well, occupied the place. The lights were dim (except in the dart alley off to the side), the music was low (The Smiths' "This Charming Man"), and a general lull had kind of halted the establishment, as if everyone inside was caught in mid-breath or mid-thought. The chess players were staring off into space, and one of the dart players stood motionless, aiming to shoot, eyeing that triple-twenty with his tongue lolling in concentration, as he held the pose, unmoving. Martin would have noticed this and thought it funny, were he not halfway in his cups, but he certainly would never have noticed, even completely sober, the second hand on the clock behind the bar suddenly come to a complete stop.

He looked up at this gentleman standing over him, this gentleman who Martin was fairly certain had not been in the bar two seconds ago (but what did he know, he had been too busy weeping like a pussy). Completely placid, serene face, narrow, kindly eyes, tanned skin.

I know you, Martin thought. And he did, he was sure of it, even firmly entrenched in an alcoholic haze. *I know you. I know I do.*

He smiled, this stranger, and the hand on Martin's shoulder squeezed slightly, and suddenly everything seemed to melt away, including his intoxication.

"Want to talk about it, partner?" The hand left his shoulder, but the feeling remained, a warm, nearly giddy sensation, like when an impacted wisdom tooth suddenly stops aching.

"You know," Martin began, embarrassed and drunk, "I'm not really in the habit of bothering anyone with my. . ." but he stopped and shifted gears, only because it felt like it was the right thing to do. Hell, the guy had asked. "Troubles at home," he said, and suddenly, and to his complete amazement, he was telling this man about his life, about his marriage, and about how both were presently sucking. It came tumbling out in a loose, stream-of-consciousness kind of rush, and as he worked his way through the monologue, beginning with his horrible teen years where he felt different from his peers and his peers sensed something different in him – something intangible yet concrete enough to alienate the shit out of him – to finding a road-to-nowhere job in a local government office, to the rapid and increasingly violent decline of his union with Maria, he felt a tremendous weight disappear from his shoulders. He stopped speaking after a while, not noticing the barkeep standing mannequin-like with his back against the room, hand frozen in the air as he reached up to grasp a wineglass from the overhead rack. The dart player continued to strike an aiming pose, the spit drying on his tongue. The music had faded; the room hummed with an ambient white noise. The bar, and its occupants, looked like a still photograph.

"You want to go somewhere?" asked the stranger. Then he said, "Wait," and walked around behind the bar, brushing past the big barkeep. He chose a bottle from the shelf, good old Canadian Club, and came back around.

The man smiled, and gestured with his head. "I live upstairs." He noticed Martin staring hard at the bottle. "They let me help myself here. I have a running tab. Let's go have a drink, it's Dullsville in here tonight." He turned and walked toward a door against the far back wall. Martin followed. His head buzzed, and as he approached the exit he heard the music fade in again. Old R.E.M., something about a green light room, and Martin stepped outside to follow this stranger.

He caught up with him at the stairs. Junk was piled on the bottom step. "You live up there?" he asked.

"For a while now. It's rundown, but cheap. I have a little fridge for my food, but except for breakfast, I eat my meals in the bar. I love pub grub: cottage pie and Buffalo wings with fries. Yum. The best."

"And Canadian Club," Martin said with a grin.

"And *especially* Canadian Club, though anything will do in a pinch." He laughed at that, some kind of joke that went over Martin's head. He was buzzing harder now, but mainly from the alcohol that seemed to be seeping back into his bloodstream.

"Um, so anyway, I don't think I got your name," Martin said.

"It would be Thomas. Sometimes it's Tomas, like Daniel Day-Lewis' character in *The Unbearable Lightness of Being*, because someone once said I looked like him."

"Um, you don't."

"I know I don't. Too bad, eh? C'mon up."

They ascended the stairs and Thomas pushed open the door. The apartment was dark, except for the front area where the street lamps provided enough light to read by if you were close enough to the windows.

"Have a seat," his host said, pulling a chair away from a card table and spinning it around. Martin sat and Thomas disappeared into the dark, flipped on a lamp that did very little to illuminate the room, and brought over two glasses with ice.

"Sorry, no mix," he said.

Martin shrugged. "I don't need mix." He accepted the drink that Thomas poured, drained half, and held out the glass for more when Thomas lifted the bottle. He poured; Martin drank. His head was buzzing like a bee convention.

"That might do it for the night," Martin said, drinking more and then putting the glass on the card table. "I'm getting considerably lit up. Like a Christmas tree."

"I'll let you know when you've had enough," Thomas said, and topped up Martin's drink. "Whiskey . . . god, I love it."

"Me too. Sometimes a bit too much, I think."

"Bah. You're fine."

"Moderation in all things," Martin said.

"Including moderation," Thomas said.

"I'm getting really drunk." Martin had picked up his glass again and was sipping. It really was quite delicious. Whiskey had never been so good. The buzz in his skull had bumped up a notch; his lips were numb, his tongue a useless piece of flesh. His lids half closed, and suddenly his head was hanging. Thomas was there to hold him up, then hoisted him from the chair and laid him down somewhere. Martin tried to speak, say that he really should be going, thanks for the hospitality, maybe again next week, but instead he only managed a few vowels.

"Never mind," Thomas said. "You've had a hard day, nothing wrong with overindulging." Thomas was cradling him, and Martin resurfaced a bit, enjoying the warmth from this man's arms and chest, soothed by the vibrations of his rasping voice, consoled by his cooing. He nearly fell asleep, but forced himself not to, just so he could enjoy the moment. He snuggled in close.

But then he did drift off, lulled by this sublime moment, and when he slipped back to wakefulness, he was keenly aware of the scent of spice, something exotic. He was alone on the mattress, beneath a thin, threadbare blanket. He was still dressed, though his boots had thoughtfully been removed.

Then suddenly Thomas was there, next to and above him, his mouth sweet and red and very close.

"How do you feel?" he said.

Martin started, then relaxed. The room tilted on some unseen axis. The taste of whiskey was strong in his throat and nostrils.

"I don't know," he said. There was a myriad of feelings, floating just beneath his drunkenness, but he went for the obvious one. "I feel safe," he said. "Secure. Like I'm in a womb."

"I bet you never feel like that at home."

"Never. Never, ever."

Thomas sat up, letting the blanket fall away from him. He sat upright, leaning full against the radiator. The wind moved his hair.

"I've been waiting for you, you know."

Martin stared blankly.

"For a long goddamn time."

Martin closed his eyes. He saw swirls of colors. Far out.

He opened his eyes. Thomas was on the other side of the room, pacing.

"I want to see you again," he said.

"Okay," Martin said.

"If you want."

"I want," he said, without a shred of doubt.

"Because I can save you. If you let me."

Martin managed a smile and then closed his eyes.

He didn't stay the night. Around two in the morning cold winter air brought him to a certain level of sobriety and he sat up, found the strength to stand, found his coat on the chair he'd been sitting in, and tiptoed toward the door. He looked back. Thomas was nowhere to be seen, but the window was wide open. He crept forward and peered out, taking in slow, cold breaths.

The night was still, the bar below long closed, the parking lot empty. A distant crunch of boots on old snow, the metal on metal sound of a car that wouldn't start.

Leave it, he thought to the fool who hadn't plugged his car in. *Go to bed.*

Then movement above. Up over the eaves, something scraping against the shingles, followed by a *thump*, a fleshy sound. The sound of bare feet slapping against a hard surface. He scanned the skeletal treetops, not sure what he was looking for and hardly aware that he had offered a tentative "Thomas?" into the frozen night.

Why would I say that?

Something slid past his field of vision, briefly standing out in bold relief against the lower gunmetal sky before flapping over the trees, riding a northern wind, and reaching up to parts of the sky that light pollution could not touch.

"Thomas?" he said again in a whisper more air than voice. As though he was afraid to be heard, afraid he'd hear his own name being whispered in return from somewhere beyond the open window.

Shivering, he left the window open and nearly ran out of the apartment.

When he arrived home, Maria was not there, but the stain on the wall certainly was, a red arterial smear that made the dining room look nearly like a murder scene.

⚗

His face was tired, gaunt, pale. The reflection shimmered in the water and for a second a school of minnows flitted by, crossing his forehead, flashing silver over his cheekbones and nose. In the last few minutes the heat had increased in intensity as the sun rose higher. The humidity was slowly becoming something to be amazed by.

Martin turned and looked back from whence he came. Lake Shore Road should have been jammed with minivans containing Speedoed children and frantic grownups; next to the beach, Centennial Park remained puzzlingly empty, its rides and swings silent.

"The water's warm," Martin said to the silence, his toes still submerged.

"This place should be packed." He thought again of taking off his clothes. When would he have such an opportunity again? To strip down in broad daylight. Maybe he'd take a swim and then sprawl out on the sand.

He thought of Thomas. Thomas should be here with him; he'd like this. They could swim together, dry off on the sand, take a walk on the beach. Swing on the swings at the park, perhaps try to power-up one of the carnival rides, fuck each other stupid at the top of the ferris wheel.

Thomas, he thought again and suddenly wanted to cry. He was afraid and he felt alone. And he felt like something was horribly, horribly wrong.

Thomas had relit the candle. They were laying back, pillows against the cool radiator, enjoying the wan glow and the breeze from the window.

Martin looked over at Thomas' dark form, lying prone, except now he was propped up on one arm, looking at him. Martin looked back. He could see a faint smile in the dark, but also a sad smile. His gaze was penetrating; his intense, prolonged looks seemed to glean thoughts from Martin's mind. Either that or he was the most intuitive person on the planet. Thomas knew him, knew his heart, knew his mind and thoughts. The first time they had fucked, for example – the day following their Canadian Club binge in the wee hours of a cold morning. Martin had found it impossible to stay away. He had sneaked in next to Maria and lain awake until dawn. After she had left for work he had showered, dressed, phoned in sick, and made his way to the Bull. He climbed the stairs, knocked on the door, and the voice from within had called his name, said, *Yes, Martin, it's open.* Thomas had been waiting for him, and there had never been a shred of doubt about his coming. He knew, that was all. Just *knew*.

And as for sex – what could he say about it? He was a married man and an alleged straight man who hadn't had penetrative sex in nearly half a year. He had gone to Thomas that morning only as a friend, an affable companion. And the day had begun with the innocence of Frank and Joe Hardy, with them laying side by side on the mattress, sharing the paper and reading the comics aloud. The day had ended with Martin feeling like he was losing his mind as Thomas did things to his cock that didn't seem possible.

Thomas sat up from his dark place on the mattress and reached for a nearby bottle of Canadian Club, poured a palm full, and washed it over Martin's face.

"What –"

"Completing the illusion. Tonight you will go home stinking drunk. Isn't that what you want Maria to believe? That you're getting shitfaced every night? It creates a terrific alibi and keeps her disgusted enough with you to not want to touch you. Isn't that your little scheme?"

Martin didn't say anything. He didn't need to. Questions from Thomas were perfunctory. He always knew the answer.

Thomas took a pull from the bottle, held it out. Martin accepted it, knocked back a large mouthful, nearly gagged.

"Easy does it, Mister Bukowski."

"I can only swallow a tablespoon at a time," he said.

Thomas forced a grin and then said, "But I can't go on like this with you." Martin's own smile fell. "What?"

"Our . . . arrangement. It can't continue. Not like this, anyway."

"But –"

"I love you too much."

"What does that mean?"

"It means I love you too much to just accept part of you. It means I want all of you, but it also means I don't want the husband hiding from his angry wife part of you."

"Jesus," Martin said. He felt panic flutter in his chest. Was he going to lose Thomas? That was an unbearable thought; he was quite positive that the only reason he was not only alive these days, but reasonably happy as well, was because of the man who now sat before him. This man who was now, it seemed, about to break it off with him. This man who was now about to break his heart.

"Thomas, I don't know what to say."

Thomas shrugged and stood up. He paced the floor, grabbing a bottle of whiskey as he went, and took pull after pull.

"I mean, these four months must mean something."

"They mean everything, Martin. But it's not four months. It's *three evenings a week* for four months. Big fucking difference. Still, in that time I have completely fallen for you and so, to be quite selfish about it, I want you every night and every day, for now and forever. I want you for eternity, Martin; that's all. That's all I want. And it breaks my heart that I can't have that, and it breaks my heart that you continue playing the game with this horrible Maria, laying next to her every night. It's sickening."

"For god's sake, Thomas, what can I do? Tell me what I can do."

"I think it's more what I can do. I *see*, Martin. I *see* hearts and I *see* souls and I can penetrate both to get to what's inside. I think you have the potential to come through, but that fear of yours, it's pretty powerful, and it's pretty fucking tenacious, and I don't know if you're up to the task."

"What are you talking about? Tell me, Thomas."

"I'm talking about getting you out. I'm talking about setting you free, by setting this Maria free."

"Setting me free?" he said.

"When we first met I told you I wanted to help you. Well, this is the help. This is how it happens."

Martin said nothing.

"You understand what I'm asking of you?"

Martin nodded slowly.

"What am I asking of you?"

Martin's voice was weak, full of fear. "To set her free."

"And then what will happen?"

"We'll be together." He laughed dryly. "You're right, you know. I'm afraid. Dreadfully so."

"Faith, Martin. I have so much of it in you."

"But what if I can't do it?"

"I think you can."

"But what if I –"

"Faith. I can see you doing it. I can see you. It's almost like I'll be there when it happens."

Martin pulled out the pillow from behind his head and slowly covered his face. Thomas watched him, smiled, and drank whiskey.

He was up to his knees in the water, the Dockers wet and heavy. He wasn't fully prepared to strip down yet, certain that the suffocating hoards would arrive at any moment and, in a collective sigh of relief, plunge into the lake. The heavy machinery that operated the rides would slowly grind to life; buskers and barkers would compete for attention, clowns would clown, children would eat ice cream and cry and piss in their pants, the mayor would swing by in his Mayormobile, a shiny new council-approved Lincoln Town Car; a celebratory summer's day would begin and carry on to its exhausted, sunburned, and stupored conclusion.

Any moment now.

Martin stood motionless, surveying the beach, taking in the silent lake, the drifting moored boats. After a long moment he thought, *fuck it,* and began un-buttoning his shirt. His fingers slipped on the buttons and he tried again.

The house was dark when he returned home, save for the diminutive light over the stove that had turned the first floor into silhouettes and shadows. He eased the door shut gently; awakening Maria on the best of nights was an unwise proposition, and he slipped off his sandals and padded silently into the kitchen for a glass of water and to turn off the light. As he did, he passed the swinging door that led to the dining room. The door was wide open and he could see someone sitting silently at the table in the dark.

He stopped and peered in. He could vaguely see the roast beef still sitting on the dinner service. He could see the gleam of wineglasses as well as the untouched dinner dishes and a half-empty bottle of red wine at the centre of the table.

The person sat quietly, both hands on the table.

"Maria? What are you doing sitting in the dark?"

She didn't say anything. Didn't move.

"Maria, it's late."

Nothing.

Martin felt an all-too-familiar surge of annoyance. This was a new stunt, but a stunt nonetheless.

"Maria, shouldn't you go to bed?"

A brief movement, like someone who had been sitting for awhile shifting from buttock to buttock. A sound: the softness of exhaled breath.

"Maria? Please go to bed."

Suddenly she stood up, pushed the chair away from her, turned and walked briskly toward him. She flipped on the dining room light, leaving it dim, and sat again. She wore nothing but panties.

"You stink," she said, not facing him.

"I'll shower before I come to bed."

"Whiskey," she said. "Did you bathe in it?"

"I said I'll shower."

"How much have you been drinking?"

"I don't know."

"Damnit, Martin." She sighed heavily and picked at a small burnt piece of roast beef.

She looked exactly as she had earlier, staring broodingly at the remains of dinner, telling him that she was –

I'm getting tired of this, you son of a bitch.

Yes. And who could blame her? He was getting tired of it too. She deserved more. And maybe he did too. And now he had a chance to make things right, to free both of them from this horrible mockery of a marriage.

"Maria, I've met someone."

He could only see her bare back, but her posture had shifted slightly, having gone from tired resignation to high alert.

Having begun, he decided to proceed. He was pleasantly surprised by his courage. "I've been with a man."

A long silence followed, except for his heart, which he was sure was filling the kitchen and dining room with its booming. He felt sick. Blood roared in his ears.

In a small, little girl voice, Maria whispered, "A man."

He swallowed noisily. "Maria . . . I have no idea what to say. I have no explanation. I –"

"There's nothing to explain." Her voice was dull, even.

"I think there's plenty to explain. I never . . . I never knew how I felt before . . . I never. . . ."

"There's nothing to explain," she said again.

He took a step closer to her. She leaned forward, picked up the carving knife and sawed off a large piece of roast.

Martin moved around to the other side of the table and stood opposite her. The dim dining room was perfect; doing this in the horrible scrutiny of brightness would have been nearly unbearable.

"There's everything to explain."

"No, there's not."

He hesitated. Then: "Don't you understand? I've been sleeping with a man."

She looked up suddenly, her baleful glare obvious in the shadows. "Shift the emphasis, fucker," she said.

"What —"

"You say, 'I've been with a man,' as though that's the issue. I don't give a good goddamn if you've been with a goat. But I'll tell you this." She stood up, poured half a glass of wine, and drank it back. "Cheating is cheating. Man, woman, winged-serpent, doesn't matter. You cheated. God! What were you expecting, some big, dramatic reaction to the fact that you suck dick? Well, dig this, sweetie, genitalia doesn't enter into it." She found this funny and blurted out laughter, but it ended almost as quickly as it began. She poured another glass of wine, raised it high, and flung the liquid into his face.

He stood up motionless, taking it.

She had picked up the wine bottle again and raised it high over her head and he knew what came next, having been on the receiving end before. He prepared to duck, but instead she merely sat down again and began to weep.

"Maria —"

"I guess I always thought this was a bad patch, that was all," she said. "An extended bad patch that somehow we'd find our way through to the other side."

Martin wiped his face with a napkin.

"But now . . . this. It's such a final act. This is the end, my friend," she whispered.

She picked up the carving knife and began cutting off another piece of meat. She looked up at him and then suddenly plunged the knife into the roast. She pulled it out, and plunged it in again. Pulled it out. Plunged it in again.

"This," she said. Out. In. Out. In. "This is what you've done to me."

Out. In.

"Maria," he began, and then watched in sick horror as dark blood began pouring from the roast. It was nearly black, like tar, and the smell was rich and metallic.

"Maria," he said, trying to get her to look, look at what she was doing. He leaned over, gently removing the knife from her fingers. He held it firmly, amazed at the dark liquid being expunged from the meat, amazed that this moment had arrived, amazed at what a hungry kitchen knife could do.

⚜

Blood. He hadn't expected there to be so much of it. Great crimson blossoms and congealing Rorschach inkblots, from collar to belt line.

Martin had just removed his shirt, knee deep in the wonderfully cool water, his fingers clumsy and slippery with blood. He peeled the shirt from his torso with one hand and it made a terrible wet, ripping sound as it came away. He tossed it aside, letting it float with the fishes, and began working on his pants. It was tough going, actually, stripping in the water while using only his left hand, but he made an admirable go of it, removing one sodden leg of the pants, then the other. The jockeys came off next and he let them go and watched them sink into the clear water and drift like some strange manta.

Some kind of instinct made him look up. There was Thomas, on the sand, naked as he. He was smiling.

Martin sank down into the lake, gasping with delight.

"You set her free," Thomas said. "I knew you would."

Doing a passable breaststroke, Martin moved toward Thomas. Thomas came closer, wading into the lake.

Martin watched him wade in deeper, watched him sink down, watched the lake take him.

Thomas. Martin wasn't sure if he got it, but he felt he was close. Like trying to wrap your brain around an impossibly large equation.

"Thomas?" he said, swimming toward him.

"Yes."

He didn't know what to ask. But Thomas knew; he always knew the questions, just as much as he knew the answers. He knew it all, because he was . . . because he was. . . .

It was there, glimmering like a pearl from many fathoms down.

"That's right, Martin, you have it."

Martin swam, thinking.

"Yes, Martin. I am you. And you are me. All this time you've been saying to yourself, 'I know this fellow; we've met before, but where?' I'm like a recording of your own voice. You know, familiar but not immediately recognizable."

Martin studied the familiar features of his love, watched them slowly meld into what they really were, watched his own face suddenly appear inches above the lake, beaded with water, smiling like a devil.

I am you.

Martin swam, and slowly the lakeshore came back to life. Vehicles up on the road had materialized out of the haze; numerous morning bathers strode along the sand in bathing suits and wraps, all pointing at something in the water, and there was a lifeguard in a red bathing suit, up on her tower, speaking urgently into a radio. He swam, the pool of blood widening, stretching thin, then diffusing. He swam, then opened the fingers of his right hand, finally, letting the long knife sink silently down.

DELICIOUS MONSTER

NALO HOPKINSON

The tree was still there. Condos and office buildings growing, floor by floor all around, formed an organics of the city – urban fractals, patterns repeating, apparently random, but inexorable; yet there in the middle of it was the tree, caged in a small empty lot scattered about with unseasonable thistles and rogue lawn grass.

Looked like that lot was slated for construction too. One of those clapboard condo sales offices had been erected at the other side of it; the kind with a storefront painted to look like a manor house in a magazine. There were stacks of lumber and fat aluminium pipes beside it.

Cars rushed past Jerry on Spadina, speeding irritably to Friday afternoon freedom. The dusky sky spat the occasional dirty snowflake which tumbled onto the sleeve of his jacket and lay there twinkling for a second, six-clawed, until it melted.

Jerry knelt by the rusting chicken wire that kept the tree in. He peered through one of the fence's rusty diamonds. He reached to steady himself, to twine the fingers of one hand in the fence, but an angry roar startled him, and he yanked the hand back. He looked up to see what had made the noise, so much louder and closer than the fractious bleating of car horns.

There it was. Bloody excavation machines, biting at the ravaged ground. The thing lurched away from the fence, bellowing. It brandished a toothed hopper, a maw on a stalk. The tree hunkered there smugly, in the lee of its machine protector. "You just wait," Jerry said quietly to the tree. "Pretty soon, it's you the excavator'll be coming for."

Once, as a child visiting the zoo, Jerry'd disobeyed his dad and stuck his hand inside the fencing of the puma cage. There had been no harm in doing so that he could see. The thick wall of clear Lucite that kept the puma penned was a good two feet beyond his reach; the wire fence just an extra precaution in a litiginous world. The gaunt great cat had lain panting behind the lucite, regarding him with a dull, disinterested stare. Its tan coat made it look baked, like biscuits. Glancing to make sure his dad wasn't looking, Jerry'd waggled his fingers at the puma.

Later, thinking about what he'd done, he couldn't say what reaction he'd hoped for, exactly, from the puma. Something. Some acknowledgment that it'd seen him. His dad had barely said a word to him all weekend. Jerry'd knelt and stared hard at the puma. Look. Look over here. He hadn't seen the other

75

one flying at him until it was a big golden blur in the corner of his eye. A millisecond later it slammed against the Lucite with a heavy thump. Jerry'd thrown himself backward onto his behind. That's when his dad had turned and asked in a puzzled voice why Jerry was sitting in the dirt. Jerry hadn't been able to take his eyes off the puma that had charged him. It had looked at him, licking its bruised nose. A fixed, hungry stare. The sunlight had played in its fur, making it glow.

It'd been a few years since Jerry'd walked this far north on Spadina. The tree's swollen middle still flowed in rolls like lava down to the ground. He could see the cincture that bit into the tree's trunk two of three feet from the ground. Something had been chained there, tight around the tree, years ago, then abandoned. The tree must have been only a sapling then. It was sturdy enough for climbing now. It had grown, the living tissue of its wood swelling around whatever it was that it now held trapped. Same as he'd done last time he'd passed the tree, Jerry peered closer, trying to see what it held in its folds.

"Mister, you got any change you can spare? I'm trying to get a coffee." The guy standing, jittering, with his hands in the pockets of a shredding jeans jacket was young. He'd shaved off all the hair on his head, except for a limp tuft of it at the front, dyed green, that flopped into his eyes.

"Uh, yeah," Jerry said, lurching to his feet. "Think I got some here." He started fumbling in his pockets. Had he put any change in there? He usually did when he was flush, to give to homeless people who asked for it. Sandor always teased him for being a softie when he gave change to beggars. Teased him and then rewarded him with a kiss or a squeeze of his hand.

"Thanks, man," said the guy. "Really 'preciate it."

Sandor didn't give money, but he always seemed to have extra smokes in his pocket to give away.

Something was funny about the way this guy stood. One shoulder was clearly higher than the other. One hip canted up at a sharp angle.

Damn. Empty pockets. "Hang on." Flushing with embarrassment at the delay, Jerry took his wallet from his coat.

While Jerry fumbled, the young man looked politely off to one side. "God, is that ever freaky-looking, eh?" he said. He was looking at the deformed tree.

"Yeah," Jerry replied. "Well . . ." There was a twenty. He wasn't going to give the kid that. He tried to surreptitiously shield the contents of his wallet from view, to riffle through the remaining bills with his other hand.

There were more snowflakes falling now. The young guy was shivering in his thin jacket. "It's a monster, that tree," he told Jerry. He said it with a familiar air. If this was his beat, he'd seen this tree before. "A monster like me, right?"

"Delicious monster," Jerry heard himself mutter. The young man had a gnarled beauty about him, like a skinny rock star who cut his own body with razors, or like a bonsai tree.

"What'd you say, Mister?"

Shit. "Uh, nothing." Perversely, the twenty kept jutting up out of the pile of grocery receipts and bus transfers in Jerry's wallet. He sighed, yanked it out. "I mean, uh, here. Hope you have a delicious dinner."

He handed the twenty to the guy, whose face brightened in delight. "Shit, thanks, man!"

"No problem."

The young man pocketed the money, then looked inquisitively at Jerry. "Not a lot of people stop to really look at stuff in the city. Not ratty old growing stuff, anyway."

"I'm curious about it, is all."

"Flower gardens, maybe. They'll look at the neat, pretty things."

"I mean," Jerry continued, "what's that thing stuck inside it?"

The young guy shrugged, his green hair tumbling onto his beautiful face. He looked at the tree's bulge, looked up at the sky. "It'll be during the eclipse," he said. "That's when it happens." Then he lurched away into the darkening day, one hip hitching higher than the other, one foot hitting the ground sooner than the other, arms windmilling awkwardly to propel him forward.

Delicious monster. That's what Jerry's dad had really taken him to the zoo to see; *Monstera deliciosa*, the massive Swiss cheese plant that flourished in the South American Pavilion. It had been warm in there, and damp. It'd smelled green, a stuffy fetor of growing, living, and dying things that clung inside the nose. Jerry'd taken his coat off. The heat had baked into his skin, his hair. It had felt like moisture was condensing on his eyelids. He'd gone heavy, slow. His dad was finally animated. "This stuff comes from my part of the world," he'd said. "From Guatemala."

When he was young, Jerry'd thought his dad had lived in the middle of a jungle, in a tree house or something. Had thought his dad had spent his days feeding orangutans, the gentle old men of the forest, and wrestling massive boa constrictors that could consume an entire child, swallow a whole person until all you could see of them was a series of lumps in the constrictor's middle. Dad was forever on about centipedes the size of snakes and eels that could electrocute you with a touch. But . . . "No," Jerry's mother had said, "orangutans are from Borneo, whatever they call it now. That's Asia. Your dad's from South America."

But Jerry still hadn't really understood. From his northern city home, where the biggest trees were the low, cultivated rowan trees that shed their orange berries in the fall, Borneo might as well be Guatemala. It wasn't until Mum had shown him pictures of Dad's family's house in Guatemala City, where she and Dad had gone on their honeymoon, that Jerry had realised that his dad was a city boy, too. Probably the only electric eel Dad had ever seen was the one right here in the Toronto zoo.

The excavator was quiet now, crouched beside the condo sales hut. The snow was heavier, but melting as it fell. Beads of freezing water hung off the thistle leaves. If he looked carefully at the water droplets, he could see brake lights reflecting red in them. Spring was pouncing in like a lion, all right.

No use putting it off any longer. Jerry turned north towards his dad's condo. The snow was turning into biting hail.

"How's your mum?" Jerry's dad took his coat, hung it in the hall closet. Jerry followed him into the living room.

"She's fine. Says she's got a new plant cutting for you, and you should go by and get it. Dunno where you'll put it, though." A ficus rioted in one corner of the living room, nearly touching the ceiling. The spider plant hanging from a nook was a veritable cathedral of foliage. Trifoliate, an ornamental shamrock blushed hugely purple. Dad grinned.

Sudharshan rose from the couch, came and gave Jerry an awkward hug. "Good to see you," he murmured. Jerry gave a kind of grunt back.

"And how's Sandor?" Dad asked.

Jerry sat on the arm of the plush burgundy couch. Sudharshan frowned.

"He's great. Settling into his new apartment."

A trilling noise came from over by the dining table. Jerry turned to see what it was. He was up and standing beside the cage before he knew it. He reached to touch the wire bars. "Yikes. Dad, what the hell is that thing?"

The bird – Jerry figured that's what it was – tilted its head at the sound of his voice. It sidled on its perch, closer to Jerry, one eye beady on him. Jerry pulled his hand back from the cage. The thing was tiny, bald, and fucking hideous. No feathers on its head, none on its wings. Looked like something out of the grocery freezer. Probably no feathers on its body, either. Hard to tell, in the weird little suit it had on. "And what's that it's wearing?"

Sudharshan laughed. He came over and stroked one of the cage's wires with a beautifully manicured hand. "You like his jumpsuit?" he asked Jerry. Sudharshan's face always made Jerry think of chocolate brownies, dark and sweet. "I crochet them for him. He'd freeze to death otherwise, wouldn't you, my numbikins?" Sudharshan cooed at the disgusting little thing. It screeched back at him, tossing its beak into the air.

"Why doesn't it have any feathers?"

"*Birdie alopecia,*" his dad said, coming up behind Sudharshan and putting his arms around him. Sudharshan put his hands on top his dad's, smiled. He leaned back into his dad's embrace. Jerry looked away.

"It's a rare condition my birdie has," Sudharshan told him. "He'd have died in the wild."

Jerry sneaked a look back at his dad and Sudharshan. They were still cuddling. He sighed and deliberately kept his eyes on them, trying to look cool.

But his gaze slid back to the creepy bald bird in its bright green wool jumper. "How does it, you know. . . ?"

"Hole in the base of the suit," Sudharshan told him. "Want some chai?"

"Uh, yeah." Something to do.

"I'll get it." His dad headed for the kitchen.

"Not too much cardamom, okay, sweetie?" Sudharshan called after him. Jerry could feel his face heating up.

Sudharshan pulled chairs out for himself and Jerry. They sat. Then he leaned over the cage, made more smacking noises at the bird. His long nose with the dip in it echoed the bird's hooked beak. He opened the cage door, reached a hand in. "Come, darling, come. Say hello to Uncle Jerry."

The bird mumbled its beak against Sudharshan's brown hand. Jerry held his breath, afraid that it would peck. The bird climbed onto Sudharshan's hand, windmilling its wings for balance. "Where'd you get it?" Jerry asked. In the kitchen, the kettle began whistling off key.

"They've been in my family for years," Sudharshan said. "His grandparents' parents belonged to my grandparents. Each new generation of children looks after the new generation of birds. It's kind of our duty. How's work?" He carefully brought the bird out of its cage. It screeched loudly. Jerry put his hands over his ears.

"Work's going okay," he said. "Sold a big mansion up in Aurora. Rich couple, one kid. Six bedrooms, that house has."

Jerry went silent. Sudharshan said nothing. The bird crab-walked up Sudharshan's arm, perched on his shoulder, and nibbled at his ear. Sudharshan giggled and chucked it under its chin. It still looked to Jerry like plucked freezer chicken, walking. He swallowed and looked around the room. One whole wall of the apartment was painted with images of suns. They flared and wheeled through space. Each one was different. They seemed hand-done. "Your art work?" he asked Sudharshan.

"We did it together," Jerry's dad said, coming out of the kitchen. He was balancing a tray, a white lace doily under the teapot, three mugs, and a saucer. The mugs were a fat, sunny yellow. He put the tray down on the table. Jerry recognized the doily. It was part of a set that his mum used to save for when they had company. "Three sugars, right, Jerry?"

"I don't take sugar, Dad."

"You like sugar."

"I never liked sugar. You always gave me too much, and I never liked it."

Sudharshan busied himself with his ugly pet. Jerry watched the way that his long black hair caught the light, gleaming. Looked at Sudharshan's handsome face, sucking in light and reflecting gorgeousness, and hated him.

With a squawk, the bird threw itself off Sudharshan's shoulder and onto the table. It started stalking Jerry, its tiny body strutting. It stared him down.

Sudharshan laughed. "Rudy, stop it." The bird ignored him. It was almost to the edge of the table where Jerry's hand was. It was bigger than he'd thought. Jerry pulled his hands away, into his lap. Sudharshan scooped the bird up and cupped his other palm protectively around it. "Stop it, I said." He beamed at Jerry. "That's his snake-eating glare." He tucked the bird back into its cage and locked the door.

"A parrot that eats snakes?"

Jerry's dad began pouring chai. "It's not a parrot, son."

Jerry took the yellow cup that his dad held out. He sipped the chai. It was too sweet. "What the fuck is it, then?"

"Jerry. Language."

"I don't know the word for it in English," Sudharshan told him. "I just call him Rudy. He knows his name. They all do."

Dad poured chai for himself and Sudharshan. As he lifted the teapot, his biceps swelled against the rolled-up sleeve of the tight white T-shirt he was wearing. He looked better nowadays, Jerry had to admit. He hadn't heard his dad complain once about his bunions. Blunt-toed army boots had replaced the pointy Italian leather shoes. Well-worn jeans sat better on his hips than the polyester dress pants that used to be his uniform. His gut had shrunk. It was now just this cute little suggestion of paunch, yet another manly bulge beneath his form-fitting T-shirts. A chain of fat silver beads encircled his neck. They shone against the warm yellow-brown of his skin. Jerry wondered where the tiny gold cross on its sallow gold chain had gone. The stiff brush cut of Dad's black hair suited his solid, square face. The lines in the corners of his eyes were the friendly signs of someone who smiled a lot, not the creases with which Jerry'd become familiar as a child; the disappointment and anger that had once been incised there. Now Dad's brown eyes were happy. Who was this man?

Dad offered Sudharshan the cup of chai along with a tender gaze. Jerry felt a lump forming in his solar plexus. The mug disappeared behind Sudharshan's long, wide hands. There was just a little bit of yellow china gleaming out from between his fingers. He sipped from his cupped hand. The color of the mug made his chin glow. Jerry thought of butter, of chocolate brownies, warm and sweet in the mouth. He pushed the thought away.

Sandor thought it was all very cute. *Your dad's one of the boys now*, he'd said. *Hey – maybe the two of them can come to the Box with us someday*. Jerry'd told him to shut the fuck up.

"Eclipse soon," Sudharshan said. "You going to watch it?"

"That's why I came," Jerry reminded him. "That's why you invited me." His dad only looked at Sudharshan, stricken.

"Where will you go?" Dad asked Sudharshan.

"I thought we'd go up onto the roof," Sudharshan replied. "We can see the sky more clearly from there."

His face remained open, friendly, but Jerry'd been looking at his dad, so he knew that Sudharshan hadn't answered the question Dad had asked. Dad stared into his mug like someone had hidden the sun in there. He looked up at Jerry, baring a too-bright smile. "Hey, Jer, you seen my *Monstera*?"

"Say what?"

Dad pointed to a shady corner of the apartment. Sure enough, there was a Swiss cheese plant there, a static explosion of large, oval leaves riddled with holes. Jerry hadn't really noticed it before, huddled in the dark like that. "Wouldn't it be better in the sun, Dad, like the rest of the plants?"

Dad sucked back the rest of his chai, put the cup down. He had an angry look. He pointedly didn't direct it to Sudharshan. "It prefers to have its roots in the shade. But it gets more than enough sun. Look at where it's growing to."

With his eyes, Jerry followed the trailing growth of the plant. It had made its way along the bottom of the wall to the big picture window, and sure enough, was climbing to the light, using a thick, succulent tree in a pot there as its ladder. The leaves of the *Monstera* were so mixed in with the leaves of the tree that Jerry couldn't tell what the tree was.

"It's a banana plant," Sudharshan told him. "The *Monstera* needs it, but it's strangling it. I'll have to have my cousin get me a new one."

Dad reached for Sudharshan's hand, but Sudharshan pulled away. "Delicious," Sudharshan said. "The chai, I mean. It was perfect, lover." He smiled at Dad, hesitated, took the outstretched hand, kissed it. The longing on Dad's face! And now Jerry was afraid, like when he was a kid. Like when his parents would fight, and then try not to fight, try to make up, but one of them would be closed, arms folded, the light shut from their face, and the other would look with longing, would try to touch, would be rebuffed and then finally taken in again, reluctantly, and the child Jerry would feel relief, but with a hard little stone of fear left there, below his breastbone.

"Isn't it about time for that eclipse?" he asked Dad and Sudharshan. In his cage, peeled Rudy screamed and flapped his raw limbs, swinging back and forth on his little trapeze.

Sudharshan checked his watch. "Yes, soon." He went to a beautiful pale wooden cabinet, all carved – the doors looked like strips of bamboo – and got out three pairs of goggles. The eyepieces had a funny gold sheen to them. "Welders' glasses," he said. "For looking at the sun." He handed one to Jerry.

"I'm not coming," Dad told them. He sat at the table, mug in his hands, staring at the window where the banana and the *Monstera* plants wrestled.

Sudharshan just stood there, looking at Dad. His face did something complicated, moved through shock and sadness to an unbending calm. "Carlos," he said softly, "don't you want to see what happens? I don't know when I'll see you again."

"Why?" Jerry asked. "Where're you going?"

"He's leaving me," Dad told Jerry.

"I am not." Sudharshan went to the front door, began pulling on his boots. "I'll come back."

"When?" Dad asked.

Sudharshan reached into the hallway closet, pulled out a long, black wool coat. He shrugged into it, stuck the two pairs of goggles into a pocket. "As soon as I can, lover."

"Where are you going?" Jerry asked again. Rudy swung harder and harder on his trapeze, warbling a harsh and complicated song. Sudharshan reached into the closet, pulled out something round and shiny, about the size of a Frisbee.

"I'm traveling for work. I have to go."

"You're leaving me."

"What's that thing you're holding?" Jerry asked. What in hell was going on?

"If you don't come outside with me now, we won't be able to say goodbye."

"You're leaving after the eclipse?" Jerry asked. Rudy hit an ear-piercing note. Dad's eyes were wet with tears. Sudharshan walked over to him, touched his shoulder.

"Please, Carlos. It's about to happen. Please come."

"Will someone tell me what's going on?" Jerry said. They didn't even look at him. Dad stood, got his coat, a sexy biker jacket in heavy brown cowhide. Jerry hated it that his dad looked sexy.

"Let's go," Dad said. "Jerry, why're you just standing there?"

Sudharshan did something to make the gold disc disappear into the inside pocket of his coat; it should have been too big to fit. Jerry slipped into his own coat, and when he turned back, Sudharshan had Rudy out of the cage again. He put the bird inside his coat and cinched the belt of the coat tight. Rudy shifted around inside, stuck his creepy little head out. "Ready?" Sudharshan asked.

"You're taking Rudy to see the eclipse? Won't it damage his eyes?"

"He'll be okay," Dad told him. "Come on."

As Sudharshan unlocked the front door, Jerry's eyes fell on the picture window. The *Monstera* was fruiting. The spike that it thrust up towards the light would plump. In a year, it would be a scaly fruit with pale yellow flesh. It would taste delicately sweet to some, like a mix of banana and pineapple. To others, it would irritate their throats and make them cough in vain efforts to dislodge the miniscule hairs with which the fruit was filled.

The three men and the bird went out into the hallway of the apartment building, heading for the elevator. Jerry remembered something. "Dad? I thought that *Monstera* never fruits if you grow it in a pot?"

Grumpily, Dad replied, "Strange things happen around Sudharshan."

In the elevator, no one spoke. Rudy peered around him with interested, birdseed eyes. Jerry wondered what Sudharshan would do if his pet pooped in his coat.

They stepped out onto the roof. The cold, bluish light of late afternoon made Jerry squint. There was a fitful wind. It poked fingers down his collar, up his sleeves. "There's the sun," Sudharshan said, pointing.

"I know where the sun is," Dad responded. But he didn't look where his lover was pointing. Instead he went to the side and looked over. They were thirty-two floors up. There was a ledge, but it'd be easy to leap. Jerry moved towards his dad.

"Carlos, come over here and put your goggles on," Sudharshan said. "You too, Jerry."

Rudy punctuated the command with a high note. Both Jerry and his dad obeyed.

The goggles made everything a calm, non-reflective yellow. The sun no longer bit at Jerry's eyes. Dad looked bug-eyed, strange. Jerry went back to the ledge, looked over. He could see the construction site, the excavator, the gravid tree.

Dad said to Sudharshan, "Aren't you going to put your glasses on, too?"

"I don't need them."

"And did you bring a pair for me?" said a voice from over by the door to the elevator. Jerry looked. It was the man from the street. He tossed the lick of green hair out of his eyes and hitched his way over to Sudharshan, scowling.

Sudharshan only nodded. "Good to see you, Gar. You'll be fine, you know that."

"You two know each other, then?" Jerry was way out of his depth. He only wished he knew whose waters he was floundering in.

Gar regarded him bitterly. "His family knows my family."

"I'd take care of Gar, if he'd let me," Sudharshan said.

"I just bet you would." This from Jerry's father. "It's him you're going away with, isn't it? The rest was just some story."

Sudharshan replied, "Carlos, it's not what you think." The sky began to darken unnaturally.

"I don't know what to believe anymore, Vic."

Vic? Victor? Wasn't his name Sudharshan?

Dad let go of Sudharshan's hand. Or Vic. Whoever he was. Dad adjusted his goggles more comfortably on his face. "Gar. That's your name, right?" he snarled.

"Yeah."

"Well, you should cover your eyes or something."

"I'll be okay," the young man replied gently. He turned his angry face full on the darkening sun. Jerry was frightened. People went blind like that, staring at eclipses.

"Hey, Gar," he whispered, but the young man ignored him.

A whistling sound came from the front of Sudharshan's coat. Rudy worked his way right out into the open, and with a happy warble, jumped onto Gar's shoulder. Gar looked to see what had landed on him, and his face softened. "Hi there, little brother," he said to the bird. He reached an open palm to Rudy, who leapt into it, chirping. The bird nibbled lightly at one of Gar's fingers, a gesture of avian affection. Gar grinned broadly down at Rudy, then up at Jerry. "He's just a fucking little sport, isn't he? He and I."

"I'm sorry, Gar," Sudharshan said. "Sometimes it happens that way." The sky was blackish-gray now. "Pollution, toxins leach into the eggs. You know." The air rushed, whooshed around them. "We look after you. All of you." Looking up at the sun, Jerry's dad gasped, put his hands to his mouth. Jerry didn't dare look. The wind beat like wings.

"Yes, you do, oh King," Gar replied. "You extend the hand of charity to us broken ones, whether we're any use to you or not."

"Well, I would, if you would take it. You don't have to beg in the streets."

"You don't get it," Gar told him.

Jerry, too unreasonably terrified to think, kept his gaze resolutely down. There, in the building lot; the tree with its swollen middle. The wrecking machine crouched over it, crane-like. As Jerry watched, a shadow washed over it, over half the city.

Out of the dusklight Gar muttered, "I could live with you and be fed serpents' tongues and sweet water."

"Amirta."

"Whatever. Sugar. I could, but I'm not Rudy. I won't die without your care. I don't *have* to stay with you."

Rudy screamed. It was almost full dark now. Whatever was arriving was big enough to blot out all the light, to eclipse the sun. Jerry's dad cried out and crouched against the roof, cowering. "I believe you, I believe you," he whimpered.

"It's all right, Carlos," Sudharshan shouted over the rushing wind. He pulled the disk out of his coat. It glowed with light. He held it high and twirled it, signaling.

There was a huge cracking sound from the construction site. By the light of Sudharshan's disk of fire, Jerry could see that the swollen tree had finally burst at the belly and split apart.

Jerry felt the weight of air above them rush down. He refused to look beyond Sudharshan's hand with its spinning circle. Something was coming. He threw himself over his dad. And finally, he looked up.

Pinions wide enough to span creation. A keel of a chest, deeper than oceans. A man's body with the dimensions of a god. Backlit by the sun it eclipsed, the bird-headed man-thing swooped down, roaring. Talons that could grasp an elephant and bear it away. A raptor's beak long enough to spear a sun. Jerry cried, but couldn't look away. Small, he was so small. The thing swept past them, the wind of its passing nearly knocking them over. The sun peeked back out. The thing's awful cawing stopped.

"Long time no see, Daddy!" Gar called out to the creature.

Jerry's dad mewled under him. Jerry hardly heard it. He had to know. He stood on noodle legs and looked over the side.

The massive bird thing looked briefly up at them. Its deep gaze, absently hungry, sucked Jerry in. A pointed tongue the length of a car snaked out and licked a hooked beak. Then it looked back down. It had folded itself up to sit in the construction site like a brooding hen in a nest. The tree stuck out from among its breast feathers. If the skeleton building or the excavator were still there, they were hidden somewhere under its body. On the street, cars were gathering to ogle. As though it bit on a toothpick, the thing pulled the top of the swollen tree away.

A smaller, ugly head covered in pinny green feathers poked out from beneath the bird-thing's breast. Crazily, Jerry thought of Rudy sticking his head out of Sudharshan's − Vic's − coat. "Oh," said Gar, "would you look at that? A healthy hatchling at last."

The smaller thing opened its beak wide. It was all red inside there. The big bird-thing retched and vomited into the ugly baby bird's mouth. Frantically, the baby gulped it down. The father fed his child.

"The long thin scrawny ones stick between your teeth, and the short thick ones just squirm . . ." sang Gar. "Whaddya figure my new brother's dining on, Vishnu?" Vishnu, not Victor. "Pre-digested cobras? King snakes? I remember how that tastes."

"He can't do it by himself," Sudharshan murmured.

Jerry's dad had stood up. He was looking down at the insane spectacle in the construction lot. Wonder made his features gentle. "That's some growing boy," he said. "How often will he eat?"

"About a ton of meat, every other day," Sudharshan said. "Garuda will need to hunt down a lot of snakes over the next five years or so. I have to help him. The baby is my new mount."

"So you are going away," Jerry's dad said. "You're leaving."

Sudharshan looked exasperated. "I told you, not for long!"

"Five years isn't long?"

"Not when you're a god, it isn't," Gar told them.

Jerry looked at his father's eyes filling, at his father bowing over again, shrinking in on himself again. He looked at Sudharshan, at the grief on the god's face. He remembered the picture albums that his mother had shown him, of his dad as a little boy in khaki shorts, grinning for the camera, proudly holding up −

"Dad," he said.

"He's leaving me, Jerry."

"Dad. Listen. Look at me."

"I'm going to be alone again."

"Dad."

"What."

"You used to hunt snakes, Dad," Jerry told him. "As a boy. Remember?"

And through his gold-lined goggles, Jerry's father *looked* at him, really saw him clearly. "My god," Dad whispered. "I did." He reached for Jerry and pulled him into an embrace, laughing, crying. Surprised, Jerry hugged back. His dad's shoulders were broader than they looked.

Over Jerry's shoulder, Dad said to Sudharshan, "I'll help you with your Garuda. You and me, okay? It's perfect."

"No," responded Sudharshan.

Stricken, Jerry's dad released him. From the street below came the sound of sirens. Jerry glanced over the side. Two fire engines were converging on the construction site. As if.

"No," said Sudharshan again. "It won't work, Carlos."

"Why not?" Jerry's dad cried out.

"It's too dangerous."

"I don't care. We'll be together. I can protect you."

The incarnation of an immortal didn't even bother to point out the flaw in his partner's logic. "You can't leave your job."

"Like they'll miss one lousy bureaucrat."

"Rudy, then. I can't take him, he's too frail. I need you here to look after him."

And now, Jerry's dad was at a loss for words. His face began to crumple.

Sudharshan was crying now too. "Rudy's my responsibility, Carlos. All the garudas are. I thought you'd help me take care of him. Please, lover."

Jerry saw Dad's broad shoulders bunch, the twist of his hip, before he realised what was happening. Dad turned, Sudharshan screamed, "No!" and Jerry reached his hands out to catch Dad, to hold him, but Dad was vaulting over the ledge before any of them could move.

"Fuck!" Gar cried out. Someone in the street screamed.

Dad spread his arms and legs. He plummeted, landed on the garuda's broad back, rolled. Jerry tried to keep breathing. Dad fetched up against a boulder-sized shoulder. He pushed himself to a sitting position. Jerry could see the moon of his upturned face, looking at them. He waved.

The garuda turned its eagle's head, peered down at its new rider. It opened its beak and struck. Carlos barely danced out of the way in time.

"Please, please," Sudharshan whispered. "He's my love. Please don't hurt him."

A god was begging for Jerry's father's life.

"Hey, Dad!" Gar called down. The garuda met his gaze. "That's Carlos! He's gonna help you feed the little one there."

The garuda closed its beak. Twisted its head sideways to regard Jerry's dad with one eye. Carlos reached a hand up, stroked the tip of its mane of feathers, each longer than Carlos was tall. The garuda allowed the touch. Turned back to feeding his son.

Sudharshan threw his head back, eyes closed. He let a breath out. His shoulders relaxed. "Oh, you smart-mouthed monster's son, you," he said to Gar. "Thank you."

"Any time I can be of assistance."

Sudharshan looked at him. Calmly, Gar gazed back. "Yes," the god replied. "I'll remember."

"You do that."

Sudharshan regarded the scene below them, his gaze fond. "Now, what am I going to do with that stubborn man? He can't come with me. Rudy needs . . ."

Gar laughed. "Is that all? Don't sweat it, Vishnu. I can housesit. Keep Rudy in birdseed and earthworms, yeah?"

Rudy skreeked.

Sudharshan glared at the two of them, the two failed garudas. He scowled down at the construction site, where Dad was stroking the garuda with one hand, and trying to wave the firemen away with the other. They had ringed the garuda and stood, holding limp hoses uncertainly. Sudharshan sighed. "All right, then," he said.

Jerry laughed. Sandor'd never believe this in a million years.

"Look, we'd better be going," Sudharshan told them. "Those people down there could get hurt. We'll send word, Gar."

Vishnu didn't so much jump as float down into the cushioning of the garuda's feathered body. Jerry's dad and Vishnu pulled the ugly baby bird into a cradle between them on the garuda's back. The garuda purred at them as they struggled. Its child was bigger than the two men combined. But they managed.

The police had arrived. They bullhorned at them to get down, pointed rifles. Dad shielded Vishnu with his body. The garuda roared again, and the people on the ground crouched and covered their ears. It gathered its taloned feet under itself and leapt into the air, its wings pumping. They flew. In seconds they were too small to see.

"You'll have to care for the *Monstera*, too," Jerry told Gar.

"What's that?"

"It's ugly, and it's beautiful. I'll show you."

Sitting in Gar's palm, Rudy made a chirping noise.

"Yeah, but he never remembers," Gar told his brother.

"Never remembers what?" Jerry asked.

"My dad. The garuda. We don't like king snakes. They have this weird sweet-ish taste to them."

Jerry laughed, trying to make out the speck in the sky. "He forgets, huh? Yeah, I know how that goes."

GAYTOWN

ROBERT BOYCZUK

Gaytown, 5 mi. Your home away from home!

"Gaytown? They've *got* to be kidding."

Two hours, and it was the first thing Paul had said since he'd slammed the passenger door of the Escort. He punched the eject button on the deck and flipped his compilation tape, starting it again.

"I mean, shouldn't the sign read, 'Your homo away from home'?"

Damien didn't smile; instead, his grip on the wheel tightened.

"Hm," Paul said, "since you *refuse* to come out, maybe we should turn around. Just in case, you know, someone might see *you* passing through *Gaytown.*"

Damien went for the light touch. "Nah. But I'm going have to ask you to get into the trunk."

"Naturally."

No trace of amusement in Paul's voice. Crossing his arms, he stared outside. Playing the temperamental artist again.

Another hour of pouting and it'll be over, Damien thought. *Paul will perk up like he always does. Then we can get on with our vacation.*

The tape whirred on, a song from a British band from the '80s whose name Damien couldn't quite recall, though he could picture the sexy lead singer clearly: tall, athletic, handsome, who'd gone on to star in a few indie films after the band had broken up.

Gaytown.

The sign had been old, weathered. An artifact from a time when the name wouldn't have raised eyebrows or invited jokes. Someone, a few years ago by the looks of it, had made a half-hearted attempt to paint out the word Gay; but the paint had faded so that now, instead of obscuring, it highlighted the word like a crucial term in a high school student's text.

The Escort's tires hissed over country asphalt, the late afternoon world drifting past. An hour and a half earlier they'd passed into cottage country, the flat, barren fields outside Toronto melting into undulating terrain. Ranks of evergreens snuck up on them, pressing in on the highway, falling away when a lake suddenly appeared at the side of the road, or retreating reluctantly for an oasis of humanity − a resort, a country store, a restaurant − although these became less frequent as the afternoon wore on. Above it all, the sky was unaccountably blue, the counterpoint of a few white clouds tacking across its sweep. A perfect

Thanksgiving weekend. Exactly the sort they'd come seeking.

Only Paul's mood had spoiled it all.

Four years we've been together, Damien thought. *You'd think he'd have adjusted by now.* But Paul had only become worse lately. How could someone so sensitive, so loving, also be so unreasonable?

"It's wrong," Paul said.

"We're on vacation." Damien tried to keep his voice even. "Can't you give it a rest?"

"You're ashamed of me, aren't you?"

"No." Of course not. Still, there were times when Paul acted – if not exactly flamboyant – then gay enough to make Damien uncomfortable. "You know that's got nothing to do with it."

"Then why not come out?"

"Jesus, Paul, how many times do we have to have the same argument?"

"You didn't answer the question," he said flatly.

"You know I can't come out." Damien shook his head. "Not right now, anyway."

"I did."

"You're an artist, Paul. I'm a high school principal."

"It's not like they can fire you."

"That's not the point." How could Damien explain it so that Paul would understand? "It's the way people would treat me afterwards."

"Okay, forget work. But you won't even introduce me to your family."

"You've met my brother."

Paul blew out an exasperated breath. "You told Jeff I was your tenant." His anger dissolved into hurt. "One time he came over. *One* time. And you made me move all my things out of our bedroom and into the study."

Damien felt a spike of guilt. He *had* made Paul do that.

"You don't give them enough credit." Paul's voice softened. Reaching over, he rested a hand on Damien's forearm. "If your family really loved you, they'd understand."

"Not all families are as understanding as yours." Paul's parents, a university professor and a social worker, were hardly cut from the same bolt of cloth as Damien's, who were sturdy small-town folk. Nor could Paul begin to fathom the kind of place Damien grew up, a circumscribed, distrustful, and disapproving world. Where, reputedly, no one was, or ever had been, gay. "If you knew them, you'd get it."

Paul yanked his hand away like it had been burned. "Not much chance of that, is there?"

"You've got to be patient." How many times had he told Paul that? It was starting to sound more and more like a lame excuse, even to him. "I promise, when the time is right, I'll introduce you."

"At thirty-six," Paul said, "I'm no longer willing to be somebody's dirty little secret."

Damien's stomach fluttered, like they'd just hit a dip in the road.

Paul pulled a road map out of the glove compartment; it had been neatly folded back to display a section of highway. On it he'd traced out a route in black marker. Paul tapped the map with his forefinger. "It's about three miles to the next junction. If we turn left there, we'll be in Coville in three hours."

Perspiration gathered between Damien's palms and the wheel.

"I'm not asking you to make an announcement or anything," Paul said, a hopeful note in his voice. "Just introduce me to your parents. Let them see my face, maybe start getting used to it."

"You said the cottage was booked for tonight. If we don't show up —"

"I lied. There's no cottage."

Damien stared at him in disbelief.

"I'm sorry." Paul fidgeted. "But it was the only way to get you up here." He brightened. "You said your mom invited you and your *roommate* for Thanksgiving. Remember?"

"Shit, Paul —"

"Just a quick visit. We grab a drumstick and we're out of there."

"No." Damien kept his eyes on the road, unable to look at Paul.

"I swear I won't act gay."

"I said no."

"Why not?"

Why not? Damien's dad would spot Paul for what he was in a second. And connect the dots. *My son the faggot.* Then all hell would break loose. Jesus, Paul really didn't have a clue.

"Because."

Paul snorted. "There's a good reason."

In a dense tangle of trees on the left, a corridor suddenly opened up, revealing a field behind. Damien knew he should have been focused on their conversation, but an odd color in the field had hooked his attention. A blotch of pink in the midst of sere grass and thick-limbed evergreens. It moved. Stood up? Or seemed to, although it was hard to tell with the motion of the car, the rapid change in perspective. *An animal?* But there were no animals that color. None that Damien knew about, anyway. He craned his neck, only the angle was gone, the field lost to sight.

"Are you listening to me?"

"Of course I am."

"I can't wait any longer, Damien. If you won't do this for me, then. . . ." Paul's voice trailed off.

"Then what?"

"Then I'm moving out."

Damien felt like he'd been sucker punched. *He doesn't mean it,* Damien thought. *He's tired, that's all.* But when he looked over, Paul returned his gaze resolutely, the map clutched in his hand, his determination plain. The Escort's engine whined as it began laboring up the back of a large broken rise.

"Well?"

I can't, Damien answered silently, his stomach churning. Only the alternative was no more palatable. *Life without Paul.* The only man he'd ever dared love. The space inside the car suddenly seemed way too small.

"Aren't you going to say anything?"

They passed another old sign that Damien almost missed, faded and barely visible through the tangle of anemic trees that huddled around it, announcing the inevitability of Gaytown in two miles. "You dump this on me out of the blue then expect an immediate response?"

"No," Paul said, flipping the map into Damien's lap. "Not immediate. You've got two miles left." The map slid onto the floor. "I've made up my mind, Damien. I can't abide half a relationship any longer. Either we turn left at the junction together, or we turn back and go our separate ways. Your choice."

The Escort continued to toil up the hill. They'd crest it momentarily. Damien was possessed by an irrational impulse to stomp on the brakes, to throw the car into reverse and back up past the start of their conversation, back to a place where everything had been all right.

Topping the ridge, they dropped into a shallow valley and came upon Gaytown.

Damien's mind numbly registered the outskirts, a scattering of clapboard houses, some dodgy trailers that had sunk cinder block roots, a lone quonset hut. Down the highway he saw more responsible-looking brick structures clustered around an intersection, a lone stop light suspended above the road by thin black wires as fine as the lines in one of Paul's pen and ink drawings. Although they were too far to make out the markings on the green highway sign posted at the intersection, Damien knew with heart-sinking certainty it marked the junction. The intersection seemed to be flying towards him. Lifting his foot from the gas, Damien eased the Escort off the road; gravel crunched under the tires.

"What are you doing?" Paul sounded alarmed, like maybe he thought Damien was going to turn around. Or ask him to climb into the trunk.

"Gas," Damien said, pointing at the pump in front of the quonset hut. "We're out of gas." Somehow his mind had registered the congruence of pump and gas gauge needle hovering just below E, and had grasped at the momentary reprieve like a drowning man would a scrap of flotsam.

Paul frowned, eyeing the gauge.

Damien pulled up beside the pump, killed the engine, and reached for the door handle.

"Yesterday —"

Damien's paused, a leg out the door.

"— when I went to the wine store, I filled up." Paul looked at Damien. "It should still be half full."

"Look at the gauge." Damien felt detached, like someone else was talking. "It says we're out of gas."

"Tell me about it."

It took Damien a second to realize Paul had just served up a shot. *Don't react,* he thought numbly. *It'll only make things worse.*

He stepped onto the dirt lot, the chill of autumn enveloping him. The gas bar seemed abandoned. For a second he couldn't remember why he was *here*, of all the places he might have been in the world.

He undid the gas cap. No one appeared from the hut.

Paul opened his door and climbed out, leaning on the roof. "Well?" He said it like he thought Damien had contrived this delay.

"It's not self serve." The pump, an old mechanical one, had no digital display, no instructions, no card swipe. On its side was a flow indicator, a small half-sphere of glass with an orange ball that would flutter the moment the gasoline started flowing.

"You know that's not what I was asking. I want to know —"

"I'll see if anyone's around," Damien said, hurrying away. The hut had a semi-circular plywood facing with a mismatched door and an oversized window cut into it. In the corner of the window's grimy pane an orange, fly-specked sign read *Open* even though it was dark inside. He heard Paul climb back into the car.

Damien tried the handle. Locked.

He leaned forward, cupping one hand against the glass to block the bedeviling reflections. Hard to make out anything, just the shadowy outlines of a cramped front office, a beat-up metal desk, sagging shelves to one side, a yellowing girlie calendar tacked to the back wall. Damien was about to turn away when, in the far corner, a movement caught his eye. He squinted, but whatever had shifted was now still. Raising his hand, he rapped sharply on the glass —

A figure reared up from the floor, cutting across the smeared field of view, in full sight for a split second, then disappearing through a backroom door.

A naked girl.

At least Damien was pretty sure it had been a girl.

Behind the glass, a second figure rose now, levering itself up tentatively, like it had just woken. It swept upwards, dwarfing Damien, practically filling the whole window, stooping as its head brushed the ceiling. Its skin was the same color he'd spotted earlier in the field, an off-pink, except now he could see it was marbled with blue veins, like the ribbons of flesh left between the ribs of an eviscerated carcass. Where there should have been a face was a vacant oval

— or at least no distinguishable features, just nubs or indentations where there should have been eyes, a nose, a mouth. For half a heartbeat, the empty visage regarded Damien impassively. Then the thing turned and wobbled drunkenly into shadows that folded around it in a protective mantle.

For another second Damien blinked at the empty room. Then he turned and bolted back to the car. Throwing himself into the driver's seat, he yanked his door closed so hard the car rocked. He felt sick.

"What the hell was that?" Paul's eyes flicked from Damien to the hut and back.

"I —" Damien started, then stopped. The whole thing seemed unreal, like he'd been watching a movie. "Nothing."

"Nothing?" Paul gaped at him in disbelief.

"A couple of kids," Damien said. "Probably the pump jockey and his girlfriend." It sounded right as soon as it was out of his mouth. What he thought he had seen couldn't have been real. Could it? "I surprised them. Caught them *in flagrante delicto*." The suddenness of it, the shock of Paul's ultimatum, had magnified everything in his already battered imagination. Sure the guy had been big —

Clutching the sleeve of Damien's sweater, Paul said, "Kids? Jesus, Damien, he had to be nine feet tall. And his skin was pink, like. . . ." Paul hesitated, searching for the words to explain what he'd seen. "Nobody has skin like that."

"You were startled," Damien said. *Like I was.* "That's all."

Paul peered at the window; his hand trembled. "Don't fuck around."

"Who's fucking around?" Damien pried his sweater free from Paul's fingers. "You're the one who saw the jolly pink giant. All I saw was a couple of horny kids."

"Bullshit. You saw exactly the same —" Paul stopped, staring at something outside.

Damien turned.

Beside his door was a kid. He wore spotless coveralls, a jean jacket. On an oval badge above the pocket the name "Jerry" had been stitched. He didn't look the sort you'd expect at a gas bar: his skin was flawless, his eyebrows as precise as if they'd been drawn on. Not a single hair out of place. He was beautiful in an unnatural way, like a perfectly symmetrical mannequin. He swirled his finger, indicating that they should lower the window. Damien cranked the handle.

"Fill 'er up?"

Damien nodded.

Paul stared at Jerry, tight-lipped. The kid sauntered over to the pump and lifted the hose from its cradle. Sliding the nozzle into the tank, he squeezed the trigger gently. Lovingly, almost. He smiled and nodded at Damien. The pump went *ching-ching-ching* with old-fashioned animation.

"Doesn't look pink to me," Damien said. "More pasty, I'd say."

Paul stared at Jerry through the back window, then at the office where the door was now open and the lights on. "That's not him." On the left side of Paul's forehead a vein throbbed conspicuously. Outside, Jerry began whistling.

"You're upset." Damien laid his hand on top of Paul's and gave it a reassuring squeeze. "We both are."

"Jesus, Damien, I know what I saw."

A movement in the rearview mirror snagged Damien's attention.

Paul looked at the hut. "I mean, I'm pretty sure I saw –"

Jerry was walking towards his door.

"– that *thing* –"

Damien pulled his hand away; Paul look startled.

Reaching Damien's window, Jerry leaned in. The slightest of wrinkles creased that perfect forehead. "There's something you'd best have a look at out here."

"Damien," Paul whispered, "don't. . . ."

"It's fine," he answered. Opening the door, he got out, following Jerry to the back of the car.

"See there," Jerry pointed at the dirt behind the car. This close, Damien smelled a whiff of something on Jerry, like the stink of rotting potatoes he'd once found moldering under the sink. "You've got a leak."

Damien looked but couldn't see anything. "Leaking?"

"Uh-huh. Gas. I'd better have a look." Jerry trotted back to the office, re-turning a moment later with a flattened cardboard carton. Placing it on the ground at the rear bumper, he lay on it face up, wriggling underneath the car. Damien heard him tinkering with something. Then he made a *tchhhing* sound. A moment later he eased himself out and got to his feet.

"Big crack in your gas tank," he said, wiping hands on a pristine rag he'd pulled from his back pocket. "Leaking like a cocksucker."

Damien glanced behind the car; a tiny rivulet now snaked through the dirt.

"So what does that mean?" Paul's question startled Damien; he hadn't heard him open his door.

"You need to get her fixed. Or you won't make it another ten miles, let alone the next gas station."

"How long to fix it?" Paul said. He sounded angry – but Damien knew him well enough to know his anger masked his agitation.

"Need to drain the tank, let her dry out overnight, and then weld a patch. You'll be back on the road by eleven tomorrow."

Paul's expression tightened; Damien felt relief.

Another distraction. Maybe a reprieve. He'd almost forgotten about Paul's ulti-matum. Maybe Paul had too.

"What's it going to cost?" It was the expected question, even though Da-mien didn't really give a damn.

"With parts and labor, and new a tank of gas, it'll run you about seventy-five." Less than Damien had guessed. "Fine. Do it."

"You'll have to leave the car overnight." Jerry nodded towards the junction. "There's a hotel just on this side of the lights." He pointed. "It has a bar downstairs. Just don't go in there expecting much *action*, if you know what I mean." He smiled, exposing a row of perfect teeth, and elbowed Damien lightly in the ribs, startling him. "Leastways, not for a couple of young bucks like you." He winked at Paul, who opened his mouth as if to say something, then snapped it shut.

"That's okay," Damien said quickly. "We need a break anyway. That's why we're bach-ing it." He handed the keys to Jerry. "Just us, a lake, and some cooperative fish." The lie slipped out before Damien realized they had no poles or tackle boxes or bait in the car.

Paul pulled his overnight bag from the back seat and started off down the shoulder of the highway, towards the hotel. He was pissed. As pissed as Damien had ever seen him. Moving at a good clip, too; Damien nodded at Jerry, then hustled after Paul, finally catching up as they neared the intersection.

"Paul?"

Eyes forward, refusing to look.

Fine, Damien thought. *Let him pout.* At least he wasn't talking nonsense about visiting Damien's parents. He slowed, letting Paul stay a few steps ahead. On the other side of the road, an old man wearing a white panama hat, tweed jacket with an ascot, and gray loafers leaned on a walking stick, waiting patiently for a miniature Scotty while it sniffed critically at the base of a sapling. It was an absurdly small dog. Not like the Rottweilers or German shepherds that Damien remembered from his own town, the sort of dogs that would have ripped a Scotty like that to pieces given half a chance. The man lifted his chin to stare, and Damien looked away, hurrying to catch up with Paul.

In silence, they passed a row of businesses – Ace Hardware, the Hi-Style Hair Salon, a dry cleaner's, the Apollo 8 Diner – coming to the last building before the intersection, a vertical art deco sign bolted to its side. The words "Town Hotel" were visible on the bottom part but someone had painted over the top bit; Damien could guess what lay underneath.

They entered a narrow lobby. To the right, through a set of open glass doors, was the bar: dark wood paneling, round tables, and curved-back chairs, the walls hung with posters of barely clad cheerleaders advertising different brands of beer that Damien found indistinguishable in taste. A few late afternoon patrons gave them no more than a bored glance.

On the lobby desk there was a bell. Damien banged it until a gray, middle-aged man in a cardigan materialized from the back room. Dust seemed to have settled permanently in his wrinkles. "Can I help you gents?" His rheumy eyes took them in with bored disapproval.

"A room with a king-sized bed," Paul said. "And fresh sheets."

The man glared at him.

"He's joking," Damien said quickly. "Twin beds will be fine."

The clerk tapped a pencil on the counter for a full five seconds, looking from Paul to Damien and back again like he was trying to decide between renting them the room and getting his baseball bat. Then he shrugged, like the bat was too much trouble, and surrendered a yellowed card for them to fill out. Damien scribbled their information in the tiny boxes as fast as he could. The clerk handed him a key, pointing wordlessly to a set of crooked stairs at the back.

"Thanks," Damien said and hurried away.

Paul followed him up. Their room, number eight, was on the corner overlooking the intersection. It was surprisingly clean. Nice even. Obviously, someone with taste had decorated it. The walls were yellow and artfully hand-stenciled; the furniture was colonial, including hand-painted quilt chests at the foot of each bed. Damien threw his bag on a wing back chair that in a Queen street vintage store would have fetched several hundred dollars.

"Why won't you talk about it? "

Damien closed the door quietly. "I'm tired, Paul. Can't we discuss going to my parents tomorrow, when we pick up the car?"

Moving over to the window, Paul lifted a green chintz curtain with his finger, his head turning slowly, tracking someone walking along the sidewalk outside. Maybe the old guy with the Scotty. "Your parents? That's not what I meant." Paul let the curtain drop. "I was talking about that *thing*."

"There was no 'thing.' I was right there. You were thirty feet away. It was just Jerry and some girl."

"A girl?" Paul took a step towards Damien. "What girl?"

"The one who ran by first."

"It wasn't a girl."

"There's no need to raise your voice." Damien glanced at the walls.

"No one's listening, if that's what you're worried about. We're the only people in this dump."

"Look, I'm as pissed as you that we're stuck here." Damien spoke in a whisper.

"Really?" Paul sniffed. "You sure don't seem to be."

"We've just got to make the best of it."

"Something's wrong. And you don't care."

"This is a small town." Damien was getting annoyed. "*Everything's* wrong here."

"It was Jerry."

"What are you talking about?"

"There was no girl. Just Jerry. Then that *thing*."

Jerry? "You're nuts." It *had* been a girl, and Jerry afterwards . . . except Jerry wasn't very tall. Shorter than Damien. And kind of skinny. While the second figure had been big. Really big. Only it made no sense. *Two men?* Not here. "You saw him, Paul. Talked to him. He wasn't rattled or upset. He was whistling. Not the way he'd act if he'd just been caught with another guy."

"He was gay. Hell, he was even flirting with you. I saw him wink."

Damien shook his head. "Christ, Paul, you can't be gay in a place like this."

"You were."

"I meant you can't be openly gay here."

"Or anywhere, apparently."

Damien's cheeks heated. "I'm not going to talk about this anymore."

"Why doesn't that surprise me?"

"I'm going to the diner to get something to eat," Damien said, opening the door. "If you want, you can join me."

"Wait." Paul's anger melted; he looked nervous, scared maybe. "I was only –"

But Damien pulled the door shut. For a second he stood in the hall, hand still on the knob, squeezing it so hard it hurt his fingers. *It's not my fault,* Damien thought. *I refuse to feel guilty.* Letting go, he thumped downstairs and stepped out of the hotel onto the street.

On the north side of the intersection, a couple walking hand in hand swung right and disappeared into a narrow laneway. Damien had only caught a glimpse of them from the back. One, from the size and shape, could have been Jerry; the other had to duck under a "No Parking" sign ten feet off the ground.

Damien's heart pounded.

He took a few halting steps toward the lane. Then stopped.

Just my imagination. Paul's got me so worked up, shouldn't come as a surprise.

Doing a one-eighty, he hurried back past the hotel, glancing over his shoulder at the laneway and almost collided with a man wearing a greasy apron, smoking a cigarette. Despite the chill in the air, he wore only a T-shirt underneath. No, not a T-shirt, more like a tank top, the kind you'd see on men cruising Jarvis Street. The guy took a long drag on his smoke.

"Did you . . . did you see a man down there?" Damien pointed to the alleyway. "A big man?"

"Nope." The guy flicked his butt onto the sidewalk and crushed it under heel. "Didn't see no one." He pulled open a door behind him and held it. The distinctive odor of well-seasoned deep-fryer oil wafted out of the Apollo 8 Diner. "Well?"

Paul would have never have gone into a greasy spoon like this, where he couldn't get a vegetarian burger with arugula and goat cheese toppings. Damien crossed the threshold.

Empty, except for a few pensioners. Despite the odor, the place had a kitschy charm. On one side half a dozen booths ran back along the wall. The seats were upholstered in vinyl and the tables had Arborite tops whose patterns had gently faded over the years. On the other side a long counter wrapped around a stainless steel grill, classic soda-shop stools with chrome trim bolted to the floor in a neat row in front of it. Hung on the wall above the grill was a blackboard listing the daily special: *Soy burger with choice of three toppings, includes side salad, hearts of romaine with sweet corn, toasted brioche croutons, and a red wine yogurt dressing - $6.99.*

Damien picked a spot near the back.

The cook brought him a menu in a maroon plastic folder, not venturing a word. Damien tried to read it, nothing registering, his eyes flicking up again and again to the plate glass windows in the front. Waiting. For Paul. Or that thing. A few minutes passed, but no one –

Damien sensed a presence hovering beside him; the stink of stale cigarettes drifted around his head. He turned. The cook stared down at him through dull, simian eyes. "Made up your mind yet?"

A figure that might have been Paul flitted past the front window, but Damien had been distracted, didn't get a good look.

"I need a few more minutes."

Six-thirty.

Paul hadn't joined him.

Cover to cover through two old *Time* magazines, retrieved from a rack at the counter, chewing and swallowing his burger and fries without really tasting them. An hour and a half since he'd stormed out of the room. Long enough, Damien supposed, for Paul to have finished his sulk. And for his own nerves to settle. He paid his bill and returned to the hotel.

On his way through the lobby he spotted Paul in the bar, wedged behind a table, his back to a musty wall that probably hadn't been painted in twenty years. In his hand was a beer mug containing a red concoction, no doubt an approximation of a Caesar, his current drink of choice. Although he looked up when Damien walked in, he didn't say a word.

"Here." Damien dropped the plastic bag he'd been carrying on the table. "I got you some take out."

Paul glanced at the bag but remained silent.

"So don't eat it." Damien tried not to show his irritation. "I'm going up to the room."

No response. Like *he* was the one who'd been wronged.

"You coming?"

Paul shook his head.

"You've made your point."

"I'm not trying to make a point."

"Then what *are* you doing?"

"Waiting."

"For what?"

Paul glanced around the bar. "You'll see."

The remnants of Damien's soy burger roiled unhappily in his stomach. Paul drained his mug, raised his hand to order another, clearly determined to get drunk.

Let him, Damien thought. In the morning he'd be hungover, too focused on his own miseries to worry about a trip to Damien's parents.

Only. . . .

Only Paul could be a lousy drunk. When he got something in his head, he just wouldn't let it go. At best, he'd make an ass of himself. At worst. . . . Damien glanced around the bar. It wasn't the sort of place where you wanted to find out about the worst. Damien plunked himself down in one of the uncomfortable seats.

"Thought you were going to the room."

"There's no TV." Damien stared at the set above the bar.

Paul hunkered down, watching the locals through restless, narrowed eyes while Damien pretended to be absorbed by the movie of the week.

The bar filled, Paul still not saying a word except to order his drinks from the dour, consumptive waiter. Damien ordered draft, like everyone else, wanting to fade into the background. But he was painfully aware that they were strangers here, marked not only by their unfamiliar faces, but also by their awkward silence and the garish color of Paul's drink, the only bright cocktail in a sea of dull beer.

⚜

It was pushing nine o'clock.

The last tables had filled an hour ago; groups formed, standing shoulder to shoulder, clotting the aisles. The waiter now had to move with his tray held above the sea of heads, and the buzz of conversation had become so loud it was hard for Damien to hear the TV.

Paul ordered another drink. His fourth – no, fifth – since Damien had arrived. Damien himself was starting to feel drunk, even though he'd just finished his second beer. He kept his eyes glued to the set. The movie was about a housewife who led a secret life as a prostitute. Her motivation for being a prostitute didn't make much sense, nor did the naïve credulity of her family. What sort of PTA meeting lasted until one in the morning?

"You're part of it, aren't you?"

Paul's question startled Damien; he'd fallen into the movie. "Part of what?"

Paul waved his arm. "This." He slurred the word slightly, but at least he was speaking low enough that there was no danger of being overheard.

"You're not making any sense," Damien said, sensing the potential scene he had dreaded. He wanted the conversation to go away, for them to lapse back into a moody silence.

Furrowing his brow in inebriated concentration, Paul asked, "Why did our car break down?"

"God, Paul, I'm not a mechanic," Damien whispered. "Why does anything go wrong with a car?"

"I mean, we didn't scrape the tank," Paul said. "I would have remembered that. Don't you have to hit something to puncture the tank?"

Damien decided to ignore him. He swiveled around to face the television screen again.

"When you went for dinner I walked back to the garage to check. I couldn't find a gash in the tank. Or anything like it. Nothing that would cause a leak. And there was something else I wanted to check. Something . . . that bothered me." Paul reached in his pocket and pulled out a piece of paper with ragged edges. Dropping it on the table, he spun it around. It was torn from their map, a thick black line running along the highway, angling right at the junction not thirty meters from where they sat. "Where's this town?"

"Paul —"

"Show me."

Reluctantly, Damien peered at the map. There was no mistaking the junction. But nothing to indicate Gaytown. "Maybe it's too small."

"We went through plenty of smaller towns, and they were all on the map."

Damien shifted uncomfortably on the hard seat. "Don't be paranoid."

"Maybe," Paul said, "it's the sort of place that never makes it onto maps."

"Come on," Damien said. "Let's go back to the room." He reached over and tried to pry the mug out of Paul's hand, but Paul snatched it back, eyes blazing.

"Where are the women, Damien?" He said it loudly; a few people glanced over.

"What are you talking about, Paul?"

"Look around. There aren't any women."

Paul was right. They were surrounded by men. Some of whom now eyed them suspiciously. "It's a small town bar," Damien said, feeling this was explanation enough. "And would you mind keeping your voice down?"

"Don't you think that's odd?"

"Sure. Whatever you say." Damien glanced around, trying to remain calm. "Why don't we go back to the room and talk about it there?"

"*No!*" Paul banged his glass down on the table. Incarnadine liquid sloshed over the side and onto the chipped veneer. A group of four men, all wearing baseball caps, glanced over. One said something and they laughed dismissively, then returned to their conversation. Paul glared at them, put his hands on the arms of the chair as if he was thinking about pushing himself out of his seat to confront them.

Leaning in, Damien whispered, "You're making a scene."

"A scene?" Paul's voice boomed out at drunken volume. The people at the table nearest them now stared openly, their smiles gone, their conversation stopped dead. In the background the hooker mom on TV droned on, talking dirty to one of her clients, while the rest of the bar, oblivious, hummed with trivial Friday night conversations.

"Please, Paul —"

"Don't you see?" He was shouting now. "There was no girl! It was two men fucking!"

Those nearest them had fallen silent. "I don't know what you're talking about," Damien said. He felt the stares of people boring into him; a drop of perspiration rolled down his temple. He rose, fighting the impulse to run, to get as far away as possible. "I . . . I'm going back to the room. Are you coming with me?"

Paul shook his head, leaving Damien no other choice.

He walked away. Or tried to. A wall of bodies blocked the aisle, deflecting him from the double doors leading back to the lobby, steering him in another direction, deeper into the bar. He tried another route, but it was plugged with people too. The crowd swirled around him, making him dizzy. Then a passage opened up and he rushed down it, coming to a door, a dead-end, with a hand-lettered sign, *Men's*. Pushing through, he found himself in a narrow, dimly lit bathroom, a bare bulb on the back wall casting watery illumination. Thankfully, it was empty. He stepped up to a urinal, just in case someone came in. The muted sounds of the TV and a dozen indistinct conversations buzzed on the other side of the thin wall like a swarm of annoyed flies.

On the wall, right in front of Damien's nose, someone had scrawled, *Jerry is a faggot.*

A scratching sound. From the row of the stalls at the back. Then a stink, like that of rotting potatoes, filled the air. Damien could hear something else now, something that sounded like an exhalation, but it went on an on, more air than a set of lungs should have been able to hold. Then silence. Damien realized he was holding his own breath.

A sharp gasp sliced the air, higher pitched — too high to have come from the same person.

No, Damien thought, stepping back from the urinal, fumbling with his zipper. *Impossible.*

A wavering groan filled the narrow space, prickling up Damien's spine. A groan of intense pleasure. It went on and on, rising in volume. Under the last stall, something — a bare foot scrabbling for purchase? — slipped into view then disappeared. It had long, twisted talons and had been absurdly pink.

Damien crashed through the door, bursting into the bar. At his back the groan changed pitch, became an unrestrained shriek, so loud it seemed to tear the air.

No one else took any notice.

The old man in the white panama hat, the one Damien had seen earlier at the side of the road, sat at the end of the bar, his Scotty curled at his feet. He cast a disapproving glance at Damien, as if Damien's hasty exit had violated an unwritten rule of washroom etiquette, then returned to idle contemplation of his beer. The howl blotted out all sound. Damien looked around wildly. Oblivious or uncaring, the bartender filled a pitcher; groups of men chatted or laughed at crude, testosterone-laden jokes. None seemed to hear it.

Damien shoved through a clutch of people –

– then stopped short.

Two locals were settling into their vacant seats, Paul's half-finished drink still on the table.

The shriek broke off. Cut with the abruptness of a slashed throat. Bar noise trickled back into his consciousness: the clink of a glass, the muted whispers of conversation (*about me, about us,* Damien thought), the jukebox now playing, the nasal whine of a country singer whose love had turned sour.

Paul was gone.

Damien felt his reality slipping away.

"Looking for your friend?"

A hand clasped Damien's shoulder. It was Jerry's. Guiding him through the crowd. The ranks of people opened, staring as he passed, then closed behind with the finality of prison doors. They emerged from the bar, Damien stumbling out into the chill night. The street was deserted, the buildings – save for the room behind him – empty and dark.

"Is he –"

"Your friend's all right. He went to the dance."

"Dance?"

"Up at the Legion hall," Jerry said. "Told me he wanted to see women. I told him there were loads – too many if you ask me – but they were all at the dance. He asked where it was, so I gave him directions. That's when he took off like a bat out of hell."

Damien's hands shook; perspiration peppered his forehead. He pulled a deep breath of cool air into his lungs. It helped calm him.

"You best go after him," Jerry hesitated. "Before he gets hurt."

"Where –"

"Over there." Jerry pointed north of the intersection, to the laneway where Damien had seen the couple earlier.

"Are . . . are you gay?"

Jerry went rigid at Damien's question; he curled his hands into fists. Damien braced himself for the blow.

"No one here is a homo," he hissed. "And you best remember that." Turning, Jerry strode back into the bar, abandoning Damien on the desolate street.

✛

The laneway became a dirt road behind the buildings on the main drag. Damien sprinted past a row of neatly groomed Andy-of-Mayberry bungalows and a field of broken corn stalks. Heavy-set Douglas fir crowded in on the road, constricting it, then fell back abruptly revealing a stubbly pasture, the flat-roofed Legion hall sitting in its middle. From around the edges of mustard curtains soft light trickled out, and he could hear the *thump-thump-thump* of the music's backbeat. Behind, the town was nowhere to be seen, hidden by the close-ranked trees. For a moment he experienced a panicked belief that the town no longer existed, maybe never had existed, and that the hall in front of him was the only real thing, the only drop of humanity in the midst of the vast, dark ocean of woods.

Shaking his head, he dislodged the unsettling notion. Leaves scratched past his feet, blown by the gusting night wind.

Hurrying up a gravel drive, Damien tugged open a wooden door. A blast of a song drained out of the building. It was the same song that had been on Paul's tape, only now he remembered the title and the band's name: "Johnny Come Home" by the Fine Young Cannibals. A young woman stood in the foyer sipping from a plastic cup, blocking his way; the stink of scotch coiled around her like a noxious perfume. Swaying slightly, she smiled at him, displaying lipstick-smeared teeth. "Wanna dance?"

Damien pushed past her.

"Cheeky!"

It was like walking into the past. Nothing had changed since he had gone to these things as a teenager, not the room, not the music, not the people. Maybe twenty couples, men *and* women – more than enough, Damien thought, to satisfy Paul – were gyrating on the dance floor. Other people were scattered around the periphery of the hall, at tables or leaning against the wall, drinking, gossiping, watching, trying hard to get laid. On the stage at the back a DJ stood behind a plywood table pulling a record from its sleeve; above his head a disco ball suspended from the ceiling dragged silver dollars of light across everything with dizzying regularity.

Damien scanned the crowd. No Paul.

Godamnit, where was he?

There, in front of the stage, saying something to a tall, thin man who just kept shaking his head. The man's face darkened and he walked away, waving his hand dismissively, like he was trying to disperse a bad stench. Paul shouted something after him that was lost in the tumult of music.

Jesus Christ. Paul was determined to get them both killed.

Scooting across the dance floor – dodging a spinning couple – Damien grabbed his arm. "What the hell is the matter with you?" On the stage behind, a large speaker boomed; he could barely hear his own words. "Are you trying to piss off everyone in town?"

"I've figured it out, Damien." Paul didn't sound drunk anymore.

Damien tried to nudge him away from the stage, over into the corner. "Figured what out?"

"This place. These people." He paused. "You."

Damien spotted the man Paul had been talking to, speaking to two of his buddies and nodding in their direction.

"It all makes a weird kind of sense."

The three men were glaring openly at them now.

"Come on, Paul. You've seen your women. Let's go." Damien tried tugging on his arm, but he refused to budge.

"You really only see what you want to, don't you?"

"Jesus, Paul. I don't know what kind of point you're still trying to make, but you've made it. Now let's get out of here."

"Okay. But first you have to do me a small favor."

"What favor?" The men began advancing towards them. Damien could tell from the look in their eyes that things were about to turn very ugly.

"I want you to get up on stage and say you love me."

"What?"

"You heard me."

Until now Damien had tried to keep his voice level, but everything was happening too fast. "Those guys coming towards us, they're going to kick the shit out of us. We've got to get out of here!"

"And go where?" Paul smiled crookedly. "This place isn't even on the map."

"For Christ's sake!" The men were only a few steps away. "You want to get us killed?"

Paul shrugged. "Too late." Breaking Damien's grip, he loped to the side of the stage and mounted a short set of stairs, taking them two at a time. He smashed his palm against the edge of the DJ's table; the needle scratched across the record, killing the song. People stopped dancing, conversations died. "Hey!" someone said. Hiss from the speakers filled the hall.

Paul raised his arms. The disco ball slashed circles of light across his chest. "Hey everyone, I have an announcement," he shouted. "I'm gay!" Pointing an accusing finger at Damien, he added, "And I love that man."

Damien felt the blood drain from his face. Around the edges of the crowd, he heard mutters. Angry, disapproving words, growing like the rumble in a tiger's chest. People eyed him with malice.

A fat woman stepped up to the stage. "Who the hell do you think you are?"

"I'm gay," he said as if that were the most reasonable thing in the world. "Like all of you!"

The woman blanched.

From the back of the room, a shrill voice screamed, "Get off the stage, homo!"

A chorus of other voices joined in, jeering.

"Go back to the city!"

"Get him!"

"Kill the faggot!"

The fat woman lurched forward, trying to snatch at Paul's pant leg, but Paul pirouetted out of the way, ducking back towards the woman and grabbing a fistful of her hair. Jerking his hand back, he pulled a wig free. Underneath, wispy brown hair circled a bald spot.

A man. Damien couldn't believe it. *A goddamn man.*

Shrieking, the man fell to his knees, his dress ballooning around him, futilely trying to cover his head with his hands.

Paul, holding up the wig like a trophy, giggled.

A big guy vaulted onto the stage and punched Paul in the mouth. He crumpled, the wig dropping from his hand. The DJ scooped it up and tossed it down to the fat man.

"Paul!"

Damien started up the steps to the stage. But someone pinned his arms from behind, dragging him back. More men surged onto the stage, Paul at the heart of the scrum, hard to see through the forest of legs, screaming as he was pummeled. The fat man, his wig askew, stepped in front of Damien and slapped him so hard his head snapped back; tears blurred his vision and the coppery taste of blood filled his mouth.

He felt himself being propelled across the dance floor. Blinking his vision clear, he craned to look back, saw a group of men carrying Paul face down, his head lolling, muttering. They passed an older man wearing a military uniform and a beret, his chest cluttered with ribbons and medals, who shook his head sadly. Another face swam up, stuck itself right in Damien's. "Too bad," said the woman who'd asked Damien to dance, her breath reeking of scotch. "You're cute." Beneath her makeup, Damien could see the start of a five o'clock shadow.

In a moment of clarity he thought: *We're going to die.*

They were in the foyer; he was thrust at the door, his chest crashing against it, knocking the wind from his lungs. Strong arms heaved him outside, the cool night air on his skin for a brief, shocking second as he tumbled through the air. He hit the ground, rolling over, skinning hands and knees on concrete, ending up on his stomach, staring back at the knot of angry men clustered in the doorway. A second group pushed to the fore, hauling Paul. They dropped him on the sidewalk like a bag of trash.

No one moved. No one spoke.

Please, god, Damien thought, hateful stares pinning him to the ground, *I don't want to die.*

Paul raised his head. One eye was already swelling shut. His jaw moved, like he was chewing on a piece of gum, and a tooth entwined in bloody strands of saliva emerged from between his lips; he spat it out onto the sidewalk. Swiveling his head slowly, painfully, to look at them, the men who'd beaten him, he whispered, "Fuck you."

Damien braced himself for a new onslaught.

Incredibly, it didn't come. Instead, they turned their backs and retreated inside the hall. The lock on the door clacked shut.

Damien couldn't believe they were still alive. He pushed himself up onto his knees, felt a stab of pain where one pant leg was bloody, wobbled, and went back down on all fours. He swore.

Paul regarded him impassively.

"I . . . I love you," Damien offered.

"Of course you do," Paul said, drawing a wheezing, liquid breath, as if a viscous fluid bubbled at the bottom of his lungs. "You just don't want anyone to know it."

Even now, he couldn't let it go. "Jesus, Paul —"

But Paul wasn't listening; his attention had shifted to something past Damien. His one good eye squinted.

"Paul?"

From behind, a scrabbling noise, like claws scratching and clicking towards them over the concrete walk. Damien froze, his own stare locked on Paul's. A fetid odor, like rotting potatoes, curled into his nose. Paul's mouth opened and closed in disbelief.

Everything went terribly, terribly still.

Don't look, Damien thought desperately at Paul. *If you don't look it won't be there.* But Paul's eyes were wide, goggling with terror.

Damien felt a familiar dread shiver through his bones. He squeezed his eyes shut.

— *don'tlookdon'tlookdon'tlook* —

A chill wind touched him, a sickening cold, like a plunge into the frigid waters of a stagnant reservoir. A ragged, slavering breath, the same one Damien had heard in the washroom, tickled the hair on his neck and cheek, passed him by —

Brief scuffling sounds, and something that may have been Paul's grunt. Then the sensation lifted. Gone. Like it had never been there. Damien snapped his eyes open.

The sidewalk was empty.

He pushed himself to his feet, pain spiking up his leg. He ignored it, looking around wildly, hobbling back and forth on the path.

"Paul!"

Behind the Legion hall, he spotted something large loping across the stubble of the denuded field, a body slung across its shoulder. The darkness washed out its color, but its shape, the shape of Damien's fear, was unmistakable. Paul began screaming then, a cry that pierced Damien's heart like the tip of a knife. The thing reached the edge of the field, vaulted over a wooden fence, and was swallowed by the woods. Paul's final cry echoed and was lost, suffocated by trees and torn away by gusting wind, scattered like the invisible leaves scudding past on the sidewalk.

This can't be real. Damien stared dumbly at the ranks of indifferent evergreens. The path rocked under Damien's feet like the deck of a sailboat foundering in a storm. *This can't be happening.*

⊹

Sometime later, Jerry stood beside him, shoulder to shoulder. Two friends who'd just wandered out of the dance to clear their heads. When he'd appeared, Damien couldn't have said.

"Looks like it'll be another few days for your car."

Damien said nothing.

"People round here aren't so bad." Jerry stared across the field, unaccountably beautiful in the moonlight. "Long as you don't go around upsetting them."

"Please," Damien croaked, even though he wasn't sure what he was begging for.

"*Shhhh.*"

In the dark a smooth, lifeless hand slipped into Damien's.

"It's best not talk about these things."

DIGGING UP GRAVES

WILLIAM J. MANN

This is how my dream begins: the sound of shovels, the stabbing of earth.

A dark blue night. The moon as odd voyeur, its light glinting off the blades of the silver shovels. It is the eye of the sky, a hole into the heavens, perchance the passageway from which he might return. I have had the same dream over and over ever since he died: I peel away my sweat-drenched sheets, placing my feet against the cold of the wooden floor, feeling my soles stick. I push myself to stand and pull on a pair of jeans, plunging head first into the blue of the night. And once there, embraced by a sweet, damp, blue fog that cools my skin, I dig up his grave, and pull him out of his coffin. He is dressed in a blue jacket, white shirt, and red tie, the clothes we buried him in, clothes that smell only a trifle musty now, like the old hand-me-downs my mother would keep in her hope chest in our basement that flooded every spring. I shake him as if he might wake, and I am not surprised that he has not decomposed: he is perfect, in death as in life.

Finally his eyelids begin to flutter, like little moths. When I awake, which I always do precisely at that moment, I feel neither disappointment nor relief. It is just the endless rush of nothing that I feel, and I am always conscious of how wet my sheets are. Sometimes, if I wake before the sun has arrived, Maria Magdalena is there with me, shaking her head from side to side as if I will never learn. She can read my thoughts: she knows my dream.

"He ain't comin' back to you," she says, sitting in the chair in the far corner of my room. "Whatcha expect? That you can just go out and dig him up and carry him back here?"

"Why not?" I ask her. "Look at you."

And she laughs — she always laughs, in such a big and marvelous, from-the-lungs kind of way. I can't see her very well in the dark, but she's wearing an old tattered floor-length dress and she's got her feet out in front of her, crossed at the ankles. I can make out that much from the light of the moon. Once, Maria Magdalena was a house slave, in her life before this one, maybe even a mammy to some silly little white boy like me. She knows how to take care of silly little boys. Ever since I dug up her grave, eighteen years ago this fall, she's been with me. On and off, before the sun comes up, in the back of my mind, here and there, in the shadow of the old tree outside my window, at the side of his bed right before he died.

So there's logic behind my question: if she can come back, why can't he?

Her grave had seemed forgotten and insignificant when we chose it under the bright white of the afternoon sun: nothing more than a slab of decaying brownstone at the far reaches of the cemetery, almost totally covered with deep green ivy. But that night, that cool October night, under an orange moon and among windswept dried maple leaves, it had seemed foreboding, sinister.

"There's not going to be anything left of her," I'd said, taking up my shovel. I was thirteen. Ned was fifteen. "I don't know why we're going through with this."

"Cause Sammy Westerholm said we wouldn't dare," Ned told me, digging at the earth with frenzied strokes. "I want to bring him the skull and set it on his lunch tray."

I had started to sweat. "This dirt is too hard," I moaned.

"Shut up and dig."

The gravestone tipped over. Its inscription faced the purple sky. It read: MARIA MAGDALENA HAWKINS 1804-1852.

"Ned," I asked, "do you believe in ghosts?"

"Oh, shut up, you lily liver," Ned snapped at me.

I didn't want to sound like a crybaby to Ned. He was a real *guy* in school. He never got picked on. Not that he was popular, but he drove a truck, even though he was too young to have his licence, and he was big, like a football player, even though he wasn't. Kids didn't mess with him. Nobody would ever call *him* a fag.

I think he hung around with me because he didn't really have any friends. He was always getting into fights, and I think there was some part of him that wanted to be more like me: good grades, stable family, never getting into trouble. Though I couldn't imagine why: I was the kind of kid who *did* get called a fag. Up until that year, the other boys in my class had pretty much ignored me, but a couple had started calling me "faggot" on the bus over the last couple of months. I'd seen what happened to kids who were labeled "fag" – and I didn't want that fate. And so Ned became my buddy: hanging out with Ned gave me masculine credentials. At least it ended the name-calling.

And so I dug harder. We'd been at it about an hour. The night had deepened and gotten colder. The crickets scolded us from the dark. Owls hooted.

"I think the coffin will have dissolved," I said, stopping my efforts and leaning on my shovel.

"Keep going. We're almost there."

We were down in a hole by now. Only our heads and shoulders remained at earth level. It was like a wound in the earth, I kept thinking. That's when the sweet, fruity smell hit us.

"It's *her*," I wheezed.

"No, it isn't, you fool," Ned snarled. "It's just roots and soil." But the smell, like rotting apples in a closed-in sun porch, was nauseating.

And then Ned hit wood.

It was a soft sound, mushy. Ned yelled for me to look. I watched as the old wood gave way like cardboard under his shovel. Something glistened in the starlight. A brass hinge.

"It's the coffin," Ned exclaimed, triumphant. "We've found it!"

"Is she inside?" I asked, terrified.

"We'll soon see," Ned said, scraping away at the sides of the hole to follow the outline of the wood. He was at a corner of the casket, either at the head or at the foot.

"Why'd we have to pick her?" I asked all of a sudden. "Why couldn't we have picked a guy? I don't feel we should be pokin' into no lady's coffin."

"You jerk. It don't matter. She was black, anyhow. This is the black section of the cemetery." I hadn't known that. I felt dizzy all of a sudden, and I covered my face with my hands.

"Listen, Jimmy-boy," Ned said, his face close to mine. "Some of the guys asked me why I hang around with you. They said you were a faggot. I said you weren't."

"Yeah?" I asked, trying to sound tough. "So?"

"You remember our little wager?"

How could I not? "Yeah," I said.

"The only way to prove you're not a little faggot is to go through with this. Otherwise, you know what you have to do."

I did. But I said nothing.

Then Ned bent down, ripping at the warped wood with his hands. He's like a savage, I remember thinking. A tiger tearing into a fallen antelope.

The wood crumbled in Ned's hands. The fruity smell became more intense. For a second, he gagged. Then it was gone. The air was pure.

"Looky here," Ned whispered in awe.

I looked down and let out a small cry.

Peeking up at us from between the ripped wood was a white skull, gleaming in the moonlight, deep dark eye sockets holding the secrets of a life from a hundred years before.

I backed up, my heart in my ears and throat. Why had I agreed to do this? Would I stop at nothing to fit in? Would I really do anything to not be the boy who always fell in the relay races, who couldn't break through the girls' hands in Red Rover?

"Oh, please, Ned, please let's get outta here," I cried. "This is really freaking me out."

But Ned was too enthralled to answer. He reached through the moldy wood and cupped the skull in his hands. With a gentle but firm snap, he broke the skull from the neck. He lifted it from the dirt, raising it as delicately as one might a pearl from an oyster. He stood and lifted the skull towards the sky.

"We've done it!" he exclaimed, holding the skull above him. "We've robbed a grave!"

And with his words, the jaw of the skull dropped open in his hands, tumbling from his grip and crashing into the soft soil of the grave. I jumped up and out of the hole and ran through the dark cemetery towards the gate.

"Faggot," I heard Ned mutter behind me, and right then, I didn't care.

"He snapped my ol' head right off," she says now, from across the room.

I was drifting back to sleep, but her words wake me. "You know, he was considering going further," she says, "poking down towards the other end of the casket to claim a hand, or to see if I'd been buried with any jewels. But I heard him say, 'She was just a nigger. Probably a slave. She didn't have any jewels.'"

I always feel bad when she reminds me how racist Ned was as a boy. I want to tell her that he changed, but I assume she knows. She seems to know everything.

I wonder how long she will stay with me this time. The darkness is tinged with pink now, the mites of dust in the air catching the first specks of new light.

"I was waiting for him at the cemetery gate," I tell her, remembering dreamily. "'Put that thing away,' I told him. He was carrying your half-skull. But he wouldn't put it away. He kept pushing it at me."

"What a terror," she says, and she gives a little laugh, slapping her thigh.

"That he was."

"And now he's got you dreamin' 'bout diggin' up graves."

"If only I could . . . and he'd be sitting there, where you are," I say.

Her voice grows kind. "But he ain't comin' back to you. You gotta accept that. You can't just go out and dig him up."

"But I *want* to," I say, squinting my eyes, trying to see her better. In all the times she's come, I've never really been able to focus on her. It's as if she'll disappear if I look directly at her. I can always see her best if I look away, when she's just in my peripheral vision, at the edge of my reality.

"Poor, lonely child," she says, with the sun just beginning to edge the horizon in red. "You've been gone and left all by yourself. Well, if you ask me, I'd say you'd better start digging up your own grave. You been sinking for far too long."

"I'm not in my grave yet," I promise her, and she laughs. I close my eyes, and I'm back on that October night, with that big orange moon up in the sky, the night I fell in love with Ned.

"You know what you have to do now," Ned said, approaching me with the half-skull as I stood at the cemetery gate. He positioned himself in front of me, thrusting the skull out at my face. The chorus of crickets started scolding us again, louder this time.

"I ain't gonna," I insisted.

"Oh, yes, you are." Ned pushed the skull at me again.

"Stop it!" I shrieked, throwing my arms up to cover my face.

"Then *do* it."

"I helped dig," I protested. "I did what I said I'd do."

"But I put my hands inside and got the skull," Ned said evenly. "You ran off screaming like a little faggot boy." He smiled. "So you shouldn't have any trouble getting down on your knees."

My breath caught short. I hesitated for a couple of seconds before dropping to Ned's crotch. His jeans were still soiled from the grave digging, and a lingering fruity smell clung to them. But I unzipped Ned's pants and fumbled through his white cotton briefs to get at his prick. I popped the short, soft bulb into my mouth and began to suck.

Ned rested the skull on top of my head. I jerked forward, trying to shake it off, but Ned used one hand to force me back down by the shoulder. I accepted the fact that the dead woman's head was going to rest on my own while I blew my friend, and I began to get into my work. Ned was hard now, and his cock slipped easily in and out from between my lips.

"Ahhhh, I'm goin' to shoot," Ned said all of a sudden, and my mouth at once was filled with a warm, salty infusion. I hardly felt it happen; I just tasted it, and it slid quickly and easily down my throat. Then Ned staggered backward a couple of steps, and, regaining his balance, tucked his softening cock back into his pants, zipping up. "C'mon," he said, "let's get going. My father's gonna wonder where the hell I am."

Ned was in fine spirits on the way home. "I can't wait to put this babe on old Westerholm's lunch tray. He's gonna shit!" He laughed and banged the dashboard. The skull was wrapped in a blanket in the back of the truck.

I wasn't saying much. I was looking out the window. Ned dropped me off and told me he'd pick me up for school the next day. "Maybe we can do that again," he said, and his voice was softer this time. It confused me; I didn't know how to answer. So I said, "Yeah, sure." And he smiled.

I understood then that he didn't mean digging up graves.

"Where have you been, young man?" my mother demanded when I walked through the front door.

She was in a kerchief and curlers and a frayed, blue quilted housecoat; she'd been up waiting for me. "Do you know it's nearly two AM?" she asked shrilly. "And you have school tomorrow?"

"I know both of those things," I said, walking past her towards my room.

"Hey! Don"t be smart with me!" my mother snapped. "Where were you?"

"Out with Ned."

"He's a bad influence on you," she said. "Go to bed. Your father will handle this in the morning." She turned into her room and closed the door. I heard my father sleep-mumble something. Then I heard the groan of the old springs as she got into bed.

In my room, I slipped my smooth body between the cool sheets and my cock raged against them. I touched it; it jumped. I thought about what I did at the cemetery gate, and concluded I must be a faggot.

"So I'm a faggot," I said to myself. It was as easy as that. I jerked off thinking about Ned, had a hard, fast climax, and then couldn't sleep.

That fruity smell seemed to be everywhere.

She's been with me ever since.

"They ever catch you?" Maria Magdalena asks.

"No, never. But it caused a big scandal in town."

"They knew it was one of you boys," she says, and if I look away, I can see her smiling at me across the room in the dark. I'm glad she's there. She's good to have around. Without her, I'd have no one. Most of my friends are dead and not one of them has come back. Especially not Ned, who I buried last summer, after ten glorious years together.

"No," I tell her, smiling now myself, "it was both of us."

And she laughs. God, how she laughs.

ARTGOD

JOSEPH O'BRIEN

"Forty thousand dead Eye-talians!"

Old Crazy Bastard at it again. Early for him. What is it, five-thirty? It's still dark. Raining? Hail maybe. What's he doing out there? It's February, for Christ's sake. He must be freezing. Head's throbbing. Clock's an orange blur. Glasses? Glasses glasses boys don't make passes at boys who wear. Two-fifteen. Barely slept at all. Felt like years. Dreamt something. Something. It'll come back. Go back to sleep.

Go back to sleep.

Go back to

sleep. Did I sleep? Am I sleeping? Heart's racing. Cold. Still in bed. Safe. Still in bed. Breathe. Dream fuck nightmare gone. It's hiding in me. Something. Something. Only two-thirty. Old Crazy Bastard. Still on the corner. Still screaming. Still raining. Running across the eavestrough. Splattering down into the gutter. I'm bleeding again.

Floor's freezing. Fucking nosebleeds all my life. Blood warm on my face. My neck. Chest. Belly. Cock. Hands. Legs. How long have I been bleeding? It's still dark. Bathroom. Switch. Light hurts. My fucking head. Dripping onto grotty tile. A cockroach skitters over my foot. Mirror. Jesus, fuck, I'm fucking covered in my own red.

Shower coughs to life. Not hot enough. Never hot enough. Bad pressure. Lukewarm. Like being spit on. Old pipes. Rust brown and red spiral down the drain. I hate shower curtains. Psycho. Anthony Perkins was a faggot with two kids and a wife. Piss a sleep erection down the drain and work up a real one. Almost clean now. Did I bleed? Am I bleeding? Soap still lathers pink. The dream surfaces through halfsleep. I think artGod and come.

Cold. Wet skin freezing. No scars today. It's February for Christ's sake. What's he doing out there? There are shelters. Towel hard friction builds heat. Can't get back to sleep. I'm hungry. Nothing in the fridge. Damnit. 7-Eleven down the street. Past the corner. Past him. I'm hungry.

Dress fast. Sweater. Pants. Coat. Hat down over my eyes. Down the stairs. Lock the door. Please don't see me. I forgot my gloves. Fuck.

Outside. Clotted blood in my nostrils. I'm breathing glass. He's on the corner. Huddled by the ABM. Sunken eyes hidden beneath curtains of matted hair, brown and black and gray and yellow. Not screaming now. Not moving. Standing there. Am I here? What are you waiting for? Cross once to get away from him. Cross again to the store. Do you see me? Do you know what I've done to you?

The store clerk is young. His face is bruised. His eyes are pink where they should be white. Red-webbed. Broken inside. All he wants is my eight dollars and thirty one cents and to not be hurt anymore. I pass him a wrinkled ten. In seventeen minutes he'll be dragged into the back room and shot. I should leave now. He will cry for mercy and squeal and piss his pants and it will take three bullets before he finally stops. I can't be here. I don't want it to happen. I can't help him anymore. Sometimes these things just start making themselves up as you go. Bullets come out of the barrel red hot. Mass times acceleration. Like a sledgehammer in your chest. They cook you inside. His last thought will be *Ishitmyself.* I almost make it to the door before I puke. Sour. White and yellow, marbled with red. I mumble "sorry" and leave.

Old Crazy Bastard's gone now. Not far, though. I can hear him screaming. I take the short way back. Past the ABM. Felt-marker tags like ancient hieroglyphs. Are they for me? Are they mine? I can smell him. Whiskey and stale shit. I run the last thirty feet. Through the door and up the stairs.

Microwaved meatball sandwich tastes like shit. Coppery vomit in the back of my mouth. I swallow it anyway. Beat the hunger back. Turn out the lights. Too tired to sleep. TV. *Tombs of the Blind Dead* in Spanish. After a while the picture melts off screen. Rotting Templars pool on the floor. Their victims lap at my toes. My shadow recoils from their touch. It's already starting. Close your eyes. Go back to sleep. It hurts to sleep. Go back to sleep.

Go back to sleep.

Go back to

sleep. Did I sleep? Am I sleeping? Still dark. Raining harder now. Breathing. Shallow and wet. In the room. Not mine. Panic. Scramble. Glasses clatter to the floor. Lamp topples, flickering. I catch him in the strobe. Old Crazy Bastard at the foot of my bed. Those eyes, they roll back. White and yellow, marbled with red. He holds a finger to his lips, black and cracked. Worms boil in his beard.

He whispers, "artGod."

I scream.

I

scream? Did I scream? Am I screaming? It's out now. Not hiding. No longer captive. Fingers find the new wound, pulsing. Above the eyebrow. Curving back and around. All the way behind the ear. Big one this time. It stings. Already closing. It's all out now. Sheets stained with sweat and piss and shit and puke and blood and come. I am empty inside. The dreams are all gone.

Bundle the sheets up. Into the hamper. Back to the bathroom. Legs weak. Everything's weak. Leave the lights off. You don't want to see this. Shower. Never hot enough. Bad pressure. Like being spit on.

Shots from outside, distant. Three of them. Like pops. Seventeen minutes. I told him I was sorry. I am.

Towel dry. Turn the lights on. No headache now. Skin pale, almost blue. Hands are shaking. Weak. What. Did I dream? What. Am I dreaming? No more dreams now. Scar thick as a finger across my head. Healing fast. Gone tomorrow. Exit wound. artGod has left the building.

God was a hack. Not mine. The other one. Yours or your parents. Seven days to build a whole world. Six really. Lazy fuck. Too many loose ends. Protagonists underdeveloped. Lacking depth and proper motivation. Vague ending. Inconclusive. Large stretches of plotlessness. Pointlessness. Mine took years. I bundle up again and leave.

artGod is still close. It tugs at me like a madness. It is still sick with the disease of me. It won't get far. It never does.

Old Crazy Bastard sleeps like a foetus beneath the ABM. Scrawled walls, chalk, crayon, broken fingernails etching stone. He's almost got it.

On the wall he's written

fOrtY tHoosnD ddEAD ITALIANS

He's written:

Fgukking biches r CUNTS

He's written:

awareness is suffering

He's written:

meaning decays

I open him, throat to groin. Carpet knife. Impulse buy. It takes me ten minutes to work my way down. He doesn't scream. He doesn't make a sound until the end; he mutters something incomprehensible through twenty years of hurting. Fuck you or thank you maybe. It doesn't matter. He's dry inside, and hollow. Like me. artGod was here. Old Crazy Bastard didn't take to him at all. All that pain and nothing to do with it. artGod is gone.

I'm unmaking already. So fast this time. Strands of me float free at the periphery. Meaning decays. It's still dark. Hold it together. It's not all about him. He picked me, remember? Not the other way around. He liked me. No. Not like. Not even love. Want. Naked and senseless. Any whore would do. I was just there when he wanted it. Stalking toward me, skin shiny and dreaming, wispy fingered shapes grasping at me. I could create. I was a maker, baby. I was good. That part was easy for me. He felt that much at least. Soulfucked his way in, tearing me open from the inside, pushing the hurt up and out through the hands, through the mouth. I made it in my mind. artGod made it real. Bleeding me dry. Emptying me. Nothing left inside now. My want is hollow.

Raining harder now. Warmer. Not like being spit on at all. Like being bled on, maybe. Drops burst into steam against cracked asphalt. My world dies around me. Nothing new. Every block just a shallow replication of the last. Walk far enough and you'll start to see the same faces, over and over and over. Everything

Dies.

Did I die? Am I dying?

Was I living?

Was I ever?

The ground turns to ash. Like me. I fall forever into it, choking on the remains. I try to scream through it. It comes out wrong. Hoarse. He hears it anyway.

artGod waits for me at the bottom of it all. Like he always has. I am nothing without you, I scream.

I dream.

Did I?

Am I?

artGod says: "You never were."

Meaning decays. It's still dark.

BLACK SHAPES IN A DARKENED ROOM

MARSHALL MOORE

The siege has been on for weeks. I won't be able to leave my apartment again. Imagine the desperate claustrophobia of a Belfast, Beirut, or Banja Luka: an acrid veil of smoke overhead, bombs and gunfire in the background, Molotov cocktails crashing through every intact pane of glass, rooftop snipers on the lookout for pedestrian targets. Impossible to venture out. My circumstances are different, but the result is the same. I can't leave. And I'm in Berkeley. Apart from the occasional earthquake or student protest, this is supposed to be a place where nothing bad ever happens.

Edward, I write in my journal. It's exquisite, this journal. Hand-tooled leather the color of chocolate, heavy gray paper. I bought it in Florence. *I'm sorry. I will spend the rest of eternity telling you that. Will you ever listen? I'm so sorry.*

I used to be a flight attendant. Home is this old apartment a few blocks from the university: old furniture I picked up from consignment shops and flea markets, candles everywhere, cobalt glass vases I filled with fragrant clusters of the white jasmine that grows semi–wild outside. Now I'm overdosing on my own hipness. I want to be above the clouds again, but work hasn't been an option for weeks. I had to call in, feign an illness, and quit. Too dangerous to do anything else.

Based out of United's hub at the San Francisco airport, I'd spend a week or two smiling and serving cocktails five miles above the world. One night I'd sleep in a hotel room in Sydney. Sometime later, Paris. Taipei. Never much time to acquaint myself with these cities, to be honest. It's not as glamorous as it sounds. I might have a couple of hours to stumble down some foreign street in search of a café or restaurant worth a second visit, maybe a friendly stranger to wake up with. After a period aloft, I'd fly home to California and sleep for a couple of days. From Shanghai, Madrid, Toronto I'd email friends to let them know when I'd be home, and soon enough the phone would start to ring. It was a life.

Now I can't go outside. The attack comes before the door swings shut behind me, invisible hands ripping at my hair, my clothes, my skin. The walls in the vestibule beyond my apartment cracked the last time I tried to leave; clouds of plaster dust drifted down from the ceiling. The beams in the walls seemed to groan as some immense weight or force bore down on them. The light

119

overhead flickered once, twice, went out. In the intangible distance, screams I couldn't hear so much as feel. Palpable rage. I slammed the door shut behind me and stayed home, praying the talisman would hold.

Last time I left this place was when . . . (*Be honest, Noel.*) . . . a month ago? Six weeks?

⚰

I write this knowing it will be my suicide note. Even if I don't do myself in, my death will be seen as the sad, solitary opt-out by a young man who lost his grip on the real world. The problem is, the real world is slippery. Your grip is never as tight as you think.

I don't want to die.

I don't.

But I don't think I'm going to get any choice in the matter.

When I met Edward Wright, we both lived in Baltimore. I had just finished college: U of Maryland at College Park, BA in psychology, useful for nothing but a future of huge student loan payments for the advanced degrees I'd need if I actually wanted to work in that field. Or retail. I wasn't sure what to do with myself next. My bookstore job turned into a full-time assistant manager gig, a professional cul de sac in the outer suburbs of hell. And in the romance department, when I met Edward, I arrived with more than my full baggage allowance. I opted to turn away at the check-in counter instead of trying to board.

I met Mr Wright while he was living with Mr Wrong. Edward's gorgeous Trinidadian boyfriend Nathaniel had lost several jobs in a row and was about to lose his visa. The INS hung overhead like the paper-slicer of Damocles. Edward, the sweet naïve fool, had been sucked into supporting the guy: apparently he gave legendary head. I have to say although Nathaniel made me a little weak in the knees, Edward was the one I wanted. Couldn't get him out of my mind. He worked fourteen-hour days as a personal trainer to keep Nathaniel in good clothes and good weed. Nathaniel, an elegant six-foot-three panther of a man with sexy, shoulder-length dreads, got by on the occasional modeling gig. He'd pose nude for sculptors or slink down a runway to debut some department store's new collection. By contrast, Edward's looks revealed themselves during the second glance: a lean and well-developed body beneath his dark clothes, fair freckled skin prone to sunburn, overcast blue-gray eyes, handsome in an offbeat way, but devastating when he broke into a grin.

I influenced Edward's decision to get rid of Nathaniel. *You're addicted,* I told him. *And you feel sorry for the guy.* When I said nobody could blame him for loving to swab his tonsils with Nathaniel's cock, Edward socked me. Gave me a black eye. I'll remember the look of mixed shame and horror on his face long after I'm dead. Edward threw his arms around me, sobbing too hard to ask me to forgive him. He dumped Nathaniel the next day.

That same week, Edward threw Nathaniel out of their apartment and changed the locks. *Solve your own problems*, he told his newly-minted ex, who bawled like he had, in fact, cared once. *Go down on the goons from the* INS *when they come to deport you. It's not my goddamn problem anymore.*

I cheered. The bruise faded. What the hell, we've all had our outbursts. You can never predict what someone's going to do next, no matter how well you think you know him. Thing was, I sort of had it coming. I led him on. But I shouldn't have forgotten he did that.

⁜

When the attack comes, it's like someone is trying to drive an invisible car through the wall. The geometry of the house seems about to fail, as if a massive pair of shoulders are forcing their way into a child's sweater. The first time this happened I called Henry, the condo association's manager. He stopped by my apartment the next day, surveyed the damage with widening eyes.

"We must have had an earthquake," he said. "Would you mind logging onto the Internet? We can confirm it."

"Earthquake," I said. The idea made sense, I guess, if you didn't know what was going on. "Sure. I've got a fast connection. Go crazy."

Of course there hadn't been one.

"I'll call the maintenance guys and get those walls replastered," Henry said.

One more attempt at leaving my apartment was enough to convince me to stay in. The hallway window imploded. Shards of glass peppered my face and arms. I'm lucky I wasn't blinded. Audible roars that time, deafening, the enraged bellows of a minotaur whose virgin sacrifice lacked a hymen.

Ever taken a really long flight, say San Francisco to Sydney or London? New York to Johannesburg? By the time you arrive, the cabin is fetid from all the farts and armpits, bits of food dropped on the floor, crotches in need of a wash. The same bad smells, exhaled over and over, assault you until you want to disinfect your tingling sinuses with a Q-tip you've dipped in peroxide. My apartment smells like the lavatory in a 777 that has just crossed an ocean. I live on the shady side of the building, and I keep the blinds closed, the curtains drawn. I'd open the window for fresh air but I'm afraid of what I'd let in.

Last week I parted the curtains and looked outside. Something struck my window hard enough to crack the glass. In my mind's eye I saw a corpse hurtling toward me, something dead and putrid, a dog flattened on the freeway, then snatched up and flung for the occasion. *Noel, you're seeing things.* For a second, I saw lurid purple-red smears across the crazed glass, clumps of fur, a pointed tooth wedged in one of the cracks. The stench of sun-baked rot underlay the armpit atmosphere of my apartment, evanescent like the cigarette aroma wafting off the clothes of a smoker you pass on the sidewalk. Now you smell it, now you don't. When I blinked, the vision passed. The roadkill stink subsided, and I saw nothing but a run-of-the-mill broken window. One more thing for Henry to take care of.

Edward, you're not going to forgive me, are you?

I tried to keep my head down for the two months between accepting the flight attendant job and moving to Dallas for training at American's headquarters – Barbie Boot Camp, my colleagues called it. (I wouldn't transfer to United for another year, when I decided I wanted to live in the Bay Area.) My excuse, I told Edward when he called: I needed to work overtime at the bookstore to pay off my credit card debt before I left. I needed some money in the bank to finance the move. Please understand, I begged him. You know I really like you. But I have to do this. Was it manipulative of me? That's a question for history, not for me; I thought I was doing what I had to do, putting the issue of this putative relationship with him on the back burner until I had put my own life together, until he had more time apart from Nathaniel, until until until. . . .

Okay, so I ran away and went looking for justifications after the fact. I had to whistle in the dark. The easy way out tempted me every time I saw the bastard. On one level, I wanted to press myself closer to him when we hugged each other hello, to turn the friendly dry kiss on the lips into something hot, wet, and horizontal. Any idiot could see how much he wanted that. His emotions hung out all raw and naked for everyone to see. When he didn't think I was looking, he'd look at me as if he couldn't believe I liked him at all. Even in conversation, his eyes would light up, letting me know there was no other place he wanted to be.

I didn't think I deserved that kind of adoration.

I see that now, Edward. How many times do I have to tell you I fucked up? That I should never have run away? It's not enough to say I thought you deserved better, is it? You made up your mind I was the one you wanted, and that was that. You stubborn son of a bitch.

In retrospect, I should have treated Edward like the miracle he was. The odds of finding a man like that . . . how can I describe it? It was like winning the lottery.

I fucking ran away and stayed gone for a long time. Did I want to punish Edward for loving me? As I said, I had baggage of my own. It's the classic pathology: you care about me, therefore there must be something wrong with you, so I must make you suffer. I didn't call him. Well, that's not true. I did, sporadically. I weakened. I couldn't get him out of my head, goddamn it. I needed to hear his voice. I needed to know he was okay. I wanted him to hope I'd come to my senses and find my way back to him. And the hell of it is, I always believed I would. Just not like this.

I didn't kill him. That's how it sounds, I know, but I didn't kill him.

Not exactly.

Edward, I write in desperation, as if an answer will appear on the page like invisible ink unvanishing. *Call them off. This isn't how our story is supposed to end.*

It's growing dark outside. This is the fogged-in time of year, here in the Bay Area. The sun gives up on the day in the late afternoon, 4:30 or so, suggesting winter even in July. Some primitive part of me panics at the coming of night. I used to enjoy lying on my sofa and watching the sky deepen with sunset; now I'm too scared. The furniture becomes a menagerie of dangerous black shapes in the darkened room. Sounds outside take on a terrifying quality. Has something evil hunkered down on the doorstep? What are those voices? Everything rational in me collapses.

Edward and I bumped into each other in Miami three months ago, after a year and a half apart. I'd barely written, emailed sporadically, never called once. The usual. I had no idea he'd be there . . . or where he'd be, to be honest. He used to email me whether I replied or not, and I loved that about him. I hated it, too, and felt guilty. He deserved better. When I noticed his emails were coming less and less often, I felt a shameful flush of relief. Part of me wanted him to move on. The other part wouldn't let go.

After a hard month of too many overtime hours, too many cities, too many languages, my hands had started to shake with fatigue. I kept myself functioning with caffeine and twenty-minute catnaps. My circadian rhythms were as misaligned as trailer trash from Biloxi trying to tango. Exhausted to the point of incoherence, for some reason I couldn't fall asleep. I left my South Beach hotel for a few drinks, to dull the clamor in my head. In the club, there was Edward, talking with a cute Asian guy he introduced as a colleague. They were in town for a conference.

"But you're supposed to be in Baltimore!" I steadied myself against the edge of the bar.

"I moved to San Diego two months ago."

I couldn't look at him without welling up. Every few minutes I'd hug him again, then turn aside to knuckle tears away from the corners of my eyes.

I called in sick, persuaded a doctor friend back in California to fax a note to my boss, and spent three days in bed with Edward. He blew off the conference. We only got out of bed to let the room service cart in, shower, and use the bathroom. We went for walks through South Beach when we were drained dry, to drink in the sun, the warmth that made us want to tug each other's clothes off again and roll like puppies in the sweaty sheets of our hotel bed, the nouveau-deco-retro architecture, the acres of browning flesh.

"I could almost live here," I told him.

He shuddered. "Too muggy. Let's stay in California."

Our time in Florida felt like the first chapter of happily-ever-after, but we both had to return to the real world. We parted with kisses at the airport and made promises to be in touch, passionately determined in the moment to see where things could go. My old habits kicked in within a month: I stopped replying to Edward's emails and got slack about returning calls. True, it's hard to be in constant touch with someone when you're on an airplane most of the time. No matter how much you love him, the constraints on time and communication technology are real. I drifted away again. I took comfort in the familiar sensation of denying myself what I wanted most.

Three weeks ago, I got home from my last full-length work-related odyssey – Vancouver, Osaka, Singapore – and found a livid Edward on the landing. My legs almost gave out when I saw him. He wore a gray sweater the color of the sky, and his nose glowed red from the midsummer chill.

I fumbled in my pocket for my keys. My overstuffed carry-on suitcases toppled over backward. (Try not shopping when you're in Singapore.)

"Where have you been?" he asked me after an awkward hug.

I couldn't answer. With effort, I unlocked the front door and motioned for him to come in. I dropped my bags on the floor and collapsed on the sofa, then let Edward move me like a big rag doll so that my head rested in his lap. He stroked my hair. I hated myself.

"I got sick of waiting," he said. "I drove up."

Edward's fingers, while slender, were stronger than they looked. He massaged the knots out of my neck and shoulders.

"Noel, I thought we had started something," Edward said after a long silence.

I tensed up again.

"We did," I said quickly. "No, wait, that came out wrong. We have." My face burned. "I'm sorry."

He stopped the massage.

"Why do you keep doing this? I know you want me as much as I want you, but you keep running away. I don't understand that."

I sat up.

"Edward," I began.

He closed his eyes and shook his head.

"Don't," he said. "Please don't say anything that sounds like your old excuses. I don't want to hear it."

"I don't have an excuse," I told him. "If I did, that would be a step up from where I am now. You deserve better than me."

His face turned hibiscus red, as it did the time he hit me. He closed his eyes.

⚛

"Edward," I tell the air in my apartment. The journal pages feel like skin. I caress them like I did Edward's back after the first time we made love. "I know you can hear me. I know you're out there."

When mediums channel spirits, a state of deep calm must be attained. I have meditated. I have attempted to clear my mind. I've lit every candle I own. The stick of champa incense burning in the kitchen has rendered the air almost too sweet to breathe. Fear clouds my thoughts, but I have done the best I can.

The talisman won't hold forever.

An eye has opened inside my mind. Something has awakened, something that can see. When I recognize Edward's backward-slanted chickenscratch on the Florentine paper, I gasp as if I've been stabbed in the face with a length of piano wire. The psychic pain almost throws me out of my trance. The tiny window of vision threatens to close.

The voodooienne diluted the recipe to make sure you'd need a new charm from her. Its power is going to wear out in a few hours. Otherwise I wouldn't be able to write through your hands like this. That woman thought you were a fool. She thought you were another stupid white boy who had read too many New Age books.

"This is Berkeley. People here aren't supposed to do things like that," I said to the paper as if I'd drawn an ear on it, wondering if I'd ever in this life or the next stop feeling so stupid. The pen in my hand feels as if someone else is holding it, and describing the sensation by whispering to me.

I love you, but you're kind of an idiot.

"We've established that."

You shouldn't have played with me for so long, Noel. You attracted attention, and once I was dead and the story got around, it pissed a lot of people off. Haven't you figured that out by now?

"What was there to figure out, Edward?"

On this side, there's nothing that infuriates people more than someone like you who could have had it so good and kept running away. You were too much of a pussy to grab the brass ring when you had the chance. AIDS and hate crimes have sent a lot of gay guys to the grave with loose ends still untied. Couples who had been together for years were separated in their prime. A lot of relationships were never reconciled. Your behavior has been a major affront to those people. They're not impressed.

My hand aches from being forced to write someone else's words. My wrists feel as taut as guitar strings. If I were to thump them, they would twang.

It's like going to prison when you're guilty of raping kids, Noel. Before the cell door even slides shut behind you, you're already done for. Your inability to deal with our romance left me at the foot of your stairs with a broken neck, and I entered the afterlife screaming. People noticed. They were insulted, and they decided to do something about it. Pretty soon we're going to be together on this side, whether you're ready or not. I'm sorry it has to be like this.

"You hit me once. I should have known you'd do something like this to me in retaliation."

It's not me, Noel. It's not about retaliation, or my temper. There's nothing I can do. I've tried, and it's like trying to change the course of a hurricane by shouting into the gale. Look at it this way: I'll be there when they're finished with you. Be brave. It won't hurt for long.

I snapped out of my trance and slammed the journal shut, wracked with cold chills, shaking.

"You're never going to pull your head out of your ass, are you?" Edward had pulled away from me. At the other end of my sofa, he hugged himself like a six-year-old boy in adult guise. "You're going to keep doing this until . . . what? Until you get tired of the game and find someone else to torture?"

"No, it's not like that!" I tried to put my arms around him, exhaustion making me feel like a statue brought only halfway to life. "I just . . . I . . . ."

"What?" He glared at me. "Finish the sentence. I dare you."

"I can't."

"That's the long and short of it, isn't it, Noel? You can't. For the last few years, you haven't been able to, and you still can't. I'm leaving now, and when I go, it's the last time you're going to see me. I'm done."

I ran after him and tried to hold on. I stumbled, lost my balance, fell against him at the top of the stairs. We teetered on the brink for a terrible two seconds; I fell backward on the floor and Edward pitched forward, crashing down the stairs headfirst. The amplified cereal crunch of his breaking bones will stay with me until the sun cools and God forgets he ever invented the universe.

"Edward, how long do I have?"

A wind has picked up outside. The talisman, contained in one of those tall, red bodega prayer candles, has burnt itself out. Inside, its glass container is smudged black with smoke from the special wick the voodooienne had prepared for me and inserted ever so carefully while I watched, doubting and hoping in equal measure, wondering if I'd make it home without being run over by a car veering out of control or eaten by someone's rabid mastiff.

They're in here. . . .

No answer comes, but the dozens of candles I've lit start to wink out one by one. Shadows are eating the room.

"Edward!" I scream. "Stop them!"

No answer comes. It's hard to breathe, my heart is beating so fast. My belly is full of rocks. I can't swallow. I have to wait and watch these little flames snuffed one after another.

Wait, Noel.

Of course I'll wait. It's out of my hands now.

I kept Edward waiting, didn't I? What choice do I have?

Fair's fair.

NIGHT OF THE WEREPUSS

MICHAEL THOMAS FORD

At first Ellen thought she was just getting her period. She woke up to mild cramps and a general feeling of being slightly irritated at everything, much as she always did when confronted with the monthly departure of one of her unfertilized eggs. As she lay in bed with the cat licking her face and breathing hot tuna breath into her mouth, she resigned herself to five glorious days of bloating and scrounging around at the bottom of her purse for chocolate.

A few minutes later, as she fished in the box under the sink for a tampon, it occurred to her with a sudden flash of insight that her last period had ended less than three weeks earlier. She distinctly remembered it, because on the worst day she had been faced not only with an important client presentation but also with a blind date with Margie's friend Jane, who made movies and talked endlessly over dinner about her last disastrous relationship. Neither the presentation nor the date had gone well, and Ellen had ended the evening in bed with a pint of rum raisin watching *Desert Hearts* for the three hundred and eighty-sixth time and still wishing the ending were different.

Still, there was no ignoring the primal stirrings deep inside her belly, which were stronger than ordinary gas and undeniable. No, it didn't make sense that her period would be upon her so quickly. But weirder things had happened than a hitch in her cycle, and rather than question Mother Nature she dutifully imitated the helpful diagram on the Tampax box, putting one foot on the edge of the tub and deftly slipping the cotton wand inside her.

Almost immediately she felt a strange grinding sensation, like the cogs in a machine chugging to life. Something inside her lurched, and the tampon shot out and landed on the floor with a soft *plop.*

Ellen stared at the wad of cotton at her feet for a moment. It looked rather like a starfish washed up on the beach. Bending over, she picked it up gingerly by the string and held it in front of her face, where it hung, swinging in a slow circle. The end was frayed, the cotton fibers puffed out into a bedraggled cloud as if a cat had been using it for sport.

With a shudder she dropped the savaged tampon into the trash can, sat on the toilet, spread her legs, and looked between them. Everything *looked* right, at least as much as she could see. There was the familiar swatch of dark red hair, always so lovely against her creamy skin, and the dark pink folds of her labia smiled back pleasantly as though greeting the morning. The grinding feeling had ceased, and although she still felt slightly ill, nothing indicated that anything was drastically wrong down there. *Maybe it's just gas after all,* she thought.

Parting her labia, she slipped a finger between them and began tentatively to explore. There didn't seem to be anything out of the ordinary going on within herself – no pain or irritation, no weird bumps that hadn't been there the last time she'd checked herself out. She moved a little farther inside. Suddenly she felt a sharp pain surround the tip of her finger, a quick penetrating sensation like a ring of needles closing around her flesh.

Pulling her finger out, she saw that she was bleeding. Looking more closely, she saw that the end of her finger was circled by a row of puncture wounds, the skin broken by a neat halo of tiny holes from which blood was leaking in shiny drops. *It looks just like a bite*, she thought vaguely.

Wiping the blood away with a handful of toilet tissue, she nursed her aching finger in her mouth while she pondered what was happening. She had just stuck her finger inside her vagina, and she had been bitten. She could form the thought in her mind easily enough, probably even say it out loud if she wanted to. But when she actually thought about it, about what it meant, all she could do was giggle.

She placed a hand on her belly. Ever so faintly, she could feel a rumbling, almost like the calling of an empty stomach, but emanating from somewhere deeper. It was as if there was another hunger inside her, another empty space needing to be filled. She looked between her legs again. Her pussy looked so pretty, so innocent. Yet it had just bitten her savagely. Not anxious to repeat the experiment, Ellen closed her legs and thought.

She knew what she'd do. She'd call Margie. Margie had read both editions of *Our Bodies, Our Selves* cover to cover. A product of the women's movement, she had viewed her vagina, and those of her friends, in dozens of hand mirrors and from every conceivable position. She knew exactly what a vagina should look and behave like. Ellen went into the bedroom and dialed her number.

"Margie, it's me," she said when the call was answered.

"Ellen?" said a very sleepy Margie. "It's seven in the morning."

"I know," said Ellen, once again feeling the urge to start giggling. "I need you to come over here."

"Ellen, I can't come over there now. I'm not even up, and all eight cats have to go to the vet today."

"You have to, Margie, there's something I need to show you. Please?"

"Can't you just tell me what it is?"

"You wouldn't believe it if I did. Just get over here. Oh, and bring your hand mirror."

Ellen hung up before Margie could protest. She knew she'd be over. Margie was nothing if not predictable, and Ellen knew that if there was one thing her friend couldn't resist it was the opportunity to help out in a time of supposed crisis. While she waited for her to arrive, Ellen made herself some tea.

Somehow she thought that a nice cup of Lemon Zinger would help smooth everything out. When it was ready, she sat on the bed and tried to think about anything except her unruly vagina. The cat wound itself around her feet, and she idly scratched him behind the ears.

When she heard Margie's knock on the door, she ran out, opened it, and dragged her friend inside. "Okay," she said, dropping her robe, "Look at my snatch."

Margie grinned. "How'd you know it was my birthday?" she said.

"Very funny," Ellen retorted. "Just take a look in there. I think something's wrong."

"Like what?" Margie asked, dropping to her knees. "Shouldn't you be at a doctor then? I know this great midwife. . . ."

"Trust me," said Ellen, spreading her legs. "I don't want a doctor in there right now."

Margie spread Ellen's labia and looked inside. "Look's alright to me," she said. "Just like a nice healthy puss should. What do you think is wrong?"

"Look closer," Ellen said. "But watch your fingers."

"Why, you going to bite me?" Margie laughed.

Ellen held up her finger, the tip wrapped in a bandaid.

"What's that," Margie said.

"My cunt gave me a chomp this morning," Ellen said.

Margie started to laugh. "Good one," she said. "You dragged me over here to tell me your pussy's gone primal? You've been reading *Women Who Run with the Wolves* again?"

"I'm serious, Margie. Take a look in there. Something's not right."

Margie spread Ellen's labia once more. She put her eyes right up to it and looked for a long time. "Holy shit," she whispered.

"What? What the hell is it?"

"Sweetie," Margie said, looking up at Ellen's questioning face. "There are teeth in there. A whole set of little pointed ones."

Ellen sat down hard on the couch. "Oh, good goddess," she said, starting to cry.

Margie sat down next to her. "How'd this happen, hon?"

Ellen's body convulsed. "How the hell do I know? It was fine when I went to bed last night. You're the pussy expert; I thought you'd know."

Margie laughed. "Don't look at me, hon. I've been between a lot of legs, but I've never seen anything like this. What's down there is way out of my league. Forget the midwife, what you need is a good vet."

Ellen glared at Margie, wiping tears from her eyes. "It's not funny," she said. "What am I going to do? I can't walk around like this."

Margie patted Ellen's leg. "Give it a day or two," she said. "See what happens." She stood up. "I have to go. I have a yoga class to get to. I'll call you later."

Ellen saw Margie to the door. "Thanks for coming over," she said.

Margie hugged her. "No problem, kid. Sorry about your pussy. Now don't go playing with yourself. You might lose a hand."

After Margie was gone, Ellen sat on the couch. She tried not to think about what was between her thighs. But the rumbling sensation she'd felt earlier was getting stronger. *Oh shit,* she thought to herself, *it's hungry.*

She went into the kitchen and opened the refrigerator. Nothing was in it except for leftover Thai peanut salad and a block of tofu. She snatched up the tofu and took it to the counter. After slicing it into cubes, she picked up a piece and gently inserted it between her legs, careful to keep her fingers out of the way. Again she felt the grinding, chewing sensation. And again she felt her pussy convulse as it spat out the tofu, like an obstinate child refusing its creamed corn.

Just my luck, she thought, *I'm a vegetarian and my cunt's a meat eater.*

Opening the freezer, she rooted around for anything she could feed to her growling pussy. At the back, behind the vegetarian lasagna and the frozen kombu stock she'd diligently made the week before, was a box of breakfast sausages, a leftover from her brief fling with a cop a few months earlier. Joan had liked her breakfasts – and her sex – hot and greasy.

Ripping the top off the box, Ellen poured the contents onto a plate, where they lay like a pile of tiny ancient mummies. She briefly wondered if perhaps she should microwave them first, but her curiosity got the better of her and she simply carried the plate back into the bathroom.

It felt odd to be sitting on the toilet holding a plate of breakfast sausages, but no odder than being bitten by her own cunt. Picking one of the sausages up, she held it between thumb and forefinger and looked at it. The skin was wrinkled and brown, the flesh mottled with dark spots that she couldn't identify and veins of white fat that marbled the surface. She shivered. She couldn't imagine ever eating one.

Spreading her legs wide, she slowly inserted the sausage into herself, trying not to think about the fact that she was putting what once used to be a happily snorting pig into her body. Almost immediately, the link was snatched from her fingers as the walls of her pussy began to gnash back and forth. There was a slight slurping sound as the sausage was swallowed up, and then all was calm again. In fact, even the cramps she had been feeling earlier were lessened somewhat.

She fed another sausage into herself, and again the tiny jaws made short work of it. Three more sausages later, Ellen felt completely fine, full, and happy. She closed the box of sausages, returned them to the refrigerator, and went back to bed.

⁜

Over the next three days, Ellen became used to feeding her pussy. While it in no way seemed normal, it became something she just did, like brushing her teeth or washing her hair. Every morning she would get up, take the box of sausages, and stick five or six of them inside herself.

After a week, she did notice that her snatch was becoming a bit more ravenous. Instead of the usual six sausages, it was now consuming at least ten, and sometimes a whole dozen, at each feeding. And twice during the previous three days it had demanded a noon feeding as well, requiring her to run out of the office to purchase a Big Mac at the nearest McDonald's. She had fed herself in the women's room at work, pushing pieces of hamburger into her pussy and hoping anyone who came in would mistake the growling sounds it made as it ate for particularly exuberant flatulence.

It was Margie who finally put her finger on what was happening, although inadvertently. They were having dinner during the third week since discovering Ellen's uninvited guest, and Margie happened to mention that the moon would be full on the following Friday night.

"That's it," said Ellen, a forkful of penne and asparagus hanging waiting before her lips.

"What's it?" asked Margie, her mouth full of artichoke.

"The full moon," said Ellen. "Our cycles are tied to the moon and the tides and all of that happy Mother Earth shit, right?"

"Yeah, sure they are," said Margie. "What's that got to do with the mouth you've got down there?"

"Don't you get it?" said Ellen. "All month this thing has been getting hungrier and hungrier. It's like it's turning into this out-of-control beast. The closer it gets to the full moon, the hungrier it gets."

She dropped the fork, scattering penne all over the table. "Oh, fuck," she said, holding her hands to her mouth and staring at Margie with terrified eyes. "I have a werepuss."

Having a name for her affliction didn't make Ellen feel any better. If anything, it made things worse. It was like finding out that a new lump wasn't just a lump, but cancer, or that a lingering cough was actually caused not by a simple virus but by something that could be looked up in a medical textbook and assigned not only a name but a likelihood of fatality.

A werepuss, of course, could not be looked up in any book, medical or otherwise. As far as Ellen knew, she was the first person to have one. Yes, the concept of a *vagina dentata* had been around ever since men began peering between women's legs and became frightened of what they found there. But this was altogether different. This was real. Nor, like cancer or bronchitis or lupus, was there any course of treatment Ellen could follow to rid herself of the beast nestled in her vagina.

Admittedly, she had a limited knowledge of lycanthropy, an educational gap she attempted to fill by giving herself a crash course on the subject. This consisted largely of going to the video store and renting *An American Werewolf in London, Ginger Snaps, The Company of Wolves,* and, of course, all of the Lon Chaney movies featuring his famous tortured lupine character.

From these movies she deduced that, first, only a werewolf could make another werewolf. Second, the only thing that seemed to stop a werewolf was death by silver bullet. Third, walking alone on the moors of England at night was really not a very good idea. Apart from that, she gleaned little from the twelve hours she spent in front of her television set, feeding herself popcorn and chocolate chip cookies and sating her twitchy snatch with the occasional cocktail wiener.

She tried to do her best with the limited information she had, but the undertaking was far from fruitful. She hadn't been to England recently, or even to anywhere particularly damp. No one had bitten her. And as for silver bullets, the very idea of firearms made her queasy.

She began again. If it took a werewolf to make another werewolf, she reasoned, then the logical conclusion was that someone had done this to her. But who? Biting had already been ruled out. But since the toothiness appeared to be confined to her nether parts, perhaps she needed to consider another means of infection. Unfortunately, her love life had been, apart from the disastrous blind date a few weeks previous, barren. No one had been inside her pussy in a long time. The opportunities to pass along a common yeast infection – let alone what she had started to call pussanthropy – were virtually nil. Perhaps, she thought idly, it was something one could pick up from toilet seats or the dressing room at Macy's.

She turned to the Internet for answers. To her surprise, typing the words *pussy* and *teeth* into the Google search engine yielded quite a number of results. Her enthusiasm quickly waned, however, when she visited the first dozen or so sites and found there either hysterical, purely allegorical, rants by men who claimed to be emasculated victims of a lover's controlling sex or else pictures purporting to show actual *vagina dentata* which, when looked at more closely, were revealed to be photographs of women clenching sets of plastic Halloween vampire teeth between their thighs. *Just like those so-called mermaids that P.T. Barnum made by sewing baby monkey torsos and fish tails together,* Ellen thought as she signed off.

Another week went by. By now she was sort of used to having a werepuss. The feedings, while not precisely enjoyable, were undeniably interesting. She progressed from breakfast sausages to hot dogs, and had on her last visit to the grocery store thoughtfully fingered a kielbasa she came across in the meat freezer while shopping for her pussy's dinner. She even found a way to keep her frequently demanding vagina quiet during work hours by slipping it pieces of beef jerky, which took a long time to chew and gave her extended periods of peace and quiet.

None of this, however, was getting her any closer to solving the real problem, which was how to get rid of the teeth. Although feeding her twat had become just part of her routine, she missed sex. Masturbation was not an option due to her pussy's tendency to nip, and letting anyone else stick a digit or tongue into her was absolutely out of the question. One night, deciding she needed to have an orgasm or go out of her mind, she tried pleasuring herself with a dildo. But she barely got the first few inches inside before the grinding started, and when she removed the toy it emerged headless, shreds of electric blue silicone hanging like skin from a shrapnel wound.

As first Tuesday and then Wednesday rolled around, and the Friday of the full moon approached, Ellen could sense that she was beginning to lose control. Her pussy ate more frequently, and demanded more substantial meals. The kielbasa she'd once hefted in her hand and viewed as an amusing but impossible fancy was now simply a midmorning snack. Prosciutto. Salami. Parma ham. All of these things, and more, she bought by the pound and fed to her ravenous cunt. It was becoming insatiable. The only item it rejected outright was olive loaf, which Ellen tried as an experiment. This was the same luncheon meat Ellen herself had despised as a child, and seeing her pussy refuse to eat it made her feel an odd kinship with it. Maybe, she thought hopefully, she could gradually wean it onto a strictly vegetable diet. Then life together might be a possibility.

She knew, though, that she was only fantasizing, just as she'd once dreamed of turning her sausage-loving policewoman into a pacifist granola eater. It would never work. She knew, too, what her pussy really wanted. It wanted live meat. The thought pounded in her head, making it hard for her to think, let alone get any work done. She knew that dead, salted flesh was simply not enough anymore. Her pussy wanted something that beat with life. It wanted to taste fresh blood.

On Friday afternoon she left the office early. The itching between her thighs had grown steadily all day, and by three o'clock it was unbearable. She could feel the tiny rows of teeth inside her gnashing and chomping, calling out for a feeding. Although the thought of giving it what it wanted sickened her, she was compelled to obey.

She drove home and showered. Taking the scissors to her bush, she whacked away at the thicket that had sprung up there as the moon had waxed to fullness, until the hair around her snatch was short and tidy, masking the ferocious interior. Then she dressed quickly, slipping the black silk dress she reserved for formal occasions and going to the symphony over her shoulders. She wore no bra or panties.

Ellen hadn't been to a straight bar since college. As she pulled her car into the parking lot of the first place she came to, she tried not to think about what she was doing. It had to be done, she reminded herself. Her pussy had to eat. She hoped that no one she knew would see her. If they did, she had contrived a story about meeting an old friend from college. The rest of the details were murky, as her head was filled with more pressing needs.

Going inside, she walked quickly to the bar and ordered a drink, a Cosmopolitan. She hated vodka, but she knew it would go to her head more quickly than anything else. It would provide her with the protective fog she needed around her to be able to finish what she'd started. Besides, wasn't a Cosmopolitan what lonely straight women drank? She sipped it quickly, hoping she looked available.

There were a number of men in the bar. Ellen considered them. She hadn't looked at a man as a potential sexual partner in years, not since her sophomore year of college. Even back then she'd basically taken whatever came along, convinced that was how things were done. It wasn't until she'd discovered the joys of sleeping with women that she'd begun to select her partners based on anything more than willingness.

"Nice dress."

Ellen turned to find a man standing beside her. In his forties, he was dressed in a business suit. His face was pleasant and completely unremarkable, one that she might see while walking down the street and forget within seconds. In fact, there was absolutely nothing to distinguish him from any other man in the world. In short, he was perfect.

"Hi," she said, trying to remember how to be flirtatious. "And thanks."

"No, really," the man said. "It looks good on you. But do you know where it would look even better?"

Ellen shook her head. The man grinned. "On my bedroom floor."

Internally, Ellen groaned. The guy was an idiot. But she forced a smile and a laugh. The man, apparently relieved that she hadn't found his come-on offensive, laughed too. Ellen smelled more than a little gin on his breath.

"I'm Carl," he said.

"Cindy," Ellen replied.

The rest of the half hour that constituted Carl's idea of courtship was totally forgettable. Ellen, or rather Cindy, listened raptly as Carl told her about his business, which had something to do with importing cheaply-manufactured clothing from India and reselling it at enormous profit. This, combined with the fact that Carl kept staring at her breasts, made Ellen remember why she was so often glad that she didn't have to suffer the burden of heterosexuality. Why was it, she wondered as she nodded and laughed occasionally, that straight men assumed everything about themselves was interesting?

Two additional Cosmopolitans, several well-timed brushes against Carl's leg, and far too many bad jokes later, Ellen found herself in her car, following Carl back to his condo. She still couldn't quite believe what she was planning on doing, but she knew that she had to see it through. When at one stoplight she was tempted to turn left as Carl signaled a right, she looked up and saw the full moon hanging above the car like a beacon. All her remaining will drained away as her pussy surged with need, and she allowed Carl's taillights to lead her on.

For the first time in her life, Ellen was pleased to find herself in bed with a lover whose idea of foreplay was to remove his underpants. She'd half feared that Carl would try to go down on her, or at the very least use his fingers to get her wet. Had he attempted either thing, he would have gotten an early indication of what she had planned, and everything would have been ruined utterly.

Carl, however, was completely focused on trying to get an erection. As Ellen lay on the bed, trying not to think about anything at all, Carl kneeled between her legs, anxiously stroking himself. His flaccid dick flopped heavily in his hand as he tried to coax it to life, and although the sight sickened Ellen, she couldn't help but be relieved that at least her pussy's meal was going, from all appearances, to be a substantial one.

After several minutes Carl cleared his throat. "I think I may need some help," he said. "Maybe you could suck it?"

Ellen looked up at his hopeful face, then down at the meaty cock in his hand. She'd never liked sucking dick, even the fake ones her lovers sometimes wore, and the thought of putting Carl's prick anywhere near her mouth made her feel nauseous. But she could feel her cunt pulsating, urging her to comply. It sensed that what it wanted was near, and it was urging her to do whatever she needed to feed it.

"Fine," Ellen said wearily.

She and Carl traded places, with him lying on his back and her between his legs. She lowered her head toward his crotch, praying that it would only take a few touches of her tongue to get him going.

Suddenly she felt Carl's fingers grab her hair. "That's right," he said. "Get daddy nice and hard."

In a moment she was off the bed. Carl, surprised, stared at her. "What's the problem?" he asked.

"No," Ellen said, snatching her dress from the floor and pointing her finger at Carl. But it was as much to her angry pussy as it was to him that she directed her words. "No. I won't be a cliché. Even if you do deserve it."

Leaving Carl on the bed, the bemused look still on his face, Ellen ran from the house. Pulling on her dress as she ran, she jumped into her car and sped out of the parking lot, leaving Carl and his bad porn film dialogue behind. Her pussy, furious at having its meal snatched away when it was so close, was churning.

"I don't care," Ellen said as she drove. "I'm not going to become that, not even for you."

She drove furiously, ignoring stop signs and red lights. She drove until she came to what she was looking for, then stopped and got out of the car. A moment later she had pushed open the door to the shop and gone inside.

"Can you do a labia piercing?" she asked the bored-looking teenaged clerk at the counter.

He shrugged. "Sure. Let me get Lydia."

The boy disappeared and returned a moment later with a woman covered in tattoos and glittering with metal.

"You the one who wants a labia piercing?" she asked, looking suspiciously at Ellen's disheveled dress.

Ellen nodded. "Right now," she said. "And it has to be silver. Pure silver."

Five minutes later Ellen was once again on her back with someone staring into her crotch.

"What the hell is in there?" Lydia asked.

"Don't get too close," warned Ellen. "And hurry." She could feel her twat gearing up for one final attempt at getting her to feed it. It was taking all of her strength just to stay still.

Lydia picked up the needle. "This is going to sting a little," she said.

Ellen gritted her teeth. As the needle pierced her labia, she felt her pussy convulse as if it had been shot. Her first instinct was to leap off the table and get out of the store. But she gripped the edges and hung on, fighting it.

"Hurry," she said breathlessly. "Put the ring in."

Lydia held the ring between the jaws of a pair of forceps.

"You're certain it's pure silver?" asked Ellen.

Lydia nodded. "One hundred percent," she said. "Sure you don't want stainless? It's easier to clean."

"Put it in," answered Ellen, straining against the invisible assailant that tried to pry her fingers from the table.

The ring pierced her flesh and Ellen screamed. It felt as if Lydia had entered her with a brand. Her cunt recoiled at the touch of the silver, and her heart swelled to near bursting. The room swam, Ellen's vision darkened, and a howl of unearthly origin emerged from her, coming from her mouth or her vagina, she couldn't tell which. For a moment she felt as if she were being torn apart, her very cells exploding with pain. Then it was over.

"There," Lydia said. "It's done. God, I've never heard someone make such a fuss."

Ellen gulped in air, trying to slow the erratic pounding of her heart. "Guess I'm just a big pussy," she said, her breathing slowly returning to normal.

⚬

"So it's gone?" Margie asked over lunch the next day.

"Totally," Ellen replied, holding up her hand and wiggling the fingers. "I came for the first time in almost a month this morning, and not a scratch."

"You must be so relieved," said Margie.

Ellen paused. "Actually," she said. "In a weird way I miss it. It made me feel wild, primal, like I was something right out of the forest."

"You can always take the piercing out," Margie told her.

Ellen laughed. "No way," she said. "I think one night of the werepuss is about all I can take."

"And still no idea how it happened in the first place?" asked her friend.

"Not a clue," Ellen said. "I don't think I'll ever know. It will have to remain one of life's great mysteries. Just promise me one thing."

"What's that?"

"The next time my period comes around, if I start baying at the moon or craving raw meat or anything, tie me down and put a stake in me."

Margie grinned. "With *pleasure*," she said.

ON BEING A FETISH

DAVID COFFEY

Here's the latest set-up: four drunk teens in a suburban bungalow. Two males, two females. Blossoming hormones everywhere. Mom and Dad are nowhere to be found. According to the detailed note on the fridge, they're getting brown on a safety-sealed deal to the Dominican Republic. The family dog has fallen asleep and is drooling on the forbidden parental bed, giving up on his post-dinner stroll. The pumpkin remains uncarved on the kitchen counter.

It's almost Halloween, a popular time for these calls. My four "clients" are finally heading toward the basement with its wood-paneled charms and musty furniture. The track lighting is off. The perfunctory white candles are burning. The Ouija board and I wait for them on the floor.

Before seating themselves, each teen removes their Hubba Bubba from their mouths so that my spirit, who they will try to summon, will hear each syllable clearly. The two long-haired sisters, only a year apart, are smiling with sad nostalgia, both reflecting on their shared past with the Ouija board. They claim they haven't used it in several years, not since they bought the board with their combined allowances to summon the soul of Tittles, the beloved family cat that never meowed back a message after her tragic fall from the roof of this home. Hopefully, both girls have given up trying to summon spirits from the animal world. Considering most animals can't spell, save a few smart gorillas, you have to stick to yes or no questions anyway.

The two visiting guys crack familiar ghost jokes and try to scare the two bosomy sisters. They pretend to hear the noise of an escaped convict or suddenly grab the girls' waists so they squeal with silly fright. Of course, the sisters aren't scared at all. They just want the boys to think they're cute and girlie.

Nothing new here. In fact, the set up is so cliché that I'm tempted to leave, but the lack of quality communication in the last year or so is making me more desperate for attention.

Each participating teen has one of those new names that all kids seem to be called now, but were never named in my day; trendy names that will quickly become unpopular in a few more years. We have something like Brittney, Ashley, Conner, and some guy I'll call Eminem because of his uncanny resemblance to the real Slim Shady himself. I feel superior in knowing that I was a far more sophisticated teen with a much stronger sense of self. Never did I duplicate my MTV contemporaries with such bland precision.

With all eight hands on the Ouija pointer circling lightly over the board, we finally get down to some scary business. Everyone has stopped chatting, but contrary to what you might think, there is never silence – always a motorist outside, the heat cutting in, or someone breathing too loud.

Eager to get the show on the road, Brittney gives a hair toss and asks, "Is there anyone here?"

I wait to see if anyone is pulling the pointer. That person can seriously disrupt my part in this pop exorcism. If steroidy Conner or Eminem want to play fake phantom and move the pointer around by themselves, my fun is ruined.

Usually, I need a certain amount of energy to move the pointer, or do anything for that matter. I can't play Ouija or cause a cold breeze or flicker the candles without a little something. I live like a rechargeable battery. I need a certain amount of human electricity before I can do anything very interesting. Not only that, I need the right electricity – fear, righteousness, anger, and, of course, horniness – teens are always good for that.

"Is there anyone here?" the girl asks, this time more impatiently.

There isn't much to work with right now. Let's just say the battery power is very low. Though I don't have enough power to get the ball rolling, Brittney gently pushes the pointer to yes.

An argument follows over who may have pushed it. No one takes responsibility. They shuffle in their seats and Connor's knee pushes up against Ashley. Eminem's baby finger comes into sweaty contact with Connor's baby finger.

"Whassup, buddy? You a guy?" Eminem asks with his phony Midwestern ghetto accent.

I feel a faint bit of electricity moving through me from the mutual hormones that have been unleashed through the Ashley-Connor knee attachment. Surprisingly, I receive a little jolt from Eminem and his finger connection to Connor's manly pinky. This charge is not mutual.

With the bit of energy I get, I glide the pointer to where it says "yes" on the board. No debate ensues. Even if the teens believe it was one of them who moved the pointer, they don't want to argue about it this time.

"Were you murdered?!" Brittney asks dramatically. A few snickers slip out of the boys, though the direct and deep-voiced way she delivers the line sends a chilly charge through Ashley.

I harness Ashley's easily induced fear and point to yes, though I don't remember a thing. That's just what I hear.

My move creates a stir of anxiety in the sisters, and I feel now that this may be a fun night after all. I usually don't get the murder question so fast.

"When did you die?" Brittney asks.

I point to the numbers 1-9-8-9, though I'm not really sure. It might have been 8-8.

"Where are you buried?"

Like almost everybody else I'm buried in a cemetery. I really hate that question.

I could tell them that I'm just outside the town near a sewage treatment plant. Nicer than you would think, but I decide to be vague about it.

H-E-R-E, I spell with the alphabet on the board.

Of course, the teens believe that means right here in the basement as if their stupid, drywall house was built on some Satanic burial ground.

The fear levels shoot up.

At this point, they return to the premise that someone must be pushing the pointer. They almost give up the game because Ashley is so freaked out that she wants to stop.

"Why are we doing this? Do we really want to speak to some murdered dead guy?" she sobs.

Ashley's fear fills me with energy – a good rush for sure, but her early panic makes me think she'll bail. Ashley's fear also makes Conner horny and from what I can tell, Eminem is getting a hard-on from the continual finger-finger action with Connor. Brittney, who I suspected would be the chicken priss of the bunch, is gently persuasive to the others. She explains her curiosity in the undead to her friends and sister, and says she'd like to help me like I'm some poor kid with polio. It seems that they are close to calling it quits, but Brittney somehow saves the day.

"Are you evil?" she asks, her hand on the board.

I'm tempted to say yes, but that would put Ashley over the edge. I'm a little worried that I came off as too scary too quickly after the burial question. So I playfully spell M-A-Y-B-E.

This time they all blame Brittney for the spelling.

Brittney swears up and down that she didn't spell a thing. Connor finds this sexy.

Now, I feel a storm. A sweet warmth moves through my empty crevices – the kind of ghostly fix that doesn't come along too often. The joy is almost unbearable, but I hold it back. Don't want to waste it. Brittney turns to the board, and places her hand lightly on the pointer. Everyone else keeps their hands at their sides.

"What's your name?"

C-H-U-C-K, I spell.

They all try to recall all the murdered Chucks they know. I mean, how many can there be? Luckily, I'm a bit of a local celebrity, like a weatherman you might see at the mall.

"That's Chuck Wachowski," Ashley says in tears, her hands over her mouth shaking.

"That faggoty kid whose head was blown off! I heard his Dad shot him," Conner explains.

"Omigod!" Ashley shrieks, her blood pressure rising.

"Shut up, Conner!" Brittney yells, "My uncle is gay. That's so homophobic!"

Visibly shaken by Conner's comments and now hard simply from sitting next to him, Eminem turns to the board and asks, "Are you Chuck Wachowski?"

No one is touching the pointer, so I use every spark of my ghostly electricity to send the pointer quickly and firmly to yes.

Fear fills the room like oxygen fills the lungs. Ashley is wailing in panic while Connor tries to engulf her in his quarterback arms. Eminem rushes to turn on the lights. His trembling fingers can barely flick the switch. Brittney snaps too. She rocks back and forth embracing a pillow, closing her eyes, pretending she's somewhere nice.

"Go away," she begs me over and over again.

I'm drunk on fear and sexual tension. It feels so good that I gotta do something, something that will rip apart their Bambi-like views of the world, something that will haunt their naïve dreams and waking lives forever. It's gotta be a real horror show.

Do something bad! Real, real bad! I command myself.

Act now! Strike while the iron is hot!

There are no knives, no dishes, no pictures, not even a pencil to throw across the room. I think about something really bloody and painful, but you can't kill your clients if you want return customers. And there's certainly no Tittles to possess. I must do something. Something subtle, yet frightening. Nothing is coming to mind. I feel rushed and panicked. The moment is slipping away.

So, I spookily blow out the candles. Unfortunately, this doesn't have much of an impact on my callers because the lights are already on and no one seems to have noticed. I end my evening drowning in frustration. How could I blow my load on such a lame-ass finale?

Weeks later I expected Brittney to try to get a hold of me, but the whole haunting inspired her to help the homeless. Somehow she believed she was going to release my ghostly being from this trapped state so I can go happily to heaven – or hell, if I really deserved it. She saw the summoning of my spirit as a kind of therapy where I, or any other ghost, would come to understand why we were stuck here in undead limbo, and then decide to take the right route. Unfortunately for Brittney, the homeless didn't like her, but I commend her on her willingness to give it a shot and come back after the first day for more verbal abuse.

Of course, Ashley stayed hysterical for days. Her tanned parents tell her repeatedly that it was just an illusion, something all four of them saw after drinking too much of the family wine. Her shrink agreed.

Conner just blocked the whole thing out, until he was around Ashley, when he would recite the night's events to scare her into letting him feel her up. It usually worked.

It was Eminem who wanted more. He bought a Ouija board of his very own. He didn't tell any of the others about it, and kept it hidden between his cushions where someone else might hide a couple of *Hustler* magazines. Despite this purchase, he didn't seem to be in a hurry to try a call of his own. I knew he would try again though, and I waited around for it.

In the meantime, I visited some Chinese exchange students and pretended to be a serial killer, but when the girls asked me to spell things in Mandarin on a sheet of paper, I knew I was in for a tough night. After insisting on English, I told them I tore apart people with coat hangers and rusty hooks, then stuffed them into an oversized, industrial freezer until I couldn't fit anymore. When I was finally caught, the detectives were so disgusted with the stench of my destruction that they threw up within seconds of stepping through the door of my rat-infested home. I even added that I picked on Chinese girls. I'm not sure they understood what I was saying, but I can say wholeheartedly that they weren't impressed with the whole serial killer thing.

I also visited an insanely religious Portuguese woman who prayed like crazy. No Ouija board this time. She kneeled for hours at the local Catholic church begging for her grandson's spirit to show up. The poor kid got his foot stuck on the train tracks on the way back from visiting her. Apparently, the whole thing was pretty messy. She also mentioned that her husband died soon after her son and that she really didn't speak to anyone, except God.

I sat around with her waiting for his spirit to show up, but I've been around long enough to know that most people don't get to be ghosts. In fact, I've never seen any others while I've been dead or alive. After a few hours of feeling sorry for myself, I really began to feel sorry for grandma, but when I pretented to be her grandson and gave her a playful hair tousle, she ran screaming from St Michael's. I guess her grandson never did such things.

So, as you can imagine, I was feeling a little depressed by my recent hauntings. I hadn't had any action since the group of teens. I've been haunting this town for over a decade now and I was feeling like a failure during this Halloween, a Christmas of sorts for a ghost.

⚰

After the holidays, I decided to hang out at Eminem's apartment. It turns out that Eminem's mother dislikes him so much that she pays for him to have a separate apartment so that she and her boyfriend can fuck in peace. Apparently he works at a gas station, but has been putting some drawings together so that he can go to art college. His drawings consist largely of two things: characters from *Star Trek* doing dirty things to one another; Captain Picard getting a blow job from Number One. These kinds of drawings were kept well hidden so that a visiting Brittney or Conner wouldn't find them. He also drew dismal landscapes – cranky rats in back allies, polluting factories under gray skies, and there's one of a kid playing at a dump. He also had a few sketches of men in open coffins – fat ones, skinny ones, black ones, white ones, old ones, and young ones. Needless to say, I wouldn't want any of these gems hanging on my walls.

After days of just hanging around his apartment, unknown to him or any of his few visitors, I was very pleased to find out that Eminem had the Ouija board set up on the floor of his apartment. Unfortunately, he was lying naked on his back away from the board. He didn't have any candles going. He just lay in the dark and used the street lamp out the window to see what he was doing. I wish I could tell him to just turn on the lights. The darkness does nothing for me, though it sometimes helps generate a horny/fear vibe in the summoners. Contrary to what you might think, ghosts can't see in the dark.

I wait and wait and wonder, why doesn't he go to the board? Wouldn't that be great to visit someone twice? So far, despite my efforts, I haven't done that.

Then, to my absolute shock, he pulls out a photo of yours truly, holds it under the lamplight, and starts tugging on his larger-than-average penis. The photo, circa 1986, has me dressed for the Love-Is-In-the-Air Valentine's formal standing next to my date, a sporty lesbian named Pam. I don't have my jacket on and my shirt is a little too tight because I borrowed it from my little cousin – so embarrassing – but to my dismay Eminem masturbates to my bad outfit and cut-to-perfection mullet.

My battery heats up. If only he would go to the Ouija board. In fact, I wish I had a Ouija board of my own. I'd like to ask a few questions right now.

As he's about to cum all over his belly, he squeezes his nipple with his left hand and repeats my name a few times as he gushes all over his chin, chest, and stomach. Following this, he slowly sits up, rubs his ejaculate over his stomach, admiring the volume and shine, then saunters toward the shower to clean up.

I'm so distracted from the scene that just took place that I hardly take the time to relish the charge I was just given. It was nothing like the one I received in Brittney and Ashley's basement weeks ago, but it was a substantial jolt. Part of me would like to use this charge to do something helter skelter on this wanker, but there are questions in my mind that cannot go unanswered. I think about what Eminem would have done to get a photo of me. Did he speak to my parents? Did they show him their forgotten photo albums of me? I can't believe that I didn't see anything earlier since I have been here for the past few weeks.

After Eminem finishes his shower, I cut to the chase. "Hey, buddy, where did you get my photo?" I spell out on the steamy mirror.

Just a simple question, but the poor rapper doesn't sleep all night.

During the next day, a tired Eminem packs a cheese sandwich, an energy drink, and some Nibs before leaving his apartment.

On a cold November day, the guy walks out of town down a few side roads until I realize he's heading to my cemetery, the Rolling Hills Cemetery near the sewage treatment facility. When he arrives, he walks directly to my gravestone, sits down beside it and starts having his lunch. Every once in a while, he looks up at my gravestone as if it was his lunch companion.

Endearing in a way, but strange to say the least. Who would have thought that a ghost could have a stalker? After he's done his lunch, he runs his fingers over my engravings and rubs his groin over my gravestone. He even kisses it gently. I wonder if he's going to jerk off again.

I'm sure many non-ghosts would be happy to see people masturbating all the time or rubbing up against their gravestone. After I first died, I learned a great deal about people just by wandering into their houses when they thought they were alone or hidden away with a loved one or a friend of a loved one. The truth is, seeing sex, solo or otherwise, gets boring after a while. It's like watching too much porn – the novelty wears off. With real sex, let me tell you, you wish you could make more than a few edits. Any way you slice it though, horniness always gives me more options to communicate.

In fact, Eminem's horniness is charging my battery right now.

I hear him apologizing to me. "I'm sorry, I'm sorry," he whispers. "I broke into your parents' basement and stole a photo from the album. There wasn't much there, so I took the first one I found."

For the first time, I am angry. Not confused about being dead, not bored, not lonely, but angry – violated. I feel like the little fucker went through my drawers. Though I've been disappointed by the living, this is the first time that I am truly upset. This new feeling leads to a new discovery. My own anger makes my energy even stronger.

"I know Conner was lying," he continues. "I know your dad didn't kill you. I know it was an accident, at least that's what the newspaper said. You were looking for a suitcase. You were leaving town. You were in the basement that night where you tripped over your father's hunting rifle in the dark and shot yourself in the head. There's pictures of you everywhere. Your room is like a shrine. Your dad belongs to PFLAG now. I don't think he would have shot you."

His explanation enrages me, but who's to say he's telling the truth? I was so convinced by the local rumors about the old man shooting me that I never bothered to return to my parent's house to look for answers. Sure, Dad could be a cranky bastard at times, but there's no way he'd do anything to land his soft, suburban ass in jail. Just the other day I thought I passed him on my way to terrorize the Chinese girls.

Could I have been so dumb as to shoot myself in the dark? I always tell everyone I was murdered. I guess I just hoped it was something dramatic and legendary. I didn't like that some kid could find out more about it than I could.

My anger brewed like indigestion and in a rage I send my gravestone crashing down on Eminem who lets out a sound like a broken bagpipe. I worry that I've hurt him. I see a bit of blood trickle from the side of his head. Even more disturbing, I realized he just came in his pants.

I carefully store up my leftover anger for another night. I know I need to store it so we can have a real conversation about what he knows.

That night, Eminem sleeps like a baby. I don't sleep at all. Ghosts never sleep. I study his face and obsess over his obsession with me.

The next night, he's got the candles going. He's got the heat up. He's sitting cross-legged in his briefs, Ouija board out in front. His eyes are closed.

"Chuck, are you there?"

Yes, I point almost effortlessly.

"Don't be mad at me," he says.

I point at nothing.

"Listen," he begins, "No one knows I'm gay. I'm not even sure yet myself. I think I might be bi."

I want to spell out "who cares?" because I want to talk about me. What else can he tell me about me? I decide to say nothing again.

"I've been on the Internet. I've met so many gay guys online. I meet them and I hate them. I have nothing to say to them."

Eminem pauses for a moment then asks, "Do you know what the Internet is?" That makes me feel old. Though I've never been "online," I've seen people "surfing" for hours. I want to tell him that I'm not a retarded ghost, but I just point to yes.

Then Eminem reaches for his laptop and removes the pointer from the Ouija board. He then places the laptop on the Ouija board and boots up his computer.

He pulls up his word program and types out, *Chuck, are you there?*

I've never tried this before and think Eminem is being stupid. I'm used to the pointer and I'm not sure you can use a computer as part of the Ouija board. It's like trying to make a phone call with a banana.

I use my reserved energy and give it a shot.

Yes, I type with ease. Wow, I can't believe he thought of that. Maybe I should give this kid more credit.

Eminem caresses his computer, then caresses himself.

"Why are you a ghost?" he asks

I don't know, I type. *It wasn't my choice.*

"Is it God's choice?"

Beats me.

"What's it like being a ghost?" he asks, freshly lit cigarette dangling from his lips, gangster style. I consider making up a series of lies about the exciting non-life of the undead, but, for a change, I decide to be honest.

It's terribly dull, I type. *It's easy to get consumed with hauntings. I can spend days trying to scare the shit out of just about anyone.*

I even confess that I was a lousy ghost at first. In my early days, I would shake tables at séances or have nothing to say when I was summoned by a medium.

Not too creative, I know, but I'm not very good on the spot. Even to this day, I wish I was quicker on my feet.

"Do you like me? Are you around me all the time?" Eminem asks.

I've spent a lot of time with you lately, I admit.

"I can't stop thinking about you. I thought you would look really gay in an '80s kinda way, but I when I saw your photo, I couldn't stop thinking about you with me. Did you see me jerk off to you?"

Yes, I type.

Eminem reaches for his cock under his underwear and starts pulling.

I'm sorry about the gravestone, I type.

This seems to wind him up even more.

He keeps tugging and tugging, sending me wave after wave of horny currents. Just when I think I couldn't siphon off anymore, he lets out these deep-down grunty noises, and falls down on his back, pushing his cock to the ceiling. The waves crash into me, practically pushing me against the wall. In my efforts to hold on to my overwhelming supply of electricity, I start to feel a warm, intense heat. Eminem's eyes open wide in astonishment as a light begins to form in front of him. It's not the sexy shape of a human body that I want to present, but more like the blob of light you'd see from a patio lantern. Nonetheless I press my blobby self up against him. "I can feel you here," he says dreamily, releasing himself all over his face and the wall behind him.

As he finishes with a final squirt, the waves stop coming. Eminem rubs the cum into his belly, smiling up in my direction as my light begins to dim before him.

"Will you stay with me for awhile? Will you be with me tomorrow?"

Yes, I type.

Eminem shuts down his computer and goes to bed.

For weeks after, I am delighted. I never had a boyfriend when I was living, and I never meet other dead people. So now I'm dating a living person. Who would have thought? Sure, Eminem isn't really my type, and he is quite young considering I would be much older if I was still alive, but I have grown to love him and his quirky ways. Besides, he is the age I was when I died.

We spend a great deal of time together. He talks out loud to me during the day knowing full well that I am beside him. At night we chat on his laptop. I confess he's my first boyfriend. I tell him I was freshly out and ready to move to New York to begin my life as a homosexual. He loves New York too, though he's never been. After we're done chatting, he climbs into bed with the covers thrown off, and I come over as a warm blob of light before he ejaculates all over the place. This goes on for a few months. I never thought I could be so happy being dead.

Then one night, after hours of tossing and turning, Eminem slides out of bed and throws on some warm clothes. How sweet, I think, a midnight walk. I wait for him to call out to me, but he doesn't say a word. Instead, he tiptoes out of the house like a thief.

I follow him through the night until he arrives at the local morgue. Standing before this unremarkable block of bricks is a jittery security guard with an odd, tight smile. He offers the guard a handful of bills. The security guard hands him a slip of paper and two keys.

"The cameras are off. You got an hour," the guard whispers.

Eminem takes the paper and keys from the guard and enters the building. I follow him down the hall to a room that requires both keys to open. After entering, he looks at the piece of paper without turning the lights on. The guard must have scribbled down what looks like "c16" on the paper. Eminem scans a wall of large metal drawers until he finds c16 engraved on one of them. He pulls the drawer out to reveal a white sheet over a freshly dead guy. Eminem removes his jacket and gloves, then continues to remove the rest of his clothes. He pulls the sheet off the dead guy then climbs on top of him. He runs his fingers over the cold skin and scars, slowly rubbing himself all over this guy while these wimpy sex noises I've never heard before start coming out of him. As the noises grow stranger and the rubbing grows faster, the burnt skin on the dead man's flesh splits open, releasing a small flood of puss and cold blood. At this point, I knew I didn't want to stick around for the rest.

Of course I was freaked out, but I decided I should try to be rational about tonight's events. I went for a walk through the graveyard thinking that Eminem must need some contact with a real body. After all, I was just light at best. He needed a little physical one on one. I try to be understanding. He must be pretending that guy was me. I'm dead, the guy's dead, and this guy's got a body. I'm sure he will offer an explanation tomorrow.

But he didn't. I waited beyond tomorrow into the next week. Did he think I never saw his little sicko act? Was he trying to get me mad so he could get off on my wrath? I waited even longer and I didn't get a word out of him, not even a lousy hello.

Days later when he places the laptop on his Ouija board, I spell out fast and furiously, *Why haven't you let me talk to you?!*

Eminems sighs.

"I can't be with you all the time," he says, irritated.

I saw you screw that ugly burn victim. What the fuck was that about?

:His name is not burn victim, it is Mr Doe."

I wonder if the fool thinks that's his real name. "Do you follow me *everywhere* I go?" he asks, "because I don't appreciate that. I need some privacy sometimes."

I thought we had a good thing going here.

"I just want to be with other dead guys," he tells me. "It's not that I don't like you. I'm still young and want to explore."

Dead guys? I think, doesn't he mean guys?

Do you like me just because I'm dead? I ask.

"For Christ sake, Chuck!" he hollers.

Nothing is said for a few moments, then a grin starts to take shape on Eminem's face.

"All this arguing in making me hot," he says, pulling out his big shlong and falling on to his back.

I'm really not in the mood right now, I type, but he isn't even looking at the screen. He's pulling away at his cock, mumbling something under his breath. As his ejaculation comes closer, I can finally make out what he's saying.

"Fuck me, dead guy! Fuck me, dead guy!"

At that point, I realize our whole relationship has been built on a fetish, his fetish for dead men. If I was alive, he would give me as much attention as those guys from the Internet. Being a fetish is worse than being objectified. I'm like leather, or feet.

I'm tempted to do something really vengeful and cruel to the weirdo, but decide that I'm too good for that. I know ghosts are supposed to be all about revenge, but I'll take the high road this time. Besides, I miss the rush of a new haunting.

So I decide to do what a ghost does best. I disappear. At first, I plan to tell him this, but change my mind. The one advantage of being a ghost is that you can disappear without a trace. The mystery will drive him crazy! It's best, I think, to hold out for a boyfriend who can appreciate my personal qualities, not just my deadness. A dismal search, I know, but one worth pursuing during my time here between the living and the completely dead.

I STAND ALONE

SEPHERA GIRON

I remember the day David joined us.

He was a handsome young man. One of those boys with a square jaw to complement his square shoulders. He was fearful, but of course, who wouldn't be?

We were all-powerful. All-consuming.

Omnipotent.

He could smell our energy the moment he stepped across the threshold.

I saw it in his eyes. The burning yearning of one who is fearful to know, yet compelled to experience it all.

My job was to welcome people. To make them feel more at ease and to educate them in the various rituals and customs so that when their time came, they could proceed with the confidence and enthusiasm of the most seasoned member.

That night, as I led him down the long, dark corridor, I could hear the tremble in his voice as he spoke.

"I have waited a long time to come here."

I nodded knowingly. It always takes people a long time to summon up the courage after they discover the existence of this place. I should know.

It took me nearly seven years of vacillation before the yearning overwhelmed the trepidation.

After all, it is a huge step to pull a man's deepest, darkest desire from his heart and into the light.

Many say it can't be done.

I am living proof that it can.

But I am not here to tell you the dark secrets of my own heart. I am here to tell you the story of David.

The smell of fear-tainted sweat was perfume to my senses as we wandered through the dank twists and turns of the cavern.

"This is what you want," I said. Simple words. Simply stated.

"Yes," he replied.

I turned suddenly and it was all I could do to keep from licking my lips as I drank in the anxious fear emanating from his large brown eyes.

"You would do well to remember your manners," I said sternly.

"I am sorry . . . Master. . . ." he said, taking my hand. He knelt down before me, those perfect bud lips pressing against the blood garnet of my ring.

His dark eyes looked up to me from beneath his curly bangs. He had the dreamy face of an angel. To freeze-frame that moment; his perfect face, the smell of his fear, my stirring blood, would not bring it the justice nor the beauty it deserved.

It was deeper.

Deeper than the yearning of loneliness.

Bone-deeper than the most urgent primal hunger.

Soul deeper – than knowing, just knowing, that there has to be someone out in the world who can mate with you, who understands your needs and desires, who could compliment your lust and fear, if only . . . if only there was a way.

A way to call them.

A way to find him.

A way to entice him into the same existence as you. . . .

I nodded at David, all these thoughts and more moving through my mind. We were all here for the same reason. We all harbored the same dream, the same fantasy, the same call of the flesh.

"Come along," I instructed.

He scrambled to his feet. I made him walk before me this time, enjoying the view of his jean-clad ass tentatively working its way through the dimly lit cavern.

At last, we came to a big room, brightly lit with flickering torches and candelabra. The musky scent of incense perfumed the air. The ceiling was a spectacle of art and glass, a mosaic of light and darkness, of man's haunted fears brought to life by the precise flick of a brush or slash of stained glass.

David sighed, staring up in awe at the ceiling, at images of rapture and despair. When at last he lowered his gaze, he saw that there were many men standing in a circle, wearing long garnet robes like mine. They stood, their faces shadows under hoods, shoulders back, waiting patiently, staring at the center where there was a stone table. To the side, ordinary men watched.

We had a few initiates this full moon. David was but one.

A bell rang and a voice called from the darkness.

"Prepare the initiates."

I touched David on the arm and he trembled. I nodded to him and he followed me. Several other men watched nervously. One by one I nodded to each and they fell into step.

I led them to a row of doors just by the main hall.

"You may prepare yourselves in privacy," I said, nodding to the doors. "You will find a robe. Put it on, then return."

The air was thick with anticipation as I watched them barelegged under the swinging change room doors, shucking street clothes to don the gowns.

One by one, they emerged. Wide-eyed, shallow-breathed, cheeks flushed, and fingers twitching. I contained my own excitement by concentrating on my duties. It would not do to lose focus of my obligations and wallow in the fuel of emotions wafting around the room.

I held out my hand, the large garnet glinting as it caught flickers of light from the wall torches. One by one, the men came to me, knelt in front of me, took my hand into theirs, and gently lay their sweet lips on the cold stone of my ring.

With each kiss, the energy in me resonated. Each kiss brought a gentle vibration, a quiver in the fabric of the universe, now passed along to me.

By the time the last man had lain his lips on the ring, my entire being reverberated. I swallowed and then licked my dry lips as I studied them. One by one, I met their gaze and one by one, they dropped their eyes, unsure of what their role was to be.

"You are here for a grand experience. The Master awaits."

They stayed on their knees. Quick learners. They would do well, or so I thought.

"You may rise, and you may take a place in the magic circle. It would behoove you to stand beside a seasoned member, one that wears the ring."

The men stood, moved slowly into the large chamber, and took their places in the circle.

I took my place in the circle as well. My job was done. Now I was one of them, one of the circle, one of the seekers and one of the masters.

We are all one another. We are all brothers together.

My senses tingled, each nerve ending fluttering with the idea of what would happen next. You could never really be certain how a ceremony would go. You could never really be certain who would be called.

The bell rang three times. The hairs on my arms stood on end. A low humming started.

We are all one another. We are all brothers together.

The Master entered the room. He was tall, his face partially covered by the hood, but I knew his face well. He had the face of a god. A dark, brooding face with dark eyes and gleaming white teeth. His darkness had both covered and penetrated my pale flesh on more than one occasion beyond the ritual. I still shudder when I remember how delicious he felt deep inside of me, how his teeth gnawed on my shoulder, his breath hot on my neck. Like most new to the fold, I felt his eyes had been only for me, that he was the one that I had been called to consummate, that he had been my missing link, the darkness for my light.

But like the others, I had mistaken his strength and power, his forcefulness for human folly, mere human emotion. He was beyond that. He was all men and every man, he was my hero and my brother. He was our leader, the one who knew the words, the one who would lead us on our journey, and nothing more.

He loved me as he loved all the brothers.

No more, no less.

And as I saw the new boys gaze upon his dark magnificence, I knew that he had captured their hearts and minds the same as he had mine.

His deep, resonant voice led us through the prayers and I felt us all melt together in our eagerness to not only please ourselves and our god, but our charismatic leader.

There was pouring of wine, burning of incense, much singing and walking and standing and hand holding. About secret ceremonies, I cannot betray what words are truly spoken nor exactly what we use to conduct our rituals.

The robes were gracefully placed around the circle, and men of all shapes and sizes and colors stood facing each other. Smooth firm chests gleamed in the candle light, hairy chests were shadows, and eyes glimmered and peered, casting little peeks at a smooth firm buttock or a well-hung cock.

I was mesmerized by David. By his hairless body, his square shoulders, his narrow hips. By the muscles of his legs, taut with every step, rippling up to his ass like he were a tiger.

"We will wait no longer," Master said.

Two men left the circle and returned with a third. This man was not part of us. This man was young, hungry, panicked. He was probably a street youth, enticed with a free meal. His eyes were wild with fear, the slick sweat of him rolling off in a delicious haze of pheromones. His back was marked from the beating that had kept him complacent until we were ready for his fuel.

The two men led him to the center of the circle. He tried to buck their grip, tried to cry out, but their hands were firm as they wrapped thick ropes around his wrists so that he was straddling the stone table.

The Master's face gleamed and he went over to a table to find an appropriate tool. His fingers plucked a riding crop from the vast array of instruments, many of which had danced along my own flesh at some time or another.

"Your pain is the fuel for our pain," Master said, readying his aim. "We absorb you and grow stronger, so that our quest may end, even tonight."

The boy flinched under the stinging slaps of the crop. As his back grew red and bloody, Master handed the crop to one of the other men to continue the flogging.

"As we prepare the sacrifice, one of you may step forward and speak his deepest desire." The men looked around at each other, each daring the other to step forward and speak.

At last, David took a hesitant step forward.

He spoke with clarity about his desire. How I pitied his simple wish.

To make an elusive lover be with him. Always.

"I had tasted him and that was the beginning of the end. I wanted him by my side, yet for him that one night meant nothing," David explained to the room.

The Master nodded. "You desire this man."

"More than anyone ever."

"How much do you want this lover?"

"As much as I can give."

The Master laughed and a shiver ran up my spine. I wanted to crawl into a little ball and roll into a corner when I heard that sound. It echoed haunted memories that made the fading welts on my own back throb anew.

David sank to his knees, hugging the Master around the ankles.

"What can I do?" he cried out.

The Master stared at David's unmarked muscular back, his smooth, firm ass.

I knew how vulnerable David must be feeling right now. To confess love in a room of strangers is never easy, yet it was what had brought most of us here.

The air was thick with smoke, thicker still with anticipation. The circle waited with bated breath. Master looked up to the skylight. I didn't want to look, but I forced my gaze.

Yes, it was there.

That cloud.

That mist that hung like a curtain between worlds.

There was a shriek, louder then any bird call, and a giant claw swooped from the cloud, scooping up the battered body of the sacrificed boy. No one said a word. There was a terrible sound of gnashing and tearing. Bloody bones were tossed down in a steady stream, rolling and shattering into shards as they landed on the floor.

David braced himself to stand, but Master lifted his foot and placed it on that halo of curls, pushing David's face to the floor. David looked over at me, wide-eyed, and I nodded solemnly. He squeezed his eyes shut.

From where I stood, I saw the glitter of tears.

⚕

The next time David attended the ceremony, his face was gaunt, his eyes hollow. When he saw me, he grabbed my arm. I was going to protest, but the shock of his icy grip kept the words from me.

"I can't believe it," he whispered, his eyes darting around as he made his confession.

"That it worked," I said snidely.

"Yes."

"Of course it works. That is why we exist. Why we continue to return."

David nodded and took a deep breath.

"But there's a problem," he said, hesitantly.

"Did you not get your darkest desire?"

"Yes."

"So what's the problem?" I asked.

"It's not . . . how I thought it would be. . . ."

"It never is," I said coldly, turning away.

David participated in the ceremony, hollow eyes darting, his fingers straying now and again to the garnet ring on his finger.

Another boy was brought forth. Another boy feeding the fuel of our darkness. Again, the feasting with noise and relish, bones dropping from the skylight.

Every full moon it was the same.

There were always new people to initiate, and there were always new victims to sacrifice.

David grew more gaunt, more nervous, more disturbed. I avoided his presence when I led new initiates into the fold, and prepared boys for their ultimate sacrifice.

The last time David came to the meeting, he grabbed my arm with iron fingers. I struggled under his clutch, amazed that such a frail, wild-eyed man had such strength. He leaned close to me, his breath rank from a hundred sleepless nights.

"You knew all along," he accused. His fingers twisted the garnet ring around and around his finger.

"Knew what?"

"I can tell in your eyes, that you know. You know for yourself. And yet, you led us here, led us to believe we will have our darkest wish."

"And do you not have your darkest wish?" I asked.

David tore the ring from his finger and tossed it at the center stone table. He looked coldly at me with narrowed eyes and made a noise, a shriek like a wounded cat, his fingers clamping around my neck. I gasped for air and felt his nails ripping and tearing through me till the blood ran down my neck. I didn't try to protest, for I understood his anger.

We all understood his anger.

Several followers had witnessed the scene and pried him away from me.

I lay on the floor, gasping, watching the blood slowly drip from my wounds. How I wished he had dug deeper, crushed my throat hard enough to collapse it, but he knew, as I did, that it was far more torturous to stay alive than to be released into sweet death.

David swore and screamed as they tied him to the stone table.

I watched strips of flesh fall from him as the studs of the flogger slapped his back.

Above, the mist gathered and as David's blood pooled on the ground, the giant taloned claw swooped down to scoop up its monthly meal.

I returned to my home that night, wondering why David had touched me in a way the others had not.

What was the link, if any? How bad could it have really been?

It was of no consequence anymore.

After all, David had received his wish and paid the price in a quicker fashion then most. How I envied him as I walked with great trepidation into my bedroom.

Every night, I dreaded going into my bedroom.

Every night, I cursed the day I had discovered I could have my darkest desire.

Every night, I wished that he would not be there on my return.

Yet there he is. Sitting in my bed.

My darkest desire.

Malcolm.

He waits for me every night. His bones gleaming in the darkness where chunks of his decaying flesh have flaked away. His beautiful green eyes long rotted. The clicking of his cracked teeth prominently protruding from shrunken lips. His bloated, pussy arms outstretched, reaching for me, showing me that he still loves me, still wants me, still desires me, though cancer had claimed him long ago.

He presses his fetid mouth against mine and I think about how much I loved him. I still love him. And he loves me.

Forever.

I have my darkest desire, yet still, I stand alone.

NUMBERS

STEVE DUFFY

BILL

Days on the ward . . . the old men in their sad pajamas, the old-fashioned ill-nesses that wind down their clocks; infarctions, carcinomas, slo-mo cerebral episodes. They've been around forever, these guys, long enough to learn the ropes and then some. Longer than me, even. They're experts, all of them, in sickness, fluent in the language of the institution. Listen while they rehearse their complaints in the day-room, ready for the doctors' rounds: how their stools are funny colors, how they can't get any sleep nights, this pill versus that pill, *yadda yadda yadda*. And then with the confidences: old so-and-so in the next bay looks like shit on that new medication, doncha think? And what about me? How do I look? I mean, how old would you say I am, go on, take a guess – and the pleading in their voices, in their crumpled-up old faces. . . . And it's the brusque and bubbling farts they can't hide, the mumbling in the night, the copious cuds they hawk up into Dixie cups, little love-tokens for the nurses; our bodies, it's our bodies that give us away. Traitors, all of them, in the end. Same thing, young or old, gay or straight.

One thing's for sure: they don't know what to make of *us*, these seniors. Us, in the far bay, with our patterned wraps and our heavy-duty hairdryers and our Mylar get-well-soon balloons; though we're still a minority, even here in a San Francisco hospital, we're gradually taking over this little corner for our own. There'll be others too. Soon, there'll be more of us. Word is, we're going to get our own space soon, a ward all to ourselves. Which is progress, I suppose; you'd have to call that progress.

Even their visitors and ours differ – like, *noticeably*. For them, the grannies in pantsuits who take away the underwear with its gravy-stains and soilings and bring it back the next night, all respectable again. Inheritance vultures, the grown-up children who bring their own kids along, and the kids don't really want to be there and get cranky and wind up banished to the TV room, and then the silence, no one knowing what to say. Old men clutching sweat-damp-ened bus transfers, gray-faced, exhausted, who just sit by the bedside, indistin-guishable from those they've come to visit. Biding time . . . biding time.

Meanwhile, on our side, it's the Macy's Day Parade. You got your clones, your musclemen, your leatherettes and disco-divas; more Studio 54 than ward fourteen. Imagine the possibilities for culture-shock down in the atrium come visiting time: furious forward-looking straights queuing with muscle-marys and scream-queens in the line at the cafeteria, jostling over the last of the bouquets at the flower stall. How they *harrumph* and look away, those straights, at the end of the evening; how they tut at the hugs and the kisses, and the teary brave goodbyes . . . palpable blasts of repugnance, of disgust, sour like a spoiled gut. (Only the sick guys seem not to mind, the really sick guys, and the ones who really love them.) A lot of people out there are more comfortable with the way it used to be, back when we were invisible. In which case I shouldn't trouble them that much; most days now I actually do feel invisible, nothing left except the signals coming in, seeing, hearing, impressions. Nothing but a spookily heightened acuity in place of that old flesh and bone, that sought-after Nautilus body tone I was so proud of, once upon a time. All that sensation I loved so well – all that precious embodiment – seems diffuse now, dispersed, given over into the surroundings of this ward, this bedside; and so as the night wears on, I'm still up watching, listening, taking it all in for the thousandth time: bed C, bay three, ward fourteen. . . .

The hospital was built, like a lot of county hospitals out west, in the thirties, in the forties: not much juice in public health care since the Depression, I guess. It reminds you of childhood in many ways, all tiles and vitaglass and Mondrian blocks of primary colors. Very grade-school. Familiar too, from childhood, is the sheer level of attention, the care; all cradled in the discreet, the sexless arms of public medicine, we eat up our health-mush dinners, sip our slightly chlorine-tasting water from the scratchy plastic tumblers, say *please* and *thank you* and *I think I need the bathroom, please* . . . and at nights the night-lights burning on the ward, like the corridor lights left on in all the houses of our childhood; we lie back in the pillows and dream ourselves to sleep, such dreams as we can spin ourselves, such sleep as we can snatch. Those of us who can't manage even that much, well, we have the new toys, the Sony Walkmans, and we can listen to the music from back when, from Before. You hear it leaking from the headphones sometimes, in the stillness at the very pit of the night; the outline of a beat, the ghost of a melody, and it's tantalizing, and it's almost-there, like music through a half-closed door, it's like a mainline into the memories of those good times, all merged into that one hot endless summer. . . .

Scott & Robert
Did you hear?
    Omigod.
    No, did you hear?
    I can't *stand* it . . . will you look at that number by the poolside? I mean, you think he knows it, or what? Oh, *please.*
    Listen . . . you know Benny from the Everhard, who we met over at Jason's that time? Barman, at the Everhard? Real cute, real short hair, no mustache . . . know who I

mean? Well, I ran into him down at the bookstore this afternoon —

Backroom of the bookstore? Lucky for you I'm not the jealous type.

Not in the backroom, it was out front, thank you . . . well, we were talking, and you know what he said? You're not going to believe this.

Oh, *that?* It's all over the Castro, Scott — Jim Bakker came out, front page exclusive in *Blueboy, Time,* and *Newsweek.* Tammy Faye says it don't matter none to her, she's gonna stand by her man like a Christian woman should, but Lord, she don't understand nothin' no more, and she just thinks it must be the flu-o-ride them Commies put in the water —

Will you listen? Benny said that he was in this leather place last week, you know, just kind of checking it out, something a little different, and he got talking to this guy, nothing too heavy, just talking, and you know what he told him?

The tension is killing me.

Well hey, Miss Snippy, if you're not interested —

Aw, come on now, Scott, don't get all sulky on me here. Sulky is not becoming. Tell the story.

What, you think this is sulky? I'll show you sulky, Robert. . . . As I was trying to say — this guy tells Benny how there's this thing that's going round the leather bars, all through the leather scene —

Oh, *not* some sordid leather queen thing, please — you know those guys are just too damn tacky for my taste. Ohhh-kay — what, are we talking hardware here? Ironmongery? Plumbing? Electricity?

Well, yeah, that's what Benny thinks at first: Benny thinks this guy is coming on to him, and before too long he's going to suggest —

— they make it back to *his* pad, take the drinks down in the *basement* and then shazam, out with the ol' Gestapo drag, right? How's about you git down over this bench here, hands behind your back, stick this big ol' leather thang rat b'tween your *teeth* there, buddy —

— absolutely. Too creepy. But . . . turns out he's just like a regular, nice kind of guy, and they have a couple of drinks, and in the end it's just that the guy needs someone to talk to more than anything, he's like freaked, cause of the stories he's hearing. What it is, he's heard these rumors going round the scene, about this guy they call the Sketchpad —

The what? The Sketchpad? What kind of a deal is that? I mean, chains I can figure, okay, not my idea of fun, but you know, whatever gets you off, right? Whips, belts, handcuffs, flex . . . but a sketchpad? I don't see where —

Listen while I tell you . . . this Sketchpad guy, what they're saying happens is, he sits at a table in the leather bars, somewhere dark, you know, over in the corner maybe, and he's got this sketchpad —

Hence the name.

Hence the name; and, and what happens, he sorta singles out this one other customer, and they say usually this is like a new guy on the scene, on his own, you know, not with anyone, and he's glancing up at him, looking down at the sketchpad, glancing up, looking down at the sketchpad . . . like he's making a picture, you know? Like he's making a sketch of him. So, this guy obviously feels kind of flattered, you know, like my god, all these really humpy numbers in the joint tonight, and here's this guy, he's drawing a picture of me . . . and he kind of sidles up a little closer, you know, and the guy with the sketchpad sort of holds up his pencil, like, stay there, I haven't finished yet, so the guy goes back to where he was, and he's thinking, oh boy, is this hot, is this a turn-on, and after a little while, the guy kind of gestures, okay, finished, and the number comes on over, and they get to talking . . . and then they're gone. No one sees them go, they're just not there anymore, like the table's empty, drinks left behind, and – get this – there on the table, there's the leaf out of the sketchpad, with just this amazingly detailed drawing of this guy. . . .

Lucky guy, right? You know, that's actually kind of hot. I mean, I could go for that. . . .

Wait, I haven't finished . . . the whole point is, that's the last anyone sees of him!

What? The guy with the sketchpad?

No – the number! – I mean, both of them! Don't you see? He cruises the bar, picks up this guy, and then, bang, that's it. Guy vanishes, no one ever sees him again. Gone. Into thin air. He picks 'em up, takes 'em off, and . . . whatever.

No. . . !?

Really. Benny said they even use the sketch the guy leaves behind for the gone-missing poster – he said he'd seen one on a lamp-post over by the Tenderloin. Très butch little number, first night in town, whatever: phfft, vanishes into thin air, never seen again. And wait! I didn't even tell you the spookiest part – each time, at the bottom of the sketch, there's just the one thing written there – and it's a number, like, number twelve, number thirteen, number eighteen, number twenty-three. . . .

Patient Zero

I remember that story. It made the rounds maybe '79, '80: actually, I figured that's all it was: just a story. I mean, there are always stories going 'round about something. But story or not, I have to admit I thought it was kind of sexy, you know? Okay, spooky, yes, but . . . kind of sexy. One of my lovers actually did make a sketch of me one time – not that I think for a minute that he was, you know, the Sketchpad guy, but still it was . . . hot. I'd never had anyone ask me to sit for them before, and I did kind of get off on it. It was a good thing for him to think of.

I mean, if I'm honest, the thing is, I wasn't always worth sketching, I guess. That makes a difference. You know, if I ever came into, like, lots of money, like, I don't know, Howard Hughes? Rock Hudson? I think the first thing I'd do is round up all the copies of my class yearbook and have them pulped or burned or something. Whole print run. Oh, but you can't imagine – I mean, Jesus, that picture? I had like the worst kind of acne, and a big cold sore just the day of the photo, and that stupid stupid haircut, and those really dumb glasses – I'd just die if I thought that anyone I know now could have actually seen the way I used to look back then. Because they'd never guess, now, to look at me. That much I do know. I'm not the same anymore. I've changed.

⚜

DON

Gerald brought me a new tape for the Walkman the other day; it's got the Rufus and Chaka Khan thing first track, you know that big hit they had, *Ain't Nobody*? Totally my kind of music: last summer, couple of summers ago, I would have been playing it all the time. Disco bunny, dance dance dance. I had a T-shirt with that once: I wore it on the float at Gay Pride. Happiest day of my life, probably.

You know what used to be my favorite time for listening to music? Early in the evening, and it's those long summer evenings and, like, the expectation . . . I'd be back across the harbor from, you know, the Joe-job in Oakland, shower, change, get ready for a night out on the trail, down the baths, maybe down the Glory Hole, wherever. I'd leave the bedroom window open, so you could hit off the smell and the noise and, and, just the whole buzz of it. Some evenings, it felt like everyone in the whole city was getting ready to come out and play, you know? And you could hear the music out on the street: *Street Life*, The Crusaders; *Good Times*, Chic; *Young Hearts Run Free*, Candi Staton – that was my absolute favorite like the whole of that year; the Teena Marie thing, *Behind The Groove* . . . love my music. All the way down to that Bee Gees soundtrack album one of my lovers bought me, once he found out I was into, Jesus, *boogying*. I don't care. Night fever, whatever. Just so's you can dance to it.

It was all a part of it, the dancing, the music, everything: the way you'd cruise the scene on a Friday night down past the Muni Metro and the Twin Peaks, and like the lyric from a song just running through your head, and the beat of it, the way you'd be in your space out on the floor and when the DJ cued your tune up you would hit it, just go into that dance, and once you were locked into that, then nothing, like absolutely nothing would matter for just that little minute, nothing could touch you –

I'm sorry; no, I do want to go on, it's okay, it's just. . . . Sorry. I'll be okay in a minute. Love my music, man.

⚜

BILL

The old poops on the ward play their music too. They listen to the oldies stations, Gordon MacRae and Mario Lanza and Nelson and Jeanette, all those Rodgers and Hammerstein songs from the shows. Rodgers and Hammerstein, Rodgers and Hart, Rodgers-schmodgers, I don't know. All those. We used to have the record albums at home when I was a kid, those thick, incredibly solid old LPs you filed upright in a wire rack by the stereogram, with the sleeve laminate you could peel off in big silvery strips. My parents loved them all, no matter how cornball; I think they represented something in their eyes (or maybe just in mine?), something you wouldn't ever express directly, that had to do with — what would you call it? — steadfastness, maturity, respectability . . . just that whole solid-citizen spread, the driver's licence, the job-with-prospects, the insurance, the two-point-four children, all the rest of it. Straightsville, Oklahoma, where the wind comes sweepin' down the plain. It was like, forget all that running wild, all that shaking your tail-feathers, you're not Artie Shaw or Rita Hayworth. This isn't Hollywood. It's not gonna happen. Just settle for being the Folks That Live On The Hill, Darby and Joan who used to be Jack and Jill. It's not anything to be ashamed of. It's okay to fall in love, to get married and raise kids. It's what you do. . . .

But. What good is love if you're thinking about how it could all be over, like *that*, tomorrow, the next day, whenever? You think about *passion*, and it's different; it's *this*, and *this*, and *this*, like the running man in the children's flickerbook, it needs the flicker to make it run. Like one of the guys on the ward said, love's alright if it lasts a while. Romance is cool, I guess, if that's what you're after; and the torchsong thing on the downside when it's over, in the wee small hours, all the what-ifs and the could-have-beens and maybe-next-times; that's all part of it, but it's not the real deal. Not that heartstopping blast when the pheromones kick in, where there's no room for anything but the truth.

What do we mean when we talk about passion? Sometimes you can't even tell what it is *you're* feeling let alone anybody else. What I call love — what I've known as love, my definition — it may not be pure, but it sure isn't cut, and when love comes it comes with nothing but love. It's like a strobe light on a dance floor, and there are no faces, no names; you don't ask for the names. In this place, in this city, there are no names; there are only strangers.

ANTHONY

Okay, it's not always like this. You don't think about it all the time, or obviously you wouldn't be able to function, you'd just go to pieces. You go whole days, well, the best part of a day, maybe, and you don't think about it at all. You do your job, if you still have a job; you bank checks, you pay your bills, you get groceries from the store and you bring them home and cook them, whatever. You watch TV in the evenings and take the trash out. You drink, probably more than you used to, start smoking again after you quit already. Maybe somebody comes round, and you keep the conversation light, try not to dump on each other. That's how you deal with it, when you're not right up against it. The thing is, though, none of that matters in the last analysis;. it's not important, it's not what you remember.

I've always thought: you know what you really see? You're on your deathbed, at the last moment, and what you see, it's not your whole life that passes in front of you, not all that day-to-day shit, those endless rainy afternoons in cities, those boring little people in those boring little rooms. It's your fantasies, your imaginings; it's all you ever dreamed you'd be. . . .

SCOTT & ROBERT

There's this guy handing out pamphlets on the Castro.

Oh, like the end of the world is nigh? Hi ho.

Pamphlets, I took one. See, it says here that it was all this experiment that the army had, the biological weapons research at Fort Detrick, you know? The army, and the Pentagon and the CIA.

Right: army and the Pentagon and the CIA, big conspiracy, government plot to rub out all the un-Americans once and for all, right? Homos, Haitians, and hemophiliacs. Operation H. Guy with the white cat in his underwater hideout, like in the James Bond movies. This kind of stuff – it's actually pretty fucked-up, Scott, you know? Like, pretty desperately lame?

Well, I didn't say I believed in it.

Oh – I'm relieved. Glad to see your brain's not turned completely into moosh. It was the same sort of thing with sickle cell, remember? Whitey's equalizer? Big fat honky plot to get rid of all the brothers? Amazing. Out of nowhere this comes. What I want to know, who is it thinks of this stuff? Every time something happens, no matter what, god, they're out there with the pamphlets and the *wooo* and the big bug eyes and the conspiracy theory – like before the dust settles, you know?

That's right . . . remember when Harvey Milk was shot? I was still working at the real-estate place off Geary? Just that same night, you know, the exact night it happened, I saw the copier boy from the office down the A&P, and he already had the joke, some really stupid joke, about knock-knock, who's there, Dan White: and they were yakkin' it up, all the jocks and punkers and whatever 'round the checkout. It made me so mad, but what you gonna do? Say anything, they'd have been on to me, and then who knows . . . you know.

Same thing. I would love to know just what the fuck goes on, really? How that kind of information travels . . . why.

People always seem to know.

People don't know, not really. Maybe that's why. Nobody knows, and they just need to make shit up, so's not to freak themselves out completely. Like, for instance, I don't know. Like it's just a spot, right? Little skin cancer, like the surfer boys get. Nothing to worry about . . . there you go.

He said fourteen days till the results. Come here. . . .

Nobody knows.

DENNIS

I heard something about it, yeah. Only the way I heard it, you have to be like mainlining or something, and I'm strictly from poppers, personally. Well. Little bit of grass still, when I want to be mellow. Toot or two, weekends, special occasions. But nothing heavy. Poppers more than anything.

The scene was really something new to me, the poppers and everything, because I guess I was a little naïve when I first came to town. I remember my first night in a bathhouse, and this really hot guy had the door open to his cubicle, and he kind of nodded at me as I went past, and I was like, duh, *who, me?* – right out and *said* it, can you believe that? – and he said, he had this really cute kind of French accent, or Canadian I guess it was, *Who do you think*, and it was like, whoa, alright, I made it. Home at last. Hoo, Mary.

I never forgot that first time, and I still get a kick out of the bathhouses and everything. They're really unbelievable, if you've never been in one: they're like this magical place where all your dreams come true. Do you remember that song, real corny old-time number, "Did You Ever See A Dream Walking?" Well, that's what it's like on a good night in the tubs. I have to pinch myself sometimes, like, is this really happening to me?

DON

I'm really very faithful in my habits, considering. I mean, I listen to all those old songs still, on the Walkman Gerald bought me. I remember how they'd get around, the way they'd move through the scene so fast, how you'd hear them first in just the one place, maybe Workingman's Groove or the Boys' Own, and then inside a week or two they'd be all over town, and you'd hear them everywhere, on the radio, on the TV, in the straight places, everywhere. And of course by then you'd have moved on to the next hot thing. That was part of the fun.

But you always remember them, each and every one of them, each and every beat. The songs, they're like benchmarks, mementos; they're how we measure the memories one from another. Like, "Down Deep Inside," Donna Summer? That's 1977, the apartment with the deck over on Egremont, and the dark-haired guy from the fire department with the scars on his back and the scuffed-up work boots. "Magic Fly?" '77, same again; the airline steward in the bathhouse that time, the French-Canadian guy that said, you look hot, you must work out, no, you're a dancer, aren't you, I can tell, and everybody was so jealous. . . .

That summer, that red-hot everlastin' '77; wasn't it just the best thing ever? Remember?

BILL

The city is Storyville, where we make ourselves over. We come in on the short-haul or the Greyhound, and we're Joe Blow from Shamokin, all tank tops and Jesus sandals, granddad shirts and granny glasses, and we see the things we desire, and we make ourselves into the image of the things we see. Work on some muscle at the YMCA, get a new haircut, get a whole new look together. Re-invention.

Pretty soon we become that something new, that thing we always dreamed. Something we knew we could be if we only had the chance to start over, away from all those things that used to hold us back, away back where we came from. It's always been the way of it, and to me it's actually very American, quintessential textbook stuff. You light out for the territories, hole up on Jackson's Island like Huck and Jim, and hey, you get your second chance. Absolutely apple pie.

Nothing could be wrong that made so many people so happy, could it? It was like our honeymoon – which means that we're allowed to be a little nostalgic for it, because after all, honeymoons don't last forever. Nothing that good ever lasts, I guess. Nothing in this culture, anyway, this TV-techno-carsmash-fuckarama excuse we have for a society. There are no working paradigms for bliss eternal – at least beyond the Hollywood thing and the sloppy slow-dance ballads at the end of the evening – there are only the accommodations we each of us make. Boats borne against the current. Shit moves on. The worm is always there, in the bud, waiting for ripeness. Because ripeness, remember, is when it's over. That summer, all those summers, it was already over, and we didn't even know it.

†

SCOTT & ROBERT
They're setting up camps.
What?
Duane says there are these camps – it's all over town. When you test positive, your name goes on the list, and once he's re-elected Reagan's gonna push the legislation through Congress and then it all comes down – San Francisco first, then everywhere. They're gonna round up everyone that's positive and put 'em into camps.
Camps . . . no shit? Well, I never enjoyed camp all that much, you know? All the rough boys and the ugly-bugs used to beat up on me, cause I used to let the side down in the communal activities or whatever . . . camps, my god. It was all too rawhide for my liking – you know I never really got off on that cowboy thing. Hundred-percent closet cases, all those steer-punchers. That's how come all their women look like drag queens.
Yeah, but – you don't believe it?
Frankly.
What, you think they'd have like the slightest scruples over –
Scruples, god, no. It's just, you know, do we really rate a special camp all to

ourselves? Do you think they even give us that much thought, Reagan and everybody? Don't flatter yourself, sweetie. It's just somebody making up tales again. No need to get paranoid. Oh hey, look, I found another spot on my leg this morning . . . it's the hundred-and-one Dalmatians all over. I'm practically piebald. I hope they don't have communal changing rooms at this camp of yours – it better be like in the bathhouse, where you can make with the towel in the cubicle first before you open the door, let it kind of drape over all the embarrassing parts –

Bathhouse . . . they closed all the bathhouses now. Everyone's going 'round town, and they're just . . . looking at each other, like, you know –

Hey. Do you remember the first time we ever met each other? It was in that bathhouse, tiny little place with, like, miniature cubicles, hardly enough room to take your clothes off in the first place, let alone –

On Folsom Street, right –

On Folsom Street, and I was with that *extremely* hot airline stew who said he came from, where in the hell was it, Quebec, and you caught me on the rebound after I waited three nights running for him to come back there again. . . .

I never figured out what you saw in him.

No? So what were *you* doing there three nights running, Little Miss Innocent? Waiting for a cable car?

PATIENT ZERO

At first you dream of a lover – one lover – I guess because that's what you pick up from all the straight stuff, you know, like the song, "One girl, one wife, one love, through life; Memories are made of this." Something like that. Isn't that how it goes? Something.

Only, once you make the scene, you realize: why one, why just one? All those amazing, gorgeous numbers, and they're all there, all available. Whatever you want, you can go right ahead. You can make it with any one you choose – you can make it with all of them, if that's what turns you on, if that's what you want – and there's no one there to say, bad boy, dirty boy, shame on you, you ought to be ashamed of yourself. What's to be ashamed of? No one's thinking like that; everyone thinks just like you think, everyone's the same. And there are hundreds of you, thousands, in every city. Thousands just like you. And no one knows your name, or no one need know it. No names, no hang-ups, no situations. It's *très* romantic.

Once you realize you're not the only one, once you find out who you really are and you start to see the possibilities, then you're free to do the things you feel; just cruise on through, coast to coast, Washington, Manhattan, San Francisco, Honolulu. All my lovers, everywhere. All my beautiful lovers.

ANTHONY

Yes, I'm ashamed of him. Yes, I could curl up and die when anyone sees him this way. Yes, I'm mean to him sometimes, I admit it. Yes. But do you really think that means I don't love him still?

He was bad today. I mean, it was one of his bad days. He insisted on going out 'round about seven, after I got home, wanted to walk down to the Chinese restaurant for dim sum like we used to. I tried my best, I told him he wasn't up to it, we could phone, but no, he had to go out, and so I had to go with him. He left his cane at home, because he knows I don't like him going out with it – he's thirty-three years old, for god's sake, and a cane just looks ridiculous – and halfway down the street he got so bad. . . . It started with him bending over, because he hadn't tied his lace properly, and he couldn't manage it, and then he just sat down in the middle of the sidewalk, and everybody was looking, and there's no way he could fix this goddamn shoelace, and I practically had to carry him back to the house with his shoes falling off. It was awful. And on top of his medication, he drank. After everything Doc Szymanski said. And then, it was just the usual thing all night, just huddled up on the couch there falling asleep and muttering to himself and, like, with the drool and everything, and all the time trying to telephone – I said to him, who in the hell do you think you're trying to call, Adam? Who have you got *left* to call? Who do you think would want to hear from you when you're this way, anyway?

I said that to him, but I know who he wants to call, I think. When he gets that way, I think he kind of loses track of time, forgets where he is, and it's as if he's in this strange room, and he doesn't hardly know me, and he panics and he tries to call up Bobby and say, where am I, I'm in this room, come get me. . . . See, he doesn't remember about Bobby, what happened. I don't think he even knows who I am when he goes into that whole thing. I'm like some stranger or something. It comes and goes, and it's just. . . .

I sat there, just watching him, making sure he didn't set fire to himself with his cigarette or take any more of his pills or choke on his damn vodka. So, anyway, his eyes started closing, and it got time for him to go to bed, and I had to more or less manhandle him off of the couch, and he was just like dead weight, not helping at all, and he's kind of slumped over sideways and I can't get a purchase, and. . . .

It was my fault. I was probably not gentle enough with him, I think. I think I might have scared him, because I had him halfway up and he said, it was the clearest thing he'd said all night, he said, "Don't hurt me." Like a little kid: "Don't hurt me." I carried him into the bedroom and got his clothes off, tucked him in under the quilt and turned the nightlight on, and then I came back into the kitchen and I cried so hard because I felt so bad. Because I really do love him, and it's like he's already gone.

Dennis

Like I say: no one need know your name. In the bathhouse, you're not a name, you're a . . . a concept, a symbol, you're like an image of whatever you want to be, or whatever someone else wants you to be. You play a part, it's like you have a role to play. They have a picture in their mind, some fantasy they've worked on, and you become a part of that fantasy. You make that fantasy a reality for them. What they just dreamed about comes real, it comes real in you. And it's the same the other way, too. Everything's moving, changing all the time, this way, that way . . . sorry, I'm not explaining this too well, I know. It's my fault – I'm really, like, still stoned, you know? From last night? Pretty out of it still. It's . . . you had to have been there, I guess.

We were saying before, that story about the Sketchpad? I'm not sure that I believe it, you know, like every detail or whatever, but there's something in it that does ring kind of true. Cause I guess we've all been in a bar someplace, or like a nightclub, and we've sat and watched someone, you know, who really turns us on, that reminds us of some number or other we've always wanted to get into, and you could say it's like we're creating them, in a way, in our mind's eye. Like we're sketching out the scenario. Just like the sketchpad thing. You could say that. What you get with that kind of scene, someone's always controlling the dream, the one who's playing the active part, and the other person, he's like the passive part, like the hanger to hang it on, you know? And to make that kind of fantasy come real . . . I guess I can see how with a certain kind of guy these certain things might happen. Fantasy into reality, that's what it's all about. What's actually real, when you stop to think about it?

Like . . . there's this one place, where the walls are all mirrors. Sometimes, when you're in there and it's really hot, just really packed out with guys, it's like you'll see someone, and you think it's your reflection in a mirror; only then he moves, comes over, and it's like your reflection just stepped out of the mirror, *shoom*, clean through the looking-glass. You really double-take for a second – it's so weird. But hot – my god.

That's the kind of thing that could only happen in a dream, right? And the weirdest thing is, really . . . really, it is you, in the mirror. It's you, all the time, if you want it to be. Pure fantasy.

Patient Zero

Every city: New York, Houston, La-la land, Miami, Denver, Seattle, Chicago . . . every stopover, there was always someplace to go. As if it was the same place: the same scene wherever you went, and whatever you wanted, you could get it. Hit town on the redeye, check into the hotel, get a shower, line or two to wake you up, pull out your address book and get on the phone. Taxi to the bathhouse; party time. The further out in the boondocks, the more pleased they'd be to see you. The bigger the city, the more choice you got. Either way, you couldn't lose. Not if you were one of the pretty ones. It was totally dreamy in there for a while; Miss Popularity, and all those open doors.

Summertime, you got your pick of the house parties on Fire Island; winter, up in Aspen for the skiing, or should I say the après-ski? And whatever time of year it was, there was always the Lavender Shuttle, Los Angeles to San Francisco for the weekend, or vice versa: wherever the party was at. Always a party, somewhere in town.

Stewarding, you got all the air miles you could use, I mean over and above the scheduled stops, and I made the most of it, believe me. One time I tried to plot it on a map, all the back-and-forth and the zig-zags and the stopovers, and even with my diary I couldn't keep track. And if you go on to think of all my lovers, *this* many at *this* place, *this* many *here*, *this* many someplace *else*; well, where do you begin?

It's strange: when I'm not with them, I really don't think about them all that much, but it just this minute struck me – imagine all my lovers, all my lovely numbers since whenever, and then try to imagine all *their* lovers. . . . Obviously, not everyone's as popular as I am, you know, but still, they must know people I haven't even heard of, let alone been with. And yet we are connected: imagine, all across the country – across the whole *world*, who knows – we have this thing we share, this thing we have in common; and we don't even know it, because we don't know who we are. It could be anyone you see on the street, in a bar, anywhere, and there's this secret, this secret thing between us that we'll maybe never know. Don't you think that's kind of spooky?

⚵

SCOTT & ROBERT
Hey, Dick Breneman says it may be the poppers.

Come again?

Poppers. There's this lab, and they've done research, and they haven't published or anything, and nobody's going on the record till they've tested on monkeys, but . . . poppers.

You're kidding – and "come again" was supposed to be a joke, by the way. Never mind. Start over. So, how'd they research poppers, Scott? Look under the bed in your apartment?

There were like these doctors from the CDC collecting, they went round every place in town. All the sex stores, all the bathhouses, they got poppers from all over. They say maybe it could have been a bad batch, or maybe somebody even spiked them, you know, like the Tylenol killer that time?

Really?

Absolutely. It's possible, no? Bad batch of Rush on the street, and bingo.

Or it's the Tylenol scenario – god says to crazyman, all queers must die, and bingo double bingo. I can swallow *that* a damn sight more than quality control at the popper factory: imagine it, there's this guy lives in back of some garage somewhere, stinkin' like a polecat, eating tuna straight out of the can, thinks Jerry Falwell talks to him through the faucets or something . . . man on a mission. Writes it all down in green ink in his Big Chief pad: Dear Diary, killed me another buncha faggots today, praise be to the ever-livin' neon drive-in Jesus –

Will you quit that? Will you please quit that, please?

No, really. Would it – do you think it would be better if it was all down to someone? If there was just, you know, someone to blame for all of this? Cause I sometimes think that, you know? That's what I think, sometimes. Nights. That's what I think.

Come on. You know it isn't really anybody's fault – you said so. You told me so.

No? Isn't anybody's fault, right? Then what the fuck is it all about, Scott? You tell me that. Like what the fuck is it all in aid of? All this? You know? Because I don't. I'm fuckin', my fuckin' lungs are full of this pneumo shit, an' I'm three parts blind already, an' I *look* like shit, an' I'm fuckin' dying here, and I, I don't know why. . . .

BILL

Remind yourself that more die of cancer, or leukemia, or from their hearts going supernova. Remind yourself that more die from dirty water, from living off of garbage dumps, out in the dust with the trash and the shit and the vermin.

I saw all that in Africa, in the Peace Corps when I was a kid. I saw them. The aid workers, the doctors and the nurses and the Catholic nuns, had a name for the people out there, all those fucked-up shuffling zombie skeletons: they called them *Les Affreux*, the scary ones, the terrifying ones. I worked mostly with the kids, and to me they were The Unanswerable Ones: unanswerable. Everything you thought about the way the world was run – or, no, everything you took for granted, more like – it was all sent flying up in the air, and you – you were nowhere. Beyond your tears, and your pity, and your righteous indignation and whatever, there was an empty place, and in that place there was nothing but the children. The children, all but dead themselves, standing in for all the dead you'd never see, now and in the future; the refugees, the orphans, crouching in the ragged tents outside the hospital, crying for their dead parents, hardly the strength to brush at the flies that clustered round them, flies all sticky on their bright and dreadful tears. How could you stand it? How could you bear to look them in the eyes?

So, more die from negligence, from carelessness. More die because we fuck up all we touch. But no single death is diminished by a thousand others, by a million, anywhere. Put them in the balance and they will all weigh the same, just exactly the same. I'd hoped never again to think about these things, or to think about the children, but then a couple of years ago – just after I took the test, those three-four weeks before the results came through – back then, I found I was thinking about them nearly all the time. This is what us educated people call *displacement*, I guess.

⚜

DON

What I suppose got me 'round to thinking about music was, Gerald was round today, and we were talking about what music to have. At the service.

Gerald says he'll handle everything, square it with my folks and all, if they come. I don't know if that'll happen, whether or not they'll stay in Allentown. I'd like for them to come out and meet Gerald, but I won't go back. I've told Gerald, and I've put it into writing, not to let them take me back. It'll be just a simple non-sectarian service-with-music at the mission, and then Gerald and some of the guys will take the ashes up on the cliffs out past the Legion of Honor Museum. It's so pretty up there. We used to go for picnics, a whole bunch of us. Most of them are gone, now.

About the music: I don't know, really. You go to these kind of services, and you hear everything from Judy Garland to Don McLean – even the Carpenters, which I think is just a little tacky. I don't know. But saying that, they played "Goodbye to Love," and I was in floods, which I never thought. . . .

My mother would like hymns, but I don't know any of the new ones they sing now, and I used to hate the old ones so much, even then. My father: all I remember is, he always used to cry, or come near as he ever came to it, at "If I Loved You," from *Carousel*. That's the one where the guy sings it after he's been killed in the knife-fight or whatever, when he comes back as a ghost, and it's for his wife, or maybe his little girl. I always used to watch it with him: I think it's the only time I ever saw him cry.

⚜

SCOTT & ROBERT

I brought you this.

What? Is that legal? My god, it looks like something you bought from a fifty-year old hippie over on Hashbury. . . .

It's made from Oriental mushrooms, this special preparation they sell in this health-food store in Chinatown. Everybody says they're the best thing you can get. They soak them in this like ginseng kind of cocktail, and then they dry them out naturally and grind them down to powder.

Sounds yummy – I guess I might as well get high on mushrooms as all this branded shit the doctors push. Okay, mushrooms, mix 'em up, dry 'em out, grind it all down – what then? What do you do with it? Smoke it, presumably?

Do with it, well, you make like a herbal tea, I guess, and drink it. Or maybe you could mix it in with juice –

Oh, you drink it? Are you sure? Only the way I feel today, it might do me more good if I poured it up the other end, you know.

Is that where it's hurting today?

Among others. It's the latest thing. Remind me never to use the expression "pain in the ass" metaphorically again. Is that it on the miracle cure front? Mushroom surprise? *Champignons à la keister?*

I'm just trying. . . .

Oh, sweetie, I know you're trying. Don't pay any attention to me – I just didn't get any sleep, that's all. Cranky-ass Robert, the billy-goat gruff. I'm sorry. C'mon.

It's just difficult . . . I never know what's for the best, you hear all kinds of stuff. There's this thing in the Advocate *about macrobiotic diets, and Bernie told me about this new drug they're testing, they say it might hold it up for years, maybe make it go into remission, even.*

Oh, drugs I got up the wazoo. I mean, literally, today. This intern came 'round – actually he was quite a dish, you know? Charlie Sheen sort of look, tough but vulnerable. Would you please take off your pajama bottoms, Mr Fullerton, while I try to find what the problem is? So I said, well, normally I like a little music at this stage of the relationship, some soft lighting, maybe a scented candle, something –

Oh, okay – sorry for intruding, how's about you get your intern to smuggle you in your Playgirls, *then?*

What, you bought me some new *Playgirls*? Well hallelujah, now you're talking. Ohh, a Special Bumper Buns issue . . . I think we might just have that miracle cure right in the bag here, Nurse. The congregation will join hands and say a novena to Our Lady of the Male Full Frontal, and we'll forget all about my stupid old keister for a while. Time enough for that later. Maybe.

ANTHONY

He had a lot of plans: all these things he planned to do once he'd finally made it to the coast. I read this diary the other night he used to keep back in Cincinnati, and he had like a timetable: by the age of twenty-five I'll be *this*, by twenty-eight I'll be *this*, thirty, thirty-one, thirty-two, thirty-three, so on and so on. Act in straight drama. Dance the lead part in a piece he'd written for himself. Find a lover. Put down payments on a house. All of that.

I knew he was fooling himself even before he got ill – basically, he just wasn't that talented, you know? Okay, he had more going for him than he had a right to have, coming from such a shitty upbringing and everything. And he was bright and witty and kind and fun to be with. But he didn't have it in him to actually do any of that stuff he wanted to. He told lies to buttress himself, all these really embarrassing oh-yeah-really stories, to me, to everyone. How he'd been with all these so-called straight movie stars incognito in the bathouse. How he'd been followed all the way home by this guy from some rock band. How he'd gotten an invite to one of the premier house parties on Fire Island for the summer from this *incredible* airline steward. How he'd met this *very famous* Broadway producer who really liked his work – just like the old stage-door musicals, where they discover Ruby Keeler dancing in the chorus line, you know?

He really did fool himself an awful lot, and he had me fooled, too, for the best part of the time we were together. Because I was so immature, and so un-sure of myself . . . and at least he sounded confident. At least he had a dream. He used to tell me all this shit, and I used to fall for it, I really did. It was only later that I'd be like, Adam, c'mon, get real here, and then it'd be arguments and walkouts and all that stuff. But I don't want to think about that now. It was bet-ter back when I still believed in him, and it was the two of us against the world, and there were all the things we were going to do, him and me. It was easy for him to be a star, when there were just the two of us: he could be a star, and me, I could have a star all to myself.

PATIENT ZERO

They say it's my fault, that I'm responsible somehow. But what else could I do? Really – what was I supposed to do? Montreal, Ottawa, Trois Rivières, Quebec; I couldn't stay in any of those places. Too uptight for me, too cold up there. So I came south, like the swallows, and I made myself into what I am today.

Now everybody knows me, and everybody who knows me, wants me. All over the country, all across the world, wherever I've been. Everybody knows my name. They watch me in the clubs and the bathhouses and they dream about me. They call out my name in their sleep at night.

DENNIS

In the bathhouse they have these cubicles. Like, they're where you go when you want to . . . okay. Obviously they have doors, you know, but if you want com-pany, you leave the door open so you can see outside, so people can see you. The feeling you get, walking past all these cubicles with, like, the hottest guys imaginable lying down inside with just a towel on – it's special, is all. It really is a special feeling. Even if nothing happens that night. Even if there are some creeps around, like there always are, the hungry ones, you know, the ones who no one goes with, the frustrated-looking ones who'll never get the door closed on anyone, know what I mean? Desperate.

Hey – you wanna know about frustration? I'll tell ya. I had this dream once, and I was in this bathhouse, enormous, great huge corridors, and I was walking down this line of open doors, and all the doors were closing one by one, just as I got level with them. So I started running, but the doors kept closing before I could see inside, and the corridor got longer and longer, and the lights kept getting dimmer and dimmer, and I couldn't even find the way out . . . whoa. It was *so* spooky, you know? Look at my arms here: goosebumps, just thinking about it. Real bringdown, really. I hope I never have another dream like that one.

⊹

BILL

So, for some of us it was non-stop Mardi Gras, heaven on the half-shell, and for others . . . well, for me, I found out a lot of things, and that was enough. Remember, I wasn't looking for storybook lovers the way some of them were, no fairytale endings and we all lived happily ever after. But what I wanted, I could get. Ancient Chinese curse, maybe.

Thinking back now . . . there was a place I found out about, down the coast past Half Moon Bay near where the Purisma comes to sea. It used to be a roadhouse back in the fifties or whenever, hadn't been open for business for a long time, and it was all boarded up, a little way back from the main road. Nobody went there anymore, but certain nights, if you drove down there, parked up in the dunes and climbed the wire fence, there was a scene . . . like lots of other places just a little way back from the main road, you know, in parks and under piers and in back rooms. Anywhere dark and quiet and anonymous. That's where it used to happen.

You got in by the window, where they'd pulled some of the boards back. Inside there was just moonlight, sometimes faint lights from the highway, and the red coals at the ends of cigarettes. There wasn't any furniture left to speak of, just a few mattresses on the floor, and in and out of the blue-black shadows came the men, maybe ten, maybe twelve, coming, going, dressing, undressing, drifting, coming together.

No one ever spoke, that was the thing that struck me, not once. They were just figures in the dark, and when you moved among them it was as if you were like them in every respect, no one, anyone. You didn't need to speak: it happened without the need for speech, firm and insistent, intuitive, the way I'd always dreamed about, the way it was meant to be. And oh, at the climax, when the stars fell in the dark, even then you could only sob out your breath in silence, so you felt it more than heard it, like a trembling, like a cooling on the skin.

This was in 1980, '81. I went back there the summer before last, after I knew for sure, before the lesions began to travel. I didn't know what to expect, or why I went, but I went anyway, earlier than I used to, in the evening while it was still light. There was spray graffiti all over the walls, a bunch of local kids parked out in their open-tops on the lot. Rock'n'roll music came back across the sand dunes, all vague and splashy and faraway, snatches at a time, swelling and ebbing with the sound of the waves, the Pacific ocean, blood-murmurous, blood-salty, blood-slow. The sun went down, and the kids revved their engines for minutes on end, shouting across the lot to one another till they finally drove away. I could hear their car horns fade like sirens off toward the highway, and then it was quiet again.

It took the light forever to go out of the sky, and not long afterwards the men came. I wasn't expecting it, not consciously, anyway. Slowly they turned up, singly, out of the dunes, very separate at first, not acknowledging one another, or me. They slipped through the gaps in the fence, vanished inside the road-house one after the other. I was out of the car by this time, pressed up against the chain-link fence, but I hung back, scared to go in, scared of leaving, scared of what I wanted most of all. Then in the dark a hand was on my shoulder, so soft and natural I hardly even felt it, I was hardly even startled. I turned around and there was a guy there, someone I thought I recognised from . . . oh, from back then. Back in the day. French-Canadian. Duggie they called him, but his real name was, Gaetan, yes, Gaetan Dugas, that was it. A steward with the air-lines. I'd heard he was one of the first, possibly even *the* first – they say he was the primary vector way back in the beginning, patient zero in the epidemiol-ogy chain. I'd heard he died, but there he was. It was him. Oh, I remembered him. He was so beautiful. . . . I looked at him, and he nodded in the direction of the roadhouse: come on. Didn't speak. For a second it was as if I could see through him, clear through to the dunes, and the luminescence of the surf away beyond. He was that insubstantial, that untouchable in all his flimsy beauty. Like a ghost, only how could I be scared?

I opened my shirt to show him the sarcoma, shaking my head no. It wasn't just the mark on my skin, it was as if I didn't really believe it was possible, that I could ever go back inside. "Doesn't matter," he said, very quiet, like a whisper, and I saw it in his eyes even before he took my hand, touched my fingertips to his own marks, his own stigmata, on the brow beside the hairline, in the angle of his jaw, in the beautiful delicate hollow where the neck's plane meets the shoul-derblade, showing me everything, taking all the shame away. "Come inside. It doesn't matter anymore." And I thought, no, it doesn't matter. Not anymore. And I followed him into the roadhouse, like it was the first time.

Now I wait here in the hospital, ward fourteen, sit out the nights remem-bering. Sometimes I see him, but then it isn't really him, it's just someone he's touched, some other lover. Men come and go, they wheel them into bed c, bay three, the bed I used to occupy, the bed where I died, and after a while they wheel them back out again, cold, not seeing, not hearing, not feeling. Where do they go, all of them? Why do they leave me here alone?

Maybe he'll come for me again, Gaetan, one last time. Maybe he'll take me away, and we'll go back to the roadhouse at Half Moon Bay. Everyone I've lost, all the numbers ever, they'll all be there, and we'll be together again, only this time it'll be forever.

WANT

RON OLIVER

Dennis shifted uncomfortably on the wooden bleacher seat, wishing he hadn't worn the stiff cotton boxer shorts his mother had laid out for him that morning. She always used too much starch when she ironed them, but no amount of his complaining seemed to change anything. His mother had her ways, and he had learned over his seventeen years to simply nod and go along with her. It was less painful that way, and Dennis certainly didn't want to cause anyone pain.

Well, almost anyone.

"Hi, Den," Lana chirped, as she delicately hopped the bleachers toward him in the way Dennis thought seventeen-year-old girls without a care in the world seemed to do with such ease in 1958. He hated being called "Den," especially by cheerleaders who wore so much gag-inducing perfume that it preceded them in a cloud. He forced himself to smile in reply.

"Hey, Lana. How's by you?"

She ignored his question and sat down beside him, adjusting her poodle skirt so the ridiculous looking dog applique straddled her leg in a way Dennis felt sure she meant to be deliberately obscene. She licked her lips, making her cherry red lipstick glisten in the harsh noonday sunlight, and ran a tanned hand across the back of her neck as she turned her attention toward the football field.

Down below, the Zephyr Hills High Zebras were having their regular noon-hour football practice, running through the grueling drills beneath a blazing sun. In spite of the woolen team uniforms and thick protective pads, the young athletes were undaunted by the heat, punctuating every tackle with the howls and yelps of their passion for the game. Dennis loved to watch them.

Alone.

"Hot, huh?" she murmured, flipping her dark ponytail with a snap of her wrist.

Of course it is, you stupid bitch, Dennis didn't say. *It's fucking noon on the fucking football field in the middle of fucking September in Florida.*

Instead, he nodded and took another bite out of his sandwich.

"You always eat lunch up here alone?" she asked, her tone almost accusatory.

Dennis considered ignoring the question as he pushed his thick horn rims back up onto the bridge of his slippery nose. In the oppressive heat, the supposedly "flesh toned" acne cream he had used that morning in a futile attempt to hide the half dozen fresh pustules that had erupted overnight made his face an oil slick.

"It's quiet," Dennis replied, gesturing at the empty bleachers around them. She didn't take the hint, looking back at the football team below.

"He's good, isn't he?" she said.

Dennis took another bite of his sandwich, the tuna fish sticking to the roof of his suddenly dry mouth, and didn't reply. He was hoping she wouldn't notice.

But she turned and looked at him. Waiting, Dennis realized with a cold, sinking feeling in his gut, for him to answer her. He forced himself to swallow and it felt like somebody had shoved a tennis ball down his throat.

"Who?" he asked, almost believing it himself.

She laughed at him. Once, sharp as a slap.

"You're funny," she said, and turned to look back to the field. Back to the young football players. Back to her boyfriend.

Cole.

⚜

"Hey, you got my towel."

Dennis remembered those words as if they were the lyrics to his favorite song. It was the first time Cole Trotter, captain of the football team and God of Senior Class, had ever actually spoken directly to him. It had made the hair on the back of his neck stand on end.

They were in the locker room after phys ed, the smell of wet teenaged boys, cheap pomade, and soap hanging in the steamy air. Dennis was sitting on the slick painted bench, trying to ignore the glistening male bodies around him as he modestly struggled to pull his damp underwear up beneath the towel wrapped tightly around his waist.

And Cole was completely, unabashedly, naked. Dripping wet, right there in front of him.

Dennis looked up and found Cole's solid, perfectly shaped cock at eye level. He whiplashed his gaze up, away from the dense patch of jet black pubic hair that trailed up Cole's slatted abdomen, past his muscular shelf of a chest, and found himself staring into the boy's emerald eyes.

"Oh," Dennis heard himself say. "Oh."

He was suddenly, uncomfortably, aware of a stirring in his crotch. He forced himself to think about his mother and it stopped as quickly as it had started.

"Yeah," Cole said, nodding at the damp towel around Dennis' waist. "That's mine."

Dennis smiled weakly.

"Sorry."

Cole shrugged and just stood there. Still naked. Still wet. Still perfect.

Did he know the dreams he inspired, Dennis wondered? Did he know he was the one the others wanted, or wanted to be? Did he know how slavishly they all copied the size of the cuff of his jeans, the style of his hair, even his loping, loose-limbed gait in order to feel closer to him?

Well. Maybe not all of them did that. But Dennis did.

Dennis suddenly realized he had to do something. Reaching into his neatly packed gym case, he pulled out a plush white bath towel, its edge folded sharply enough to cut butter.

"Take mine," he said, handing it over.

Cole shoved a thick hand through his damp black hair, looking at the towel with distrust.

"It's okay. You can keep it. My mother won't even notice," Dennis lied, all but cringing as the words left his mouth. His mother would have a shit fit, but it was worth it if it meant he could imagine Cole Trotter's naked body wrapped in a towel he himself had touched.

"Thanks," Cole muttered, unfolding the towel with a snap that made the vein in his taut bicep pulse. Dennis swallowed, hard, and watched Cole walk back across the locker room, drying himself with the towel.

Dennis masturbated six times that night, his final climax coming as the image of the twin white globes of Cole Trotter's muscular ass flexing in retreat pushed him over the edge.

⚶

"What do you mean, funny?" Dennis suddenly asked her.

Lana didn't turn away from the football field, her eyes following Cole's every move.

"Nothing, I guess. It's just that, well, you knew who I was talking about. He is my boyfriend, after all."

She turned at that moment, smiling, and the sun caught her braces. Dennis felt itchy and found himself pulling at his argyle sweater vest, the one his mother had given him for Christmas. He had hated it then and he hated it now.

"Everybody knows that," Dennis said, nodding.

Lana kept looking at him, still smiling, her braces gleaming. Dennis suddenly realized she wasn't blinking and he felt the tuna fish backing up in his throat.

"Do they?" she finally said.

She returned her gaze to the football field as she stood up, her absurd skirt rustling around her, and walked away.

She knows, he thought. *She knows what I am. She knows about the* Physique Pictorial *magazines I have hidden in my room between the box spring and the mattress. She knows about Mr Nelson the Scout Troop leader, and Frank, the guy who painted our garage last year, and my cousin Eddie from Bowling Green, who spent the whole summer with us when I was thirteen and when he left I made mother angry because I cried for two days.*

Dennis couldn't eat any more. He wrapped the rest of the sandwich in its waxed paper shroud and jammed it into his black lunch pail, crushing the miserly triangle of his mother's rubbery lemon meringue pie resting on the bottom.

He is my boyfriend, after all.

Dennis smirked. *My* boyfriend. Like being in love with somebody meant you owned him. It was a simplistic, childish notion, he thought, just the sort of thing that filled the blonde heads of simplistic, childish cheerleaders in Florida.

My boyfriend.

Okay, Dennis thought, closing his lunch pail after checking to make sure his gift for Cole was still safe inside. He's your boyfriend.

For now.

⚜

By his own reckoning, Dennis had been plotting his mother's death for at least ten years. In fact, the only reason she was still around at all was that he'd been unable to come up with an acceptable method.

He'd imagined her demise in various ways, but each had its drawbacks.

Drowning was out. Betty hated the ocean, which was why she wouldn't even hear of moving their coral-colored, doublewide mobile home away from the stifling humidity of Zephyr Hills and closer to the beach. She said she couldn't trust water of any kind, and only bathed when she was overwhelmed by the stench of her own obese body.

A car crash would've worked nicely had the woman ever bothered to apply for a driver's licence. But to Dennis' everlasting shame she was quite content to ride the bus back and forth to her job at Mr Earl's Hair-Porium every single day except Sunday when she, like her close personal friend and savior Jesus Christ the Lord Almighty, slept until noon.

Dennis had finally settled on fire and to that end had been working on a fool-proof arson plot for quite some time until he realized he'd have to sacrifice his entire model car collection to the cause; he'd be giving himself away if he'd just "coincidentally" taken them out for cleaning shortly before the flames had consumed his mother.

No, there had to be another way. Something clean, simple, and completely, utterly, accidental.

Which was how Dennis had found himself inside Miss Natalie's Natural House of Cures and Magic, Miss Natalie, Proprietor.

Normally, of course, he wouldn't have gone into that part of town. Not that Dennis had anything against colored people; he'd once enjoyed a vigorous twenty-five minutes in the toilet stall with a young black theatre usher named Delbert over at the Webb City Vista. But you just never knew, he reasoned. After all, he'd heard some of the Negroes in the neighborhood still practiced voodoo.

Still, the ad in the paper clearly said "Sleeping Potions Made To Order." And the shop was out of the way, far enough from his home that nobody would recognize him later, when the police started to ask the inevitable questions. But the moment the torn screen door slammed behind him, Dennis had felt he'd made a mistake. He had turned to leave when a voice suddenly squeaked from somewhere beneath a dusty, glass-topped showcase.

"You want?"

Dennis' eyes hadn't yet adjusted from the piercing sunlight to the darkness in the shop, and he squinted through his glasses.

"Uh . . . yes. Yes. I want . . ." he started, but stopped abruptly as Miss Natalie lifted herself up into view.

It wasn't her skeletal frame that silenced him, despite being draped in a garishly bright muumuu that played hide and seek with her razor sharp, ebony shoulders. It wasn't her shock of white hair clamped tightly against her head with two glistening scarlet barrettes, nor the eerie azure eyes that stared at Dennis from deep within her coarsely lined black face. And it wasn't even the incongruously large teeth slipping back and forth inside her wide mouth, as perfectly white as they were perfectly false.

It was her left arm. Or what remained of it.

Little more than a stump torn away at the elbow, the ragged limb dangled from her sleeveless dress, occasionally moving as if it had a life of its own.

Dennis realized he was staring, but before he could look away she rubbed at it with her good right hand and nodded at him.

"My boyfriend," she said, and suddenly gave him a dazzling smile. Dennis found himself wondering if she was referring to how she had lost her arm or, even more grotesquely, if she was talking about the arm itself. "Bad boyfriend," she said, shaking her head. "Now, you want?"

Dennis had been about to ask for the sleeping potion from the newspaper ad, ready to tell the old woman it was for himself, he was having a hard time getting to sleep you see, and certainly not mentioning anything about his plan to drug his mother, shove her down the concrete steps of the cellar where she was sure to at least break her neck, and then pretend to return home without his key and call on Mrs Clarey next door to use her duplicate to let him in, only to find Betty's twisted corpse in a pile next to the burlap sack of potatoes she kept in the basement, where she'd fallen in what was obviously a complete, utter, accident.

But before any of this, before he said even a single word, he saw something else. Something he needed more than a sleeping potion. Something he felt sure he needed more than anything else in the world.

He pointed at the tiny glass bottle on the third shelf, and found himself quivering as he spoke, as if ice water had been poured down the back of his stiffly starched plaid shirt.

"I want," he said, and as Miss Nathalie's eyes followed the direction of his hand, her porcelain smile disappeared.

⚓

"What's this?"

Cole squinted at the paper bag held out toward him like it was a rat. He was wearing dark blue jeans, cuffs turned up, and a T-shirt stretched so tightly across his chest that Dennis could actually make out the wiry tufts of hair around each nipple.

"A gift," Dennis said with as much nonchalance as he could muster. "For you."

Cole looked around the school parking lot almost nervously, Dennis thought, as if the idea of accepting a gift from the Senior Class Treasurer was a crime or something. If it had been anybody else, Dennis would have been insulted.

But it was Cole Trotter.

"For me? What's the catch?"

"No catch," Dennis lied. "I just . . . I felt kinda bad, you know, about the other day."

Cole looked at him dully, the thick pomade glistening in his hair.

"What other day?"

Dennis grinned, lowering his voice as if they had a secret to share.

"You know. Your towel?"

A full second passed before Cole nodded, remembering.

"Oh. Yeah. Right."

A car horn honked from across the lot. Cole's football buddies had piled into his Corvair and were hollering for him impatiently.

"Trotter! Let's go, daddyo!"

Cole started to move toward his car, and for one horrible moment Dennis felt sure he had failed.

"Well, it's okay," Cole mumbled, retreating. "You know, don't worry about it —"

He started to turn away, shoving his fists into the front pockets of his jeans, and Dennis felt the words leap out of his throat-

"It's booze!"

Cole stopped in his tracks. He turned back and looked at Dennis again, cocking his head slightly as if he wasn't sure what he'd just heard.

"Vodka," Dennis said, holding the bag up again. "Good stuff too. Mother buys it by the case. I thought maybe you'd like it, you know, to celebrate. After you win today."

Cole's lip turned up in a smirk as he walked back toward Dennis.

"Who says we're gonna win?"

Dennis grinned, and hated himself for the way he looked, the way he sounded, the way he dressed, the way he drew air into his lungs.

"You'll win. I know you will."

Cole shrugged and took the bag, not noticing the damp imprint of Dennis' hand staining the crumpled mouth.

"Okay, well. Thanks, I guess."

The Corvair's horn was blaring now, and Cole headed off toward it.

"Alright, alright!" he yelled, breaking into a loping run. He didn't look back, but Dennis didn't care. All he really cared about was that Cole wouldn't examine the vodka bottle too carefully, wouldn't check the seal around the cap too closely.

And that he wouldn't notice Dennis' handiwork if he did.

"See you around, Cole," Dennis said, almost to himself.

Laying in bed later that night, taut sheets crackling beneath the paisley flannel pajamas his mother insisted he wear, Dennis laughed into the darkness. He was remembering Miss Nathalie's face when she had understood what he wanted to buy.

"Too powerful. Too strong maybe, even for young man," she'd whispered, shaking her head.

"Yeah, but does it work?" he'd said, and it had sounded like a threat.

"Forever," Miss Nathalie had nodded, rubbing at her stump again. "Your whole life. Maybe more. But you, young man, too young. Too much for you."

Dennis had reached into his pocket and pulled out his hand-stitched leather wallet, the one he'd made at summer camp, the one onto which he had burned his name in large, awkward letters. He had flipped it open and had showed her the contents.

Fifty Andrew Jacksons, lined up neatly inside.

If Miss Nathalie had ever even seen a thousand dollars all at once before, she certainly did a good job of hiding it. Her lip had twitched as if she'd bitten into something rotten, but her eyes had stayed on the money.

She hadn't even questioned what a seventeen-year-old was doing with that kind of cash in his wallet, Dennis thought. And he certainly didn't tell her about his visit to Mr Nelson, his old Boy Scout leader, nor the threat that had made the man involuntarily piss himself, the dark, wet stain spreading unheeded at the crotch of his Sansabelts as Dennis reminded him what the police did to men who touched little boys.

"How much?" he'd said to her, riffling his thumb across the crisp bills and letting the musk of treasury ink drift up out of his wallet. "How much do you want for the love potion?"

"All," she'd croaked, her voice suddenly rasping. "All of it."

Dennis had smiled then, just as he was smiling at the memory, and nodded agreement.

"Throw in a bottle of sleeping powder and you've got a deal."

⚜

"Dennis!" his mother barked, her knock on the bathroom door amplified by the grape-sized fake emerald she wore on her wedding ring finger. She'd never married his father, didn't even remember exactly what his name was, but she told people he had simply "run off with some no good piece of business from Tampa." Dennis had never even been to Tampa.

"Dennis, what the *h* are you doing in there?"

He bent himself over almost double on the closed toilet seat lid to add to the effect.

"I don't feel good, Mother. I think something I ate —" he answered, cutting the sentence off with a gagging, retching sound. "I'm sick."

He could almost imagine Betty's face on the other side, grimacing at the idea of bodily fluids of any sort. She wouldn't even try to open the door, but Dennis had still taken the precaution of locking it and jamming the quilted laundry hamper under the knob just to be safe.

"Well, do it in the toilet, for heaven's sake! I just shampooed that rug!"

He listened as her rhinestone sandals clattered down the tiled hallway of their shitty mobile home in their shitty mobile home park, and returned his attention to the carefully opened mickey of vodka in front of him.

To his relief the love potion had vanished almost as soon as he'd poured it in, but now he had another problem on his hands. According to the tiny parchment instruction card, he was to add some of his own "*essence*" to the love potion: saliva, sweat or, for an even stronger response, blood.

Dennis looked at the bottle dubiously. He felt certain that he was going to have to use more than just his essence; Cole was, after all, not even a homosexual. No, Dennis was definitely going to have to use something stronger than spit.

He looked at himself in the mirror and tried to ignore how pasty his naked body looked in the ugly yellow fluorescent light. A voice suddenly echoed through his head.

If only it didn't have to be this way, it said. *If only we lived in a world where homophiles weren't freaks, where what we felt wasn't so horribly, horribly wrong. Where a boy didn't have to jerk off into a vodka bottle just to make out with the captain of the high school football team.*

Yeah, well I don't, Dennis thought, shutting the voice up as his hand lowered toward his crotch and he began to imagine what Cole would be doing later.

The big game would finish and the Zephyr Zebras would win; they were first in their division, with a clear shot at the State Finals. The boys would celebrate, of course, after a long, hot shower. Soaked with sweat, Cole would strip off his football jersey and pants, unfasten the belts holding his pads in place, and stretch as he stood there naked except for his bulging jock strap, dark and wet. Slowly he would peel it off, his firm cock and heavy balls swinging, and maybe, just maybe he would raise the cotton jock to his face and breath deeply, the aroma of his own musk causing his cock to begin to swell –

"Dennis!!" Betty shrieked outside the door. "Dennis, *now* what are you doing in there?"

Shut up shut up shut up, he thought, *as Cole let the hot spray course over his taut muscles, splashing down his bulging pectorals, cascading off his firm, round ass –*

"You can't still be sick?" his mother bellowed. "You know I have Yahtzee tonight –"

Jesus Christ mother, shut up, can't you see Cole's dressed in his tight black jeans, no starched boxer shorts for him, in fact no underwear at all, it just gets in the way of packing his cock firmly to the left and he's leaning back in his car and staring at the bottle of vodka I gave him and thinking of me –

"*That Dennis,*" Dennis imagined Cole saying. "*What a cool cat. The coolest. Man, I'd do anything to make him happy –*"

– and he's lifting the vodka to his mouth and wrapping his luscious red lips around –

"Oh god, oh god, oh god!" Dennis blurted out, loud enough to be heard in the hallway, as he grabbed the open vodka bottle and took aim.

"What did you say?" Betty demanded. "What did you just say? Young man, are you taking the Lord's name in vain in the toilet?"

"*Fuck!*" he shouted because it was all he could think of to say.

Who is Dennis?

That was the first thing Dennis thought as he woke, disoriented, in his taut bed. But of course it was him, wasn't it? He was staring at his wallet, propped in a pool of moonlight on his bedside table, the jagged letters burned onto its worn surface like an epitaph.

DENNIS

A thought crossed his mind and he picked it up and flipped it open, shocked for a moment to see it empty. It hadn't been a dream, he realized, remembering the visit to Mr Nelson and his trip to Miss Nathalie's and the screaming match with his mother that had ended with him storming into his room and locking the door.

He'd never uttered a profanity in her presence before, of course, and it had shocked and upset them both. But it hadn't kept him awake that night. In fact, he'd slept without dreams, for the first time in as long as he could remember.

So why, he wondered, was he sitting upright in his bed, as alert as if it was noon?

Skrittch skrittchhh skriiiitch. . . .

Dennis looked across his room, toward the faded orange curtains hanging at the window. Probably just a branch, he thought, or a bird?

"*Dennis. . . .*"

A soft voice from somewhere outside. Barely a whisper, but definitely not a bird.

Dennis wrapped himself in the same ugly red plaid housecoat he'd worn since junior high and moved to the window. And as he pulled the curtains back and looked out of his ground floor window, he saw that Miss Nathalie's love potion had been well worth the thousand dollars.

Because there was definitely someone standing in his backyard.

He couldn't make out the face, a dark silhouette pierced by gleaming eyes set deep within shadowed sockets. But the firm, naked body, shining wetly in the moonlight, could only belong to one person.

"*Dennis,*" Cole Trotter said again. "*I want you. . . .*"

Dennis stood at his window, frozen in shock. Although he'd secretly dreamed of a moment like this since he'd first met Cole on the playground when they had both been kids, this was different: this was real. He wasn't sure what to say, what to do, or exactly why Cole was naked. But Dennis had never been the kind of boy who worried about the small details.

He pulled the window open and felt his nipples harden in the cold night air.

"Cole . . ." he said. "Cole."

All those football drills had paid off. Cole ran across the grass and, in one graceful leap, he vaulted into Dennis' bedroom with ease.

In the dim street light filtering through the curtains, Dennis could barely make out Cole's body, still glistening slick with sweat. *He must have come straight from the game,* Dennis thought with excitement, as Cole's coppery smell filled the room. *He couldn't wait to get here!*

"Did you win?"

"Want you," was all Cole said as he lunged through the darkness at Dennis, tearing the red flannel robe away from his body. Suddenly embarrassed to be naked in front of the other boy, he instinctively covered himself, but Cole pulled his hand away, grabbing at Dennis' cock.

"*Want you . . .*" he murmured, jerking roughly on Dennis' thickening shaft.

"Okay, sure, it's just that we have to be quiet or my mother will —"

Cole shoved him down onto the bed and straddled him, pinning his arms back beside his head. Dennis started to protest, but found himself hypnotized by Cole's piss slit as it opened and shut with each throb of his huge, rock hard dick. Dennis had never seen him erect before and it was breathtaking.

"*Want you . . .*" Cole murmured as his head lowered toward Dennis' nipples. Dennis closed his eyes and tried not to come.

Ringggg. Ringggg.

No.

OLIVER + WANT

185

Ringgggg. Ringggg.

Dennis tried to ignore the phone, focusing on what Cole was doing with his tongue, but then remembered his mother. She was in the next room, asleep he hoped, but one more ring and she'd come barging in, demanding to know who was calling him so late at night, and how dare they don't they know what time it is – ?

Ringgggg. Ringggg.

Dennis snatched the phone from the cradle.

"Hello?"

"I hope you're happy," the female voice accused. She sounded as if she'd been crying.

"Lana? Is that you?" He looked down for a reaction from Cole, but saw only the top of the quarterback's head disappearing under the covers, heading south.

"It's your fault! It's all your fault, you asshole!!"

Dennis gritted his teeth as he felt Cole chewing on the soft muscle above his pubic bone.

"What? What are you talking about?"

"You did this! It was you," she screamed, her voice distorted through the telephone earpiece. "Miss Cooper saw you giving him the bottle after school!"

Cole was using his teeth along the top of Dennis' stiff cock shaft, and it wasn't entirely pleasant –

"Bottle? What bottle – ow!" He jerked, as Cole bit down, a little too hard. "Hey, take it easy," he grunted, unsure if he was talking to Cole or Lana.

"Take it easy? Take it easy?! You sonovabitch, how am I supposed to take it easy?!!! My boyfriend is –"

Zzzztcccchhhh.

Dennis wasn't sure what she'd said; her voice had been so loud it made the telephone crackle.

"What? What did you just say? He's what?"

Suddenly, Dennis felt a sharp pain in his gut, as Cole jerked hard on his cock.

"Fuck! Jesus, man, not so rough –"

Something warm and wet sprayed across his thigh, and Dennis felt a twinge of disappointment. Five minutes and the great Cole Trotter was already shooting his load?

"I said, there was an accident," Lana continued, and Dennis could tell she was forcing herself to stay calm. "He and the guys on the way back from the game. Cole had the vodka you gave him and they were all drinking and they must have had the radio going or something and they didn't even hear the train –"

Dennis' groin was really hurting now, as if Cole had pulled hard enough to give him a hernia. But he still heard what she had said.

"Train?"

"Dead, you fucking piece of nerd shit!" she screamed.

He dropped the phone, but he could still hear her talking.

"He's fucking dead!" she shrieked over the phone.

Dennis scrambled away from Cole, slipping on the sweat-soaked sheets as he grabbed for the Lone Ranger lamp that had sat next to his bed since childhood. Lana's voice still crackled over the phone.

"They're all fucking dead!"

Dennis turned on the light and saw what was left of Cole.

Empty eye sockets. Shattered face. Chest cavity torn open like a window display of the organs dangling within. Cole's heart hung limply in a nest of rubbery aorta and veins: whatever had brought the thing that was once the Zephyr Hills High quarterback back to life, it certainly wasn't there.

And then Dennis saw the gore dripping from the boy's soundlessly churning mouth, the blood trickling down his chin, the tendons turning to gristle between his teeth – and the horribly familiar shape of a severed penis dangling from Cole's mouth.

Dennis looked down at himself and felt the scream rise up in his throat like vomit.

A scarlet sea of blood covered the sheets, his legs, his torso – and the gaping canyon at his crotch.

"No!"

He suddenly thought of Miss Nathalie and her horribly tattered arm.

Bad boyfriend.

"Aw, god no! God no!"

Dennis grabbed a pillow and pushed it against his bleeding groin –

First Aid. Lesson one. Apply pressure.

He tumbled from the slick, bloodied sheets and landed hard on the floor. Cole lurched toward him, his bloodied mouth grinding with a sickening, smacking sound.

"*Want you.*"

Dennis staggered to his feet, the torn, pulsing root of his cock turning the pillow a deep scarlet, and made his way to the bedroom door.

"*Want you.*" Cole gurgled, staggering toward him. The morgue tag tied to the big toe on his left foot made an incongruously gentle "skiffing" sound as he approached. "*Want. . . .*"

Dennis slammed his bedroom door and stumbled across the narrow corridor of the trailer toward his mother's room.

"*Mother!! Oh god, Mother help me!! Help me!!*"

He forced her door open and then remembered the sleeping powder, the one he had slipped into her traditional night time daiquiri. Her shallow breathing hissed in the dark room and Dennis knew he wasn't getting any help from his mother. As usual.

He felt warm breath on his neck.

"Want you —"

Cole was behind him, ghoulish hands reaching out to graze his naked shoulder. Dennis jerked his elbow back, knocking Cole against the wall, and the sudden move sent a bolt of molten fire through his guts. He pushed past the shambling corpse of the quarterback and lurched out of the room.

Stumbling down the hallway, he felt the stabbing pain in his crotch subside as tiny darts of light shot around his eyes, and he suddenly felt very, very tired. He was losing blood fast, and he knew he was going to die.

If he could just get to a hospital, he thought. They could sew him up, yes, of course they could. They could sew him up and maybe make him a new penis out of his big toe, a transplant or something. They did all kinds of things like that nowadays.

He pushed the screen door open even though it felt like it weighed six hundred pounds. But he didn't get any further than the back steps before he stopped, staring in horror at the sight that greeted him in the driveway.

The whole defensive line of the Zephyr Hills Zebras was waiting for him.

Once beautiful naked bodies, now torn and shattered. Cream and sugar faces ripped into halves, limbs hanging limply from shredded tendons, morgue tags dangling from their toes.

But their penises stood at sharp, throbbing attention, varying shapes and sizes straining from the dark gardens of their pubic hair and glistening with wet pearls of desire.

"Want you," they all said. *"Dennnisss. . . . We want you."*

And with the same speed and grace Dennis had seen them display so many times on the football field, they fell upon him and began to satisfy their lust.

Miss Nathalie poured herself another cup of tea, sat down in her favorite chair, the one she'd brought with her from Martinique, and began counting her money again.

One thousand dollars. It seemed like a lot, but she knew it wasn't really enough. Would there ever be enough to bring back her Delbert?

She glanced at his photo on the wall, her favorite one, from when he was chosen employee of the month at the Webb City Vista. He had been so proud of that job, proud of his uniform and, for the first time since his daddy had died, proud of himself.

It had almost broken Miss Nathalie's heart to see her boy come home so upset that day.

He'd told her the whole terrible truth, how he'd fallen a victim to the Devil's temptations in that filthy toilet stall, engaging in unnatural pleasures of the flesh with that white boy, and she knew for certain it had obviously been Satan's agent in human form.

Even his name had sounded Satanic. Dennis.

Miss Nathalie wasn't exactly sure what that name meant, but she knew it had to be something evil. Just the way it had looked burned onto that hand-stitched leather wallet, the one Delbert had told her about, the one the boy had taken a ten dollar bill from and tried to pay her son as if he was some kind of whore of Babylon; that was enough for her.

But Delbert's sins had been forgiven, Miss Nathalie was sure of that. When she'd come home early the next day and found him in the garage, hanging from the cross beams, his tongue black, his eyes glassy, she had cried for quite a few days, to be sure.

But she knew there would come a day of reckoning. There would come a time when that evil boy, that tempter of unnatural pleasures, would meet his very own angel of retribution.

And Miss Nathalie had been more than happy to wear the wings on that particular deal, that was for sure.

She chuckled a bit to herself, considering what exactly the love potion would have done by now. Although she didn't have a crystal ball, hadn't used one since she'd worked the State Fair circuit back in '44, she felt certain that the love potion would have done the Lord's work by now, and probably not for the better.

She wondered if Dennis had had enough love yet?

She rubbed her stump, remembering the first time she'd used the love potion for herself.

He'd been a nice boy at school, but the potion had made him nasty, not the kind of fellow she was interested in at all. But no matter how she tried to dissuade him, the boy had returned again and again, unable to get enough of her until she had stabbed him with her nail file, again and again, and then he was dead.

But that still hadn't stopped him. He had returned the next night, wanting her again, until he had finally simply tried to devour her. He'd chewed off her hand and most of her arm before her own beloved daddy had come in with a shotgun and blasted his head off.

"You've had enough love for one lifetime, Nathalie," was all her daddy had said as he dragged her thwarted paramour's body out of the house. "Enough."

She wondered if Dennis had had enough love yet.

By the time Cole made it out of the trailer, the rest of his teammates had reduced Dennis to a few ropes of intestine and a wet, gray spot of brain matter on the grass.

Cole picked up a piece of Dennis and chewed it absently as he followed the others out of the trailer park, looking for somebody else to love.

OH YES, MY EYES

DAVID QUINN

Don't make me crave the cutting a moment longer. Razor me. A little blood, and you can live with the awareness, keen as your caressing tool, that I'm addicted to you. To your engraving.

Finger the red latticework down my back. My scab tattoo rises to meet your friction, dry and cat's tongue rough. Draw my flesh taut, feed it your keen edge. Blood streams, washes the wounding, transforming me.

You never slash. You never gouge. You cut, I heal, we repeat.

The lip of the line you traced down my spine is raw and ragged. But a pearl of a scar is waiting to grow there, bright and hard, a permanent reminder of the frayed pleasure in pain. To not provide skin to your razor's trace would be to give up on living.

The cutting gets me hot. I'm a man when you're in my veins. But the healing – healing, I am a god on fire. So don't make me wait – don't take your touch away.

Before last night's art is fully healed, I beg you to open me again.

The razor. Now.

Your blade fills me. I succumb to inward, tactile drift, floating on claret, as you etch fine, new filigree into the scar tissue lining the inside of my thighs.

Your metal closes all the world but your cutting edge. You seal me. Free-fall, lost in feeling, I tap a primal vein. Nothing has, nor needs, a name. Your kind cutting edge silences conversation. Born in a rush of blood, I enter red and disappear, hearing only the score and scratch of my mesh of wounds. A tattoo of bloodletting, with no other identity, that's all that remains – all older desires dim compared to the etching blade.

What did identity ever bring but the dullest kind of ache, anyway? Before the ecstasy of your razor I wandered cozy in a coma. You stirred me from that gray scrawling when I bit through my own tongue on our first night.

You woke me up, sunshine.

So-called medical professionals called me "self-destructive." Uncivilized hacks. I wouldn't wish the numb monotony of their calculated attentions on a baby-raping ethnic cleanser.

Doctors get all the best toys . . . but do fuck all with them.

I mean, understand the pleasure one might push. Imagine adrenal stimulation to the mesocortex, while razoring, rushing chemical pleasure in pain, in synch with the keen blade.

Skin grafts.

Bone manipulation.

Living autopsy.

But fuck that —

Anticipating your engraving is a far, far better high than stimulants, sutures, and bonesaws, so trace the scabs that etch your name along the shaft of my cock, rust-red from repetition, come on, cut me, till roiling liquid fire stirs inside, so ready to let go I convulse high geysering and my full-body blood tattoo tangos ancient dances as my heavy lids lift to reveal virgin territory, the last unscarred flesh, no, don't make me crave the cutting a moment longer razor me a little blood and you can live with the awareness keen as your caressing tool that I'm addicted to you to your engraving crave covet yearn and tonight I want you eyes wide open to razor fine-lined calligraphy on the wide white canvas of, oh yes, my eyes, my eyes.

ONE OF THE BOYS

EDO VAN BELKOM

I'd been able to pass on, or at least graciously bow out of attending the last three conventions.

After all, I had no interest in spending three days in a hotel with a bunch of middle-aged men whose idea of a good time was a weekend away from their wives, getting drunk to Bobby Darin songs, and pulling the tassels off of every stripper on the block.

That just wasn't my scene.

But the boys are a persistent lot, had to be in their line of work, and this time they wouldn't take no for an answer.

They began by asking me when a good time of year would be, then hounded me until I gave them an answer. In the end I told them some time around April, knowing full well that all of the major insurance industry events were held either in the middle of the summer, or the dead of winter. But damned if Rickards didn't find a convention for insurance adjusters being held in Las Vegas the first weekend in May.

"You're already registered," Rickards told me. "We've all got rooms on the same floor of the Landmark, two of them suites connected by doorways. . . . Best of all, Billy says he knows a few girls in town." Rickards, a shortish sort of man with a crew cut and a taste for checkered jackets, winked and jabbed a bony elbow into my stomach. "If you know what I mean."

Oh, I knew exactly what Rickards meant. If the women were acquaintances of Billy Macklin, then they were likely five-dollar whores who would hang off a man's arm all night for a sawbuck, some gin, and a warm bed to sleep in.

I forced a laugh for Rickards' benefit. "Sure, I know what you mean. Sounds great."

"You bet it does," Rickards said. "We've got a couple of wild nights planned for you, palsy, hotter than our usual."

"Can't wait!" I said, flashing the smile I'd perfected over the years, the one I used whenever clients, people in the office, or any of my mother's friends asked when I was going to get married.

"When I find the right girl," I'd say, flashing that smile and putting everyone off for another day.

The truth was I'd never find the right girl. Hell, I wasn't even looking for her. And as far as this little convention was concerned, I really couldn't wait . . . for it to be over.

But it was inevitable, I suppose.

I'd been playing the part of "one of the boys" for six years now, even going so far as to bring a friend of my sister's to the annual "Salesman of the Year" banquet just to keep the gossip mongers on their toes.

Still, people were beginning to talk. Even more so than usual. And I didn't blame them, really. In 1965 Cleveland, Ohio, what was someone to think about a twenty-nine-year-old former college tennis player, who was single, owned his own house, and was rarely been seen in the company of women?

Probably that he was a little strange, a communist, or queer – and not necessarily in that order.

So no matter how much of a nightmare going to a convention with the boys and making whooping noises at the striptease artists was going to be, it was still a small price to pay to keep my secret safe.

After all, what was the worst that could happen?

That I'd have to touch a boobie and pretend that I liked it? I'd been pretending about such things all my life and, even if I did say so myself, I'd gotten pretty darned good at it.

"And when we get back," Rickards said, slapping me on the shoulder, "you're going to be beggin' us to take you along on the next one."

I doubted that, doubted that very much, but I said, "Hey, you guys better watch out, I just might show you a thing or two myself."

Rickards' eyebrows rose up and his mouth became a twisted mask of shocked surprise, as if Uncle Miltie had come out on stage wearing a dress for the very first time. "Whoa, baby! This is going to be one weekend to remember."

How right he was.

⚜

I arrived early on the Friday afternoon, and after checking into my hotel room, I went down to the pool to have a swim and exercise. There was another man there, passing the time on a stationary bike.

We talked for a while.

His name was Ronnie, he was from Phoenix and worked in sales too. Plumbing supplies. He'd come to Las Vegas for the weekend, just to spend some time. If it were any other weekend I might have asked him out for dinner, or perhaps even up to my room, but on this weekend it was out of the question.

I did take his business card, though, in case I ever find myself in Arizona.

You never know.

I was in the steam bath when Rickards finally caught up to me. "Hey, there you are, palsy!" he said through the open door.

"Hello Benjamin," I answered.

"There's registration in the room next to the bar at six, a seminar at eight, and at nine. . . ." He paused, a gleeful smile on his face.

"What happens at nine?" I asked, only because I knew he wanted me to.
"Can't tell."

I showed him my biggest and best boyish grin. "Nothing illegal, I hope."

"Not in this state," he said.

And with that he closed the door.

I stayed in the steam bath a few more minutes, wondering what these jokers had in mind. There were plenty of things that were legal in Nevada that weren't everywhere else in the country. My immediate thought was gambling. A game of craps in somebody's hotel room perhaps, or an all-night poker game with fairly high stakes. Well, I was up for that. In fact, I wouldn't at all mind taking some money from the boys.

Maybe it might convince them to leave me home next time around.

The seminar was all about processing claims quickly.

You might think that processing a claim in a timely manner would simply be a hallmark of good service, but the real reason is because the more time that passes after a fire, or home break-in, the more time people have to discover what's been destroyed or stolen. Even in personal injury cases, the statistics show that the longer a claim goes unsettled, the bigger the eventual payout.

"So pay up, and get out!" the man conducting the seminar concluded. "Today's dime is tomorrow's dollar!"

There was a polite round of applause for the man whose bit of jingoistic advice would probably save companies millions, and then the room quickly cleared as people headed for the bar, the casino, or in our case, our rooms.

I dragged my feet across the lobby carpet as I headed for the elevators – I was in no hurry to go anywhere. My next stop would be a few hours with the boys in which I would drink large amounts of alcohol and make crude remarks about various women in the office. But while the boys would be talking about their boobs and legs, I'd be more interested in discussing their fashion sense and choice of perfumes.

I took a good long look at the front door of the hotel. It was less than fifteen paces away. It would have been so easy for me to slip out the door, hail a cab, and find some crowded bar in which to be alone. It was tempting, but it would be no escape. I'd eventually have to return and then the boys would insist I make up for lost time.

"There you are, palsy," Rickards said, coming up behind me.

"Where have you been?" I said, jabbing him in the arm.

"Gettin' everything ready."

I glanced at Rickards' face and didn't like the look on it. His nose was scrunched up like he'd been up to no good, and he was all giddy, like a teenager who had just learned the combination of his father's liquor cabinet. The boys had been on plenty of these trips before, but there was something in Rickards' expression that said this one was going to be something different.

"And is everything ready?" I asked.

"Oh, man . . . more than ready," he said. "It's all ready to pop."

"Mind if I go to my room and freshen up first?"

"No way, palsy," he said, grabbing firm hold of my arm. "I've got instructions to escort you up to the room personally. We're not letting you get away."

"What did I do to merit the royal treatment?"

"Nothing." He pushed the button for the elevator. "It's just that since you don't usually come with us to these things, we thought it might be nice to let you go first . . . you know, to show you how much your being here means to us."

I was flattered, even though I wasn't sure why. "Thanks," I said.

We rode the elevator up to the eighth floor and turned left after stepping into the hallway.

"We got the suite at the end."

"Nice."

"You ain't seen the half of it."

As we neared the end of the hall, I could hear a jumble of voices coming from one of the rooms.

When we reached the door to the suite, Rickards knocked on it in some complicated pattern, as if he were trying to gain admission to the neighborhood treehouse. The voices on the other side quieted down, and there was a knock on the door from inside. Finally, Rickards answered with one more hard knock.

And then, as if by magic, the door opened.

The sound of voices instantly got louder, but now mixed in with the others was a different-sounding voice.

A woman's voice.

I followed Rickards through a left and right turn, and then I was in the room.

I didn't want to act so surprised, but I couldn't help it. I stopped dead in my tracks, and felt the blood drain away from my face.

The rest of the boys were in the room.

And they were all naked.

Each of them was sitting comfortably in a chair, or on the couch set against the right wall. They were drinking beer and hard liquor and smoking cigars.

And most of them were sporting erections.

That's because in the middle of the room was a middle-aged woman with a decent figure, dressed in nothing but a black bra, panties, garter belt, and stockings. She was dancing slowly to a Bobby Darin song, moving her hips as if she were having sex, and smiling at each one of the boys as she faced them.

"Okay, he's here," someone said. "Now we can get started."

"Started?" I said.

Rickards slapped me on the back. "She's all yours, palsy," he said. "Take your time, but hurry up . . . if you know what I mean."

I felt the need to vomit.

I could feel the sweat starting to soak through my shirt. In minutes it would be running down my face like I'd just run a marathon.

"Hot damn," I said, weakly. "You boys sure know how to paint the town red."

The woman smiled at me then. She had probably been a working girl for most of her adult life, and looked worn out and tired, but there was still something sweet and matronly about her face. And if things weren't already bad enough, she somehow reminded me a bit of my mother.

"Go on!" said Rickards. "She's waiting for you. Hell . . . we're all waiting for you."

I had hoped that this was all some sort of gag. An adults-only version of *Candid Camera* that you could order from the back of magazines, but that didn't seem to be the case. The boys had hired a hooker for the night, all night, and they wanted me to get the ball rolling. And from what I understood, they not only wanted me to have sex with this woman, but they wanted me to have sex with her in this room while the rest of them watched.

My dinner was creeping up my throat again.

I needed to get out of there, even if it was just for a moment.

"You caught me off guard here, fellas," I said. "You have to at least give me a chance to drain the snake before I put it into action."

Laughs all around.

Glasses rose up in approval.

"Sure, go ahead," Rickards said. "But don't take all night."

The woman climbed up onto the dining table that the boys had covered with blankets and moved into the middle of the room. "I'll be right here waiting for you, sugar," she said with a smile I recognized well. It was the one she used on clients when she told them how much she enjoyed what they did to her, and it was just like the one I used on people who asked me if there was a special little lady in my life.

"I'll be back," I said.

"Can't wait," she said, slipping off her panties.

I headed for the bathroom.

Behind me, someone turned up the music. The room came alive with whistles and cheers.

⚬

I locked the door to the bathroom, turned on the water in the sink and fell to my knees. I wanted to throw up, but my body wasn't co-operating. It seemed content just to let me feel sick to my stomach.

This couldn't be happening.

There had to be some explanation for it.

Maybe it was just a gag. Maybe I'd go back out there and the boys would be dressed and the woman would be serving drinks and everyone would be having a good laugh at my expense. I wanted that to be true, but of course I knew it wasn't.

They'd picked Las Vegas because prostitution here was legal, or at least as legal as was possible in the United States. They'd come here not for some insurance seminar, but to screw this woman collectively. They would all mount her, affirming their manhood in plain view of the others. Then they would refer to it in innuendo around the office for months. . . . Their dirty little secret.

And they wanted me to be in on it. Not just be in on it, but to lead the charge.

As if I didn't already have enough secrets of my own.

I thought about that for a moment, thought about just coming right out and telling them. I could admit to them what I was and simply avoid this whole situation.

Right, and then my life would be over.

It would start with a change in attitude. The golden boy would be awash in pink. The top accounts would slowly be handed off to other agents. Clients would call up and ask to be served by other representatives.

And that was if I was lucky.

If I wasn't so lucky there would be endless ignorant remarks made behind my back, even right under my nose. People would laugh and giggle, make limp-wristed jokes and apologize by saying, "No offense." And then there would be others who would watch me and follow me just for the chance to beat me to within an inch of my life. Then my work would really suffer. I'd be chastised for showing up looking like hell (somehow a broken nose on a queer doesn't look as tough as it does on a straight man) and there'd be hints that I didn't get along with co-workers, and then . . . then they'd suggest I leave the company and ask that I do it quietly and without a lot of fuss.

Or maybe they'd just fire me on the spot, then spread the word I was queer.

No thanks.

Telling the truth was not an option.

And I couldn't bluff my way out of this one.

I had to go through with it. Had to do it in front of the rest of them to prove to them I was a man.

Just then there was a knock on the door. It was Rickards. "Hey, palsy, we're waiting. . . . She's practically startin' without you."

"I'll be coming out in a minute," I said, smiling miserably at the irony of the statement.

⚓

I decided that I'd do it, or at least my mind decided that I would. My body had ideas of its own. I'd never had trouble getting an erection before, but of course I'd never been in such a circumstance before.

After stalling for as long as I could, I came out of the bathroom and stepped into the room. All eyes were upon me. Normally I would have been thrilled to be the focus of three naked men, but this time it wasn't having any effect on me.

That's because along with the three men, was a single woman.

"There he is," someone said.

"Show us how it's done, palsy."

It seemed like such a simple thing, to get an erection and slip it inside her, but at that moment it was the most difficult thing in the world.

"Come on, sugar," the woman said. She had both her hands between her spread legs. They were turned palms up and she was curling her fingers at me as if summoning me onto the ride of my life. "I won't bite."

I smiled at her, feeling that patented self-assured smile that had served me so well over the years fading. I reached down between my legs and stroked myself, hoping that by some miracle I'd respond.

"Why don't you let me do that, honey?" she said, rising up into a sitting position and reaching out to touch me.

I hesitated a moment, then realized I probably looked as if I were afraid for my life. Of course, I was terrified, but I couldn't let on. I put my hands to my side and let her touch me . . . touch it.

It was obvious she was pro, but no matter how good she was with her hands it wasn't going to change a damn thing. I made eye contact with her then, and felt myself getting sick once more. I closed my eyes and raised my head. The boys took it as a sign I was getting into it.

And then I suddenly felt something warm and wet sliding over the head of my penis.

I had to swallow to keep from throwing up.

The boys had moved in closer for a better look. None of them seemed to be having any trouble getting hard and after I was done, this woman would probably work her way through them in less than an hour.

I closed my eyes again and thought of the boys, all of them hard and watching me. That seemed to help, because I could feel the first tingling of excitement building down there.

Maybe I could get through this, I thought. Get it over with. . . .

"Lie down," I said.

The boys voiced their approval.

"Sure, honey," she said. "Anything you say."

She lay down on her back, but the sight of her like that wasn't helping at all.

"No, on your stomach," I said.

"Whatever you say."

She dutifully turned over, set herself onto her knees and elbows and lifted her rear into the air. It was a better view, but I could still feel myself going soft.

So I closed my eyes again, but instead of the boys I thought about the man I'd met at the pool, Ronnie from Phoenix. Instead of this woman, I imagined it was him crouched in front of me. That seemed to help, a lot.

I was hard.

With my eyes closed I tried to enter her, but I was missing the mark. Then a hand, her hand, grabbed me and directed me home.

It felt, interesting . . . but only because I imagined I was in Ronnie's mouth.

I was practically home free.

Three . . . four more strokes and I was ready.

I pulled out, finished myself off with my own hand, and slowly opened my eyes.

There were streaks of white across the woman's back and the boys were all cheering their approval.

"Okay, palsy," said Rickards, pushing me aside. "My turn now."

Someone thrust a drink in my hand. A double scotch, straight. I emptied it in a gulp and asked for another.

More drinks.

Within an hour I'd passed out on the couch, fogging the memory of what I'd done and making sure I wouldn't have to do it again.

Because I had done it.

And it was over.

Unfortunately, the real nightmare was just beginning.

I woke up in the morning with a pounding headache. I was wrapped up in a hotel bathrobe with half the covers strewn across the floor. I felt terrible, like death warmed over, but at least I was in my own bed and there was no one else in the room.

I checked my watch and saw it was already eleven. I'd missed the morning seminar, but I didn't care. To hell with that farce. There'd been only one reason why the boys came out here and that had been for last night's entertainment. Now that was over with and we could drop the pretenses. I had little over a day before my flight home and I was going to keep a low profile between now and then. No more fun and games for me, fellas. I'd had my fill and it had left me feeling sick to my stomach.

I rolled over in bed and saw that the little orange light on my telephone was blinking. That meant there was a message for me at the front desk. It was probably from one of the boys inviting me to their next bit of fun.

No thanks.

I closed my eyes and tried to get some sleep, but thoughts of the previous night didn't allow me a moment's peace. So I got up, showered, and headed to the hotel restaurant for something to eat. On the way I stopped by the front desk, just in case the message was legit.

Turned out it wasn't from any of the boys, but from the woman who'd entertained us last night. It was written in an elegant scrawl, but the message was anything but tasteful.

I know what you are, it said. And if you don't want your friends to know too, maybe we should talk. There was an address of a home in the city. And that was all.

Apparently she must have suspected I was queer and she was going to tell the boys if I didn't . . . didn't what, I wondered.

Blackmail?

It was incredible. I'd heard that such things happened to movie stars and entertainers, people who had money and careers to protect, and who would pay anything to stay away from a hint of scandal. I was just an insurance agent from Ohio for crying out loud.

I supposed it was all a matter of scale. Instead of asking for tens of thousands, she'd ask for thousands, maybe even hundreds. Maybe that's how she really made her living, shaking down executives by threatening to tell their wives and children what they'd done on their last trip to Las Vegas.

And here she'd found a queer. It must have been like hitting the jackpot.

I tracked down Rickards and asked to borrow the car he'd rented. He complained a bit at first, saying there were a few burlesque joints in town he wanted to visit, but he gave up the keys when I promised I'd be back before dinner.

She lived in a decent neighborhood. The homes looked new, if a bit on the small side. I wasn't crazy about parking in her driveway, but I guessed there were strange cars parked there all the time. Who would notice one more?

When she opened the door, she had on a silk kimono, probably a gift from some serviceman on his way back from Vietnam. It looked good on her, and I couldn't help but think she'd bounced back from the night before a lot better than I had.

"You sure didn't waste any time getting over here," she said, almost as if she were surprised to see me. "Care for a drink?"

"Thought you might want to do it again," I said, almost managing to make myself sound sincere.

"Ha!" She laughed hard at that. "Oh, you're good. I bet you've got everyone fooled in your little corner of the world."

"What do you mean?"

"Look," she said, pouring herself a drink. "You know you're queer, and I know you're queer. The only people who don't know are those boys you hang out with."

"I don't know what you're talking about —"

"I've had my share of men, pal, and I know when one of them is scared out of his wits. You managed to get it hard, even managed to pop, but through most of it you were closer to throwing up than you were to climaxing. . . ."

I couldn't deny it. She was too sure of herself for that. And I could easily picture her telling Rickards and the others why she was so sure. And they'd believe her too. With that smile and body, who wouldn't? And then it would be game over for me.

All of it, gone!

Unless . . .

"You're a pansy," she continued, lighting up a cigarette, "and if you don't pay big, I'm going to let the world know it."

Unless I did something about it.

"See, I know lots of queers. This town's got more than its fair share. Nothing wrong with it, except none of you like people knowing about it. That's where I come in."

I glanced around the room. There was an ashtray on the table. It was big, black and heavy.

I picked it up . . .

"A couple hundred dollars and your secret's safe with me. Unless of course I need some extra cash, then I might ring you up every so often for another installment —"

. . . and brought it down hard against her skull.

Spittle flew out of her mouth.

The cigarette fell from her fingers.

And she hit the floor like a silk-wrapped side of beef.

⁘

Luckily, what blood had leaked out of her head had pooled on the wooden floorboards and was easy to clean up. It was also lucky that she didn't weigh more than one-twenty, one-thirty. After I wrapped her head in a towel, and her body in a bed sheet from the hall closet, it was easy to put her over my shoulder and take her out to the car.

I popped the trunk first, then carried her out into the driveway. I was worried about people watching me, but I figured the more nonchalant I was about it, the less people would notice.

Once she was in the trunk, I locked the door to the house and headed east looking for a hardware store. Before I hit the city limits I stopped to buy a shovel and pick. When the clerk asked me if I was going to do some prospecting, I told him it was for a gag for one of my buddies.

"Want I should spray 'em with gold paint?" he asked. "Do that all the time for ground-breakings and such."

I told him no and left as quickly as I could, getting back on the highway headed east. It was only about twenty miles to the Hoover Dam and Colorado River. The river would give me an excuse for being away all afternoon as well as options about what to do with the body. I could either weigh it down and toss it into the river or I could just bury it out in the middle of desert where no one would find it for years.

Another little secret I'd have to keep to myself.

About ten miles out of town the adrenaline that had been pumping through my body seemed to have run its course and I felt weak and faint. I was tempted to pull over until the feeling passed, but that would be like waving a flag to anyone passing by that here was a man with a problem.

So I kept on driving.

Before the dam I made a left at Boulder City, turning off the main highway and heading north into the desert. I traveled about five miles when a suitable rock formation appeared on my left. It was big enough to hide the car from the road, and remote enough to allow me to do the job without interference.

I pulled off the road and headed out across the flat.

Only when I had picked my spot and started digging did I realize how hot it was outside. The sun beat down on my aching head like a hammer and every swing of the pick and shovelful of dirt seemed to send white-hot spikes piercing through my skull.

"Serves you right, you bitch!" I said. "Who did you think you were messing with?" I laughed a little then. She'd been so smug, so self-assured about how she was going to string me along as an extra source of income. I bet she thought queer meant spineless, that I'd roll over and beg her not to tell. My only regret was not being able to see the expression on her face when I hit her with the ashtray. That must have been some sight as all at once she realized that she'd been both right and wrong about me – Yes I was queer, but no I wasn't going to play ball. And I hoped she didn't die right away. Not that I wanted her to suffer or anything like that, but I wanted her to live long enough to realize she'd made a mistake. A big mistake. She'd probably made it a habit to push queers around, . . . well sugar, I haven't been pushed around since the first grade and I'd be damned if I let some cheap Las Vegas whore ruin my life for a few c-notes.

I threw the dirt onto her body with relish. She was taking my secret to her grave, which was the very same thing that I was planning on doing with it.

"Got just what you deserve, you scheming bitch!" I said, as I tossed the last few shovels of dirt onto her grave.

"Who are you talking to?"

The voice came from behind me. It belonged to a man.

"Is there somebody here with you?"

Another voice, this one female.

I slowly turned around.

They were hikers, wearing heavy boots and carrying backpacks and canteens.

"Were you burying something, mister?" the man asked. He was a young kid, early twenties maybe.

"I told you," the woman said to the man, a hint of fear in her voice. She was as young as he was, and blonde, with her hair tied up with a kerchief. "We were watching you. We saw you take something out of the trunk of your car."

"I'm just doing a little prospecting, that's all."

The man looked at me strangely. "Then why are you putting dirt into the ground?"

The woman took a few steps to the right . . . and gasped.

I looked down into the hole in the ground and saw a hand still exposed to the sun.

"Don't worry, mister," she said, her eyes as wide as poker chips. "We won't tell anybody." She turned to look at the man. "Will we?"

He was shaking his head. The look of fear on his face was unmistakable. "No, we didn't see anything here. Your secret's safe with us, mister."

I didn't believe them for a second. "Promise?" I said.

"Yeah, yeah," he answered. "We promise."

She was nodding.

"Okay," I said.

"Well, we'll be going now. We're on are way to the dam."

"Have fun," I said, then swung the shovel, just like Mickey Mantle, catching the guy right about the ear. His head split open like a melon and the top of his skull fell onto his shoulder, held in place by a flap of skin.

The woman screamed and started to run, but I caught her in four or five strides, then used the shovel to knock her feet out from under her. One hard downward thrust and the shovel blade cut her head clean off her shoulders.

When it was done I took a moment to catch my breath. Two more holes would take an hour, at least. Rickards was going to be upset about missing his striptease.

To hell with him.

He might have been missing out on enjoying life, but I was out here preserving mine.

My throat was dry, my clothes were soaked, and I was dying for a drink.

Three people were dead.

But my secret was safe.

I left the shovel and pick on the other side of the rocks and hopped in the car. It was after five and Rickards wouldn't be too happy, but he'd get over it.

I started the car up and headed back for the road, reveling in the feeling of the air blowing hot and dry on my skin.

In just over twelve hours I'd be out of this nightmare and everything would be back to normal. Back to the way it was. I couldn't wait.

I got back onto the main highway and read the sign that said Las Vegas was fifteen miles away. I stepped on the gas a bit, trying to make up for lost time. . . .

And that's when I noticed the flashing red light in my mirrors.

I pulled over onto the shoulder and the Nevada state trooper pulled up behind me.

With the car stopped and the wind gone, I began to sweat again. I could feel the salty drops running down my temples and into my eyes. I wiped my face with a sleeve, realized it was dirty, and tried to hide it from view.

"Hey there," said the trooper. He was slimmer and fitter than what I had thought a Nevada state trooper would look like. He had dark glasses, and he smiled, but the thing that struck me most were his black leather driving gloves. They seemed to fit his hands like second skins.

"Hello," I said.

"You sure are in a hurry."

I nodded. What could I say?

"Question is, are you in a hurry to get somewhere, or to get away from something?"

"I was out at the dam," I said. "Lost track of time. I promised my friend I'd have his car back by dinner. I'm running a little late."

"This your friend's car, is it?"

"A rental."

The trooper nodded. Then he bent over and rested his elbows on the bottom of my open window. "You looked like you worked up quite a sweat. Little dirty too."

"Oh, well," I looked at my shirt and saw the patches and smears of brown from the dirt I'd been shoveling. "It's the silliest thing . . . I climbed up these rocks to get a better view of the dam. I slipped and rode down the rocks on my rear end."

I laughed, but the trooper didn't think my story was all that funny.

"Taking pictures, were you?"

I realized he was being clever, and felt my stomach tighten. I had no camera with me, no touristy things at all. If I said yes, he might ask to see the camera, so I had to stay as close to the truth as possible.

"No, just went for a sight-see. But after seeing the dam, I wished I'd had a camera with me."

"Water level's high this time of year, ain't it?"

Another tricky question. I had no idea what the water level of the dam was. It might be high, it might be low. One thing was for certain, the trooper would know, and he'd know if I was lying. There was about an even chance I'd pick the right answer, but since it was still spring, it made sense that the water level would be high. "Oh yeah," I said, putting a hand on my stomach to calm it. "Somebody told me how deep the water is, and I just couldn't believe there was so much of it there."

The trooper nodded, and looked me over again.

"I know the speed limit don't mean all that much out here with the roads as flat and as straight as they are, but it is the law."

What? It sounded like he was letting me off with a warning. "Oh, yes, absolutely." I was able to take a deep breath for the first time in minutes.

"You respect it," he said with a wink. "And get back to the city safe and sound."

"Yes sir," I said.

He walked back to his car, and honked his horn at me as he pulled away.

I waited until his patrol car was a tiny dot on the highway in front of me, then I leaned over, opened the passenger side door, and threw up onto the highway's shoulder.

⁜

I arrived back at the hotel around 6:30. Rickards was in the lobby watching out for me.

"Hey, palsy, where the hell have you been?"

"I drove out to the dam for a look around . . . lost track of time."

"I've been waiting for you for a couple hours now."

"I know, I'm sorry."

"Ah, never mind that now. How's about a drink?"

My throat was full of sand and grit. A drink sounded good. "I'd love one."

"Good." He punched the Up button and the elevator doors opened immediately. "The boys are already upstairs. We got food, drinks, and some special entertainment all lined up."

The food and drinks sounded good. I was almost as hungry as I was thirsty. I didn't like the sound of "special entertainment" since that was almost the same way they'd described the previous night's fun.

"Nothing like last night, I hope."

"Nah, that was kid's stuff. We got something better for tonight."

Better was good. Maybe it was a high-stakes poker game, or maybe one of those close-up magicians who performs sleight-of-hand tricks for three or four people at a time. That would be nice. And at least it would be closer to my idea of entertainment.

We got off the elevator and headed for the same suite as we'd had the night before.

"In fact, tonight's entertainment is twice as good last night's."

Twice as good, I thought. What the hell did that mean?

He opened the door and I stepped into the room.

The boys were all there, once again naked.

Only this time, instead of a hooker dancing in the middle of the room, there were two.

"Feast your eyes, palsy," Rickards said.

I shook my head in disbelief.

"We were going to play cards, but you looked like you had such a good time last night, we thought . . . why not two girls?"

I would have thrown up right then and there if I hadn't cleaned out my stomach out on the highway. I couldn't believe I'd made it through one nightmare, only to have it played out again, this time in – what was that new sound system called – hi-fi stereo.

Of course, instead of going through with it all, I could just admit I was queer. Consequences be damned. Things wouldn't really be that bad, would they?

"C'mon, palsy, what are you waiting for?" Rickards asked.

I hesitated a moment, then said, "After you."

TILL HUMAN VOICES WAKE US

STEPHEN DEDMAN

Cowboys tell stories – there's not much else to do, on most ranches – and sometimes they even tell the truth, even if they don't always know it. And they love sad songs, ballads; those are the best ones to sing to the cattle at night, to soothe them. Cattle don't know shit about music, or maybe they just have better manners than some audiences I could tell you about, so cowboys don't have to sing *well* – but sometimes you hear one who does, and this one had a voice sweet enough that I listened for a minute or more before I heard what he was singing.

I was working as a trail cook because there were some people on the *Natchez* who thought me too lucky at cards for their liking, so I'd left the boat, changed my fancy duds for Levis, an old patched red shirt, and a coat that might have been blue or gray once, and headed towards California. I had some money, my pistols, and a wicked deck of cards, but none of them were much good in a land where there's nothing left to buy or steal. I signed on for the drive team because we were heading the same way and I knew they'd do twenty miles or more a day for the first few days, just so the cattle would be tired. Besides, no one would think to look for the Professor on a chuck wagon in Kansas . . . not that I was still using that name. I don't know what the cowboys called me when I wasn't listening, but to my face, I was Mr Morgan, sir.

Anyway, this cowboy looked prettier than me, and much younger than I owned to, and he was singing in Spanish too soft for me to catch all the words, though I made out most of them. He had a good voice, and it was a pretty song – about how beautiful this woman looked as she bathed in the river – until he reached the end where they found the young man gutted like a fish . . . no, that couldn't be right. I must have misheard, or misunderstood.

He came to the wagon for coffee a couple of hours later, and I asked him what he'd been singing. "Pretty song . . . something about a woman crying?"

"'La Llorona,'" he said, softly.

"That's it. How does it end?"

He looked at me for a moment, uncertainly. Like I said, he was young and pretty, prettier than most mattress girls I'd seen, and he'd probably had men try to seduce him before. Then he sang the last few verses quietly, as though they were a threat. As I'd thought, the story ends with the young cowboy going down to the river to see the beautiful crying woman – alone, despite everyone's advice – and being found a few days later, a few miles downstream, torn almost in half.

I shook my head. "You make that one up?"

"No. Heard some women singing it once, but it was another cowboy who taught it to me. I guess it's an old song; Aaron, the tall black guy, he sings it in English."

I had to smile at that. Aaron had a fine bass voice, a good few octaves deeper than this boy's. "And what's – Dulcea? A woman's name?"

"Dulce agua. It means 'sweet water' . . . it's the name of a river where this happened."

"That's a true story?"

He shrugged. "The women, they say so. On the Rio Dulce Agua, near the Puerta Del Diablo."

I stared at him. "Devil's . . . Gate? On the Sweetwater River?"

"I don't know. I just hear the song, and the cattle, they like it." He shrugged, then poured the dregs of the coffee into the dust. "Graçias, senor."

Aaron stood more than six feet tall in his old worn boots, and weighed nearly two hundred pounds without that big LeMat revolver he carried, though he didn't eat any more than the other cowboys or a grizzly bear that's just woken up in spring. He was older than the trail boss, and smarter, and as black a man as I'd ever seen . . . but his eyes weren't any darker than mine, just sadder.

They were swapping stories, and I told them about the ranch I'd heard of in Texas which was owned and worked by women, and some of them said that beat all and some just called me a liar, but I could tell who wished it were true. Not as many of them as you might think, either. A lot of cowboys have only one use for women, and a few have none at all. Some of the cowboys told stories about women they'd known and Indians they'd killed, and if I had a dollar for every one that was true, I probably wouldn't have enough to buy a shot of whisky. Then I asked Aaron if he knew the song about the weeping woman. He looked at me warily, then began to sing it softly, his voice as low as new-mown hay. He knew verses that the young Mexican hadn't, but the story was the same, and so was the setting: a ford across the Sweetwater, a valley known as the Devil's Gate.

I nodded when he was finished, while some of the cowboys grimaced at the thought of the mutilated young cowboy. "Do you remember where you first heard that song?"

His eyes became darker, and I realized – too late – that he didn't want to talk about his past. It was barely two years since the war had ended, and I wondered if he'd been a slave, or maybe a runaway. "No," he said. "Heard it a few years ago, know that much."

"Have you ever been to Devil's Gate? In Wyoming?"

"No. Is it a real place?"

"Yes. It's where the Oregon Trail crosses over the Sweetwater."

A few of the cowboys looked at me curiously, and one asked, "You been there, Cookie?"

"Ridden through there," I said. "Years ago. They talked about the weeping woman then, but I hadn't heard that song before."

Another cowboy snorted. "You see her?" he asked.

"No," I lied. "No, I rode through, I didn't stop. And I haven't been back in years."

They were silent for a moment; none of them so much as broke wind. Then one of the wranglers laughed. "Hell, I'd probably go that far to see a beautiful woman myself."

That got them back to boasting and bullshitting about what they'd done for women and what women had done for them and I looked up at the north star and didn't say anything and wondered how soon I could get back to Devil's Gate.

I left the cattle and the cowboys at some town which wasn't much more than a railhead and a street full of saloons: no school, no church, and mine was probably the only Bible - maybe the only *book* - for miles. Like the red shirt, it was a souvenir of my Pony Express days, but it was also a useful prop when I wanted to pose as a preacher. The cowboys had headed for the saloons and the dance halls, but I'd declined to go with them, even though one of the prettier saloon girls had given me a look that said she could see through my clothes and liked what she saw. Instead, I paid for a bath and emerged from one of the town's hotels as the Professor, in time to catch the next train north. I caught the train as far as I could – it felt good to wear clean clothes and sleep in a real bed again, even if it was just a bunk on a Pullman car – then bought a horse and rode most of the rest of the way.

I saw the cemetery up on the hill before I saw the town. It wasn't much of a cemetery, never had been, but even from here I could see it wasn't much of a town anymore either. There was but one street, Front Street, and that was empty. I couldn't see a living soul, even in the shade of the porches, but I could hear the piano. The tune was unfamiliar, and the player was pretty damn good. The saloon was next to the old stable which had once been the swing station; there was one man behind the bar, and no one at the piano.

"What'll it be, Mister?"

I looked at the barman, who was sitting on a stool watching the door. He looked to be a few years older than me, and looked a few years older every step I took in his direction. "Feed and water for my horse, mostly."

"Water I got, if your horse ain't particular, but no feed. You want a drink?"

"Stable closed?"

"Three or four years, now," he replied, as he slowly walked behind the bar. "There are ranches hereabouts, but hardly nobody comes across the river. Folks're scared of the lady."

I looked around the saloon, wondering how long it had been since a lady, or anyone who claimed to be a lady, had been in town – unless he was referring to the painting above the bar. I don't know if she was a lady, but she was sure enough a woman, and even ladies have to be naked sometime. The piano was being played by some roll of paper, playing the only tune it knew, and the whiskey was vile stuff, made from cask alcohol and water and God alone knew what else, but I drank the glass down, somehow. "Tell me about the lady."

"Well, I ain't never seen her misself, but they say she comes down to the river and has herself a bath, sometimes. Beautiful gal, they say, though it's mostly women who sees her and tells the story, and nobody ever seems to see her long or up close."

"What does she look like?"

"Long dark hair," he said, softly. "They all agree on that. Hair down past her waist, so it waves in the water when she sits down. Pretty face, but sad: some say she's crying, or maybe singing something sad, though nobody ever hears the words . . . leastways, nobody remembers them." He shrugged. "Mebbe it's some Indian language, or Mexican, or something, but most folks say she's pale, and some say her eyes are blue or green."

"Does she ever speak to anyone?"

"Not that I ever heard. Most folks say as how she might turn and look at them, then she disappears into the water. Guess she don't want them looking at her tits – and I hear tell they're nice tits. You want another whiskey?"

I slid a coin across the bar. "And this is out by the ford? Either the water must be deeper than I remember, or she must be as skinny as a snake."

He shrugged again, then poured me another whisky. "All I know is what folks say. I wouldn't advise you to go looking for her, though."

"Why not?"

He was silent for a while, then poured himself a glass of whiskey. "I've seen three men, boys almost, young like you, who went to the river looking for her. One of 'em was likkered up, and he drowned, and he was lucky. Two . . . two were jaybird nekkid and ripped open, from their neckerchiefs down to where the good Lord split 'em. The doc told me that maybe they drowned first, and lucky for them, cause if they'd lived they'd have been steers."

"Indians?"

"Mebbe," he allowed. "I've heard tell that squaws do that sort of thing in some places, but not around here – and even the Indians are scared of that valley."

"Why do *you* stay?"

A shrug. "Lived here all my life. Most of my kin are up in the cemetery; don't want to leave 'em. Reckon somebody'll find me and bury me when my time comes. I never was a traveling man."

Me neither, I thought, but I didn't say it. I slid some coins across the bar. "Will this pay for a bath, a bed, a meal, and some water for my horse? I'll be riding on in the morning. I'd like to see this lady."

He shook his head, but took my money; I couldn't help but think of Romeo's apothecary. The room faced onto Front Street, so I couldn't see the cemetery, but I dreamed about the funeral anyway.

We were all there, even some older boys who'd stopped going to school a year or two earlier, but who'd stayed on at the ranches near Benedict or gone to work in the mines instead of going off to war. Johnny McKillian, whose father was the sheriff as well as running the faro game at the Silver Dollar saloon, tried not to grin, but he whispered in my ear as we walked away, "You know what this means? No more school!"

"They'll get another teacher."

"No they won't, not just for eight or nine children. The town won't pay for it, my father said. No more school!" he crowed again, this time more loudly, now that we were outside the cemetery's rickety gate.

"What will you do?"

"I'm going to go sign up," said Frank, the blacksmith's son. "There's not enough work here for two smiths, and not enough silver left in the mountain to be worth the digging. Or hunt buffalo, drive a stagecoach, find a mine isn't worked out yet. . . . Or be a sutler, maybe; they make all sorts of money. What're *you* going to do?" he asked me, managing not to smile.

I turned away and looked at the rough wooden cross they'd given Miss Towers as a marker. She'd been the prettiest woman I'd ever seen, and though I've seen a lot of women, I never saw another I felt the same way about until I saw the weeping woman at Devil's Gate. . . .

Johnny grabbed me by the shoulders, turned me around, and kissed me. His teeth clashed against mine, his tongue felt like a slug, he tasted of. . . . I twisted in his grasp, and brought my knee up as hard as I could between his legs. He made a horrible gurgling sound and backed away from me, half bent over. "Why'd you do that?" he gasped, then he laughed. "You're just a girl! That's all you'll ever be, and all you can ever do is. . . ."

I looked down at him — even standing, he was an inch shorter than me, and now he was a foot or more down the slope — and past him to the town. I thought of all the things that he could do that I. . . .

I rode out of town the next morning, wondering what had happened to Johnny and Frank since I'd run away that day. Had they joined the army? Hunted buffalo? Ridden with the Pony Express? Ridden shotgun on stagecoaches? Apprenticed to a printer? Played the piano in saloons and brothels? Sold corsets, guns, whiskey, patent medicines, barbed wire? Been a deputy sheriff, a trail cook, a railroad gambler, Lady Macbeth and Desdemona and Viola and Rosalind? How many women had they known and loved the way I had?

The wind changed, and I could hear the player piano churning out the only song it knew, a slow, sad song. . . . I spurred my horse on to a gallop, and headed for the river.

She wasn't there, but I was prepared to wait for as long as I had to: after all, she'd been waiting for me for years. If I'd known her name, I would have called it out, but we'd never actually spoken.

She appeared just as the sun was setting, and stared at me across the river with eyes the same color as the water. She was as beautiful as I remembered, and I wondered how I'd ever ridden away that first time.

I wore much the same outfit as I had when I was with the Pony Express, blue jeans and red shirt, but no guns. I slapped my horse on the rump and sent it running back to town, then pulled my boots off and threw them away. My Levis and my shirt and my long-johns went into the water without me, then I unbound the bandage around my breasts and let them free.

I heard what sounded like laughter as I stepped naked into the river, though it might just have been water flowing. The woman looked at me, then down at her breasts. Her dark nipples were swollen, and a drop of water balanced on one like a magnifying lens. We walked towards each other, her brown body glistening with moisture, mine sheened with sweat. She stopped when the water was just above her knees. She had the broad, strong features of an Indian, but I had a feeling she was much, much older, maybe as old as the Sweetwater itself. The black tangle of hair at her crotch was dripping, and I wanted to fall to my knees and catch every drop in my mouth. "It's me," I said, stupidly. "Josie."

Silence, then, *Where have you been some mortals have been here here in the water some were young and strong and I thought they were you but they weren't I removed their disguises looking for you but they still weren't you they lied.*

I reached out and touched her; she was warmer than the water, and sweeter. "Don't worry about them," I said, softly. "There were things I had to do, but I've done them, and I'm here now."

The river seemed to rise and engulf me as she kissed me, and I realized that not only could I do almost anything a man could do, I could do at least one thing they couldn't: I could give comfort to the weeping woman, and more than comfort.

There was another woman at the ford today. Few people stop here, now; they rush past, usually in little carriages faster than any train I ever saw, or sometimes – like this woman – on a two-wheeled iron thing they ride like a horse. But this woman stopped and looked at the water for a moment, so we rose out of the water and looked back at her. She was young and strong, as I had been when I first came to this river, and dressed in leathers and Levis like a cowboy. She looked at us, and we hoped that she might join us, but another woman called out to her and she just smiled and shook her head and walked away.

She's beautiful.

"Yes," I said, softly, and wondered how long it would be before she came back to swim in the river, and whether she'd bring her friend. I can't leave the river, and I wouldn't if I could, but sometimes I miss having other people to talk to. And maybe they can sing.

SLICE

WARREN DUNFORD

He was pulling on the T-shirt – his left arm above his head – when his hand hit the ceiling fan. A sharp jolt, not exactly pain. He pulled the shirt the rest of the way on and looked at the side of his hand.

A clean two-inch slice. Deep enough to see under the skin to a layer of blood and maybe bone.

He sat on the edge of the bed and looked up at the metal blades, still circling on high speed. He squeezed the ends of the cut and watched the line gape open like a mouth.

It didn't bleed.

Ken came out of the bathroom, rubbing gel into his gray hair. "Put on your shorts. We have to get going."

Doug looked down at his cock, still slimy with cum. He was naked except for the shirt. He didn't say anything.

"Phil and Randy are waiting for us."

"I cut myself."

"Where?"

"On the fan."

"Let me see."

Doug held up his hand.

"It looks bad."

"It's no big deal."

"Did you pack any Band-Aids?"

Doug shook his head.

"Don't wash it. You never know what's in the water down here. Come in the bathroom. You can rinse it with Listerine."

"I'll do it later."

"We're late already. Phil and Randy said they'd wait outside their hotel."

"I'm not going."

"Of course you're going. You told me you'd do this."

"I don't want to."

"They want to meet you. That's why I brought you."

"I don't feel like it right now."

"Half an hour. Go to the drugstore and buy some Band-Aids."

"I need money."

Ken took his wallet off the dresser and pulled out some bills.

Doug flipped through the strange-colored paper. "How much is this?"

"Seven hundred pesos. A hundred bucks."

Ken bent down and kissed him hard on the mouth, grabbing a handful of his hair as if they were still having sex. "Take care of the cut and come meet us for a drink. At the bar on the beach. You remember where it is?"

"I can find it."

"Half an hour, okay?"

Ken left the room, shoving his wallet and key into the front pocket of his shorts.

Doug lay back on the bed. Stared up at the ceiling fan and then out at the sky. No clouds. Just hard blue. He could hear waves crashing on the rocks beneath the balcony.

He held his hand up in front of his face. Stared at the cut.

His stomach felt weird. He needed food.

He found his cut-offs on the floor under a pile of bed sheets. He put them on, pulled on his running shoes, and left the room.

He went downstairs to the lobby. The hotel was totally white except for chipped, red clay tiles on the floor.

Doug walked down the street. A mix of cobblestones and dirt.

All the buildings were old and painted white. There were cracks in the walls and holes in the sidewalk. The streets were narrow and motorbikes kept zooming past him.

He didn't know where anything was. They'd arrived last night in the dark. These friends of Ken's had taken the ferry over this morning.

It was hot. The sun was glaring and he'd left his sunglasses in the room.

He found a grocery store on the corner. Small, dirty, with no lights on. He walked up and down the aisles. He didn't know what he wanted. He grabbed a package of baby cookies and a bottle of Coca-Cola.

He took them to the cash register. There was a woman sitting on a step ladder. Shiny black dress. Long black hair and red lipstick.

She said something in Spanish and jabbed her finger at his hand. Suddenly it was pouring out blood.

"I cut it."

She said something else he couldn't understand.

"I cut it on the ceiling fan. Do you speak English?"

She shook her head. She reached under the counter and brought out a roll of paper towels. She ripped off a sheet and handed it to him.

He pressed it over the cut. Right away the paper turned red.

"*Farmacia,*" she said.

"What?"

She went to the door and pointed a couple of different ways and said more stuff he didn't understand. He gave up paying attention.

"How much?" he said, pointing to the food.

Who knows what she said. He held out his money and she took a bill marked with a 20. She gave him back some coins. And she put another paper towel in the plastic bag.

He looked up and down the street. No sign of any drugstore.

He headed back towards the hotel, towards the water. The rocky side of the island where waves crashed over big brown boulders.

There was a paved walkway along the shore, but nobody was there. All the tourists were over on the other side, on the sandy beach. The whole island was only six blocks wide, maybe a mile long.

He set the plastic bag on the ground and sat on a rock. He ripped open the roll of baby cookies and ate three of them. He opened the bottle of Coke.

The money he had left might pay for the ferry ride and a taxi to the airport. But it wouldn't fly him back home.

He looked out at the waves.

He felt hot pinpricks on his forehead and across his scalp. He drank some Coke and the feeling went away.

Two people were coming along the shoreline. A man – short and pale – and a large, black woman.

Doug looked out at the water and then back at them. There was nothing else to look at.

The man had a handsome face. Big muscles, even though he was short. The woman was over six feet tall and she must have weighed 300 pounds. She wore a loose blue dress and a straw hat.

"*Hola*," the woman said.

"Do you speak English?" Doug asked.

"We certainly do," she said with a wide smile. "It's our mother tongue."

"You want one of these?"

He held out the cookies and they each took one.

"What happened to your hand?" the guy said.

It was still bleeding, dripping.

"I cut it on the fan in my room. It's a low ceiling."

"You're going to need stitches." The guy had a high-pitched voice.

"It's not that bad."

"There's a doctor on the main street."

"It doesn't hurt."

"It might leave a scar."

"It's no big deal."

The woman took another cookie. "Have you been here on the island long?" she asked.

"Since yesterday."

"It's very peaceful, don't you think?"

"I was thinking it's fucking boring."

The man smiled. "You haven't got the spirit yet."

"Come back to our hotel," the woman said. "I'll take care of your hand."

He went with them.

They walked down a deserted street into the middle of the town. They turned a corner into a busy marketplace. Sombreros and shawls, maracas and leather sandals.

"Most of it's junk," the woman said. "But yesterday I bought the most beautiful black clay vase."

The woman went into a store. Doug and the man continued walking a few steps farther before they stopped.

"So what do you do?" the man asked, his fingers massaging the muscles of his chest.

"Back home? I work in a club, a bar, sort of. What do you do?"

"I teach music. At a university."

"What about her?"

"She's an opera singer."

"For real?"

"She just came back from a concert tour in Italy."

"Is she famous?"

"When she's in Italy."

Doug laughed.

"So are you here by yourself?" the man asked.

"No."

"With a lover?"

"I've only known him a couple of days. It's sort of weird."

The opera singer was back. "I bought some antibiotic cream for your hand," she said.

"You didn't have to."

"I wanted to."

Their hotel was another block away. Just a gap between two storefronts. They climbed a staircase to the third floor. The woman climbed slowly, taking deep breaths.

The man went down the hall and opened a door. "I'm taking a shower," he said. He closed the door and left them alone.

The woman led Doug into her room. The curtains were closed. The room was small and dim.

The hot pinpricks were back, all over his face.

She poured him a glass of tequila. "Cleaning it might hurt," she said. "Sit there on the bed."

She went into the bathroom. He took an extra mouthful from the bottle.

"Have you been to this place before?" he asked her through the doorway.

"The island? I come here every year."

"What for?"

"It's so quiet. I find it soothing to the soul."

She came out of the bathroom, holding a white towel and a few Band-Aids.

"That guy said you're an opera singer."

She smiled gently. "Yes, that is what I do."

"Can you sing something?"

"Sometimes I don't like to sing."

"Why?"

"Sometimes I like to rest."

"I don't know much about opera."

She sat beside him on the bed. She smelled like flowers.

He jerked when she took his hand.

"Don't touch the blood, okay?"

She looked steadily into his eyes. "All right," she said. She poured tequila on the towel and wiped his hand. "Does that hurt?"

"No."

"You can relax with me," she said.

"I am relaxed." He drank more tequila.

She squeezed cream from the little tube and rubbed it firmly into the cut. She used two Band-Aids to cover it.

"I can make it heal faster," she said.

"How?"

"A secret I learned."

She moved her hand down the length of his arm, not touching the skin. She played her fingers above the cut, as if she were sewing it together with invisible thread.

He closed his eyes.

She sang. Some language he didn't understand. Her voice was light and piercing. It felt like a shiny metal tube running through his brain.

He was crying.

She stood and kissed him on the top of his head. Her breasts pushed against his face. He pressed back with his open mouth, his teeth in the beginning of a bite.

She pushed him gently away.

He picked up the glass of tequila and swallowed what was left.

"I have to meet some people," he said.

"You're very sweet."

"I have to go."

"I'm sure I'll see you," she said. "The island is so small."

He left the hotel.

He didn't know where he was. How could you get lost on a tiny fucking island? He walked a few blocks, trying to find the water.

A car sped around the corner – nearly knocked him down.

He could feel the tequila in his head. He looked at his hand.

The cream had made the Band-Aids slippery. They were peeling off. He balled them up and pitched them onto the sidewalk.

No sign of the ocean in any direction.

It was hot. His face was dripping with sweat.

A high white wall spread along the block in front of him. When he reached the far corner, he found a metal gate.

He went inside.

A graveyard. Cement coffins on top of the sand, side by side, just a few inches apart. On top of each coffin was a red glass box holding a picture and a candle.

He walked down the first row.

Out of nowhere, he saw a wild-looking old man. Brown skin. Messed-up black hair. Scraggly mustache. White shirt with dirt marks all over it.

"Hey, man. You like dead people?"

"I was just looking around," Doug said.

"We got lots of dead people. You want to see a pirate?"

"A pirate? For real?"

"Yeah, man, pirates used to come to this island. Long time ago. Bring the stuff they stole. You want to see?"

"Okay."

"Come on, I'll show you."

He led him through the narrow paths, cutting between the coffins.

He stopped in front of a gray stone box with a skull and crossbones carved on one end.

"Been dead 300 years. Oldest one here. You want some weed, man?"

"You got some?"

"Five dollars U.S."

"I only have Mexican."

"A hundred pesos."

"Sure, okay."

"Sit down. I'll go get it."

Doug sat on the sand, his back leaning against the pirate's coffin.

He put his hands over his face, his palms pressing into his eyes.

"Hey, man, you're bleeding."

"Yeah."

The guy sat on the coffin across from him and lit up two joints.

They smoked.

"I live here," the guy said.

"On the island?"

"In here – with the dead people. Empty box right over there."

They both started laughing.

"That's sick, man," Doug said. "Really sick."

Smoking and laughing.

"So you like Mexico, man?"

"I don't even know what the fuck I'm doing here."

They both laughed as if that was the biggest fucking joke in the world.

Doug closed his eyes.

When he opened them again, the guy was gone.

He was sitting there alone, leaning on the pirate's coffin. His hand was coated with sand – stuck in the left-over cream.

He checked his pocket. The money was gone. The key to his room was gone.

His face was hot. His stomach was churning.

He looked for the guy's empty grave. They all looked the same.

He had to find Ken.

He left the graveyard.

How can you get lost on a fucking island?

He saw a bunch of tourists. "Where's the beach?" he yelled.

They pointed back behind them.

He walked down the street. There was an empty lot piled with garbage. Skinny, sick-looking dogs were ripping open green garbage bags and chewing on bones. A tiny brown dog with patchy hair rushed towards Doug's ankles and barked.

He started to run.

On the edge of the beach, he found the bar they'd gone to last night. Palm leaves for the roof. Tree trunks for seats.

"Hey, get over here! Where've you been?"

Ken was at a table with his two friends. Old guys. Laughing. White hair and pink shirts. Drunk old men – just like at the bar back home. One of them was pale and skinny and had dark red scabs all over his face.

He didn't want to talk to them. Didn't want to think.

His head felt weird.

"I'm going swimming," he said.

He stumbled out to the beach. Light blue water, bright and glaring.

The cut was stinging. Salt water would be good.

He took off the T-shirt and dropped it in the sand. Stepped out of his shoes and walked into the water.

A splash on his hand and the salt burned.

No matter how far he walked, the water stayed shallow. He dove in and did the front crawl – strong and hard – his arms moving like blades.

His denim shorts were heavy in the water. He pushed them off and let them go.

His head was swirling. He could hear singing. Hard blue sky. The ceiling fan spinning, chopping off his fingers, his hand, his arm.

His head was swirling.

He choked and spit up what he'd eaten. Salt water filled his mouth.

The burning changed to throbbing.

The water was deep now. He heard waves on the shore. Saw a big wooden ship – a pirate ship – crashing onto the rocks.

A knife-sharp pain went through his hand.

He stopped swimming and put his hand to his mouth, pressed his tongue into the line of the cut, as if he was kissing a lover, as if holding his mouth to his hand was the only thing that would keep him afloat.

VEGGIE MOUNTAIN

THOMAS S. ROCHE

On the outskirts of the mid-sized city of San Esteban at the intersection of Northern California's Napa and Sonoma Valleys lie the southernmost estates of the Monteverdi family. Certainly these estates are only the physical manifestation of a much greater empire, for any dedicated wine drinker from Berkeley to Beijing would instantly recognize the name Monteverdi.

It should perhaps be no coincidence that at the edge of that famous empire lie the grounds of the Monteverdi Institute, a series of research and treatment facilities for the mentally ill, and that on the southern border of the Monteverdi Institute grounds is the Monteverdi Institute Lockdown Facility – known more colloquially as Mount Murder, for the Facility was established to incarcerate and study only the most violent cases of mental illness. Despite its somewhat gloomy location – the Lockdown Facility overlooks the Monteverdi Cemetery, the largest final resting place in Northern California – the Facility is today considered the premier institution for postdoctoral fellows doing work on the violently insane, and a place where those dangerous inmates can receive the best possible care.

But it is coincidence that it was the eldest Monteverdi who founded the Facility – pure coincidence – for it was opened prior to the scandal that all but ruined the Monteverdi family. That Old Man Monteverdi, only three years after opening the Facility, saw his own brother and, later, his son, incarcerated there before taking his own life – that is a matter of consternation to tourists, certainly, but a mere footnote in California history, and of only passing amusement to those who use the Monteverdi Institute Lockdown Facility today, both as inmates and employees. Fate has its way of playing tricks on us.

The hall lights in the Monteverdi Facility are on. They're always on.

Martin Warren makes his rounds, peering through the tiny, reinforced window in each steel-plated door, noting each room found occupied on a clipboard he carries with him. Warren's institutional whites are cleaner than they look – the dirt and stains are but the intractable detritus of his two years there. He's not much of a housekeeper; he skimps on bleach and washes his whites on cold to save on the gas bill.

Warren performs his rounds without much interest. He's eager to get back to the poker game in the staff room, and not once in his two years at Monteverdi has there been a serious attempt at escape from the Lockdown Facility. He yawns as he makes notes on his clipboard.

He pauses outside cell 915, reading the name on the clipboard several times over. Can it be? No, it's impossible.

Warren puts his face right up against the reinforced window, tries to glimpse the face of the inmate. But Charles Quinn is sound asleep, his face buried in his pillow.

Warren goes downstairs.

"We almost started the hand without you, slowpoke," jabs Trev Altman as Warren enters the staff room.

"One buck ante too rich for your blood?" asks Ramon Gutierrez, shuffling the cards.

"Hey, anything's too rich for Marty's blood," says Stevens, riffling through a stack of crisp one dollar bills he's brought especially for tonight. "But you'll cough up, won't you? Martyboy can't bear to be left out of a poker game."

He takes his place at the poker table. His plastic chair's still warm.

"That new loonie up on nine," says Warren. "Charles Quinn."

"Oh, Marty wasn't here for the big show," laughs Trev Altman. "The big serial killer, comin' in all peaceful. Pretty yawnsville."

"That's him."

"Correctomundo." Trev picks his teeth as Gutierrez deals the cards. He was a blackjack dealer in Tahoe for ten years; each card sails effortlessly into position in front of the players.

"*The* Charles Quinn."

"Right."

"The fucking homo serial killer."

"What part of 'yes' don't you understand, motherfucker? Didn't you know he was being transferred here?"

Warren shakes his head.

Gutierrez: "And in case you didn't know, Marty, serial killers prefer to be called gay."

The table erupts in laughter.

"No, I didn't know he was coming here. That's fucking disturbing."

Trev: "We've got a guy on six who filleted his wife, Marty. Ate her with a side of mustard greens. A girl on four beat her mother to death with a plastic light saber. Why is it any more disturbing than either of those, or any of the other half a zillion fuckin' nut cases we got bending the bedsprings at this dive?"

"Because he's a fuckin' homo."

"Hey, Trevelian on seven's a homo. He sucked alien cock. At least he thinks he did."

More laughter around the table. "You got jacks or better, motherfucker, or has serial murder somehow become more important than a good game of poker?" Laughter.

Warren hasn't even looked at his cards. He picks them up, leafs through them. "No good."

"I've got 'em. Three bucks," says Stevens.

Everybody tosses their cash into the bedpan in the middle of the table.

"Besides," says Stevens. "The guy's not technically a serial murderer. I guess you'd call him a mass murderer, but he ain't very mass."

"What the fuck do you mean," snaps Warren, "that he's not a mass murderer?"

"Hey, lighten up, motherfucker! He's just not."

"How is he not a mass murderer?"

"He only killed two people, dumbfuck. The ambulance driver and the EMT."

"Yeah, but he fuckin' ate them."

"Oh, come on, he barely ate them at all. Just their dicks and part of their faces."

"That sounds like a mass murderer to me."

Stevens snorts in disgust. Gutierrez and Altman laugh hysterically.

"I'm afraid our diminutive friend is correct," says Altman. Stevens shoots him a dirty look; he's incredibly sensitive to any comment about his height. "Charles Quinn does not qualify as a mass murderer. Two victims does not a slaughter make."

"Marty! Marty!" It's Gutierrez, screaming at the top of his lungs.

Warren jumps, looks at Gutierrez blankly.

"Do you want any fucking cards?" shouts Gutierrez.

"Oh," says Warren. "Fuck. You scared the fucking shit out of me. Don't shout like that."

Stevens: "Yeah, Ramon, don't you know you're not supposed to scream in an asylum unless you're tryin' to eat someone?"

"In more ways than one," laughs Altman, and makes a mock-fellatio gesture with his hand around his mouth and his head bobbing up and down while his tongue jabs his cheek.

"Hah! Now that you mention it, I am gettin' kinda hungry – hey Warren, you mind if I nibble on your earlobe a little?"

"Don't even fuckin' joke about that shit," snaps Warren. "That's fuckin' disgusting. I'll take four."

"Jesus, Marty, you just want me to deal you another hand?"

"Just give me the fucking cards."

A round of betting goes by in silence, dollars piling up in the bedpan. Marty stares at his cards, unseeing, and grinds his teeth.

"Why is he here? Shouldn't that bastard be at a prison facility? Full security, guards with real guns and shit?"

"Jesus, Warren, what's with you? The sonofabitch was found not guilty by reason of insanity. He hasn't committed a single bit of violence in five years. Takes his meds on time, goes to therapy, and talks about his best friends the corpses who love him and want to have sex with him." Altman giggles. Gutierrez and Stevens just smile.

Warren fumes, his lips pursed tight. He's a big guy, well-suited for working in the Facility. Well over six feet, about two-fifty. Good with his hands.

"You've got to admit, it's a fucking disturbing case."

Altman, grinning: "I've got to admit that you think it's fucking disturbing for some reason." He's known Warren the longest. He's worked the night shift the entire two years that Warren has. He knows how to annoy him.

Warren stares at Altman accusingly. "And you don't, motherfucker?"

"Hey, I do, motherfucker. Some underaged pervert eats a couple of paramedics, swallows their dicks, eats their faces – yeah, okay, I'll be the first to admit that's a little disturbing. But you seem to be obsessing over it."

"You've got to fucking kidding me. I am not obsessing."

"Sure you are. You read every article published on the case when it happened."

Warren stares like a trapped rabbit; his face twists in anger. "So I'm fascinated by fucked-up shit. You telling me you're not?"

"Oh, I just think it gets old after five years of working at Monteverdi. Guys eating other guys' genitals . . . blah blah blah. Give me some lesbian pro-wrestling serial killers – that'll get my motor going."

"You think it's all right what he did?"

"Hey! Hey! Hey!" Gutierrez. "Are you going to fucking bet, or are you just going to argue all night?"

"I'll call," says Warren. "Pair of kings."

Altman laughs hysterically.

"Full house, cocksucker. Read 'em and weep."

Warren looks like he's about to hit Altman in the face, but he just yells and smacks the table instead. The bedpan jumps and dollar bills scatter everywhere. Altman, Gutierrez, and Stevens look at Warren and laugh. Warren just shakes his head slowly back and forth, his face the color of blood.

"Fucking disgusting, a guy like this," mutters Warren, staring through the tiny window at the sleeping Quinn. It's three hours later, the poker game long since ended with Warren forty-three dollars down. Altman's the big winner, a hundred-something ahead. Son of a bitch just has to be cheating, Warren knows it.

"Motherfucking faggot. Sucking dead dick," mutters Warren, staring. "How could someone do that? Absolutely fucking disgusting."

Five years ago: Charlie Quinn was nineteen or twenty years old, working as a night-shift security guard at the Guerneville morgue, taking delivery of stiffs, watching horror flicks on late-night TV. Easy job, right? Easy as pie. Well, it turns out this sick motherfucker was screwing the bodies – and not the chick corpses

— that, Warren could understand. He wouldn't think it was okay, mind you, but if you gotta fuck a body Warren could sure understand wanting to do some chick, right? Especially a young one, kinda sexy. Anyway, this ambulance driver and this EMT — Sanders and Coltrane, their names were — seems they walked in on Charles Quinn doing his thing. Quinn went berserk. Little weasely kid, maybe 125 pounds, but he managed to kill both Sanders and Coltrane without sustaining any injuries to himself. He did it with his bare hands. Then — and here's were it got really disturbing — he started doing it. Warren shudders every time he thinks about that sicko's teeth digging in to dead flesh. What the hell could be a bigger perversion against God and man and everyfuckingbody?

But it didn't stop there. That was just where it got really weird. Seems when Charles Quinn had finished his meal — and things got a little hazy here, since Quinn was obviously either lying or hallucinating, probably both — he must have stumbled to the john and puked it up, flushed it. They couldn't find any human tissue when they pumped his stomach, so that was the only explanation anyone could figure out. Then after Quinn's done with his little purge, he pops open all the coolers, and starts dragging out bodies. Men, women — old, young. Buries himself, and the two ambulance jockeys too. Just lays there with the chilled corpses getting room-temperature on top of him for the next three hours until the morning shift comes in. They found him sobbing, curled up naked with the half-eaten EMT underneath him and the ambulance driver on top.

And what did Charles Quinn claim happened?

"The bodies did it, your honor. They came alive, and . . . and . . . crawled out of the drawers. . . ."

Warren unclips his keychain, turns the lock, opens the door to 915 — slowly.

⚬

"Where's Marty?" Stevens has his feet up on the desk. He's reading *Hustler*.

"Three-o'clock rounds," says Altman, crashed out on the couch reading a Stephen King novel. Gutierrez is snoring loudly across the room. "He likes to take his time."

"Don't even joke about that shit," giggles Stevens. "That's disgusting."

Altman shrugs.

⚬

Warren hopes none of the others will notice he's killed the alarms; he figures even if they do, they'll cover for him. Besides, the alarm'll be back on in fifteen minutes, when Warren finishes what he's going to do to that sick little bastard.

The mammoth guard has serial killer Charles Quinn restrained to the bed by his wrists by the time the little fuck wakes up. He starts to yell, but Warren sits down on his legs and gets Quinn's ankles strapped in while Quinn demands, then begs to know what's going on.

"I haven't done anything, I haven't done anything," he keeps saying, his voice hoarse with sleep.

Warren stands up, whips the remaining covers off of Quinn's body, and looks down at him, one key jutting between his fingers like a short knife. He reaches into his back pocket, brings out his other hand. It holds a black plastic stun gun – 250,000 volts.

Warren stares down at Quinn, his face twisted in disgust. Quinn looks up at him, quaking. Warren smiles – a look on his face so wrong that it makes him seem like some kind of clown from a child's nightmare – from Charles Quinn's nightmare.

"Oh, yes you have," growls Warren, his voice inhuman. "You sick faggot."

Charles Quinn takes a deep breath and screams at the top of his lungs.

"What's that noise?" asks Altman.

Stevens shrugs, his attention buried in a motor-oil-drenched, full-color threesome. "Alarm didn't go off."

Altman puts down his book, gets up, walks into the other room. He comes back a minute later, shaking his head angrily.

"That son of a bitch," says Altman. "Warren turned off the alarm. He shouldn't be able to do that without all three keys."

Stevens doesn't look up from his porn mag. "Well, then, how'd he do it if you and Ramon still have yours?"

Altman feels in his pocket. "Oh, fuck," he says. "Son of a bitch must have taken them when I was in the can. Hey, Ramon!"

Gutierrez wakes up with a start, looks around nervously, closes his eyes again.

"You got your alarm key?"

"Huh?"

"I said, do you have your fucking alarm key?"

"It's hanging in my locker."

"You don't even lock your locker, Ramon. You're supposed to have the key on your person at all times."

"Who gives a fuck?" says Gutierrez, and goes back to sleep.

Altman goes into the locker room. Stevens can hear him cursing. Altman comes back in.

"All right, all right. I'll go up and get him. Son of a bitch is probably paying a visit to that Charles Quinn guy right now. I knew he was up to something. I'm going to get him for this. I'll be back in a minute."

"Yeah, whatever," says Stevens.

Charlie Quinn still hasn't stopped screaming. Warren's stun gun flashes again.

"You like dick, motherfucker? You like to suck dick? Suck this!"

Charlie Quinn gags, tries to scream, can't. Outside, somewhere, he can hear sobs. He starts to curse, deep inside.

"Yeah, you fuckin' cocksucker. You like this, don't you?"

Marty Warren laughs.

⚜

Stevens jumps like a jackrabbit when he hears the pounding on the steel-reinforced door. Gutierrez jerks once, sits up, then lays back down, closes his eyes.

"What the fuck was that?" asks Stevens, grabbing his Maglite and going over to the door.

The pounding comes again, and Stevens screams and jumps back, watching as cracks appear in the door jamb on either side of the door.

"That's fucking impossible," he says to himself. What was it Altman told him, once? You could drive a Mack truck into that door at fifty miles an hour, and it'd hold.

Stevens tells himself this can't be happening. He tells himself this can't be happening. He's still telling himself that when the door explodes off its hinges.

⚜

"Marty! What the fuck do you think you're doing?"

Warren laughs. "I'm teaching this little pervert something about the wrath of God, motherfucker. I will repay, sayeth the Lord. Ain't that right, Charlie?"

Charlie gurgles.

"Marty, don't do this to me! You know I'm technically night-shift supervisor! I could be up to my ears in shit for this, pal. Get out here!"

"Soon as I'm finished."

Altman stalks into the room, his face red with fury. "Don't pull this shit, Marty! You and me'll both be in a hell of a lot of trouble for this, you son of a bitch! Lay off!"

"What's the matter, you want a piece?"

Something in Altman cracks, and he starts for Warren, his fists balled. "Yeah, I want a piece, motherfucker!"

Charlie Quinn begins to sob as Warren's bulk lifts off of him. "No," he says. "Not again. . . ."

⚜

Gutierrez is still waking up. He looks all around – figuring he's dreaming.

He feels the cold tile under his sock-clad feet. He feels the air-conditioned air. He's not dreaming.

He has to be dreaming.

Ten feet from him lies the shattered body of Stevens, the jellied limbs bent in ways they shouldn't be. The steel door has been lifted off his body; it's leaned up against the wall, on its front a distorted imprint of Stevens' body – in blood.

Three men in suits crowd around Stevens, their faces powdered with make-up, their ancient flesh drawn taut over bone. Their flesh crawls – no, seethes. Their jaws work as they crouch and crawl over Stevens' ruined corpse, one of them clawing at his face and taking a mouthful.

Other men and women are approaching Gutierrez – all of them well dressed, powdered with pancake makeup and blush. Many old, a few young. A dozen of them, two dozen. More crowding through the open doorway. Three dozen.

One of the men on Stevens gets a flap of the boy's cheek between his eagerly-working teeth. He bites, rips flesh. A spray of blood erupts over the old man's face. Stevens' body spasms in convulsion – and a pathetic moan escapes the boy's lips.

Gutierrez's eyes go wide. Stevens is still alive.

Another old man digs his teeth into Stevens' arm.

"Hail Mary," says Gutierrez as the walking corpses advance on him. "Full of grace . . . the Lord is with thee. . . ."

Then he too screams, as he feels the teeth – and he goes down in a shudder of fear and agony.

Altman is not a small man, but Warren still has fifty pounds on the guy. Of course, Warren has his pants around his ankles, but that barely hinders him as he shoves his fist into Altman's groin, pushes the guy off, and dives on top of him.

He's got his hands locked around Altman's throat, and Altman's trying desperately to scream for him to stop. But he can't get air into his lungs. And to his dismay, Warren's laughing.

"You want to stick up for the little faggot eh? You want to stick up for the faggot? Maybe you're a fuckin' faggot, too! All you goddamn queers stick together –"

Altman's vision goes dim, and he tells himself over and over again that this can't be happening, this has to be a bad dream. Warren can't have cracked, not like this – not tonight, not ever.

His ears ring, loud; all he can hear is the sound of Charles Quinn's weeping. "No, no, no, no," the kid moans. "Please God, don't let it happen again –"

Then the grip on Altman's throat disappears, and the weight of Warren on his body vanishes as someone hauls him off. Altman is too far gone to scream, but somebody does, and it's not Charlie Quinn.

Altman's not sure at what point he blacks out, but what he sees next simply has to be an anoxia-induced hallucination. It just has to be.

It fucking has to be.

Trev Altman can see dawn through the barred window as he comes to his senses. His throat feels like its been cut. He massages it, takes a few experimental deep breaths, feels his lungs burning. It feels like there's sandpaper inside his body.

He sits up, looks around the wrecked room.

Charles Quinn is gone, the restraint rent – not by a knife, but ripped apart by brute force. And Marty Warren lies in the place once occupied by Charles Quinn. It takes a good five minutes of staring in disbelief at what has happened to the body of Marty Warren before Altman feels his stomach clenching, his midnight lunch coming up.

Altman stumbles numbly through the corridors, making his way to the elevator. He goes back down to the first floor, walks into the staff lounge, already knowing what he's going to find.

"Oh, Jesus. Jesus."

Gutierrez and Stevens sprawl ruined amid the wreckage – the smashed tables, the clawed-open sofa. And Charles Quinn is nowhere to be seen. The steel door to the outside world leans up against the wall, the blood-pressed imprint of a human face and body coagulated upon it.

There in the door stands Judy Breckenridge, the morning supervisor. Her face is white as a sheet.

"Trev . . . what the hell happened?"

Trev chooses that moment to faint, falling unceremoniously across Stevens' shattered body. Judy rushes to grab him.

Even if they didn't put him on administrative leave pending review of his actions on the night in question, Trev Altman never would be able to go back to the Facility. He will doubtless eventually end up as far away as San Esteban as he can possibly be, and will try – unsuccessfully, of course – to scourge the incident from his mind.

But for the first seven years, they'll keep him in Monteverdi North. Where Trev Altman sits, and stares. And occasionally screams.

On the outskirts of the mid-sized city of San Esteban at the intersection of Northern California's Napa and Sonoma Valley lie the estates of the Monteverdi family. On the edge of those estates is the Monteverdi Institute, that famous series of research and treatment facilities for the mentally ill founded by the patriarch of California's most famous wine-growing family. At the northernmost extension of the Monteverdi Institute's ground lies Monteverdi North, where only those most non-violent of patients are taken for long-term treatment, care, and study when they show not the slightest possibility of clinical recovery. The poor prognosis for residents of Monteverdi North has led that facility to be called, in the jocular slang of Institute employees, Vegetable Mountain. Or sometimes just "Veggie Mountain."

That there should be, incarcerated deep in the bowels of Monteverdi North, a former attendant from the Monteverdi Institute's Lockdown Facility, where a famous mass murderer further solidified his legendary contribution to the annals of American violence by committing an atrocity so horrible as to render his previous crimes a mere prelude – and then vanishing without a trace – is perhaps the cruelest and grimmest of ironies. For if the keepers of the madhouses become, through their experiences, mad, then who is to draw the line between guard and guarded?

Most of the time, Trev Altman stares blankly at the wall. He has to be fed, and changed. Sometimes doctors talk to him. Most of the time, they leave him be – since in the years since the incident at Mount Murder, he has not once uttered a single coherent sentence.

Sometimes he makes noise, though.

They turn out the lights sometimes at Monteverdi North. Trev Altman screams at the top of his lungs when they do that.

EXIT WOUND

MICHAEL MARANO

For Marian Anderson (1968-2001) – neighbor and friend during the dark years.
You linger in our hearts, though you left us to endure darker years without you.

Though I know he hates when I watch, each time my eyes drink the glory of him taking the gun in his mouth, it excites me.

What contrition do I owe, if he does not fully close the door of his studio?

And though it excites me, I also know the betraying thump of remorse to see him committed to anything I am not. His attention to anything but me severs me from myself. The weakness in my knees and the emptiness in my loins are born of famishment for his gaze.

The shot that bursts apart his head bursts apart my heart. In that smothered limbo, my consciousness burns as would shadow-eternal flesh in sunlight.

I share the music of the red fog in which he drifts, his song of self-killing from which he wakes to begin his Art while the thunder-shot he limits through his Will lingers in my hearing.

Thus, do I share his Art. But never completely. His creativity defines my heart. It is right that I shatter for it, that I die during his hymns to immortality. I leave him to his Work as he replaces the gun, still oozing blue smoke, upon the table before him; I leave him to the earth-marrow pigments and scabbing shade-forms he has freed.

And afterward – when he has done taking brushes crafted of his own hair and bone to what the shot has thrown of him to the canvas, and he has patched the hole made by the bullet as it passed through the canvas – it excites me again to come to him . . . to taste gun-oil on his lips and powder-burns on the back of his scalp and to kiss coagulate paint from his fingers.

Often, in the studio perfumed with cordite, I reach down to find his Art has given him release. I touch him as if *I* have brought him release, and claim by proxy the beauty of his Work. To taste the gun-oil distilled through his blood into the saltiness of his release is to hold his Art upon my tongue and take it as Communion.

It is only after I have given him chilled fruit and mineral water to cleanse his palate that I dare a horizon-glance upon his work. *My* cleansing comes as I am burned by the russet fires the bullet has cast as layered vistas upon his canvas . . . the passions of his vision risen as living earthtones. At times, the exhaltation from the back of his head strikes the canvas so that, with a few brush strokes, working this day's red vibrancies into yesterday's browns, he creates swirling infinities that breathe as if the paint still pulsed as it had within his body.

November dawn-fire dims to ash all that surrounds it. The white of the studio walls becomes smoke-stained and sad beside his Art. It scalds my eyes.

"It's beautiful," I *wish* to say. I'd not let my words sully air through which his vision has just warmly flown, even if I *could* free my voice from the snare, my throat becomes before his Work. The canvas is a well of genius. Images at varying depths overlap.

Here, painted upon rough fabric and branded upon the rough gel of my eyes, the oft-painted "house of the suicide" is reclaimed by my lover's light. Here, the folded, churning clouds of trite dusks on the Hudson are infused with the depths of desert canyon walls. Here, a lily in a French garden flowers the colors of both new and old scars, floating upon a pond of iron-rust. Here, hidden like images within the game-pictures children love, a Starry Night made a Starry Twilight . . . with a firmament of red-crystal flecks.

Life and movement, granted by his drying blood. The blood of his life, the blood of his Art. The skill of his long and nimble fingers summon Truth. Patches of singed hair give texture to waving copper grass. Bits of teeth are pebbled to fairy-land cobblestones. A spiral of skin dances with cochlea. A scrap of eye, the pupil and iris, had, on one marvelous day, struck the far right corner of the canvas, so the painting became a kind of mirror (so he explained), able to gaze back at the viewer with the reflexivity unique to great Art.

While he sips mineral water and tastes fruit, I clear the art books that have offended him as I would dirty dishes . . . the collections of images created by mediocrities whose work has been lauded over the ages . . . images my lover salvages, then unfetters with his vision and will. Fools would call my lover's Work "pastiche" – the taking of images into himself, so he can re-use them his own way; I rightly call it "redemption."

It is my art to serve him and his Art.

As he showers the powder and flecks of himself from his hair, I clean his brushes and his gun. Then I go off to work . . . and so ensure him the solitude that gives the world such Beauty, even though the world is not yet ready to see it.

⁜

He met me on his porch.

The porch was *his*, though others eddied upon it as they fumbled with keys to mailboxes and to the converted house's front door of molded wood and fine leaded glass.

He parted my loneliness and asked, "Do you wish to be sired?"

His first words to me, swimming stars in my awareness, burning through years of smothered want. I'd made coming to Berkeley my pilgrimage to find myself; that my self could find me seemed too impossible to hope for.

Desire for him rewrote me. His question pushed all I'd been before coming to Berkeley into dream. My history, my life, became soft-edged and fogged. I was afraid.

A patch of sunlight had drawn me to his porch – I'd found it an attractive place to read of those dark angels for whom the sun is destructive. The light of this moment scattered the ash of what I'd been as would wind. I held up the book, invoking a barrier of the mundane (despite the profound truths the book itself held), so he and I could chat as if we'd met in a café, speaking in hushed, awed tones of the passions within the book. Muddy flirtation, to candle-dim the incendiary terror of that moment, to hold onto the dust-cool world in which I'd lived, because leaving it seemed too frightening.

"We won't talk about the book," he said, blocking my parry, sitting next to me. "And we won't talk about the movie. *Do you wish to be sired?* Do you wish to take the Gift of my blood . . ."

". . . *into* your blood?" would have been a more complete statement of his question. More complete, yet less True. The Beauty of the thought lay in *my* completing it . . . and thus allowed my mind to touch his as our bodies would touch while he sired me.

I drew a breath to speak my Completion when the rough tread of one of his neighbors intruded. The thud of work boots approached the door of molded wood behind us. I glanced over my shoulder. A brutish head was framed in the leaded glass.

I dropped my worn paperback shield as the door scraped open and muttered, "I should go." I walked away as the oafish neighbor clodded onto the porch. He who would become my lover smiled as I fled to a familiar landscape of want.

"You know where to find me," he said. As I backed away, his neighbor gave him the quizzical look the ignorant so often throw at artists.

I waded into Berkeley, my Promised Land whose Promise I'd forsaken. I let Berkeley huddle me as a vixen would her cub. Berkeley's hills and her trees were diamond-sharp in my sight now that my past had become so dream-diluted. The foundations of my existence seemed no stronger than the floss of long-dead spiders.

Berkeley carried me till evening, when I'd next meet *him* in a way that could not be called Fate, as *Fate* implies a thing from which one can charade an escape. I found myself at a reception honoring an artist whose work honored his own caricature. I understand that, now. I'd then been impressed by all art, no matter how facile.

I wasn't "drawn" to that small gallery. I felt as if I was refracted there, an illusion suddenly visible to my own perceptions.

Yet once in the gallery, I *was* drawn to a group of beautiful men who stood about, talking. I was drawn by their looks, the musk of their bodies, and the scented oils they dabbed on themselves. I was drawn by the confidence they exuded and the sweet smoke of clove cigarettes woven into the clothes they wore, by the knowledge that these were men who could *create* . . . who could give the gift of what they saw with their hearts to the world.

I stood within earshot of them, wanting to be desired by at least one of them. To be wanted so would be a trinket to replace the life-treasure I'd lost that afternoon.

A lovely man, ashen-skinned with green eyes, spoke to a man with golden hair.

"You're obliged to keep a journal," he said, "for the sake of those who will study your work. Your life is your art."

The golden-haired man said, "No! I'll not make the study of me or my work less of a challenge for anyone. Even *myself*. My work is my journal."

The other men listened with the solemnity of oaks. Their looks breeze-cast to one another were a web of intensity in which I longed to be entangled. I wanted to be taken into that emotional matrix that has existed among artists and their lovers throughout history, and that has defined subsequent eras of creative thought.

I stepped toward that grove of men and felt something unfold behind me. It was as if a rose the size of a cloak had unfurled. My imagination told me such a miracle had transpired, yet when I turned, I saw a miracle of another sort.

He whom I knew would become my soul-mate stood before canvases that suddenly seemed drab. No great rose had unfurled. Just his hand, extended. To me.

"Your red hair was how I found you," he said as we walked to his home. "Your red hair and your green eyes. They're a beacon. *You* called *me*. I answered. Now things must be finished." His hand gripped mine tighter. "Now you must be finished."

To be finished . . .

. . . a prize much greater than what I'd just sought within the web of artists I'd left behind. An eternal moment of fulfilment, like the interrupted moment in which I had, in my mind, finished his question to me: ". . . *into my blood?*"

Completion.

"I . . ."

"Don't say anything," he said. "Don't say a word."

We took the steps to his porch. The paperback I had no recollection of dropping was still there like a small altar. It filled me with something like nostalgia. I'd spent many hours holding it as a totem. Yet, when had I first opened it? Did it have the smell of a new book, or the musk of a used one? I reached through the dream-floss of my memory just as my hand was let go. My companion snatched up the book. He flipped through it. Smiled.

Then molded wood was pressed against my spine. The small spaces in the leaded glass caught the hairs on the back of my head as he followed the fluid motion of seizing me and pressing me against the front door with the cupping of his mouth over mine, with the rubbing of the back of his hand that held the book against my crotch.

His beautiful face came back into the focus; the rapture that had blurred him had also made the trees on the halogen-lit street a backdrop of velvet green.

"Seized first . . ." he said.

He shook me in reply to my silence. The hand that held the book pressed harder against me.

"Seized first . . ."

". . . then . . . sired."

An instant of *Completion* that brought stem-drops of pre-ejaculate from me.

His apartment was home. The jumble of canvases was welcome in my sight as would be the faces of family. Each canvas was blank. I loved them for what I knew they would wear, and the depths they'd acquire.

"Do you *see?*" he asked.

"Yes."

"I need you to see more."

He showed me the studio that been a kitchenette before he had sheathed the space in rubber foam and clear plastic. The Great Canvas, for I knew what it was despite it leaning against a far corner, a tarp draped over it. Like a magician producing a card by sleight of hand, he drew forth a postcard promoting the reception we'd left. The card reproduced a painting I'd seen at the reception: a lifeless portrait of a lifeless face. It had no character, for the subject had no character: I suspected it to be a self-portrait.

He hung a blank canvas behind a small paint-smeared table and chair. Rough, scarred, and much-spackled plaster marked the wall.

"Leave," he said. "You'll know when to come back in."

I stood outside the French doors separating the studio from the living room. Foam obscured the windowlettes of the doors, yet spaces allowed me to peer through – as must have been his intent. The man with whom I wished to spend my redefined life came to the table with a tray holding his gun and brushes. He seated himself and placed the postcard before him. The sight of his raising the gun to his mouth was as agonizingly slow in my suddenly brimming sight as would be the sight of him driving nails through his own flesh.

My vision ripped with the ripping of his skull.

I hung in the eye of the sun, unblinking in the forever of the shot.

A lifetime of dawns erupted behind my sight.

Then the grain of the wood floor onto which I'd collapsed filled my vision.

Consciousness was a sodden burden I did not want.

I stood from the fallen bundle I'd become, opened the French doors.

Through the blue veil of smoke, I saw the beatitude of him standing from the table, rising as red and rose-pink matter slowed its cascade upon the canvas.

Within the viscous, blossomed smear, the face of the portrait scabbed itself into visibility. No longer a self-portrait, it was now made valid by a true artist having seen it and transposed his pure sensibility upon it. The image on the postcard was reborn, revisualized to be what it *should* have always been. I came to myself as I saw in the crimson portrait's eyes a new profundity.

The portrait's eyes were now those of the man who would make me his lover this night. I would be granted an infusion of the same spirit through his blood. The immortality of great Art would be attainable for me through the angel-destructive taking of his spirit.

"We'll burn this canvas in the morning. I'll not dirty my brushes with it. But I needed you to see."

"I'm glad I saw." My words were church-whispered soft.

He smiled. "I'm glad you're brave enough to be glad. But *thi*s is not my Art," he said, hefting the canvas off the wall. "I'd not summon you to my life if it were. You are more worthy than that." He dropped the canvas by a pile of rubbish near what had been a wooden ice box, then crossed the studio to where the tarped canvas leaned. "*This* is my Work," he said, pulling away the tarp.

Masterpieces as collage, *Completed*. Transposed, dragonfly-wing translucent. Works that had been wrongly called "Great Works" were made valid by their being rewritten and repainted in my mentor's perceptions and blood.

His vision and his courage recast Renaissance Madonnas and cubist landscapes. Still-lifes and portraits were fully realized and improved by his giving himself to their redemption. The images shifted and blazed in front of each other, as if each session's work had been done on panes of air-thin glass.

He offered me this Beauty. He offered to let me take it within me – *my* Completion, like that which he'd given to the "great works" the world had misguidedly thought to be already timeless and eternal.

Blood is his Art. And his Art is his Gift.

What matter that the body may be too fragile to endure the immortality the Gift offers? What matter the eventual loss of life to become as eternal as his Art? His Art sustains him. It resurrects him each day as he lifts Art from the dust in which it had been buried.

That night, for the first time, I knew pleasure unmitigated by latex. He bestowed the Gift of his Blood and Art to me. Sired, complete, I woke the next morning knowing I'd found a Homeland nourished by the rivers that flowed within my lover. I left his bed to find my Sire placing my battered book upon his shelf, next to other books by the same prophetess who had germinated in me the desire I'd just known fulfilled. He slid the book in a space on the crowded shelf, as if he'd just taken it from there.

"Your first item moved in," he said.

We laughed. Embraced. Made love and requickened my blood with his blood. My veins felt cut into my flesh, etched as are the depth-giving grooves my lover makes upon his canvas with trowels fashioned from shards of his own jaw.

⚜

It happened on Monday morning. A bourgeois joke. Fodder for greeting cards and coffee mug slogans to amuse those whom my lover's Work was destined to elevate. The banality of the moment when disaster chose to strike pained him the most, at times. I shared his anguish that Mediocrity had dealt him such humiliation.

As always, on that Monday – my furtive glance and the single shot. The shattering red fog and the willow-tree spray of blood and bone and flesh. Then, in the world-stunned silence, the rustle of his brushstokes as he redeemed an image of Redemption as painted by a medieval primitive.

I waited while he worked, in a place where time seemed to sleep. Then I heard the distinct click of him setting down his brush crafted from a splinter of his femur. I took fruit and mineral water from the mini-fridge in the living room – a gesture that served Art more than did entire lifetimes nominally dedicated to Art – and heard the rare treasure of him calling me by name.

I went through the French doors, and glanced upon Beauty – the new layer added this day to the Work. It was the image of a dying knight carried to Heaven by the reputed mother of Christ. My lover had dared the ancient fresco to magnificence, finding a way for it to truthfully catch the fires of Heaven it had tried to portray.

He stared at the canvas as I placed the tray upon the book of medieval art I'd freed from the library.

"I can't find it," he said.

I looked. The kit with which he patched the canvas sat by his brushes and gun. A lesser lover of a lesser man would have said, "*It's right there.*"

Yet I failed him in another way by saying nothing.

"Look . . . at . . . the . . . *Work,*" he said.

My eye was drawn to the scrap of eye in the painting's far corner. His martyred iris still reflected his soul.

"*Look. . . .*" he said.

I ran my eye over museums-worth of sublimity.

And realized with a shock . . .

. . . no patch today.

I turned. His patching kit was unopened in its ribboned box, as I'd placed it for him.

"I can't find the *bullet,*" he said.

Together, we ran our fingers over the wall, to see if the bullet was embedded in the plaster beside the canvas, in wood or a metal stud behind the plaster. The abattoir-perfume of the canvas made me giddy as I stood closer to it than I ever had. Yet still I kept my focus to his task.

As one, we both looked to the floor.

And I felt a burning migraine-like pain as he lowered his head . . . a sharp, weighty pressure atop the loam of my brain.

The pain I felt was an echo, reaching me from his blood. The cry I let out was a leakage of the cry he held tight in his throat.

The sudden pain that subsided in me endured in him as it made twisted branches of his body. His knees fell from under him and he held his head in his blood-caked hands.

"It's still inside me."

The days that followed still shame me.

I was jealous of the bullet.

Jealous of his obsessive thinking of it, of the constant circular caresses he made upon his scalp as it gnawed him from within. I hungered for the caresses he no longer gave me.

The bullet sported in the paradise *of his mind*. An unthinking bit of stone had, through accident, attained the beatification for which I prayed. Yes, it hurt his thoughts – yet it was closer to him than I was . . . entangled in the lattice of his genius. It was an unborn half-self to him: what I longed to be, above and beyond our conjoining of blood.

And through that which is and ever shall be his Gift to me, I felt the bullet change his blood. Since he had Sired me, my own blood had the sweetness of honeyed milk in my veins. Now that was tainted with metallic hurt, a sour buzzing eroded from the stone lodged in his mind. Lead infused my vision. At times, all Berkeley itself became tinted with grayish cobalt in my sight.

My lover's Work dried upon the canvas – it took on an opacity that dimmed its layers. Though still beautiful, since it failed to be renewed each morning the Work lost vividness – rearing suns aligned in harmony became as one sun.

And I lost something as well, no longer replenished by the exquisite spirit he granted me each time our lovemaking re-enacted the moment of his Siring me. Even with the taint of the bullet in him, I hungered for such renewal.

Yet my needs were unimportant. My lover was not painting. Art was not being redeemed. That to which I'd dedicated all I ever could be suffered into stasis. I felt cut off from my own life – a bluefly tapping against the window of where I as a person should live. To re-enter, I tried to awaken his passion . . . for his Art, and for me.

I brought him new books of art to look upon and redeem.

The person I *had* been might not have suffered the wound of my lover leaping from the couch and flinging into my face the damp, oil-and-blood-stained cloth that had been on his brow. The person I *had* been might have said what he said to me: "Why are you hurting me like this?"

He grabbed the books and flung them to the floor. His teeth ground like a handful of pebbles. "You're happy," he said. "You're fine. I gave you all of me I can. You have parts of me I can't touch anymore. And you resort to cheap taunts?"

"I want you to work."

His voice became like that of a sick child. "That's very funny, coming from you."

"Your work is important to me."

"So, I should work?" Again, his voice was child-like, like that of a boy sorry he has broken the favorite plaything of another.

"Yes."

"You'd just love that, wouldn't you? If another shot got stuck? Why not let me have two hot little pebbles in my head? You'd like that, wouldn't you? To be the strong one? You jealous. . . ."

He held his head, sat on the sofa. ". . . jealous little shit," he finished. He glared at me. "*Two hot little pebbles.* That's not very good, is it? Certainly not worthy of *you*." He stood, walked shakily to the bookshelf and pulled from behind a row of novels the rolls of paper upon which I'd begun this account. He held them to me. "*You're* the artist now? You're trying to write like the 'poetess?'"

"I'm . . . trying . . . to document what you do."

"I gave you *this*." He shook the papers that I'd made into scrolls, so they'd have the solemnity they deserved. "I gave you your words. But you can't use them to describe what I do. I gave you all I'd learned from 'your' precious 'poetess,' because you're that important to me."

"You're everything to me. . . ."

"Then why do you bring me art to look at? You taunt me with a need to create that I can't fulfill?" He looked down upon the art books I'd freed for him . . . looked down upon the images only half-finished by Cézanne the way a starving man would a full and steaming plate. The images seemed to hunger for my lover as well . . . desiring his vision and blood to dream them into wholeness.

He dropped the scrolls and fell to his knees, touching the books. He sobbed the way I had when he rewrote my blood. I tried to hold him, to help him to the couch.

He pushed me away, then pressed his hands against the back of his head.

"You're worse than the fucking bullet."

I returned to work. I rode the train from Berkeley to my empty job, which seemed all the more hollow now it had no purpose other than to support our basic living. The drudgery I endured had once served the redemption of Art. Now it served the mere paying of rent. I sat surrounded by drones never touched by the sublime as I had been. I looked to the empty faces my lover's Work would have touched with fire. I pitied them. They were not ready to receive the Work that would free them from their prisons, that would bring *them* to the higher plane for which they were too afraid to reach.

And I pitied myself. I was suddenly, in fact, that which I had mimicked.

I tried to read a newspaper. The words blurred to a wall of gray. Yet as I tried to read, the roar of the train . . .

. . . took a solidity . . .

. . . that stood upon the loam of my brain. The sound of the train became the buzzing of the bullet in my lover's mind; it compressed itself into an impacted tooth of metal in my mind.

Sublimation . . . the passing of a thing from one state to another. Isn't that what my lover's blood does? What Art itself does? The pain at the back of my head was the call of my body for the bullet – just as the dull eyes of those around me was the call for the semblance of life my lover's Art would bring. The bullet's sound, its sourness, its pain, infused me through my lover's blood. Could it not crystallize into me? Could it not flow as solution to me and metastasize in my mind? Drawn as gold was once believed to be from base lead?

Thus, could my lover be free to create his Art?

I changed platforms at the next stop and returned home to realize I'd no idea we owned so many mirrors.

That was the thought that jangled in my shattering mind as I arrived to tragedy and desecration.

My lover had taken the mirrors from the bedroom, from the medicine chest, from the hall, even a shaving mirror I'd forgotten we owned, and placed them on easels of varying height so he could see reflections of reflections of his newly-shaven head as he brought the electric hand-saw I used to make his canvas frames to the base of his skull.

The buzzing in my mind externalized itself; it left me to become the light-strobing buzz of the hand-saw as it lay jammed with a thumb-sized shard of skull. In that strobing light, my lover writhed, unable to raise his hands to the shark-bite wound he had inflicted upon himself and gouge the hated nugget from his mind.

I knelt to him, held him as the Madonna held her Son in the *pietà* my lover had once amber-trapped in his blood.

Spray had geysered the studio that was no longer a studio, now that my lover's blood and tissue had haphazardly smeared the Work. His palsied hand, unlike the sure hand that brought the gun to the loving smooth roof of his mouth, had splashed gaudy rain upon the canvas. The translucent layers had blended into each other, had made the Work appear nothing more than cloth dropped on the floor of a slaughterhouse.

I unplugged the saw. The lights above stopped strobing. The buzzing fell silent. I replaced the shard of skull from where it had been torn.

"Don't speak," I said. "Don't say a word."

In that place where time held itself hostage to our plight, I knew what martyrdom he wished.

✙

A woman screamed at us, apparitions smeared with what she could only know as "blood." Yet it was also our Gift – our shared legacy. I'd not let anyone steal or sully it.

It was wasteful to spill our Gift upon the train platform. My lover, his head bandaged with duct-tape and dishtowels, paid the mid-morning commuters no heed as we shoved past them. All we could focus on was the oblivion promised by the track down which eighty tons of careening metal rushed.

I stood behind him as he dove before the train as if into pure and cleansing waters.

I knew joy, and release, as my lover was pulped to moist, red clay . . . as he found the sublimation that would free him. No one could steal his Gift, now that the Art it allowed him to create had been taken from him. No lesser talent would ever desecrate or appropriate his blood for their own revisualizations. He'd not become paint for lesser talents, not while his flesh and blood and marrow were dispersed so thinly. I smiled to know he was free.

And I split along that smile, casting my blood upon the wind-swift metal canvas of the train. I shattered along my skeleton as the *first* flesh from which my lover had crafted me burst upon the track. My dissolution had none of my lover's fire, had none of the profundity of his Art.

I hoped to ascend, to find myself in the sublime heaven my lover had painted with that Gift from which I'd been conjured.

But I found myself earthbound by a small metal nugget with the weight of a thousand suns. I . . . my lover's least creation . . . reached to him through the liquidity that joined us, through the blood-spirit-thought that defines our Gift and that now forms my words.

We cooled together, two careless smears, blended as are cheap pigments by the hoses of those who washed us away.

FRESHETS

BRETT ALEXANDER SAVORY

Okay, so I'm fucking this guy in the ass, over a chair, you know? Just fucking him hard and fast, like we're –

No, wait a sec. That's not right.

So I'm banging the piss out of this chick, right? Just railing on her, pulling on her tits from behind and really giving it to her, like –

Hang on. That's not right, either.

Alright, so I'm licking this cunt, don't care whose, just some cunt, and there're two of them, these hot lesbos, just really on fire. One's taking my whole cock while I'm lapping her up; the other's got three fingers in my ass-hole, knuckle-deep, trying to wear me like a glove, and she's pumping in hard, twisting her nipples between her fingers, trying to rip the poor fucking things off, and –

Nah, that ain't happening, either.

Dirty dishes, though, that's for sure. Right over there in the sink. Stacks of them. Filthy. Shit growing on them. Moldy green crap, you know? Nightmare mountain, looming over me, over everything in the kitchen. My tiny kitchen, with its doorless, empty cupboards, wide open, staring at the dishes, hungry, wishing I'd wash them so the cupboards could have some sort of purpose.

Yeah, sure, but fuck them. I have more pressing shit to deal with.

Like, hey, where'd these people come from? These fornicating freshets, splayed out all over my living room. My living room where nothing lives. Just a dusty television, which I leave tuned to the nature channel cause I like to learn things about other animals.

No pizza boxes, though. You want pizza boxes, go read someone else's chop-py-sentenced, no-plot story. This one only has dirty dishes, empty cupboards, a dusty television, wildly bucking males and females in decidedly provocative positions, and me, the poor bastard in the middle of it all, wishing I knew what was happening and why it was happening to me.

For the most part, I just sit on my ratty, old, cigarette-burn-holed couch and watch. No bag of chips in my lap, though. Same as the pizza boxes, so don't even think it. The shit the freshets get up to is not particularly relaxing, and my perpetual erection makes it hard to concentrate on lifting food to my mouth, anyway.

Erection. There, I said it.

But I'm not a man. Can't be a man. I have fantasies about men. Like when

I'm fucking that guy over the chair in the corner of the living room, really ripping into him, you know, and –

But it's not true. Fucking cocksucking homos.

And there's dad talking, there's my brother talking, there's everyone in my life talking.

Some days I pinch the lips of my pussy, slide a finger or two inside and grin, grin like mad, lift my other hand to my tits, heft their weight. Oh, yeah, I'm all about breasts, me. Even the dishes turn away when I'm doing this, shrink into the grimy crusts of their dried-on foodstuffs. Then I feel some other woman's sex toy in me – a long, fat dildo – and it's sliding in so slowly, just feeling around in there, spelunking, digging for treasure, scoping out the joint, and she's gonna invite some friends over, too, cause –

But that's not true, either. Sick-ass lesbos. Just need a good fat sausage up the ass to turn them back to the straight and narrow.

Hi again, Dad.

Hey, best friend.

Howdy, world.

I just sort of float around every day with different genitalia attached to me – man, woman, both, neither, in between, upside down, inside out, on top, below, from behind, whichever way and in whatever body presents itself. I'm a sexual chameleon, baby. Pussy, dick, all the same to me. I have no shame. But then, that's not even me talking. That's the person I want to be. I have yet to discover what I actually am. What do you prefer? Does it matter? Is there even a difference?

Let's ask the dishes. Let's ask the cupboards. Wide-eyed, accusing mother-fuckers, all of them. Staring, watching, leaning, looming, dirty, and dirty-minded. Not everything is about sex, I tell them. Not everything.

There's a picture on top of the dusty television of someone I don't recognize. The freshets never look at it, never even turn their heads in its direction. Two guys. Smiling. Happy. As if.

One of the guys seems like he's gone. Seems like he hasn't been in this apartment for a long, long time. So long, I can barely remember him. I think the other guy might be me. I look like a discarded beer can – sort of crumpled at the edges, pinched in at the waist and leaning to one side – and many years younger.

I can barely remember him, either.

So there's dead-or-missing guy and empty, young maybe-me. We're quite the couple. I have no idea who could have taken this picture, because no one else exists except me (or the thing that pretends to be me), dead-or-missing guy, and the ever-present host of fabulous freshets.

The American Heritage Dictionary of the English Language has this to say on the subject:

fresh_et (fɾɛʃhɪt) *n.*

1. A sudden overflow of a stream resulting from a heavy rain or a thaw.
2. A stream of fresh water that empties into a body of salt water.

The picture on top of the dusty television has thawed, and I'm M/Mme Salt-water. Pleased to meet you.

On an end table next to one of my frayed and crappy chairs is a pile of bills. The bills do not even come close to competing with the dishes, but they're trying. Yes, sir. Trying hard to loom and be menacing, but achieving only a sort of semi-threatening almost-leer that doesn't do much to stir any sort of fear inside me. I'm far more terrified of the dishes. Dirty dishes were born to terrorize, created to instill a sense of doubt in humans, designed to challenge our control of the situation – whatever situation we're deluded enough to feel that we're in control of.

Far off in one corner of the living room, leaning against a grimy gray wall, are the cupboard's doors. Looking forlorn. So sad. Ripped from their homes then crammed close to one another against their wills.

Surely there's symbolism in there somewhere, but I can't be bothered to figure it out. I know I must have ripped the cupboard doors from their hinges for some symbolic reason. I'm such a pretentious twat when it comes to emoting. Fuck it, who am I kidding? I am the doors and the doors represent my disconnection from reality for whatever pathetic, self-centered reasons I feel like telling myself this week.

Because cupboards without doors do not exist. Carpenters do not build such things. They are aberrant. Against nature.

On the television, a fat man talks about zebras, motions to them in the background behind him. Black and white stripes. Something about mating. On television, everything is about sex. And yeah, fat man, black and white stripes. Sure. Like anything is so simple.

I reach inside my disgusting couch, pull out the VCR remote, point it in the general direction of the television, having to lean around a few sets of freshets twisting nipples, reaming assholes, moaning about how good it feels, how it's never been like this before – having to lean around these monsters to shoot my infrared at the screen.

I press Record.

After a few minutes, I rewind the tape and watch zebras run across my screen in Fast Forward. They're gray. Not black and white at all.

Gray. Just like the rest of life, fat man.

Everything is about perspective.

The way I see it, sitting on this beer-stained, shit-brown couch, a distinct chunk of myself dead or missing, I'd say I'm about ready to kick these freshets out on their asses, out my door, out of my life. This isn't a porno movie, you fucks. Get out.

Now I'm standing, I'm livid, motioning with my arms, pointing at the door, get out, get out, you've been here too long. No one invited you, anyway. Nobody wants you.

But they ignore me, the lot of them. White and black and brown limbs, flailing, groping. I sit back down on my couch, defeated. Deflated.

There's a video camera on the floor, in front of the television. I get up again, push naked bodies out of my way, collecting sweat as I go, like stamps or foreign coins.

Picking up the camera, I check to see if there's a tape inside. Of course there is. This isn't the sort of story where the protagonist isn't prepared, boring everyone by running around hunting for a fucking videotape. That story, and the one with the pizza boxes and chip bags, is somewhere else, in some other book, on some other guy's bookshelf.

I press Record on this machine, just like I did on the VCR. This extension of my memory, this chunk of my psyche that will never grow old or become damaged by time. Only accident or violence can smear this recollection of my existence.

Film's rolling. Tape's moving. I'm the director. Let's see if these freshets can stand the glare of the spotlight. Let's see if they can prove their substantiality by not being ghosts, by not being just the boring, filthy furniture of my diseased living room and kitchen. Let's see what these little bastards are really made of.

Rolling, rolling, several minutes of film, from several different angles all around these two-rooms-in-one. I make sure the microphone is working too, so I'll be able to hear, upon playback, all the promises of love, fidelity, affection, loyalty, monogamy, and other things people should be smart enough not to believe in.

I want to film the dishes and the cupboards and the bills, but I'm afraid of what they'll look like on camera. They're scary enough without adding ten pounds to their weight.

I press Stop, fight my way through the fleshy freshies, eject the zebra tape, and pop this new one in.

Press Play.

Somehow the fat man has weaseled his way onto this tape (and, presumably, into my living room). He's pointing behind him at the freshets, smiling, discussing their mating rituals. Now switching his attention to the picture on top of my dusty television.

Dennis, he says. That's the only word I can make out because the live porn in my living room-kitchen is getting out of hand with the moaning and cussing and smacking and biting. Settle down, I want to say. Settle down or get the fuck out.

Dennis.

The camera closes in tight on the picture, and I remember the name. But the tears in this story are with the pizza boxes and all that other crap. Not here, buddy. No tears for dead-or-missing lovers in this recreation of events that may or may not have happened.

Dennis.

Fuck.

I rewind the tape, watch the fat man and the freshets in fast forward. Gray and gray and gray, like the zebras. All those limbs thrashing, meshing, melting, crumbling into one another, crushing the flesh hues into a colorless paste of humanity.

How profound.

I feel sick to my stomach. I'm going to vomit all over my shitty couch.

I rewind the tape again, watch it at normal speed. I point at the screen and tell the fat man to piss off. Get off my screen, you fat fuck; just go back to your nature show and leave me out of it.

But the fat man isn't listening. I let the tape run longer than before, and soon the camera zooms in on Dennis, it's now just his face. I remember touching that face. I remember kissing those lips. I remember wishing my eyes were like his eyes. Sharp. Crisp. Colorless. Gray.

I press Pause now. A new button. Mixing it up a little.

Dennis stares at me, his face filling the screen.

If dishes could laugh, they'd be busting a gut right now. Laughing at my confusion. Laughing at my loss.

Dennis looks like he's trying to say something, like maybe he's going to apologize, or tell me when he's coming back. Or maybe he's trying to open his mouth to tell the freshets to piss off and leave me be.

Dennis would have done that for me.

My Dennis.

The VCR starts chewing the tape up. I hear it munching. Dennis' face crinkles, warbles, flickers.

Disappears.

And that fat fuck from the nature show is suddenly back on the screen. Now he's talking about giraffes.

Somehow, between the last time I checked and now, tears have sprung from my eyes.

More freshets. More overflow.

Why am I crying, Dad?

What about it, bro?

How about you, Ma? What's up with me? Why can't I keep hold of anything? My cup constantly runneth over with the shit that's been poured into me.

I stand up, wipe the tears from my cheeks, looking around my living room-kitchen, seeing nothing but gray, nothing but Dennis' cold, crisp eyes in every one of the freshets' heads. Nestled in there, buried deep, gripping the sides of their sockets, refusing to change color.

I'm flitting around the room again, sucking this hole, fucking that one, trying to remember what this all used to be like back when there was more to my life than this. Trying to hold on to all these pairs of drained, gray eyes.

But resolution is something else missing from this story. Maybe it's rotting inside the pizza boxes, growing mold. Growing old. Growing tired of being pulled like a simple rabbit out of the writer's hat.

Suddenly, my tongue aching, my dick throbbing, my pussy bleeding, my tits bruised, I feel overwhelmed with warmth, with comfort. Color bleeds back into the room. I close my eyes for a second, take a deep breath, then release it, slowly.

Freshets pop all around me like balloons. Red splashes streak my walls, drench me, splatter the windows.

In a world of red, there can be no black and white. There cannot even be gray.

When I open my eyes, I'm standing at the sink, staring at the dirty dishes. Up close. Watching them watch me.

Turning around, I see there's only one freshet left unpopped. He's naked and standing there amidst all the gore. He flexes his toes, squishes around in the blood. Smiles at me.

He has Dennis' eyes, but he's not Dennis. I don't know who he is. But when I look at him, I feel something close to attraction. The closest thing to attraction I've felt in such a long, long time.

He walks toward me, confident, sure of who he is, sure of who I am. I am unable to do anything but watch him, like I watched the dishes a moment ago. Powerless. Completely at his mercy.

He extends his naked red arms to me, pulls my head close to his, strokes my hair, my neck. I feel Dennis' eyes, in this man's head. Heavy. Concentrated. Fierce.

The way his hand moves against my skin, I know he's thinking about the dishes when he speaks. He's thinking about the cupboard doors. He's thinking about me, of what I used to have, of what he's not going to try to replace.

Looking directly into the face of my crisp, gray past, he says something; his lips move, but I don't hear what they say. Not a word.

Just his breath on my neck, smooth, soothing, forgiving.

BAYOU DE LA MÈRE

POPPY Z. BRITE

The bayou twisted through the green sward of Vermilion Parish, brown and slow as a snake basking in the sun. On its left bank sat the town, very small and picturesque, and just now, very very hot. The midday sun bounced off neatly whitewashed buildings and sizzled up from narrow streets like heat rising from a well-seasoned iron skillet. Ancient moss-bearded oaks made shady tunnels over the sidewalk, but if you stood in one of these tunnels too long, a small cloud of midges and mosquitoes would form around you. All in all, it seemed a hell of a place to spend an August vacation, but it had been highly recommended by the bartender.

Said bartender was spending *her* vacation in Colorado, and the two cooks intermittently cursed her name as they trudged around the little town. They had only been successful restaurateurs for about a year. Before that their existence had been pretty much hand-to-mouth, and they'd never taken a real vacation. When they decided to close the restaurant for two weeks during the slowest part of the summer, they felt as if they should go somewhere for at least a week, and friends urged them to get out of New Orleans for once in their lives.

"We can't be more than, like, four hours away," Rickey had said. "Something could come up." Mo convinced them to visit the little town, a three-hour drive from New Orleans.

They were staying on the second floor of a 160-year-old hotel that looked out over the bayou. The place smelled of lemon floor polish and genteelly decaying wood. "I gonna show you up to y'all room," said the proprietress when they checked in. The accent out here was nothing like the exuberant, full-throated New Orleans one; rather, it was low and musical, with a hint of the French spoken here less than a century ago. The woman's jet-dark eyes, curious but not overtly hostile, kept slipping back to them as she showed off the room with its double bed. *We might not like everything y'all do in New Orleans,* Rickey imagined her thinking, *but we need y'all money.*

When she had gone, G-man set his suitcase on a marble-topped end table and started unpacking. "You think she ever met a couple of fags who were less interested in all these damn antiques?" he said.

"I kinda like the bed," said Rickey. It was a wooden four-poster with knobs carved into tortured flower shapes.

"That's cause you got an interior design queen inside you, just dying to get out."

249

"Yeah, right." Rickey had decorated the restaurant's dining room almost singlehandedly, choosing everything from the silverware pattern to the shade of green on the walls, but he had never spent more than fifty dollars on anything for their house and couldn't imagine doing so. They weren't home often enough to enjoy nice décor.

Although it was nearing the hottest part of the day, they forced themselves out of the hotel and into the slow-baking streets. That was when they started cursing Mo's name. The bayou, the cannons in the square, the old Catholic church: all were lovely, but all seemed to waver behind a cell-thin, sticky layer of heat. G-man, whose eyes had always been painfully sensitive to light, could hardly see through his dark prescription glasses. Within thirty minutes they were in a rustic but air-conditioned oyster bar gulping cocktails even though happy hour was still far away.

"How can it be hotter here than in New Orleans?" Rickey said.

"It's not," said G-man. "We just got time to notice it here."

"We stand over goddamn stoves all day. I thought I was immune to heat."

"Y'all from New Orleans?" called the manager of the seafood restaurant, who was over in the corner playing video poker. "Y'all don't even know what real heat *is* way up there."

Rickey and G-man looked at each other in half-drunken amazement at having suddenly become Northern aggressors. "I guess that's what we get for calling Tanker a Yankee," said G-man. Their pastry chef had been born in Covington, about forty-five miles north of New Orleans.

They sat at the bar a while longer, feeling somewhat out of place, but not uncomfortably so. There was nothing obviously touristy about them; to all outward appearances they were just a couple of working-class guys in their late twenties. They both wore black chef pants – Rickey's patterned with a thin blue stripe, G-man's with a variety of mushrooms – and they might have been about to work the dinner shift, if this place were slack enough to let workers drink before shifts. However, Rickey felt sure that they were as conspicuous as a couple of dorks in Acapulco shirts with cameras hanging around their necks. He didn't really care, though. He wasn't supposed to feel like a local; he was on vacation.

The thought began to sink in as he sipped his third bourbon and soda. He was on vacation! They didn't have to worry about the restaurant for a whole week. They could drink and eat and wander around aimlessly and do whatever they liked. Thinking about it, he began to feel horny. "Let's go back to the room," he said.

Once there, they cranked up the air conditioner and pulled the curtains shut. The room filled with cool afternoon shadows. Rickey rummaged through his bag. "Did you bring the lotion?" he said.

"I thought you put it in that Ziploc bag of toothpaste and stuff."

"I don't see it." They had used hand lotion as a lubricant since they were teenagers, and had never quite graduated to K-Y, Astroglide, or any of the raunchier products.

"Well, we gotta have it or I'll be walking around here like a guy with fatal hemorrhoids," G-man said sensibly. "I saw a Wal-Mart on the way into town – we could go get some."

"Dude, I don't want to go to Wal-Mart and buy nothing but a bottle of lotion. You know how that's gonna look?"

G-man shrugged.

"Wait a sec," said Rickey, digging deeper into his suitcase. "Here it is. I forgot I put it in its own bag in case it leaked."

They undressed and lay on the bed kissing, but the alcohol, sun, and twelve straight days of work before the vacation had begun to kick in. Their caresses went from languid to exhausted. "Damn, I'm sorry," said Rickey when he realized he had just dozed for a few seconds. "I want to do it, but I can hardly keep my eyes open."

"Me neither. Maybe we could just nap for a few minutes."

They settled against each other and allowed themselves to drift off. By the time they awoke, the room was fully dark, the town outside was still, and every restaurant and bar within a twenty-mile radius had been closed for hours. They went out onto the balcony and sat smoking a joint. At the other end of the street, a traffic signal cycled through its colors several times before a lone car came along, paused briefly at the red light, then went on without waiting for the green. The bayou was invisible in the night, signaling its presence only with a damp, organic smell and an occasional flash of moonlight on water.

"Let's go for a walk," said G-man.

"A what?" Rickey wasn't being a smart-ass; the concept of taking a walk late at night simply hadn't occurred to him in many years. It wasn't as dangerous as critics of New Orleans suggested, but it wasn't the sort of thing most people did if they could help it.

"I feel like stretching my legs. Then we can come back here and finish what we started."

The second-floor landing was decorated with an antique mirror, a spray of wildflowers, and a rather large, gory plaster statue of Jesus exhibiting his Sacred Heart. They walked softly down the old wooden staircase and let themselves out of the still hotel onto the silent street. "You know what's different here?" said Rickey after they had gone half a block toward the town square. "Even after a really fucking hot day, it doesn't stink. There's no shitty garbage vapor rising off the asphalt."

"The bayou stinks a little."

"Well, what do you expect? We're still in Louisiana."

"I don't think these people even believe you and I are from Louisiana. They think New Orleans is a whole 'nother country."

"They might have something there."

"Seriously." As they neared the square, G-man looked up at the spire of the eighteenth-century church. "It's so Catholic out here. I don't think I could live in a place that takes its religion this seriously."

"What you talking about? Your mom takes religion as seriously as anybody I ever knew."

"That's what I'm talking about," said G-man. "That's why I couldn't stand to be around it. Sure, New Orleans is Catholic, but it's different there. More . . . I don't know . . . more adaptable. You're a lapsed Catholic out here, they're gonna make you think about it every damn day of your life. You never really get away from it anyway – they get you by the time you're five, they got a part of you forever."

"Yeah?" As they passed in front of the church, Rickey made a grab for G-man. "Which part?"

"Quit it!"

"How come? There's nobody out at this hour."

But G-man was looking at something on the other side of the square. Following his gaze, Rickey saw a serene-faced white statue of the Blessed Virgin Mary seated in the center of a little bubbling fountain. "Oh, no, dude. You don't want me grabbing your ass in front of *that?*"

"It's just not nice," G-man said uncomfortably.

"Sorry. I didn't know you were still ashamed of me when the goddamn Catholic Church was watching."

"Course I'm not ashamed of you. Don't even say that."

"Don't act like it then."

They walked over to the statue and examined it in silence. Rickey couldn't remember ever seeing the Virgin Mary seated before. People in New Orleans put little statues of her in half-buried bathtubs in their yards, and while her robes might be painted either the traditional blue or a more festive pink, she was always standing. He refused to ask G-man about it, though. Instead he circled the fountain and entered a small floodlit garden behind it. On the whitewashed wall of the nearby church, dozens of flesh-colored lizards lay in wait for nocturnal insects. A little door on the wall was labeled CHAPEL OF PERPETUAL ADORATION, but Rickey didn't know what that meant.

G-man followed Rickey into the garden. He saw the sign and the stained glass window beside the door, where the ornate tabernacle holding the consecrated Host cast a weirdly-shaped shadow. Remembering the bland, dusty taste of the Host on his tongue, he looked away. "This place makes me nervous, that's all," he said. "It's hard to explain. You remember I told you about the last time I ever went to Confession?"

"Yeah. I think that was about a week before the first time I fucked your damn brains out."

Rickey was being crude because his feelings were hurt, and G-man ignored it. "Well, that was what? Thirteen years ago? That was the last time I ever felt like the Church could see what I was doing —"

"The Church?" Rickey said dubiously. He had not been raised in any particular religion. "You mean like God, or what?"

"Sorta. Not exactly. It's more like management." The critical gaze of management was something they both understood all too well. "Like a bunch of 'em all sitting on some kind of advisory board, deciding whether your sins are venial or mortal, how many Our Fathers or Hail Marys you gotta say, counting up every filthy thing you ever done. And even if you leave the Church, your family's still Catholic, so you know you're gonna get a goddamn funeral Mass when you die."

"Dude, you're twenty-nine. What are you thinking about funeral Masses for?"

"I'm not. That's not what I'm trying to say." Frustrated, G-man turned his back on the Chapel of Perpetual Adoration. "It's just that when I walked out of that confessional, I knew it was the last time, and all of a sudden I didn't feel like they were watching anymore. Out here, it kinda feels like they are again."

"Yeah, and you're not the first homo tourist they ever saw. Get over it."

They walked the rest of the way around the square in silence and turned onto the deserted Main Street, here called Rue Principale. Rickey stopped to peer through the window of a darkened restaurant. "Cheap-ass flocked wallpaper," he muttered. G-man didn't say anything, and Rickey turned on him. "Well, what? Do you hate it here cause they got a lot of serious Catholics? It's our first ever vacation. I hope you don't hate it."

"No. No, I don't hate it. I'm happy we're here. I just never been to Cajun country before. I didn't know it would be so —"

"So what?"

"Catholic."

Rickey threw up his hands in disgust and started walking back toward the hotel. G-man followed, feeling guilty. "It doesn't matter," he said after a few minutes. "It's not gonna ruin anything."

"It better not."

Neither of them said a word until they got back to the room, but it wasn't a particularly uncomfortable silence; they'd been together long enough to get annoyed with each other and get over it in the space of a few minutes. G-man was thinking about a small white rosary his mother had given him for his first Communion. He'd tried to say his penance on it after leaving the confessional for the last time, but had only been able to get through five Hail Marys before realizing he couldn't be a Catholic anymore, not if what the priest had just told him was true. He'd put the rosary away and hadn't thought of it for years, until one day Rickey was looking for something in a dresser drawer and found the little velvet-lined jewelry box. Anyone would have thought Rickey had found condoms or maybe a come-stained copy of *Huge & Uncut.* "What do you still have *that* for?" he'd demanded, and G-man finally just said in as sharp a tone as he ever used, "Look, my mom gave it to me. Shut the fuck up about it." But that wasn't the only reason he had kept the rosary. He could no more have thrown it out than Rickey could have gotten rid of his father's old Army dogtags, even though Rickey's parents had been divorced for a quarter-century and he never talked to his father.

Rickey was thinking about a conversation he'd had at the restaurant a few months ago. One of the cooks wondered aloud why G-man (who was elsewhere at the time) wouldn't try to extort a little lump crabmeat or something from a purveyor who'd sent them some wormy fish, and Rickey said, "You gotta understand, G's just a nice Catholic boy at heart." He was surprised to hear himself say that, because he always thought of G-man as his partner in crime, his lieutenant of degeneracy. Not so much in a sexual way – he supposed they were actually pretty vanilla in that respect – but they had gone through a considerable amount of liquor, drugs, scams, and sleaze during their tenure in the kitchens of New Orleans. To suddenly think of G-man in a whole different light was strange and somehow arousing. He went home that night and fucked his nice Catholic boy until they were both sore.

The hotel room felt very cold after the simmering night. The sweat on their skin turned clammy and they burrowed under the covers, shivering. "I don't know about you," said Rickey, "but I'm wide awake now."

"Same here. You want to do something?"

"Yeah."

It was years since they'd had sex in unfamiliar surroundings – usually they were lucky if they could find the time and energy to do so in their own bed. They'd done it once in the restaurant before opening night, but that was mostly just to make the place theirs, and Rickey had been too worried about the carpet to really get into it. Now, though, he found that he liked being in a strange room. There was something vaguely illicit about it, something that hinted of affairs and assignations without any of the pain these things would cause were he to actually seek them out. The mattress was a little too soft, but it was wider than the one they had at home, allowing them to roll around without fear of falling off the edge. Only after several minutes did they notice that one of the bed's wooden legs was banging quite loudly against the floor.

"Goddamn uneven floorboards," said Rickey. "Goddamn broken-down place. We should've stayed in a Holiday Inn."

"Don't worry about it," said G-man. "Here, let's try that daybed by the window."

They moved over to the daybed. "That's better," Rickey said, testing its firmness. "The springs aren't all busted in this one."

"I'm sure we'll bust 'em."

"Probably so . . . oh. There. You like that?"

"Yeah," said G-man. "I like that a lot." He braced himself against the windowsill as Rickey fucked him. He could barely make out the dark slow shape of the bayou through crooked oak limbs, and above it all, a crescent moon hanging high in the predawn sky. For the first time in years he remembered his mother telling him the moon was God's eye, and that whenever he saw it, he should remember God was watching him. He closed his eyes, but the white crescent's afterimage still hung there. "Let me turn over," he said to Rickey.

"Aw, c'mon, G, we *never* do it this way - "

"Okay, let me lay down then."

Rickey did. G-man pressed his face into the upholstery and concentrated on Rickey's mouth against his neck, Rickey's hand on his dick, Rickey's dick in his ass. God wasn't watching them, and if He was, it didn't matter. G-man had not stopped believing in God when he left the Church; he'd left because he did not believe that God wanted him to have a loveless life, and he'd never once felt that being with Rickey was wrong. He didn't feel it now. He just felt more self-conscious out here, somehow, than he'd ever felt in New Orleans.

They returned to the old four-poster bed to sleep, but their dreams were not peaceful. Rickey dreamed he was back at the restaurant on reopening day. Dinner service was about to start, but no one else in the kitchen had shown up, not even G-man. Rickey was on the line by himself, wondering how in hell he was going to work all the stations, trying to stifle his fury at his negligent crew because he knew it would incapacitate him if given free reign. He could already see the tickets piling up, could hear the waiters yelling for their orders. *Didn't I go on vacation?* he thought, but realized he had no memory of it.

G-man dreamed of Sts Peter and Paul, the church he had attended as a child. His name was still Gary Stubbs, he had just barely started learning to cook, and his knees were sore from kneeling, waiting to take Communion. Again he tasted the crumbling wafer, the musky sweet wine. He could smell the sweat on the priest's palm, could count every hair on his wrist. It was supposed to be flesh, blood. Wasn't that as intimate as anything you could do with a person? He had always wondered.

It was Sts Peter and Paul, but for some reason the Stations of the Cross were all in French. *Jésus condemné à mort . . . Jésus chargé de la Croix . . . Jésus tombe une 1e fois. . . .* He wasn't sure if he was reading the words or if a voice was whispering them to him. The Stations themselves were set into walls that towered high above his head, the carved wooden faces of the figures precise in their anguish.

Then he was outside the church, out in the night long past even midnight Mass, and it was no longer Sts Peter and Paul, it was the old church in the bayou town. The weirdly backlit tabernacle rose up behind the window, wavering as if an unseen figure had passed between it and the glass. The statue of the Blessed

Virgin sat placidly in the center of the fountain. Her mantle and her shoulders were worn almost smooth, like the soapy-looking lambs that mark children's graves. *Jésus recontre sa Mère*, the voice whispered, or had he just thought the words? Her eyes were wide, blank, white, fixed upon him as she began to rise, her stone knees crumbling, her lap cracking apart. Her shadow appeared on the stained glass window, blotting out the tabernacle. She reached out to him –

"Jesus!" he said, sitting up in bed, his heart hammering, his right hand at his throat. A second later, he realized he was groping for the Saint Christopher medal he hadn't worn since he was twelve.

"G? You okay?" He felt Rickey's hand on his back. "What's a'matter?"

"Nothing. I'm fine."

"Sure?"

"Yeah."

"C'mere. . . ."

Rickey pulled him down and wrapped a warm arm around his chest. Fitted into the curve of Rickey's body like a spoon, G-man began to relax, his heart slowing, his eyes growing heavy again. By morning he remembered nothing of the dream, and Rickey did not remember waking at all.

Since they'd never had a proper meal the day before, they woke up ravenous and headed immediately to the oyster bar, which was just opening for lunch. "Y'all cooks?" the waitress asked, noticing the baggy shorts they had made from worn-out chef pants. In her musical half-French accent she chatted to them about local restaurants, recommended the boudin, warned them away from the crawfish stew. Throughout the meal she kept their cups filled with strong chicory coffee. By the time they finished eating, the strangeness of yesterday had receded and they felt almost comfortable in the town.

Out on the square, they stood looking up and down Rue Principale. It began to dawn on them anew that they had absolutely no responsibilities, no plans, nothing to guide them except whatever they felt like doing. "You want to check out the church?" said Rickey, though he had shown no interest in it the day before.

G-man looked up at the wooden spire. He realized he really didn't want to go in there; certainly he'd been in Catholic churches since his last Confession, but he felt a reluctance to enter this one. Almost an aversion, for what reason he couldn't imagine. "What for?" he said.

"Well, I don't know. It's old. It's one of the things you're supposed to see – Mo said so." Rickey pointed at a nearby sign. "Look, it's on the Historic Register."

"I guess," said G-man with no enthusiasm. But Rickey had already set off toward the church, apparently determined to be a dutiful tourist despite his lack of experience. G-man followed as he always had. The heavy front doors sighed shut behind them and they were enveloped in dimness, in the smell of candles and old wood. G-man could not help dipping his fingertips in the font and genuflecting as he entered; it was as automatic as brushing his teeth or wiping the edge of a plate after he had arranged food on it.

"Hey, check it out," said Rickey. "The whaddaya call 'em, the Stations of the Cross are in French."

G-man edged into a row of pews; he didn't feel quite capable of walking around the church. He sat there and watched Rickey roam around the place admiring the architecture, the history, the craftsmanship of the carved and painted wooden statues. It must be nice to enjoy such a beautiful place at face value, without the heaviness of lapsed faith. His head had begun to ache dully. He could not think why this church felt so much more oppressive than others he had been in.

"May I help you?" someone said. G-man looked up and saw an old priest with eyes nearly as blue as Rickey's. The priest was smiling benignly at him, offering no threat.

"Uh, we were just looking around," he said. "It's a beautiful church . . . Father."

"Yes, it is. You're from New Orleans?" G-man nodded. "I recognize the accent. I was pastor of Saint Rosalie's in Harvey for ten years before I came here. What brings you to our town?"

"We're just tourists."

"Well, I'm so glad you stopped in. The church is very old, you know. So many stories about it. Some of them are even a little crazy." The priest chuckled. "Did you see the statue of the Blessed Virgin out front? The one by the fountain?"

"Sure. It's kinda unusual —"

"Because she's seated, right. You don't see that too often in America. The statue was carved in Italy in the style of the *Pietà*, but alone, without the body of Christ in her arms. It represents her sorrow after He was taken from her. Anyway, there's a legend about it."

"I bet there is," said G-man. He really didn't want to hear it, but he knew he was about to.

"It's said that the Virgin will stand if a sinner comes before her." The priest chuckled again, then broke into a hearty laugh. Up near the altar, Rickey turned to see what was going on. "But she's never stood up yet, so apparently all of us in town and all who visit us must be without sin!"

G-man rose and stumbled out of the pew. "I'm sorry, Father," he said. "The sun. . . ." But he welcomed the sun after the shadows of the church and sat with his face turned up to it until he heard the door open behind him. He tensed, afraid it might be the priest, but it was Rickey.

"You okay?"

"Yeah."

"You sick?"

"I'm fine."

"I'm sorry I made you go in there. I guess you didn't really feel like it."

"No," said G-man. "I really didn't."

He rubbed his hands over his face. Rickey patted him on the back, and G-man could feel the worry in his touch. After a few minutes he let his head fall back against Rickey's shoulder. Out of the corner of his eye he could see the fountain and the soft eroded shape of the statue. Its blank gaze was upon him again, but the Virgin stayed seated. He wondered if she understood that she must either sit forever or stand up for everyone in the world.

THE NARROW WORLD

GEMMA FILES

And then I did a strange thing, but what I did matters not.
– *Oscar Wilde*

It's always the same, always different. The moment you make that first cut, even before you open the – item – in question, there's this faint, red-tinged exhalation: cotton-soft, indefinite, almost indefinable. Even more than the shudder or the jerk, the last stifled attempt at drawn breath, this is what marks a severance – what proves, beyond a shadow of a doubt, that something which once considered itself alive has been physically deleted from this tangle of contradictory image and sensation we choose to call "reality."

Cut away from, cut loose. Or maybe – cut free.

And this is the first operating rule of magic, whether black, white, or red all over: for every incision, an excision. No question without its answer. No action without its price.

Some people fast before a ritual. I don't. Some people wear all white. I wear all black, except for the purple fun-fur trim on my winter coat (which I took so long to find in the first place that I really just couldn't bear to part with it). Some people say you have to be a psychopath to be able to draw a perfect circle – so I hedge my bets, and carry a surveyor's compass. But I also don't drink, don't smoke, haven't done any drugs but Tylenol since I was a Ryerson undergraduate, getting so bent out of shape I could barely talk straight and practicing Crowleyan "sex magick" with a similarly inclined posse of curricular acquaintances every other weekend.

Effective hierarchical magicians like me are the Flauberts of the Narrow World – neat and orderly in our lives, *comme un bourgeois*, so that we may be violent and creative in our work. We're not fanatics. There's no particular principle involved, except maybe the principle of Free Enterprise. So we can afford to stay safe . . . and for what they're paying us to do, our customers kind of prefer it that way.

Three thousand dollars down, tax-free, for a simple supernatural Q&A session, from U of T Business pre-grad Doug Whatever to me, Hark Chiu-Wai – Jude Hark, as I'm known down here in Toronto the good-for-nothing. That's what brought me where I was when all this began: under the vaulted cathedral arch of the St Clair Ravine Bridge, shivering against the Indian winter air of early September as I gutted a sedated German shepherd in preparation for invoking the obsolete Sumerian god of divination by entrails.

The dog was a bit on the small side, but it was a definite improvement on Doug and his girlfriend's first try – a week back, when they'd actually tried to fob me off with some store-bought puppy. Through long and clever argument, however, I'd finally gotten them to cave in: if you're looking to evoke a deity who speaks through a face made of guts – one who goes by the slightly risible name of Humbaba, to be exact – you'd probably better make sure his mouth is big enough to tell you what you want to hear.

Since I hate dogs anyway – tongue-wagging little affection junkies – treating one like a Christmas turkey was not exactly a traumatic prospect. So I completed the down-stroke, shearing straight through its breastbone, and pushed down hard on either side of its rib-cage till I heard something crack.

Behind me, the no-doubt-soon-to-be-Mrs Doug made a hacking noise, and shifted her attention to a patch of graffiti on the nearest wall. Doug just kept on staring, maintaining the kind of physical fixity that probably passed for thought in his circles.

"So what, those the . . . innards?" he asked, delicately.

"Those are they," I said, not looking up. Flaying away the membrane between heart and lungs, lifting and separating the subsections of fat between abdomen and bowels.

He nodded. "What'cha gonna do with 'em?"

"Watch."

I twisted, cut, twisted again, cut again. Heart on one side, lungs (a riven gray tissue butterfly, torn wing from wing) on the other. Pulled forth the gall bladder and squeezed it empty, using it to smear binding sigils at my north, south, east, west. Shook out another cleansing handful of rock salt, and wrung the bile from my palms.

Doug's girlfriend, having exhausted the wall's literary possibilities, had turned back toward the real action. Hand over mouth, she ventured: "Um – is that like a hat you can buy, or is that a religion?"

"What?"

"Your hat. Is it, like, religious?"

(The headgear in question being a black brocade cap, close-fitting, topped with a round, grayish satin applique of a Chinese embroidery pattern: bats and dragons entwined, signifying long life and good luck. The kind of thing my ma might've picked out for me, were she inclined to do so.)

"Oh, yes," I replied, keeping my eyes firmly on the prize, as I started to unreel the dog's intestines. "Very religious. Has its own church, actually. All hail Jude's hat – bow down, bow down. Happy holiness to the headgear."

She sniffed, mildly aggrieved at my lack of interest in her respect for my fashion sense.

Said: "Well, excuse me for trying to be polite."

I shot her a small, amused glance. Thinking: *Oh, was that what you were trying to do?*

Ai-yaaa.

The dog had more guts than I'd originally given him credit for. Scooping out the last of them, I started to shape them into a rough, pink face, its features equally blurred with blood and seeping digestive juices.

"You ever hear the four great tenets of hierarchical magic?" I asked her, absently. "'To know, to dare, to will, to be silent.'"

Then, pulling the mouth's corners up into a derisive, toothless grin, and conjuring a big smile of my own: "So why don't you just consider yourself Dr Faustus for a day, and shut the fuck up?"

She gasped. Doug caught himself starting to snicker, and toned that way down, way fast.

"Hey, guy," he said, slipping into Neanderthal "protective" mode. "Remember who's footin' the tab here."

"This is a ritual," I pointed out. "Not a conversation."

"Long as I'm payin', buddy, it's whatever I say it is," Doug snapped back.

Thus proving himself exactly the type of typical three "c" client I'd already assumed him to be – callow, classist, and cheap. Kind of loser wants McDonald's-level ass-licking along with his well-protected probe into the Abyss, plus an itemized list of everything his daddy's trust-fund money was paying for, and special instructions on how to make the whole venture look like a tax-deductible educational expense.

To Sumer's carrion lord of the pit, He Who Holds the Sceptre of Ereshkigal, one dog's soul, for services rendered, I thought, shooting Doug a glance, as I finished laying the foundations of Humbaba's features. And: *Try writing that one off, you spoiled, Gapified snakefucker.*

Well, I wax virulent. But these rich boys do get my goat, especially when they want something for nothing, and it just happens to be my something. Though my contempt for them as a breed may well stem from a certain lingering sense-memory of what I used to be like, back when I was one.

In the seven years since my rich old Baba Hark first paid my eventually prodigal way from downtown Hong Kong to RTA at Ryerson, I've dealt with elementals, demons, angels, and ghosts, all of whom soon proved to be their own particular brand of pain in the ass. The angels I called on spoke a really obscure form of Hebrew; the demons decided my interest in them meant I was automatically laid open to twenty-four-hour-a-day Temptation, which didn't slack off until I had a sigilic declaration of complete neutrality tattooed on either palm. Elementals are surly and unco-operative. Ghosts cling – literally, in some cases. I remember coming to see Carraclough Devize one time (in hospital, as increasingly ever), only to have her stare fixedly over my left shoulder where the spectre of a dead man I'd recently helped to report his own murder still drifted – hand on the gap between the base of my skull and the top of my spine, through which most possessive spirits first enter. And ask, dryly: "So who's your new friend?"

She dabbled in magic too, ex-child medium that she is, just like the rest of us – helped me raise my share of demons, in some vain attempt to exorcize her own. Before the rest of the Black Magic Posse dropped off, that is, and I turned professional. And she decided it was easier acting like she was crazy all the time than it ever was trying to pretend she was entirely sane.

Now I make my living calling on obsolete gods like Our Lord of Entrails here: they're far more cost-effective, in terms of customer service, since they don't demand reverence, just simple recognition. The chance to move, however briefly, back from the Wide World into the Narrow one.

Because the Wide World, as Carra herself first told me, is simply where things happen; the Narrow World, hub of all influences, is where things are *made* to happen. Where, if you cast your wards and research your incantations well enough, you can actually grab hold of the intersecting wheels of various dimensions, and spin them – however briefly – in the direction your client wants them to go.

Meanwhile, however –

"Way it strikes me," Doug Whatever went on, "in terms of parts and labor alone, I must be givin' you a thousand bucks every fifteen minutes. And aside from the dead dog, I still don't see anything worth talkin' about."

And: *Oh no?*

Well. . . .

I closed my eyes. Felt cold purple inch down my fingers, nails suddenly alight. My hands gloving themselves with the bleak and shadeless flame of Power. That singing, searing rush – a kindled spark flaring up all at once, straight from my cortex to my groin, leaving nothing in between but the spell still on my lips.

Doug and his girlfriend saw it lap up over my elbows, and stepped back. As they did, a sidelong glance showed me what I wanted to see: Doug transfixed, bull-in-a-stall still and dumb, while Mrs Doug's little blue eyes got even round-er. But she wasn't staring at my sigil-incized palms, or the flickering purple haze connecting them – no, *she* was seeing what Doug's testosterone-drunk brain would have skipped right over, even if he'd been looking in the right direction: the twilit bridge's nearest support girder, just behind me, lapped and drowned in one big shadow that drew every other nearby object's shadow to it . . .

. . . except for where *I* stood.

Snarky Chinese faggot, bloody knife still in hand, smiling up at her under the non-existent brim of that unholy hat. With my whole body – burning hands included – suddenly rimmed in a kind of missing halo, a thin edge of blank-bright nothingness. The empty spot where my own shadow should be.

Noticing. Noticing me *notice* her noticing. Trying desperately to put two and two together and just plain getting five, over and over and over.

She wrinkled her brows at me – helpless, clueless. I just pursed my lips, gave her a sassy little wink. Telling them both, one last time: "I said, *watch*."

And shut my eyes again.

⊹

February 14, 1987. For the *gweilo* rubes of Toronto, it was time to hand out the chocolate hearts, exchange cards that could make a diabetic go into shock, buy each other gift-bags full of underwear made from atrophied cotton candy. For us, it was just another night out with the Black Magic Posse.

Carra Devize, her pale braids stiff against the light, stray strands outflung in a crackling blue halo. Bruisy words crawling up and down her body as she spun a web of ectoplasm around herself, reel on reel of it, knotted like dirty string in the whitening air. Jen Cudahy, crying. Franz Froese, sweat-slick and deep in full chant trance, puking up names of Power, ecstatic with fear. And me, laughing, so drunk I could barely kneel.

With my left hand, with my bone-hilted hierarchical magician's knife, I cut my shadow from me – one crooked swipe, downward and sideways, pressing so hard I almost took part of my heel off along with it. I heard it give that sigh.

I cut my shadow from me, without a second thought. And then . . .

. . . I threw it away.

⊹

"One for Midnight Madness," I told the girl behind the Bloor's window, slipping her one of Doug Whatever's crisp new twenties. She smiled, and ripped the ticket for me.

I smiled back. There's no harm in it.

Hitting the candy bar, I stocked up with an extra-large popcorn, a box of chocolate almonds, and a cappucino from the café upstairs. My ma always used to tell us not to eat after midnight, but the program promised a brand new Shinya Tsukamoto flesh-into-metal monster mosh-fest – and after tonight's job, I was up for as much stimulation as I could stand.

Back down in the ravine, meanwhile, Doug and his girl still stood frozen above the remains of their mutual investment – their blood reverberating with a whispered loop of intimate-form Sumerian, heavily overlaid with mnemonic subtitles: Humbaba's answer to their question. The same question I hadn't wanted to know before they asked it, and certainly didn't care to know now.

I didn't exactly anticipate any repeat business from those two. But for what I'd made tonight, they could both disappear off the edge of the earth, for all I cared.

I took a big swallow of popcorn, licked the butter off my hands. A faint smell of Power still lingered under my nails – like dry ice, like old blood. Like burned marigolds, seed and petal alike reduced to a fine, pungent ash.

Then the usher opened the doors, and I went in.

⊹

I used to be afraid of a lot of things, back when I was a nice, dutiful little Chinese boy. Dogs. Loud noises. Big, loud dogs that made big, loud noises. Certain concepts. Certain words used to communicate such concepts, like the worst, most unprovable word of all – "eternity."

Secretly, late at night, I would feel the universe spinning loose around me: boundless, nameless, a vortex of darkness within which my life became less than a speck of dust. The night sky would tilt toward me, yawning. And I would lie there breathless, waiting for the roof to peel away, waiting to lose my grip. To rise and rise forever into that great, inescapable Nothing, to drift until I disappeared – not only as though I no longer was, but as though I had never been.

So I read too much, and saw too many movies, and played too many videogames, and drank too much, and took too many pills, and made my poor ma worried enough to burn way too much incense in front of way too many pictures of my various Hark ancestors. Anything to distract myself. I took my Baba's *feng shui* advice, and moved my bedroom furniture around religiously, hoping to deflect the cold current of my neuroses onto somebody else for a while. Why not? He was a professional, after all.

And I was just a frightened child, a frightened prepubescent, a frightened adolescent – a spoiled, stupid, frightened young man with all the rich and varied life experience of a preserved duck egg, nodding and smiling moronically at the next in an endless line of prospective brides trotted out by our trusty family matchmaker, too weak to even hint at what really got my dick hard.

On the screen above me, bald, dark-goggled punks took turns drilling each other through the stomach as yet another hapless salaryman turned into a pissed-off pile of ambulatory metal shavings. Japanese industrial blared while blood hit the lens in buckets. I could hear the audience buckling under every new blow, riding alternate waves of excitement and revulsion.

And I just sat there, unconcerned; crunching my almonds, watching the carnage. Suddenly realizing I hadn't felt that afraid for a long, long time – or afraid at all, in fact.

Of anything.

⁓✠⁓

Somebody came in late; I moved my coat, so he could sit down next to me. A mere peripheral blur of a guy – apparently young, vaguely Asian. Hair to below his shoulders, temples shaved like a samurai's, and the whole mass tied back with one long, thin, braided sidelock – much the way I used to wear it, before Andre down at the Living Hell convinced me to get my current buzz-cut.

I never took my eyes off the action. But I could feel the heat of him all the way through the leg of my good black jeans, cock rearing flush against the seam of my crotch with each successive heartbeat.

The screen was abloom with explosions. A melting, roiling pot of white-hot metal appeared, coalescing, all revved up and ready to pour.

Some pheremonal envelope of musk, slicking his skin, began expanding. Began to slick mine.

More explosions followed.

I felt the uniquely indentifiable stir of his breath – in, out; out, in – against my cheek, and actually caught myself shivering.

Above us, two metal men spun and ran like liquid sun, locked tight together. The credits were beginning to roll. I thought: *Snap out of it, Jude.*

Run the checklist. Turn around, smile. Ask him his name, if he's got a place.

Tell him you want to taste his sweat, and feel his chest on your back till the cows come home.

Then the lights came back up, much more quickly than I'd been expecting them to – I blinked, shocked temporarily blind. Brushed away tears, as my eyes strained to readjust.

And found I'd been cruising an empty seat.

The next day, I picked Carra up at the Clarke, signed her out, and took her for lunch at the College/Yonge Fran's, as promised. She looked frail, so drained the only color in her face came from her freckles. I bought her coffee, and watched her drink it.

"Met this guy at *Tetsuo III*," I said. "Well . . . met is probably too strong a way to put it."

She looked at me over the rim of her glasses, raising one white-blonde smudge of brow. Her eyes were gray today, with that moonstone opacity which meant she was not only drugged, but also consciously trying not to read my mind – so whatever they had her on couldn't really be working all that well.

"I thought you were taken," she said.

I snorted. "Ed? He says I broke his heart."

"I don't doubt it."

I shrugged. I could never quite picture anyone's soft little musclebox as brittle enough to break, myself; it's an image that smacks of drama, and Ed (though sweet) is not exactly the world's most dramatic guy. But be that as it may.

"Dumb *gweilo* told me I had something missing," I told her, laughing. "You fucking *believe* that?"

Now it was her turn to shrug.

"Well, you do, Jude," she replied, reasonably enough. Adding, as she took another sip: "I personally find it quite . . . restful."

Carra Devize, my one and only incursion into enemy territory – lured by the web that halos her, the shining, clinging psychic filaments of her Gift. The quenchless hum of her innate glory. Most people want to find someone who'll touch their hearts, enter them at some intimate point and lodge there, mainlining instinct back and forth, in a haze of utter sympathy. And Carra, of course – congenitally incapable of any other kind of real human contact – just wants to be alone; enforced proximity, emotional or otherwise, only serves to make her nauseous. So she bears my enduring, inappropriate love for her like some unhealed internal injury, with painful patience. Which is why I try not to trouble her with it, anymore often than I have to.

That calamitous December of 1989, when I knew the Hark family money tree had finally dried up for good – after I came out, a half-semester into my first year at RTA, and the relatives I was staying with informed my ultra-trad Baba that he had a rebellious faggot son to disinherit – I moved in with Carra for some melted mass of time or so, into the rotting Annex townhouse she then shared with her mother Geillis, known as Gala: Gala Carraclough Devize, after whose family Carra was named. We'd sit around the kitchen in our bare feet, the TV our only light, casting each other's horoscopes and drinking peach liqueur until we passed out, as Gala moved restlessly around upstairs, knocking on the floor with her cane whenever she wanted Carra to come up. I never saw her face, never heard her voice; I guess it was sort of like being Carra, for a while. In that I was living with at least one ghost.

And this went on until one particular night, she turned to me and said, abruptly: "So maybe I'm like that chick, that Tarot-reading chick from *Live and Let Die*. What do you think?"

"Jane Seymour."

"Was it?" We both tried to remember, then gave up. "Well?"

"Have sex, and the powers go away?"

"It's the one thing I never tried."

In a way, we were both virgins; I think it's also pretty safe to say we were probably both also thinking of somebody else. But when I finally came, I could feel her sifting me, riding my orgasm from the inside out, instead of having one of her own.

The next time I saw her, I'd been supporting myself for over a month. And she had an IV jack stuck in the crook of her elbow, anchored with fresh hospital tape.

There were a couple of movies playing that Carra was interested in, so we ended up at the Carlton – but none of their twoish shows got out early enough for her to be able to keep her six o'clock curfew.

"So what happens if we stay out later?" I asked, idly.

Another shrug. "Nothing much. Except they might put me back on suicide watch."

That pale gray day, and her gray gaze. The plastic ID bracelet riding up on one thin-skinned wrist, barely covering a shallow red thread of fresh scar tissue where she'd tried to scrub some phantom's love-note from her flesh with a not-so-safety razor. No reason not to wear long sleeves, cold as it was. But she just wouldn't. She wouldn't give her ghosts the satisfaction.

I looked away. Looked at anything else. Which she couldn't help but notice, of course.

Being psychic.

"This guy you met," she said, studying the curb, as we stood waiting for the light to change. "He made an impression."

"Could be," I allowed. "Why? Something I should know about?"

She still didn't look up. Picking and choosing. When you see so much, all at once, it must be very confusing to have to concentrate on any one particular sliver of the probable — to decide whether it's here already, or already gone, or still yet to be. Her eyebrows crept together, tentative smears of light behind her lenses, as she played with her braid, raveling and unraveling its tail.

". . . something," she said, finally.

We started across, only to be barely missed by a fellow traveler from the Pacific Rim in a honking great blue Buick, who apparently hadn't yet learned enough of North American driving customs to quite work the phrase "pedestrian always has the right of way" into his vocabulary. I caught Carra's arm and spun, screaming Cantonese imprecations at his tail-lights; he yelled something back, most of it lost beneath his faulty muffler's bray. My palms itched, fingers eager to knit a basic entropic sigil — to spell out the arcane words that would test whether or not his brakes worked as well as his mouth, when given just the right amount of push on a sudden skid.

I felt Carra's hand touch mine, gently.

"Leave it," she said. "It'll come when it comes, for him. And believe me — it's coming."

"Dogfucker thinks he's still in Kowloon," I muttered. Which actually made her laugh.

We got back just a minute or two later than my watch claimed we would, and the nurse was already there — waiting for us, for Carra, behind a big, scratched wall of bulletproof glass.

Needle in hand.

After which I went straight home, through this neat and pretty city I now call my own — even though, having long since defaulted on my student visa, I am actually not supposed to be anywhere near, let alone living in. Straight home to (surprise!) Chinatown, just below Spadina and Dundas, off an unnamed little alleyway behind the now-defunct Kau Soong Clouds In Rain softcore porno theatre, whose empty storefront is usually occupied by either a clutch of little old local ladies selling baskets full of bok choi or a daily-changing roster of FOB hustlers hocking anything from imitation Swiss watches to illegally-copied anime videotapes.

Next door, facing Spadina, the flanking totem dragons of Empress' Noodle grinned their welcome. I slipped between them, into the fragrant domain of Grandmother Yau Yan-er, who claims to be the oldest Chinese vampire in Toronto.

"Jude-ah!" She called out from the back, as I came through the door. "Sit. Wait." I heard the mah-jong tiles click and scatter under her hands. It was her legendary Wednesday night game, played with a triad of less long-lived *hsi-hsue-kuei* for a captive audience of cowed and attentive ghosts, involving much stylish cheating and billions of stolen yuan – garnished, on occasion, with a discreet selection of aspiring human retainers willing to bet their blood, their memories, or their sworn service on a chance at eternal life.

Grandmother Yau's operation has been open since 1904, in one form or another. She's an old-school kind of monster: lotus feet, nine inch nails, the whole silk bolt. One of her ghosts brought me tea, which I nursed until she called her bet, won the hand with a Red Dragon kept up her sleeve, and glided over.

"Big sister," I said, dipping my head.

"Jude-ah, you're insulting," she scolded, in Manadarin-accented Cantonese. "Why don't you come see me? It's obvious, bad liars and tale-tellers have got you in their grip. They have slandered my reputation and made even fearless men like you afraid of me."

"Not so. You know I'd gladly pay a thousand *taels* of jade just to kiss you, if I thought I'd get my tongue back afterwards."

"Oh, I'm too old for you," she replied, blithely. "But you'll see – I have the best *mei-po* in Toronto, a hardworking ghost contracted to me for ninety-nine hundred years. Good deal, ah? Smarter than those British foreign devils were with Hong Kong. We will talk together, she and I, and get you fixed up before I get bored enough to finally let myself die, with a good Chinese marriage to a good Chinese. . . ."

She let her voice trail away, carefully, before she might have to assign an actual gender-specific pronoun to this mythical "good Chinese" – person.

"I don't think I could afford your *mei-po*'s fees," I pointed out, tucking into my freshly-arrived plate of Sticky Rice with Shrimp and Seasonal Green. To which she just smiled, thinly – patted my wrist with one clawed hand – and went back to her game, leaving me to the rest of my meal.

A fresh ghost brought me more tea, bowing. I bowed back, and sipped it, thinking about Toronto.

Hong Kong was everything my Ryerson fuck-buddies ever thought it would be – loud, bright, fast, unforgiving. When I was five years old, my au pair took me out without calling the bodyguards first; a quarter-hour later, I buried my face in her skirt as some low-level Triad thug beat a man to pulp right in front of us, armed only with a big, spiky, stinky fruit called a dhurrian. Believe me, the experience left an impression.

In Toronto, the streets are level, the use of firearms strictly controlled, and swearing aloud is enough to draw stares. Abusive maniacs camp out on every corner, and passersby step right over them – quickly, quietly, without rancor or interest. It's a place so clean that US movie crews have to import or manufacture enough garbage to make it pass for New York; it's also North America's largest center for consensual S&M activity. But if you stop any person on the street, they'll tell you they think living here is nothing special – nice, though a little boring.

The truth is, Toronto is a crossroads where the dead congregate. The city goes about its seasonal business, bland and blind, politely ignoring the hungry skins of dead people stalking up and down its frozen main arteries: vampires, ghouls, revenants, ghosts, wraiths, zombies, even a select few mage's golems cobbled haphazardly together from whatever inanimate objects came to hand. There's enough excess appetite here to power a world-eating competition. And you don't have to be a magician or a medium to recognize it, either.

"Dead want more time," Carra told me, long after yet another drunken midnight, back in her mother's house – both of us too sloshed to even remember what a definite article *was*, let alone try using it correctly. "'S what they always say. Time, recognition, remembrance. . . ."

Trailing off, taking another slug. Then fixing me with one blood-threaded eye. And half-growling, half-projecting – so soundlessly loud she made my temples throb with phantom pain –

"Want blood too. *Our* blood. Yours . . . mine . . ."

. . . but don't mean we gotta give it to 'em, just cause they ask.

The longer I stay in this city, the more I see it works like a corpse inside a corpse inside a corpse – the kind of puzzle you can only solve by letting it rot. Once it's gone all soft, you can come back and give it a poke, see what sticks out. Until then, you just have to hold your nose.

About an hour later, I was almost to the door when Grandmother Yau materialized again, at my elbow. Laying her brocade sleeve over my arm, she said, softly:

"Jude-ah, before you leave, I must tell you that I see you twice. You here, drinking my tea. You somewhere else, doing something else. I see you dimly, as though through a Yin mirror – split, but not yet cut apart. Caught in a mesh of darkness."

I frowned.

"This thing you see," I asked, carefully. "Is it . . . dangerous?"

She smiled a little wider, and withdrew the authoritative weight of her sleeve. I saw the red light of the paper lanterns gild her upper fangs.

"Hard to tell without knowing more, don't you think?" she said. "But there are many kinds of danger, Hark Chiu-wai-ah."

⚜

Off Spadina again, and down the alley, fumbling for my key. Upstairs, the clutch of loud weekend hash-smokers I call my neighbors had apparently decided to spend tonight out on the town, for which I was duly grateful. Locking the door to my apartment – and renewing the protective sigils warding its frame – I took my bone-hilted knife from its sheath around my neck, under my Nine Inch Nails T-shirt, and wrapped it in a Buddhist rosary of mule-bone skulls and haematite beads, murmuring a brief prayer of reconsecration.

My machine held a fresh crop of messages from Ed, both hopeful and hateful. *Poor lonely little* gweilo *boy*, I thought, briefly. *No rice for you tonight.*

Then I lit some sage incense, peeled a few bills from the wad of twenties Doug Whatever had given me, and burned them as makeshift Hell Money in front of an old Polaroid of my grandmother – the only ancestor I care to worship anymore, these faithless Canadian days.

Own nothing, owe nothing. Pray to nothing. Pay nothing. No loyalties, no scruples. And make sure nothing ever means more to you than any other nothing you can name, or think of.

These are my rules, all of which I learned from Carra Devize, along with the fluid surprise of what it feels like to be gripped by vaginal muscles – the few, accurate, infinitely bitter philosophical lessons which she, psychic savant that she is, can only ever teach, never follow.

Magicians demand the impossible, routinely. Without even knowing it, they have begun to work backwards against the flow of all things: *contra mundi*. A price follows. Miracles cannot be had without being paid for. It's the illogic of a child who asks *why* must what is *be*? Why do I have to be just a boy, just a girl? Why is the sky blue? Why can't I fly, if I want to? Why did Mommy have to die? Why do *I* have to die?

We call what we don't understand magic in order to explain why we *can't* control it; we name whatever we find, usually after ourselves – because, by naming something, you come to own it.

Thus rules are discovered, and quantified, and broken. So that when there are enough new rules, magic can become far less an Art . . . than a science.

And it's so *easy*, that's the truly frightening thing. You do it without thinking, the first time. Do it without knowing just what you've done, till long after.

Frightening for most. But not for me . . . and not for Carra, either.

Once.

﹣⚙﹣

I was laying in bed, almost asleep, when the phone rang. I grabbed for it, promptly knocking a jar full of various complimentary bar and nightclub matchbooks off my night-stand.

"*Wei?*" I snapped, before I could stop myself. Then: "I mean – who is this?"

A pause. Breathing.

"Jude?"

"Franz?"

Froese.

And here's the really interesting part – apparently, he thought he was returning *my* call.

"Why would I call you, Franz?"

"I thought maybe you heard something more."

"More than what?"

With a slight edge of impatience: "About *Jen.*"

The Jen in question being Jen Cudahy, fellow Black Magic Posse member, of lachrymose memory – a languid, funereal calla lily of a girl with purple hair and black vinyl underwear who spent her spare periods writing execrable sestinas with titles like "My Despair, Mon Espoir" and "When Shadows Creep." She'd worked her way through RTA as a dominatrix, pulling down about $500 per session to let judges and vice cops clean her bathroom floor with their tongues. The last time I'd seen her, over eighteen months prior, she was running a lucrative new dodge built around what she called "vampire sex shows" – a rotating roster of nude, bored teenage Goths jacking open their veins, pumping out a couple of CCs for the drones, and then fingerpainting each other. Frottage optional. She asked me what I thought and I told her it struck me as wasteful. But she assured me it was the quickest way she currently knew to invoke the not-so-dead god Moolah.

Franz had loved Jen for what probably only seemed like forever to outside observers, mostly from afar – interspersed, here and there, with a few painful passages of actual physical intimacy. They'd met while attending the same alternative high school, where they'd barricade themselves into the students' lounge, drop acid, and have long conversations about which of them was de-evolving faster.

"Okay," I said, carefully. "I'll bite. What about Jen?"

"She says she's possessed."

I raised an eyebrow. "And this is different . . . how?"

Way back in 1987, shortly before I cut my shadow away – or maybe shortly after (I'm not sure, since I was pretty well continuously intoxicated at that point) – Jen petitioned for entrance to the Black Magic Posse. She'd been hanging around the fringes, watching and listening quietly as Carra, Franz, and I first planned, then dissected, our weekly adventures in the various Mantic Sciences.

271

I was all for it; the more the merrier, not to mention the drunker. Franz was violently opposed. And Carra didn't care too much, one way or the other – her dominating attitude then, regarding almost any subject you could name, being remarkably similar to the way mine is now.

Jen quickly demonstrated a certain flair for the little stuff. She tranced out easily, far more so than Franz, who usually had to chant himself incoherent in order to gain access to his own unconscious. This made her an almost perfect scryer, able to map our possible future difficulties through careful study of either the palpable (the way a wax candle split and fell as it melted – carromancy) or impalpable (the way that shadows scattered and reknit when exposed to a moving source of light – sciomancy).

But when it came to anything a bit more concrete, it would be time to call in the founding generation: Franz, with his painstaking research and gift for dead languages; Carra, with her post-electroshock halo of rampant energy, her untold years of channelling experience, her barely-controlled psychometric Gift; me, the devout amateur, with my gleeful willingness to do whatever it took. My big mouth and my total lack of fear, artificial though it might have been – at that point –

– and my bone-hilted knife.

"It's bad, Jude. She needs an exorcism."

"Try therapy," I suggested, idly slipping my earrings back in. "It's cheaper."

There was a tiny, accusatory pause.

"I would've thought you'd feel just a little responsible," he said, at last. "Considering she's been this way ever since you and Carra let her help raise that demon of yours . . ."

"Fleer? He's a mosquito with horns. Barely a postal clerk, in Hell's hierarchy."

". . . without drawing a proper circle first."

I bridled. "The circle was fine; my wards held. They always hold. Carra even threw her the wand when she saw Jen'd stepped over the outer rim – Jen was just too shit-scared to use it. So whatever trauma she may have talked herself into getting is her business."

"It's pretty hard to use a wand when you're rolling around on the floor, barking!"

"So? She stopped."

Another pause. "Well, she's started again," Franz said, quietly.

I swung my legs over the side of the bed and retrieved my watch from the night-stand, squinting at it. Not even three; most of my favorite hangouts would still be open, once I'd disposed of this conversation.

Which – knowing Franz – might well be easier said than done.

"Gee, Franz," I said, lightly, "when you told me you never wanted to see me again, I kind of thought you meant all of me. Up to and including the able-to-exorcise-your-crazy-ex-girlfriend part."

"Cut the shit, you Cantonese voodoo faggot," he snapped.

"Kiss my crack, Mennonite Man," I snapped back. "For ten years, you cross the street every time you see me coming – but now I've suddenly got something you want, that makes me your new best friend? We partied, Franz. We hung around. The drugs were good, but I'm not sure how that qualifies you to guilt me into mowing your lawn, let alone into doing an expensive and elaborate ritual on behalf of someone I barely even liked, just because she happens to get your nuts in an uproar."

"But . . . you. . . ." His voice trailed away for a minute. Then, accusingly again, "You already said if I found out what was wrong with her, what it was going to take to make her better – you'd do it. I didn't even know about any of this, until *you* called and told me!"

I snorted. "Oh, uh-huh."

"Why would I lie?"

I shrugged. "Why wouldn't you?"

Obviously, we had reached some kind of impasse. I studied my nails and listened while Franz tried – not too successfully – to control his breathing long enough to have the last word.

"If you change your mind again," he said, finally, "I'm at my mother's. You know the number."

Then he hung up.

⚬

Inevitably, talking to Franz sent my mind skittering back to the aftermath of Valentine's Day, 1987: A five AM Golden Griddle "breakfast" with the Black Magic Posse, Carra sipping her coffee and watching – with some slight amusement – while Franz blurted out: "But it was your *soul*, Jude."

"Metaphorically, maybe. So?"

"So now you're just half a person. And not the *good* half, either."

At which I really just had to laugh out loud, right in his morose, lapsed-Mennonite face. Such goddamn drama, all because I'd made the same basic sacrifice a thousand other magicians have made to gain control over their Art: nothing more serious than cutting off the top joint of your finger, or putting out an eye, except for not being nearly as aesthetically repugnant or physically impractical.

"And that's why you'll always be a mediocre magician, Franz," I replied. "Because you can't do what it takes to go the distance."

"I have *never* been 'mediocre.' I'm better than you ever were –"

"You used to be. Back when Carra first introduced us. But now *I'm* better, and I'm *getting* better, all the time. While *you*, my friend . . . are exactly as good . . . as you're ever going to get."

Simple, really. My fear held me back, so I got rid of it. My so-called "friends" *wanted* to hold me back – the ones still human enough to be jealous of my growing Power, at least. So . . .

. . . *thanks for the advice, Franz, old pal. And fuck you very much.*

⚜

Sleep no longer an option, I hauled my ass out of bed, ready to pull my pants up and hit the street (so I could find myself a nicely hard-bodied reason to pull them down again, no doubt). That guy from the theatre, maybe; hot clutch of something at my sternum at the very thought, moving from throat to belly to zipper beneath. Itching. *Twisting.*

If only I knew his name, that was. Or could even remember more than the barest bright impression of his shadowed face. . . .

But just as I grabbed for my coat, a thought suddenly struck me: how hard could it really be to find my nameless number-one crush of the moment, if I put some – effort – into it?

The idea itself becoming a kind of beginning, potent and portentious, lazy flick of a match over mental sandpaper. Synaptic sizzle.

Beneath my bathroom sink is a cupboard full of cleaning products and extra toilet paper; behind these objects, well-hidden from any prying eyes, is a KISS lunchbox Carra gave me for my twenty-fourth birthday. Made In Taiwan stamp, cheap clasp, augmented with a length of bicycle lock chain.

And behind that –

A glass key made by a friend of mine, who usually specializes in custom-blown bongs. A letter from the Seventh Circle, written with a dead girl's hand. The ringing brass quill from a seraph's pin-feather. A small, green bottle full of saffron. A box of red chalk.

If you want to raise a little Hell – or Heaven – then you're going to need just the right tools. Luckily, I've spent years of my life learning exactly which ones are right for my particular purposes. And paying, subtly, for the privilege of ownership, once I finally found them.

I took my little tin box of tricks back into the living room, where I gathered up a few more select items, and arranged them around me one by one: TV remote on my left, small hand-mirror on my right, box at due north. Chalk and compass in one hand, bone-hilted knife in the other. I flipped on the TV – already cued up to my favorite spot on one of my favorite porno tapes – sat back, and drew yet another perfect circle around myself. Made a few extra notations, here and there, just inside the circle's rim: the signs of Venus, Inanna, Ishtar, Astarte, Aphrodite. As many of the ancient significators of desire personified as I could remember, off the top of my increasingly aroused head. Words and images to help me focus – names of power to lend me their strength.

More magician's rules: as long as you're not looking to change anything irrevocably – cause real hate or true love, make somebody die, bring somebody back to life – you can do it all on your own. For minor glamours, for self-protection, willpower is enough.

For larger stuff, however, you need help.

Going by these standards, it's always tricky doing a negative spell – unless you make sure it's on someone else's behalf, so you have no direct stake in its outcome. Making the rebound factor fall entirely back on them.

Obviously, it takes a special kind of detachment to pull this off. But ever since I cut my shadow away, I truly do seem to have a knack for not caring enough . . . about *anything* . . . to get hurt.

Besides, love – true or otherwise – was the last thing on my mind.

As I wrote, a red dusting of chalk spread out across my hand, grinding itself into the lines of my palm. Shrugging off my shirt, I brushed the excess off down my chest, onto my abdomen. Five scarlet fingers, pointing towards my groin.

On the screen, an explicit flesh-toned tangle was busily pixilating itself into soft focus through sheer force of back-and-forth action. I turned the mirror to catch it, then zapped the TV quickly off, wrapping my chosen lust-icon up tight in a black silk scarf I keep handy for such occasions. Then I leaned the mirror against my forehead and repeated the time-honored formula to myself, aloud: "Listen! Oh, now you have drawn near to hearkening – your spit, I take it, I eat it; your body, I take it, I eat it; your flesh, I take it, I eat it; your heart, I take it, I eat it. Oh, Ancient Ones, this man's soul has come to rest at the edge of my body. You are to lay hold to it, and never to let it go, until I indicate otherwise. Bind him with black threads and let him roam restless, never thinking upon any other place or person."

The spells don't change. They never change. And that's because, quite frankly –

"Bring him to me, and me to him. Bring us both together."

– they never really *have* to.

Already, I felt myself stirring, sleepily. Jerking awake. Arching to meet those five red fingers halfway.

Purple no-halo raising the hairs on the backs of my forearms, then slipping down to slime my palms with eerie phosphorescence; my wards holding fast, as ever, against the gathering funnel of Power forming outside the circle's rim. My Art wrapping 'round me like a cold static coccoon, sparking and twinging. A dull scribble of bio-electricity, followed by a wash of gooseflesh. Nothing natural. All as it should be.

Until: something, somewhere, snapped.

The mirror cracked across, images emptied. The funnel suddenly slack as a rubber band, then blown away in a single breath-slim stain – dispersed like ectoplasm against a strung thread, or brains on a brick wall. Just gone, baby, gone.

Which was odd, granted – annoying, definitely; left alone and aroused once more, laid open for any port in a hormonal storm. Even sort of intriguing, for all that I wasn't exactly all that interested in being *intrigued* right now, this very minute. I mean, damn.

But no, I wasn't scared. Not even then. Why should I be?

I sat back on my heels, suddenly remembering how I'd once met my former aunt on the street, just after Pride, arm still in Ed's, my tongue still rummaging around in the dark of his mouth. How she'd clicked her teeth at me, spat on the sidewalk between us, and called me a banana. How Ed had blanched, then turned red; how I'd just laughed, amazed that she even knew the term.

And how I couldn't understand, later on, why he was still so upset – about the fact that I hadn't been upset at all.

Because that's how things go when you're shadowless: how trouble slides away from you, finding no purchase on your immaculate incompleteness. How the only thing you can hear, most days and nights, is the bright and seductive call of your own Power – your Art, your Practice. How it lures and pulls you, draws you like a static charge, singing: follow, follow, follow.

And how I do, inevitably – without fail – even at the cost of anything and everything in my way. Like the lack of a shadow follows a black hole sun.

This is probably worth looking at, sometime, I thought. *Got the words wrong, maybe, one of the symbols; have to do a little research, reconsecrate my tools, re-examine my methods. All that.*

(Sometime.)

But . . .

. . . not tonight.

An hour later, I swerved up Church Street, heading straight for the Khyber. Wednesday was Fetish Night, and though nothing I had on was particularly appropriate, I knew a brief flirtation with Vic the bouncer would probably get me in anyway. The street glittered, febrile with windchill, unfolding itself in a series of pointilescent flashes: bar doorways leaking black light and Abba; a muraled restaurant wall sugared with frost; parks and alleyways choked with unseasonably-dressed chain-smokers, shivering and snide, almost too cold to cruise.

Past the bar and out through the musically segregated dance floor (the Smiths versus Traci Lords, standing room only), I finally found my old RTA party partner Gil Wycliffe – now head of creative design for Quadrant Leather – strapped face-down over a vaulting horse in one of the club's back rooms, getting his bare ass beaten red and raw by some all-purpose daddy in a Sam Browne belt and a fetching pair of studded vinyl chaps. The paddle being used looked like one of Gil's own creations; it had a crack like a long-range rifle-shot, and left a diamond-shaped pattern of welts behind that made his buttocks glow as patchily as underdone steaks.

I must admit that I've never quite understood the appeal of sadomasochism, for all that "they" – those traditionally unspe̤ ꞁied (though probably Caucasian) arbiters of societal lore – would probably like to credit me with some kind of genetic yearning toward pain and suffering for fun and pleasure, just because the whole concept supposedly originated in the Mysterious East: the Delight of the Razor, the Death of the Thousand and One Cuts. All that stale old Sax Rohmer/James Bond bullshit.

Then again, I guess there's no particular reason anyone else really has to "get" it, unless they *are* a masochist. Or a sadist.

The daddy paused for a half-second between licks, catching my eye in open invitation; I signed disinterest, leaned back against the wall to wait this little scene out, let my gaze wander.

And there he was.

First a mere lithe flicker between gyrating bodies, then a half-remembered set of lines and angles, gilded with mounting heat: vague reflections off a high, flat cheekbone, a wryly gentle mouth, a bent and pliant neck. That whole lambent outline – so neat, so trim, so invitingly indefinite. It was my Bloor mystery man himself, swaying out there at the very heart of the crowd. Head back, body loose. Shaking and burning in the strobelights' glare.

Oh, *waaah.*

Every inch of me sprang awake at the sight, skin suddenly acrawl with possibilities.

The way he stood. The way he moved. The sheer, oddly familiar glamor of him was an almost physical thing, even to the cut and cling of his all-black outfit – though I couldn't have described its components if you'd asked me to, I somehow knew I might as well have picked them out myself.

I know *this man,* I thought, slowly, sounding the paradox through in my mind. *Even though I do* not *know this man.*

But I *wanted* to know this man.

Lit from within by sudden desire, I closed my eyes and bit down hard on my lower lip, tasting his flesh as sharply as though it were my own.

Movement stirred by my elbow – Gil, upright once more, reverently stroking his own well-punished cheeks. He winced and grinned, drowsily ecstatic, blissed out on an already-peaking surge of endorphins.

Turning, I screamed, over the beat: "WHO'S THE DUDE?"

He raised a brow. "TONY HU?"

Definitely not.

"I *KNOW* WHO TONY HU IS, GIL."

"THEN WHY'D YOU *ASK*?" He screamed back, shrugging.

Obviously, not a night for subtlety. I waved goodbye and stepped quickly off, resolved to take matters firmly by the balls. I wove my way back across the dance floor, eyes kept firmly on the prize: Mr Hunk of the Millennium's retreating back, bright with subtle muscle; the clean flex and coil of his golden spine, calling to me even more clearly with every footfall.

He was a walking slice of pure aura, a streak of sexual magnetism, and I followed him as far and as quickly as I could – up the ramp, just past the coat-check stand, and into the washroom at the head of the stairs, not the large one with the built-in shower stalls (so useful for Jock Nights and Wet Diaper Contests) but the small one with the barred windows, built to cater to those few customers whose bladders had become temporarily more important to them than their genitals.

The place had no back door, not even an alcove to hide in. But when I finally got there, I found the place empty except for a man crouched half on his knees by the far wall, wiping his mouth and wavering back and forth above a urinal full of fresh vomit.

Annoyed by the force of my own disappointment, I hissed through my teeth and kicked the back of the washroom door. The sound made the man look up, woozily.

"Jude," he said. "It *is* you. Right?"

I narrowed my eyes. Shrugged.

"You should know," I replied. Adding: "Ed."

He said he'd planned to spend the night waiting for me, but that the Khyber's buy one drink, get another one of equal or lesser value free policy had begun to take its toll pretty early on. I agreed that he certainly seemed in no shape to get himself home alone.

As for what followed, I've definitely had worse – from the same source too. He didn't puke again, either, which is always a big plus.

That night – wrapped in Ed's arms, breathing his beer-flavored breath – I dreamed of Carra hanging between heaven and earth with one foot on a cliff, the other in the air, like the Tarot's holy Fool. I dreamed she looked at me with her empty eyes, and asked: What did you *do* to yourself, Jude? Oh, Jude. What did you *do*?

And I woke, shivering, with a whisper caught somewhere in the back of my throat – nothing but three short words to show for all my arcane knowledge, in the end, when questioned so directly. Just *I*, and *don't*, and *know*.

But thinking, resentfully, at almost the same time: *I mean*, you're *the psychic*, *right? So . . .*

. . . you tell *me*.

The next morning, Ed came out of the kitchen with coffees and Danishes in hand, only to find me hunting around for my pants; he stopped in his tracks, striking a pose of anguished surprise so flawless I had to stop myself – from laughing.

"You heartless little bastard," he said.

I sighed.

"We broke up, Ed," I reminded him, gently. "Your idea, as I recall."

"So why'd you even call me, then – if you were just planning to suck and run?"

"I didn't."

"You fucking well *did.*"

I glanced up from my search, suddenly interested – this conversation was beginning to sound familiar, in more ways than one. Shades of Franz, so sure I was the one who'd called him about Jen. So definite in his belief that I'd actually told him I would help her out with the latest in her series of recurrent supernatural/psychological problems . . . and for free, no less.

"You called last night, when I was studying for trig. Said you'd been thinking about us. Said you'd be down at the Khyber anyway, so show up, and you'd find me."

"Last night."

"Oh, Jude, enough with this bullshit. You're telling me what, it just slipped your mind?" He grabbed his desk phone, stabbed for the star key and brandished it my way. "How about that?"

I squinted at the display. "That says 'unknown caller,'" I pointed out.

Ed dropped the phone, angrily. "Look, fuck you, okay? It was you."

With or without evidence, there was something interesting going on here. A call from somebody who claims to be me being received once is a misunderstanding, maybe a coincidence. But twice? In the same night?

By two different people?

I see you twice, Grandmother Yau had said.

And Carra, weighing her words: . . . *something.*

My pants proved to be wadded up and shoved under the bed, right next to Ed's cowboy boots. I shook them out, pulled them back on, buttoned the fly. Ed, meanwhile, kept right on with his time-honored tirade, hitting all the usual high spots: my lack of interest, my lack of loyalty. My lack, out of bed, of anything that might be termed normal emotional affect. My *lack*, in general.

Adding, quieter: "And you never loved me, either. Fuck, you never even really wanted me to love you."

"Did I ever say I *did?*"

"Yes."

Coat already half done up, I looked at him again, frankly amazed. Unable to stop myself from blurting –

"And you *believed* me?"

⚜

Heartless, I found myself repeating – a good half-hour later – as I fought my way east through the College Street wind tunnel, back from Ed's apartment. *Heart-lost. Heard last. Hardglass.* Then, smiling slightly: *Hard-ass.*

The word itself disintegrating under close examination, melting apart on my mental tongue. Like it was ever supposed to mean anything much – aside from Ed's latest take on the established him/me party line: "I used to quote-quote 'love' you, but now I quote-quote 'hate' you, and here's yet another lame excuse why."

Annoyed to realize I was still thinking about it, I shrugged the whole mess away in one brief move, so hard and quick it actually hurt.

Chi-shien gweilo! I thought. *What would I want with a heart? You don't need a heart to do magic.*

Which is true. You don't.

No more than you need a shadow.

A sharp left turn, then Church Street again: going down, this time. My Docs struck hard against the cracked concrete, again and again – each new stride sending up aftershocks that made my ankles spark with pain, as though that shrugged-away mess were somehow boomeranging back to haunt me with its ever-increasing twinge. And because I couldn't moderate myself, couldn't control either my speed or my boots' impact, the ache soon reached my chest – after a couple of blocks – and lodged there, throbbing.

Rhythm becoming thought, thought becoming memory; memory, which tends to shuck itself, to peel away. You get older, look back through a child's tunnel vision, and realize you never knew the whole that tied the details together. You were just along for the ride, moving from experience to experience, a flat spectacle, some kind of guideless tour. You remember – or think you remember – what happened, but not where, or why. What you did, but not with who. Details fade. People's names get lost in the white noise.

Reluctantly, therefore – for the second time in as many days – I found myself thinking about that shell of a thing I'd once been, back before the big split: that fresh-faced, fresh-scrubbed, fresh-off-the-boat Chink twink with his fifteen pairs of matching penny-loafers and his drawer full of gray silk ties. And just as smiley-face quiet, as neat and polite, as veddy, veddy, Brit-inflectedly *restrained* as he'd always been, the homegrown HK golden boy mask still firmly in place, even without a Ba and Ma immediately on hand to do his patented straight-Asian-male dance for anymore. . . .

Up till he'd met Carra, at least. Till she'd sat down beside him in study hall, her sleeves pushed up to show the desperate phantom scribble circling one wrist like a ringworm surfacing for air; looked right through him like his head was made of glass, seen all his ugly, hidden parts at once, and shown him exactly how wrong he'd always been about the nature he struggled to keep in check at all costs, the fears – formless and otherwise – he'd fought against tooth and nail all his relatively brief, bland, blind little life.

How restraint wasn't about powerlessness in the face of such terrors at all, but rather about being afraid of your own power. Its reality, its strength. Its endless range of unchecked possibilities, the good, the bad –

– and the indifferent.

I remember how freeing it felt to not "have" to watch myself all the time, at long last; nobody else was going to do it for me, and why should they? My first impulse, in every situation – as I well knew – was always to the angry, the selfish, the petty. I tried to be kind, mainly because I'd been so rigidly inculcated with the general Taoist/Christian principle that doing so was always the "right" thing *to* do. But even when I managed a good deed here and there, I knew it to be just so much hypocrisy, nothing more. *It was the least I could do, so I did it.*

Parental love is a matchless thing; if it weren't for that, most of us wouldn't have a pot to piss in, affectionately speaking. But even at its most irreplacable, it's still pretty cheap. Any ape loves its children; spiders lie still while theirs crawl around inside them, happy to let them eat their guts.

The only reason anybody unrelated is ever nice to anyone else, meanwhile, is as a sort of pre-emptive emotional strike – to prevent themselves from being treated as badly, potentially, as they might have treated other people. Which makes love only a lie two brains on spines tell each other, a lie that says: "You exist, because I love you. You exist, because you can see yourself in my eyes."

So we blunder from hope to hope, hollowed and searching. All of us equally incomplete.

And after all these years, still the sting comes, the liquid pressure in the chest and nose, the migraine-forerunner frown. Phantom pain. The ghost without the murder.

But what the fuck? That's all it is, ever. You want to be loved. You tell other people you love them, in order to trick them into loving you back. And after a while, it's true. You feel the pull, the ache.

The vibrato, voice keening skyward. The wet edge. Every word a whine. Weak, weak, weak, weak, weak.

When I say "you," of course, I mean "me." This is because everything is about me. To me. Why not? I'm the only me I have.

Truth is, none of us deserve anything. We get what we get.

And the best you can ever hope for . . . is to train yourself not to care.

Ahead, Ryerson loomed; residence row, with a Second Cup on either side of the street and competing hookers on every corner, shivering aslant on their sagging vinyl boot-heels.

I paused at Gould, waiting for a slow light, and put one itch-etched palm to my chest – telling myself it was to chart the ache's progress, rather than to keep myself from jarring the light's signal free with a sudden burst of excess entropic energy. Felt the charge building in my bones, begging for expression. For expulsion.

Some opportunity to turn this – whatever I felt myself tentatively beginning to feel – safely outward, without risk of repercussion. To evict the unwanted visitor, wash myself clean and empty and ready for use again, like any good craftsman's basic set of tools; make myself just an implement once more, immune to the temptations of personal desire.

What had I cut myself in half *for*, in the first place, if not for that? Scarred my heel, halved my soul, driven Franz and Jen one way and Carra the other, busted the Black Magic Posse back down to its dysfunctional roots so I could be this arcane study group's sole graduating student, its unofficial last man standing. And all to immunize myself from stress and fear and lack of focus – to free myself from every law but that of gravity, while still making sure I could probably break that one, too, if I just put my back into it. Dictator For Life of a one-person country, my own private Hierarchical Idaho.

Because if the effect wore *off*, however eventually . . . well, hell; that would mean none of the above had really been worth the effort. At all.

I hissed through my suddenly half-clogged nose at the very idea, but nothing happened. The ache remained.

And grew.

But: *something* will *present itself*, I forced myself to decide, more in certainty than conjecture. *The way it always does.*

And sure enough – soon enough –

– something did.

Just past Ryerson proper and into the shadow of St Mike's, moving through that dead stretch of pawnbrokers' shops and photographic supply warehouses. I glance-scanned the row of live DV hand-helds mounted in Henry's window, and caught his lambent shade flickering fast from screen to screen to screen: Him from the theatre, from the Khyber. That particular guy. He Who Remained Nameless, for now.

But not, I promised myself, for much longer.

I was already turning, instinctively, even as I formed the concept – half-way 'round where I stood before I even had a chance to recognize more than the line of his shoulder, the swing of his hair, the sidelong flash of what *might* be an eye: a mirror-image glance, an answering recognition. And stepping straight into the path of some ineptly tattooed young lout coccooned in a crowd of the same; Ry High jocks or proto-engineers out for a beer before curfew, with gay-bashing one of the options passing vaguely through what they collectively called a brain. Who called out, equally automatic, as I elbowed by him: "Hey, faggot!"

An insult I'd heard before, of course, far too many to count easily – not to mention one for which I currently had both no time and exactly zero interest, within context. So I tried to channel the old Jude, who'd always been so wonderfully diffident and accommodating in the face of fools, especially whenever violence threatened; dodge past with a half-ducked head and an apologetic, "no speakee Engarish, asshore" kind of half-smile, teeth grit and pride kept strictly quashed, as long as it got me finally face to face with my mystery man at last. . . .

Except that Mr Hetboy Supreme and his buddies didn't actually move, which meant I couldn't do much but hold my ground, still smiling. And when I took another look, the guy, my quarry, that ever-elusive, unimaginably attractive *him* – *he* was long gone, of course. Anyway.

And the ache was back.

"Faggot," the doofus said again – like he'd always wanted a chance to really sound it out aloud, syllable by un-PC syllable. And I just nodded again, my fingers knitting fast behind me, weaving hidden sigils in that empty place where my shadow used to be, feeling them perfect themselves without even having to check that I was doing it right.

Immaculate. Effortless. Like signing your name in the dark.

"Something I can help you with?" I asked. Adding, for extra emphasis: "Gentlemen."

One of them sniggered.

"Well, yes," said the one with the big mouth, all mock-obsequious. "See, the guys and me were just thinkin'. . ."

Unlikely.

". . . about how just seein' you come swishin' along here made us wanna, kinda – y'know – fuck you –"

Before he could finish his little game of verbal connect-the-dots, I'd already upgraded my smile to a – wide, nasty – grin.

"Over?" I suggested, coolly. "Or was it . . . up? The ass?"

More sniggers, not all of them directed at me. "You wish," my aspiring basher-to-be snapped back, a bit too quick for his own comfort.

I shrugged, bringing my hands forward. Rubbed my palms together, deliberately. Saw them all shiver and step back as one as my skin ignited – and winked, letting a spark of the same cheerless color flare in the pupil's heart of each flat black eye. Allowing it to grow, to spread. To kiss both lids, and gild my lashes with purple flame.

And oh, but the ache was chest-high and higher now, jumping my neck to lodge behind my face: a hammer in my head, a hundred-watt bulb thrown mid-skull. Like a halo in reverse.

"Not particularly," I replied.

Basher-boy's buddies broke and ran as one, pack-minded to the last. But I had already crooked a burning finger at him, riveting him to the spot, a skewer of force run through every limb. Using them like strings, I walked him – a reluctant puppet – to the nearest alley. Paused behind a clutch of trash-cans, popped my fly to let it all hang out. And leaned back against the wall, waiting.

"Down," I told him. "Now."

He knelt, staring up. I stroked his jaw.

"Open up," I said, sweetly.

And kept right on smiling, even after his formerly sneering lips hit the neat-ly-trimmed hair on my pubic ridge – right up until my sac swung free against his rigid, yet helplessly working, chin. I wasn't thinking of him, of course, but at least I wasn't thinking of that *guy* anymore – or myself, either. When I felt my orgasm at last, I came so hard I would have thought I was levitating, if I didn't already know what that feels like: off like a rocket, all in one choking gush. I held his head until I was done.

Then I stepped back, him still down on his knees in front of me, leaving him just enough room to pivot and puke back up everything I'd just given him.

My ache, conveniently enough, went along with it.

"You think you're going to do something about this," I told him, as I or-dered my cuffs and tucked my shirt back in. "Not that you'd ever tell your bud-dies, of course. But you're sitting there right now, thinking: 'One day I'm gonna catch him in an alley, and he'll have to eat through a straw for a month.'"

Closing my coat, I squatted down beside him, continuing. "But the thing is . . . even now, even with me right in front of you, you can't really remember what I look like. And it's getting worse. An hour from now, any given gay guy you meet might have been the one who did this to you. Am I right?" I leaned a little towards him, and felt him just stop himself from shying away; that little jerk in his breath, like a slaughterhouse calf just before the bolt slams home. "Can't tell, can you?" I asked, quietly.

He didn't answer.

"And do you know what that means?" I went on, sitting back on my heels. "It means that the next time you see somebody coming down Church Street, and you want to say hello – I think you're going to modify your tone a little. Lower your eyes, maybe. Not make any snap judgments. And definitely . . . un-der any circumstances at all . . . not call this person by insulting names. Because you never know." I paused. "And you never will, either."

Leaning forward again, I let my voice go cold. And whispered, right in his ear: "So be polite, little ghost. From now on, just be very – very – polite."

⚜

By the time I got home, one quick whiff was enough to tell me my neigh-bors were not only back, but already smoking up a storm. No '80s nostalgia dancemix filtering up through the floorboards as yet, though – so between the relative earliness of the hour and the obvious intensity of their hash-induced stupor, I figured I had about an hour before their proximity made it difficult to give the ritual I had in mind my fullest possible attention.

Because, morally repulsive as my pre-emptive strike on the engineer might have been – even from my own (admittedly prejudiced) point of view – the plain fact was, it had done the trick. Back in that alley, the emotional cramp temporarily hampering my ability to plan ahead had flowed out of me, borne on a blissful surge of bodily fluids. And inspiration had taken its place.

So I picked up the phone, and discovered – somewhat to my own amusement – that I really *could* remember Franz's mother's number, after all.

"You're actually going to help?" he repeated, obviously amazed.

"Why not? Might be kicks."

"Yeah, right. For who?"

"Does it matter?"

Planning it out, even as we fenced: use a two-ring circle system, with Jen sequestered in the inner, Franz and I in the outer. Proceed from Franz's assumption that Fleer was the demon in question, until otherwise proven; force him to vacate by offering him another rabbit-hole to jump down, one far more attractive to him than Jen could ever be. . . .

Making the connection, then, mildly startled by the ruthless depths of my own deviousness. And observing, to myself: *now,* that's *not nice.*

But I knew I'd have to try it, anyway.

I gave Franz a detailed list of what I'd need, only to be utterly unsurprised when he immediately balked at both its length and its – fairly expensive – specificity.

"Why the hell don't you ever practice straight-up Chinese magic, anyway?" He demanded. "Needles, herbs, all that good, *cheap* stuff. . . ."

"Same reason you don't raise any Mennonite demons, I guess."

He invited me to suck his dick. I gave an evil smile.

"Oh, Franz," I said, gently. "How do you know I never did?"

Next step was getting all the appointment-book bullshit dealt with: setting a time, date, and place, with Jen's address making the top of my list in terms of crucial missing information. According to Franz, she'd been living in some Annex hole in the ground for most of the last five years, vampire sex shows and all – though not an actual hole, mind you, or the actual ground. But only because that kind of logistical whimsy would have been *way* too interesting a concept, for either of them.

"And what are *you* planning on bringing to the party?" He asked, grumpily.

To which I replied, airily: ". . . . I'll think of something."

⚶

Which is how I came, a mere three hours later, to be sitting side by side with Carra in the Clarke's inaccurately-labelled Green Room – her slump-shouldered and staring at her scars against the gray-painted wall, me trying (and failing) to stop my feet from tapping impatiently on the scuffed gray linoleum floor. We were virtually alone, aside from one nurse stationed on the door, whose eyes kept straying back to the static-spitting TV in the corner as though it exercised some sort of magnetic attraction on her, and a dusty prayer-plant whose leaves seemed permanently fused together by the utter lack of natural light.

"I need a reading," I told Carra, briskly.

Toneless: "You know I can't do that anymore, Jude."

"I know you *don't*."

"Same difference."

It seemed clear she probably sensed ulterior motives beneath my visit, even though she knew herself to be always my court of last resort, when faced with any inexplicable run of synchronicity. But she didn't seem particularly interested in probing further, probably because this just happened to be one of those mornings when she wasn't much into seeing people; not live ones, anyway.

"Look," I said, "somebody's been doing stuff, and taking my name in vain while they do it. Sleeping with Ed, even after I already kicked him to the curb. Volunteering my services to Franz, even after I already told *him* to take a hike." I paused. "I even tried to do a spell, on that guy – the one from the movie?" As she nodded: "Well, *that* was all screwed up somehow, too. Like, just . . . weird."

"Your magic was weird," she repeated, evenly.

"Abnormally so."

She looked up, brushing her bangs away. "Told you there was something about that guy," she said, with just a sliver of her old, evilly detached, Ryerson-era grin.

I snapped my fingers. "Oh yeah, I remember now – you did, didn't you? Just never told me what."

"How should I know?"

"You read minds, Carra," I reminded her.

"Not well. Not on short notice."

"Also bullshit."

She turned to her hands again, examining each finger's gift-spotted quick in turn, each ragged edge of nail. Finally: "Well, anyways . . . it's not like I'm the only one who's told you that."

"Grandmother Yau did say she saw me twice," I agreed, slowly.

A snort. "I'm surprised she could even see you *once*."

"Why?"

"For the same reason I can hardly see you, Jude. You're only half there. Got no shadow, remember?"

Hair back in her eyes, eyes back on her palms – scanning their creases like if she only studied them hard enough, she thought she could will herself a whole new history. Then wrinkling her forehead and sniffing, a kind of combined wince/flinch, before demanding — apropos of nothing much, far as I could tell —

"God. Can you smell that, or what?"

"What?"

"*That,* Jude."

Ah, yes: *that.*

Guess not.

Yet — oh, what *was* that stupid knocking inside my chest, that soft, intermittent scratch building steadily at the back of my throat? Like I was sickening for something; a cold, a fever . . . some brief reflection of the Carra I'd once known, poking out — here and there — from under her hovering Haldol high.

I knew I could still remember exactly what it was, though, if only I let myself. That was the worst of it. Not the innate hurt of Carra's ongoing tragedy — this doomed, hubristic sprawl from darkness to darkness, hospital to halfway house and back again. Carra's endless struggle for the right to her own independent consciousness, pitted as she was against an equally endless, desperate procession of needy phantoms, to whom possession was so much more than nine-tenths of the law.

"The biggest mistake you can ever make," she told me once, "is to ever let them know you see them at all. Because it gets around, Jude. It really gets around."

(Really.)

Remembering how she'd once taught me almost everything I know, calmly and carefully — everything that matters, anyway. Everything that's helped me learn everything I've learned since. How she broke all the rules of "traditional" mediumship and laid herself willingly open to anything her Talent brought her way, playing moth, then flame, then moth again. After which, one lost day — a day she's never spoken of, even to me — she somehow decided that the best idea would be for her to burn on, unchecked, till she burned herself out completely.

How she'd spent almost all her time since the Ryerson Graduation Ball struggling — however inefficiently — to get her humanity "back," even though that particular impossible dream has always formed the real root of her insanity. And how I pitied her for it — pitied her, revered her, resented her. How I held her in increasingly black, bitter contempt, anger, and resentment over it, all because she'd wasted five long years trying to commit the unforgivable sin of leaving me behind.

No, I knew the whole situation a little too well to mourn over, at this point; almost as well as Carra did, in fact, and you didn't see her crying. She held her ground instead, with grace and strength, until the encroaching tide threatened to pull her under. And then she took a little Thorazine vacation, letting the Clarke's free drugs tune the constant internal whisper of her disembodied suitors' complaints down to a dull roar. Putting herself somewhere else, neatly and efficiently, so the dead could have their way with her awhile – and all on the off-chance that they might thus be satisfied enough, unlikely as it might seem, to finally leave her alone.

What I felt wasn't empathy. It was annoyance. I had things to talk about with Carra, business to attend to. And she made herself – quite deliberately – unreachable.

Besides which: feeling sorry for Carra, genuinely sorry . . . well, that'd be far too normal for *me*, wouldn't it? To feel my chest squeeze hot and close over Carra's insoluble pain, just because she was my oldest Canadian acquaintance, my mentor, and my muse. My best, my truest, friend.

My one. And my only.

(A memory loop of Ed's voice intervening here, thick and blurry: "Tell you what, Jude – why don't you surprise me: name the last time you felt anything. For somebody other than yourself, I mean.")

And when was it we had that conversation, exactly? Two hours ago? Two months?

Two years, maybe. Not that it mattered a single flying fuck.

Ai-yaaah. So inappropriate. So selfish. So, very –

"Still walking around out there, like any other ghost," Carra continued, musingly. "Looking like you, acting . . . *sort* of like you. . . ."

– *me.*

"So," I said, slowly. "What you're telling me is – this guy I've been after, for the last couple of days –"

"*He's* your shadow."

And: ohhhh.

Well, that explained a *lot.*

Rubbing a hand across my lips, then stroking it absently back over my hair. And thinking, all the while: could be true; why not? I mean – who did that guy remind me of, anyway, if *not* myself? Certainly explained the attraction.

Running after myself, yearning after myself. Working *magic* on myself.

Man, I always *knew* I was a narcissist.

All the lesser parts of me: weak where I was potent, slippery where I was direct, silent where I was vocal, acquiescent where I was anything but. Myself, reflected backwards and upside-down in a weirdly flattering Yin mirror, just like Grandmother Yau said.

Caught in a mesh of darkness.

"My 'evil twin,'" I suggested, facetiously.

She shrugged. "Kind of depends on your definition." Then: "Christ! What *is* that smell?"

In other words: If *he's* the evil one –

– then what's that supposed to make *you*?

I shook my head yet again, flicking the idea away – such a smooth-ass move, and one that really does get easier and easier, the more diligently you practice it. Then propelled myself upwards and outwards, brisky brushing the room's dust from my clothes, like I was simultaneously scrubbing myself free of her aura's leaking, purple-brown, depression-and-defeat-inflected stain. Saying: "Well, anyway – gotta go. Things to do, rituals to research, shopping lists to compile. Exorcisms don't come cheap, you know."

". . . don't."

"Why the hell not?"

Hesitant: "I mean, it's just. Not. Not, uh . . ."

(. . . safe.)

Riiiiight.

Cause that was the big concern, these days: staying safe, at all costs. Even when the best way to make sure *I* stayed safe, if it really concerned her so much, would be to sign herself out of this shithole – the way we all knew she could, at a moment's fucking notice – and come help out. Instead of just sitting there all smug with dead people's handwriting crawling up and down her arms like some legible rash and the air around her starting to thicken like a rind, to crackle like a badly-grounded electric fence. . . .

Bitch, I thought, before I could stop myself. And saw her flinch again, as the impact of my projected insult bruised her cortex from the inside-out; saw blood drip from one nostril, as she blinked away a film of tears.

I shut my eyes to block it all out, feeling that *ache* squirm inside me, twisting in on itself. Knotting tight. Feeling it ripple with fine, poison-packed spines, all of them spewing a froth of negativity that threatened to send my few lingering deposits of tenderness, sorrow, and affection flowing away at a touch, leaving nothing behind but emptiness, and rot, and rage.

If I *let* it, that is. Which I wasn't about to.

Not when I still had even the faintest lingering chance of getting what I wanted.

"Listen," I began, carefully. "We both know the main reason you put the Posse together in the first place was because it was the only way you could blow off steam, stop devoting all your energy to just protecting yourself. . . ."

Leave it open as sin and let the ghosts rush in at will: babble and float, vomit ectoplasm and sprout word-bruises like hickey chains, laugh like a loon, and know no one was actually going to treat you like one for doing it.

Good times, baby. Good, good times.

"But now the lid's back on all the time, because you're afraid to let it come off, under any circumstances. And the steam's still building. And pretty soon it's going to blow either way, and when it does it'll hurt somebody, which'd be okay if it was just you. Except that it probably won't be."

Carra cast her eyes at me warily. There was an image lurking somewhere in her downcast gaze, half-veiled by lash and post-meds pupil dilation: past, present, maybe even future. It took all my remaining self-restraint not to tweeze it forward with a secret gesture, catch it between my own lids, and blink it large enough to scry. But that would be impolite. We were friends, after all, me and her.

And: like that actually *means* anything, some ungrateful, traitor part of me whispered – right against the figurative drum of my mental inner ear.

"You know," she said, finally, "if you hadn't caught me on an off-day . . . that probably would have worked."

Adding, a moment later: "And speaking of reading minds – you think I don't know what you're planning, by the way? An open medium, a vessel with no shields; couldn't ask for a better demon-trap, not if you ordered it from *Acme Better Homes & Banishments*. I walk in, Fleer jumps me, you cast him out and toss him right back through the Rift again – and what the hell, huh? Because I'm *used* to having squatters in *my* head."

"So what – would you have agreed if I'd said it straight out?" I shot back, reasonably enough. "But c'mon, admit it: be a fuck of a lot more interesting than just hiding in here, where you're no use to anybody."

"I'm sick of being 'of use.' I've been 'of use' since I was born. And now – now *you* want to use me; Jesus, Jude. Is that what 'friends' do to each other these days?"

I shrugged. Well, when you put it *that* way. . . .

Softly: "I'll always be your friend, Carra."

She shook her head. "That other part of you, sure. But you . . . you've changed."

Shadow-coveting vibe just pumping off of me by now, no doubt – extruding at her through my pores, like Denis Leary-level cigarette smoke at a hyper-allergenic: sloppy-drunk with wanting him, distracted with seeking him, enraged with not finding him. Forgotten emotions colliding like neurons, giving off heat and light and horror. Making me feel different to her, all complicated and intrusive, instead of the calming psychic dead-spot whose absence she'd gotten all too used to basking in. Making me feel just like . . .

. . . everybody else.

"I never change," I said. Contradicting myself, almost immediately: "And anyway, should I have just stayed the way I was: that fool, that weak child? Too scared of everything, including himself, to *do* anything *about* anything?"

"I liked him."

So simple, so plaintive. Her barely-audible voice like an echo of that dream I'd had the night before, the one where I'd seen her hanging between earth and air. Asking me: What did you *do* to yourself, Jude? What did you *do*?

You know what I did, I started to say, but froze mid-word. Because just then – at the very same time – I finally caught a hint of something unnatural in the air around us: some phantom stink skittering from corner to corner like a rancid pool-ball, drawing an explosive puff of dust from the center of the prayer-plant's calcified Cry to Heaven. Making the nurse look up, sniffing.

Carra hacked, hands flying to her nose; her fingers came away wet, stained with equal parts coughed-out snot and thick, fresh blood.

"Fuck," she said, amazed. "That *smell* –

"– it's *you*."

And she began to rise.

The nurse's eyes widened, fixing; she made a funny little "eeep" noise, and scuttled back against the wall. To her right, static ate the TV's signal entirely, turning *All My Children* into Nothing But Snow. I took a retreative half-step myself, fingers flashing purple: wards, activate! Ghosts, disperse!

Thinking – projecting – even as my flared nostrils stung in sympathy: oh, baby, don't. Please, do *not*. Do not *do* this to *me*. . . .

Carra's heels hooked the seat of her chair, knocking it backwards with the force of their upswing; she gasped, blood-tinted mucus-drip already stretching into hair-fine tendrils that streamed out wide on either side, wreathing her like impromptu mummy-wrap. The chair fell, skipping once, like a badly-thrown beach rock.

Rising to stick and hang there in the center of the room, her heels holding five steady inches above the floor. Head flung back. Ectoplasm pouring from her nose and mouth. While all around, a psychically-charged dust devil scraped the walls like some cartoon tornado-in-a-can, its tightening funnel composed equally of frustrated alien willpower and whatever small, inanimate objects happened to be closest by: plastic cutlery, scraps of paper. Hair and thread and crumbs. Garbage of every description.

A babble of ghostly voices filling her throat, making her jaw's underside bulge like a frog's. Messages scrawling up and down her exposed limbs as the restless dead took fresh delight in making her their unwilling megaphone, their stiff and unco-operative human note pad.

She looked down at me, cushioned behind my pad of defensive Power, and let the corners of her mouth give an awful rictus-twitch. And as her glasses lifted free – apparently unnoticed – to join the rest of the swirl, I saw ectoplasmic lenses slide across her eyes like cataracts, blindness taking hold in a milky, tidal, unstoppable ebb and flow.

Forcing her lips further apart, as the tendons in her neck grated and popped. Wrenching a word here and there from the torrent inside her, and forcing herself to observe:

"Not . . . ever . . . ything. Is . . . ab . . . out. *You*. Jude."

Believe it –

– or not.

And I, as usual, chose not.

The primary aim of magicians is to gather knowledge, because knowledge – as everyone finds out fairly early, from *Schoolhouse Rock* on – is power. To that end, we often conjure demons who we use and dismiss in the same offhand way most people grab the right implement from their kitchen drawer: fork, cheese-knife, slotted spoon; salt, pepper, sulphur. Keep to the recipe, clean your plate, then walk away quickly once the meal is done.

But even if we pursue this culinary analogy to its most pedantic conclusion, cooking with demons is a bit like trying to run a restaurant specializing in dishes as likely to kill you as they are to nourish you: deathcap mushroom pasta with a side of ergot-infested rye bread, followed by the all-fugu special. They're cruel and unpredictable, mysterious and restless, icily malignant – far less potent than the actual Fallen who spawned them, yet far more fearful than simple elementals of fire, air, water, earth, or the mysterious realms which lie beneath it. Like the dead, demons come when called – or even when not – and envy us our flesh; like the dead, you must feed them blood before they consent to give their names or do your bidding.

Psellus called them lucifugum, Those Who Fly the Light. I call them a pain in the ass, especially when you're not entirely sure what *else* to call them.

On the streetcar ride from College/Yonge to Bathurst/College, I chewed my lip and flipped through my copy of the *Grimoire Lemegeton*, which lists the names and powers of seventy-two different demons, along with their various functions.

Eleven lesser demons procure the love of women, or (if your time is tight) make lust-objects of either sex show themselves naked. Four can transport people safely from place to place, or change them into other shapes, or gift them with high worldly position, cunning, courage, wit, and eloquence. Three produce illusions: of running water, of musical instruments playing, of birds in flight. One can make you invisible, another turns base metals into gold. Two torment their victims with running sores. One, surprisingly, teaches ethics; I don't get a whole lot of requests for that one, strangely enough.

Glasyalabolas teaches all arts and sciences, yet incites to murder and blood-shed. Raum reconciles enemies when he's not destroying cities. Flauros can either burn your foes alive, or discourse on divinity. Or Fleer himself, indifferently good or bad, who "will do the work of the operator."

If it actually *was* Fleer inside Jen, that is. If, if, if.

Practicing the usual injunctions under my breath, while simultaneously trying to decide between potential protective sigils: *Verbum Caro Factorem Est*, your basic quadrangelic conjuration, maybe even the ultimate old-school reliability of Solomon's Triangle – upper point to the north, Anexhexeton to the east, Tetragrammaton to the west, Primematum anchoring. Telling your nameless quarry, as you etch the lines around yourself:

"I conjure and command thee, oh spirit N, by Him who spake and it was done; Asar Un-Nefer, Myself Made Perfect, the Bornless One, Ineffable. Come peaceably, visibly, and without delay. Come, fulfill my desires and persist unto the end in accordance to my will. Zazas, Zazas, Nasatanada, Zazas: exit this vessel as and when I command, or be thrown through the Gate from whence ye came."

The streetcar slid to a halt, Franz visible on the platform ahead – looking worried, as ever. A shopping bag in either hand testified to his having already filled out my list. Which was good; proved he wanted Jen "cured" enough to throw in from his own pocket, at least.

And: I've *done* this, I thought. Lots of times. I can do it again, Carra or not – and what the fuck had I really thought I needed Carra for, anyway? As she'd (sort of) pointed out, herself.

Easy. Peasy. Easy-peasy.

But none of the above turned out to matter very much at all, really. In the end.

⚜

Stepped off the streetcar at six or so. By midnight I was back at Grandmother Yau's, sucking back a plate of Glass Noodle Cashew Chicken and washing it back with lots and lots of tea, so much I could practically feel my bladder tensing yet another notch with each additional swig. Starting to itch, and twinge, and . . . ache.

(Ache.)

"So, Jude-ah," came a soft, Mandarin-accented voice from just behind my shoulder. "Seeing you seem sad, I wonder: how does your liver feel? Is the general of your body's army sickening, tonight?"

And: tonight, tonight, I found myself musing. What *was* tonight, at the Khyber? Oh, right . . . open bar. No bullshit restrictions. I could wear that tank-top I'd been saving, the really low-cut one.

Wick-ed.

Grandmother Yau reached in, touching her gilded middle claw to my ear, brief and deft; I jumped at its sting, collecting myself, as she reminded me –

"I am not used to being ignored, little brother."

Automatically: "Ten thousand pardons, big sister."

She narrowed her green-tinged eyes, shrewdly. "One will do." Then, waving the nearest ghost over to top up my teapot: "My spies tell me you had business, further east. Is it completed?"

And waaah, but there were so very many ways to answer that particular question, weren't there? Though I, typically, chose the easiest.

"*Wei,*" I said, nodding. "Very complete."

"The possessed girl, ah? Your friend."

That's right.

My friend Jen, laying there on the tatty green carpet of her basement apartment; my other friend Franz, leaning over her. Shaking her — a few times, gently at first, then harder. Slapping her face once. Doing it again.

Watching her continue to lie there, impassively limp. Then looking back at me, a growing disbelief writ plain across his too-pale, freckled face — me, standing still inside my circle, with no expression at all on mine. Watching him watch.

She's not breathing, Jude.

Well, no.

Jude. I think . . . I think she's dead.

Well — yes.

"Turns out," I told Grandmother Yau, "she wasn't actually possessed, after all."

"No?"

"No."

Ai-yaaah.

Because: I'd taken Franz's word, and Franz had taken Jen's — but she'd lied to us both, obviously, or been so screwed up that even she hadn't *really* known where those voices in her skull were coming from. So I'd come running, prepared to kick some non-corporeal butt, and funnelled the whole charge of my Power into her at once, cranked up to demon-expelling level.

But if there's no demon to be *put* to flight, that kind of full-bore metaphysical shock attack can't help but turn out somewhat like sticking a fork in a light socket, or vice versa. If that's even possible.

Franz again, in Jen's apartment, turning on me with his eyes all aburn. Reminding me, shakily: you *said you could* help.

If she was possessed, yes.

Then why is she dead, *Jude?*

Because . . . she wasn't.

You — said —

I shrugged. *Whoopsie.*

He lunged for me. I let off a force-burst that threw him backwards five feet, cracking his spine like a whip.

You don't ever lay hands on me, I said, quietly. *Not ever. Unless I want you to.*

He sat there, hugging his beloved corpse with charred-white palms, crying in at least two kinds of pain. And snarled back: *Like I'd want to* touch *you with some other guy's dick and some third fucker pushing, you son of a fucking bitch.*

(Yeah, whatever.)

Fact was, though, if Franz hadn't been so cowardly and credulous in the first place — if he hadn't wanted an instant black magic miracle, instead of having the guts to just take her to a mental hospital, the way most normal people do when their girlfriends start telling them they hear voices – then Jen might still be alive.

Emphasis on the might.

I can call demons. I can bind angels. I can raise the dead, for a while. But just like Franz himself had observed, more than once, I can't actually *cure* anybody – can't heal them of cancer, leprosy, MS, old age, mental illness, or color-blindness to save my fucking life. Not unless they *want* me to. Not unless they *let* me.

The other way? That's called a miracle, and my last name ain't Christ.

Franz, crying out, tears thick as blood in his strangled voice: *You promised me, you fuck! You fucking promised me!*

Followed, in my memory, by a quick mental hit of Carra, half the city away: still floating, still wreathed. And think: *If I could do something for people like that, you moron, don't you think I would?*

She *wants* to be nuts, though. Long and short of it. Just like, on some level, Jen wanted to die.

But hell, what was Franz going to do about it, one way or another? *Shun me?*

I took a fresh bite of noodle while the ancient Chinese spectre I'd come to think of as Grandmother's right-hand ghost flitted by, pausing to murmur in her ear for a moment before fading away through the nearest lacquer screen. And when she looked at me, she had something I'd never seen before lurking in the corners of her impenetrable gaze. If I'd had to hazard a guess, I might even have said it looked a lot like – well –

– surprise.

"Someone," she said, at last, "is at the maître d's station. Asking for you, Jude-ah."

Glancing sidelong, so I'd be forced to follow the path of her gaze over to where . . . *he* waited: He. It. Me.

My shadow.

My shadow, highlighted against the Empress' Noodle's thick, red velvet drapes like a sliver of lambent bronze – head down, shyly, with its hair in its eyes and its hands in its pockets. My shadow, come at last after all my fruitless seeking, just waiting for its better half to take control, wrap it tight, gather it in and make it – finally – whole again.

Waiting, patiently. Quiet and acquiescent. Waiting, waiting . . .

. . . for me.

I met Grandmother Yau's gaze again, and found her normally impassive face gone somehow far more rigid than usual: green-veined porcelain, a funerary mask trimmed in milky jade.

"The Yin mirror reflects only one way, Chiu-wai-ah," she said, at last. "It is a dark path, always. And slippery."

I nodded, suddenly possessed by a weird spurt of glee. Replying, off-hand:

"*Mei shi*, big sister; not to worry, never mind. Do you think I don't know enough to be careful?"

To which she merely bowed her head, slightly. Asking –

"What will you do, then?"

And I couldn't stop myself from smiling, as the answer came sliding synapse-fast to the very tip of my tongue, kept restrained only by a lifetime's residual weight of "social graces." Thinking: Oh, I? Go home, naturally. Go home, dim the lights, light some incense –

– and *fuck* myself.

⚜

So soft in my arms, not that I'd ever thought of myself as *soft*. I pushed it back against the apartment door with its wrists pinned above its head, nuzzling and nipping, quizzing it in Cantonese, Mandarin, ineffectual Vietnamese – only to have it offer exactly nothing in reply, while simultaneously maintaining an un-broken stare of pure, dumb adoration from beneath its artfully lowered lashes.

Which was okay by me; more than okay, really. Seeing I'd already had it pretty much up to here with guys who talked.

Feeling the shadow's proximity, its very presence, prickle the hairs on the back of my neck like a presenitiment of oncoming sheet-lightning against empty black sky: all plus to my mostly minus, yang to my yin, nice guy to my toxic shit. And wanting it *back*, right here and now; feeling the core-deep urge to penetrate, to own, to repossess those long-missing parts of me in one hard push, come what fucking might.

Groin to groin and breath to breath, two half-hearts beating as one, two severances sealing fast. Unbreakable.

Down on the bed, then, with its heels on my shoulders: key sliding home, lock springing open. Rearing erect, burning bright with flickering purple flame, all over. And seeing myself abruptly outlined in black against the wall above my headboard at that ecstatic moment of (re)joining, like some Polaroid flash's bruisy after-image: my inverse reflection. My missing shadow, slipping inside *me* as I slipped inside *it*, enshadowing me once more.

Ten years' worth of trauma deferred, all crashing down on me at once. Showing me first-hand, explicitly, how nature abhors a – moral, human, walk-ing – vacuum.

⚜

And now it's later, oh *so* much, with rain all over my bedroom floor and beads of wood already rising like sodden cicatrices everywhere I dare to look. Rain on my hair, rain in my eyes – only natural, given that the window's still open. But I can't stand up, can't force a step, not even to shut it. I just squat here and listen to my heart, eyes glued to that ectoplasmic husk the shadow left devolving on my bed: a shed skinfull of musk and lies, rotting. All that's left of my lovely double, my literal self-infatuation.

I've done the protective circle around myself five times now, at least – in magic marker, in chalk, in my own shit. Tomorrow I think I'll re-do it in blood, just to get it over with; can't keep on picking at these ideas forever, without something starting to fester. And we don't want *that*, do we?

(Really.)

Because the sad truth is this: my wards hold, like they always hold; the circle works, like all my magic works. But what it doesn't do, even after all my years of sheer, hard, devoted work – all my Craft and study, not to mention practice –

– is *help*.

Once upon a time – when I was drunk, and young, and stupid beyond belief – I cut my shadow, my *soul*, away from me in some desperate, adolescent bid to separate myself from my own mortality. And since then, I guess I haven't really been much good for anybody but myself. I bound up my weakness and threw it away, not realizing that weakness is what lets you bend under unbearable pressure.

And if you can't bend . . . you break.

My evil twin, I hear my own arrogant voice suggest to Carra, mockingly – and with a sudden, stunning surge of self-hatred, I find I want to hunt that voice down and slap it silly. To roll and roar on the floor at my own willfully deluded stupidity.

Half a person, Franz chimes in, meanwhile, from deeper in my memory's ugly little gift-box. *And not even the* good *half.*

No. Because *it* was the good half. And me, I, I'm – just –

– all that's left.

My shadow. The part of me that might have been, if only I'd let it stay. My curdled conscience. Until it touched me, I didn't remember what it was I'd been so afraid of. But now I can't think about anything else.

Except . . . how very, very badly, no matter what the cost . . .

. . . I want for it to touch me again.

Thinking: is this *me*? Can this possibly be *me*, Jude Hark Chiu-Wai? *Me*?

Me.

Me, and no-fucking-body else.

Thinking, finally: but this won't kill me. Not even this. Much as I might like it to.

And maybe I'll be a better person for it, a better magician, if I can just make it through the next few nights without killing myself like Jen, or going crazy like Carra. But that's pretty cold comfort, at best.

Sobbing, retching. All one big weakness – one open, weeping sore. And thinking, helpless: *Carra, oh Carra. Grandmother Yau. Franz. Ed. Someone.*

Anyone.

But I've burned all my boats, funeral-style. And I can't remember – exactly, yet – how to swim.

The Wide World converges on me now, dark and sparkling, and I just crouch here beneath it with my hands over my face: weeping, moaning, too paralytic-terrified even to shield myself from its glory. Left all alone at last with the vision and the void – crushed flat, without a hope of reprieve, under the endless weight of a dark and whirling universe.

Ripe and riven. Unforgiven. Caught forever, non-citizen that I am, in that typically Canadian moment just before you start to freeze.

Keeping my sanity, my balance.

Keeping to the straight and Narrow.

NOTES ON CONTRIBUTORS

ROBERT BOYCZUK is a Toronto writer. He has previously published stories in *On Spec, Trans-versions*, and *Prairie Fire*, and in the anthologies *On Spec: The First Five Years*, *Erotica Vampirica*, *Northern Frights 4*, *Tesseracts 7*, *Northern Suns*, and *Queer Fear*.

POPPY Z. BRITE is the author of six novels, three short story collections, and a great deal of miscellanea. She lives in New Orleans with her husband Chris, a chef. If you liked the characters in "Bayou de la Mère," you can read much more about them in her novels *The Value of X* (available from Subterranean Press) and *Liquor* (forthcoming from Crown). Find out more at *poppyzbrite.com*.

DAVID COFFEY is a Toronto-based writer who has flirted with journalism, radio, and television. He is a graduate of York University's MFA program in film. Currently he works as a producer at CITY-TV's *Book Television* and *MuchMoreMusic*.

STEPHEN DEDMAN is the author of the novels *The Art of Arrow Cutting* (a Bram Stoker Award nominee), *Foreign Bodies*, and *Shadows Bite*. His short stories have appeared in an eclectic range of magazines and anthologies, and thirteen of the best have been collected in *The Lady of Situations*. Would you believe they let him write children's books too? Stephen, his wife, and her wife all live in Western Australia. He enjoys reading, travel, movies, complicated relationships, talking to cats, and startling people.

STEVE DUFFY's tales of the uncanny have appeared in magazines including *Ghosts & Scholars*, *All Hallows*, *Supernatural Tales*, *New Genre*, and *Darkness Rising*. Ash-Tree Press have published two collections of his short fiction (both solo and collaborative), and Steve has contributed to several of Ash-Tree's hardback anthologies of original work. His stories have also been included in Ellen Datlow and Terri Windling's *Year's Best Fantasy and Horror* anthologies. In 2001 Steve won the International Horror Guild's Award for Best Short Story of the year 2000. "Numbers" is dedicated to the trailblazers, with admiration; to the sufferers, with sympathy; and to those who carry on, with hopefulness.

WARREN DUNFORD is the Lambda Literary Award-nominated author of the novels *Soon to Be a Major Motion Picture* and *Making a Killing*. He lives in Toronto.

After a nine-year flirtation with film criticism, GEMMA FILES has finally settled down into a far more rewarding pattern of teaching scriptwriting and film history at Toronto's International Academy of Design and Technology by day, and scaring the pants off people by night (or any other time she has the opportunity). Her two short story collections, *Kissing Carrion* and *The Worm in Every Heart*, will be available from Prime Books as of 2003. She is hard at work on a first novel.

MICHAEL THOMAS FORD is the author of numerous books, most notably the *Trials of My Queer Life* series of essay collections. His fiction and essays have been included in many anthologies, including *Mirth of a Nation 2*, *Brothers of the Night*, and *Queer Fear*, and his first novel, *Last Summer*, will be published in summer 2003. He lives in San Francisco with his partner, Patrick, and the world's largest black Lab. He can be viewed at *michaelthomasford.com*.

SEPHERA GIRON is the author of *The Birds and The Bees* (Leisure Books), *House of Pain* (Leisure Books), *Eternal Sunset* (Darktales Publications), and the non-fiction book written under her pen name, Ariana, *House Magic: The Good Witch's Guide to Bringing Grace to Your Space* (Conari Press). Some of her erotic horror stories appear in *Hot Blood 11*, *Decadance*, *Sex Macabre*, *S/M Futures*, *Unnatural Selection*, *Tooth*, and *Claw 2: The Asylum* (volumes 1 and 2). Sephera lives in the suburbs of Toronto.

NALO HOPKINSON, from Canada by way of the Caribbean, is the author of novels *Brown Girl in the Ring*, *Midnight Robber*, and *Griffonne*, and of the short story collection *Skin Folk*. She recently edited an anthology of short fiction by other writers: *Mojo: Conjure Stories* which will be out from Warner Books in spring 2003.

JAMES HUCTWITH, who painted the cover image, is an artist living and working in Toronto. Trained at the University of Guelph, he has shown his figurative oil paintings in Vancouver and Toronto and has collectors across North America. *Queer Fear* and *Queer Fear II* mark his first entry into the world of book illustration. Mr Huctwith is currently working on his next solo show at O'Connor, his home gallery in Toronto. When he's not painting, you can catch him working as a leather-clad bouncer at Toronto's most popular gay bar. His website is *jameshuctwith.com*.

WILLIAM J. MANN is the author of several novels, including his latest, *Where the Boys Are*, as well as two acclaimed books on the Hollywood film industry, *Wisecracker: The Life and Times of William Haines* and *Behind the Screen: How Gays and Lesbians Shaped Hollywood*. He lives in Provincetown, Massachussets.

MICHAEL MARANO is a freelance writer who divides his time between Boston and Charleston, South Carolina. Primarily a movie reviewer and pop culture commentator, Marano has published in such venues as *The Charleston City Paper*, *The Boston Phoenix*, *Science-Fiction Weekly*, and *Horror Garage* (among many others). Marano's punk/heavy metal style of criticism has been described as "combining the best of *Cahiers du Cinéma* with the spirit of pro-wrestling." His "Headbanger Movie Reviews" have been a regular feature of the *Public Radio Satellite Program Movie Magazine* (which is syndicated in 111 markets throughout North America) since 1990; his popular "MediaDrome" column appears in *Cemetery Dance*. Marano's first novel, *Dawn Song*, received both the International Horror Guild and Bram Stoker Awards; his short fiction has appeared in Peter S. Beagle's *Immortal Unicorn*, *The Mammoth Book of Best New Horror 11*, *Queer Fear*, and *Gothic.net*. He receives email at: dawnsong@mindspring.com, and his web page is located at *mindspring.com/~profmike*.

MARSHALL MOORE is a North Carolina native now living in the San Francisco Bay area. He buys too many books and collects ink in the form of tattoos and passport stamps. His debut novel *The Concrete Sky* is set to appear in spring 2003 from Southern Tier. For more information about Marshall and his work, please visit his website: *marshallmoore.net*.

DAVID NICKLE's stories have appeared in two previous Michael Rowe anthologies: *Queer Fear* and *Sons of Darkness*. He's also had stories in the *Northern Frights* series of anthologies, *The Year's Best Fantasy and Horror*, and magazines such as *Cemetery Dance*, *Transversions*, and *On Spec*. He won the Bram Stoker Award for his short story (co-written with Edo van Belkom) "RatFood," and he's the co-author (with Karl Schroeder) of the novel *The Claus Effect*. He lives and works in Toronto.

Due to a recent bout of existential angst, JOSEPH O'BRIEN is unable to confirm nor deny the existence of said person. As "WideScreenPig" he continues to be a regular presence on the alt.horror newsgroup. Most recently he embarked on the online graphic adaptation of Don Coscarelli's *Phantasm* film series. Joe remains convinced that this book should be subtitled *Queer Fearer*, and no one is more surprised to find his story in its pages than he is.

RON OLIVER, whose writing and directing credits include everything from *Queer as Folk* to *The Chris Isaak Show*, says he's been forced to create short fiction for over ten years as a condition of his long friendship with the editor of this very book. "Want," written during a very warm spring weekend in Palm Springs, owes its existence to Frank, Dean, and Sammy, several bottles of Jack Daniels, and a long lost crush, Ed Legate, the cutest sixth grader of 1970 at New Lowell Central Public School, Ontario. But in spite of his literary passions, Ron insists he's still madly in love with his husband and, according to California law, "domestic partner," Anthony – which is all anybody could ever want.

Up the river from NYC, DAVID QUINN, the writer behind comics' trailblazing adult horror franchise *Faust*, is currently writing a sequel to *Faust: Love of the Damned* (2000).

THOMAS S. ROCHE's more than 150 published short stories have appeared in such magazines and anthologies as *Horror Garage*, *Blood Muse*, *Gothic Ghosts*, the *Hot Blood* series, as well as *Queer Fear* (his story "The Sound of Weeping," which appeared in that volume of the series, is a prequel to the story that appears in *Queer Fear II*). His own books include three volumes of the *Noirotica* series of erotic crime-noir stories as well as the short story collection *Dark Matter*. He is currently at work on a series of crime novels and a book of interconnected horror stories. He lives in San Francisco.

BRETT ALEXANDER SAVORY is a twenty-eight-year-old Bram Stoker Award-winning editor. His day job is as an editor at Harcourt Canada in Toronto. He has had roughly twenty-five stories published in numerous print and online publications since 1998, and recently completed his first novel, *In and Down*. His latest book is a novelette from Prime Books called *The Distance Travelled*, which he is currently expanding to novel length. Short story collaborations with British authors Tim Lebbon and China Miéville are in the works, as is a dark comic book series with artist Homeros Gilani.

SCOTT TRELEAVEN is a Toronto-based writer and filmmaker. He has produced numerous published articles, zines, and award-winning films and videos, including the much-acclaimed *Salvation Army*. Scott has also curated events in conjunction with Pleasure Dome, media culture icons Arthur and Marilouise Kroker, artist Floria Sigismondi, and counterculture legend Genesis P-Orridge. New projects can be found at *scotttreleaven.com*.

C. MARK UMLAND lives and writes in Toronto. His non-fiction has appeared in *Fangoria*, and his fiction previously appeared in *Queer Fear*. He is at work on a novel.

EDO VAN BELKOM is the Bram Stoker and Aurora Award-winning author and editor of more than twenty books and over 200 short stories. His short stories have appeared in such publications as *Years's Best Horror*, *Best American Erotica*, *The Best of Northern Frights*, as well as the gay-themed anthologies *Brothers of The Night* and *Queer Fear*. His novels include *Teeth*, *Martyrs*, *Scream Queen*, and *Blood Road*, while non-fiction titles include the how-to books *Writing Horror* and *Writing Erotica*, and a book of author interviews *Northern Dreamers*. Edo lives in Brampton, Ontario, with his wife and son, but his homepage is located at *vanbelkom.com*.

Michael Rowe is the three-time Lambda Literary Award-nominated author and editor of several books, including the vampire anthologies *Sons of Darkness* and *Brothers of the Night*, the essay collection *Looking for Brothers*, and the groundbreaking study of censorship, pornography, and popular culture *Writing Below the Belt*. He is also the guest literary judge for *Best Gay Erotica 2003*. An award-winning journalist and essayist, his work has appeared in *The National Post*, *The Globe & Mail*, and *The Next City*, and he is currently a frequent contributor to *The Advocate*. A lifelong afficionado of the horror genre, his essays, articles, and reviews have appeared in *The Scream Factory, Rue Morgue, All-Hallows*, and *Fangoria*. A member of both PEN Canada and The Horror Writers Association, he is married and lives in Toronto with his life-partner, Brian McDermid. He receives email at Mwriter35@aol.com, and his website is located at *michaelrowe.com*.

photo by Bruce Macaulay